The TREASURE *of* CHRISTMAS

A 3-in-1 COLLECTION

MELODY CARLSON

Revell

a division of Baker Publishing Group
Grand Rapids, Michigan

Published by Revell
a division of Baker Publishing Group
P.O. Box 6287, Grand Rapids, MI 49516-6287
www.revellbooks.com

Combined edition published 2010

Previously published in three separate volumes:
The Christmas Bus © 2002
The Gift of Christmas Present © 2004
Angels In the Snow © 2006

Printed in the United States of America

Library of Congress Cataloging-in-Publication Data
Carlson, Melody.
    The treasure of Christmas : a 3-in-1 collection / Melody Carlson. — Combined ed.
        p.   cm.
    ISBN 978-0-8007-1947-0 (cloth)
    1. Christmas stories, American. I. Carlson, Melody. Christmas bus. II. Carlson, Melody. Gift of Christmas present. III. Carlson, Melody. Angels in the snow. IV. Title.
PS3553.A73257T74 2010
813'.54—dc22   2010022465

10   11   12   13   14   15   16   7   6   5   4   3   2   1

The
CHRISTMAS
BUS

Stay on good terms with each other, held together by love. Be ready with a meal or a bed when it's needed. Why, some have extended hospitality to angels without ever knowing it!

Hebrews 13:1–2

PROLOGUE

December 20

"Where in the world are we?" asked Amy as she pulled the wool blanket she was using as a shawl a little tighter around her shoulders. She looked out the dirt-streaked passenger window, gazing at the bleak, brown rolling hills all around them.

"Like I told you . . ." Collin pulled into the slow-moving vehicle lane to allow a short string of cars to pass him. "We're in northern Oregon now. We'll be heading into the Cascade Mountains in a few minutes. I just hope we can make it over without too much trouble. Ol' Queenie almost bought the farm going over the Rockies."

At the beginning of their cross-country trip, they had christened their revamped school bus the "Queen Mary" but had since shortened it to "Queenie." The name worked since the makeshift motor home was as big as a ship and probably used about as much fuel too. Collin hadn't told Amy that they were almost out of money, due to the recently inflated gas prices, or that he was worried about Queenie's transmission going out before they reached their final destination in San Diego.

"I just hope I can make it over without *another* rest stop." Amy rubbed her hand over her large taut belly, silently promising her unborn baby that everything was going to be okay, that they would be settled in sunny Southern California in time for Christmas, which was only five days away.

"So why did we come this way?" she asked as they started the ascent into the foothills. More vegetation was growing here. Mostly evergreens, but the change of scenery was welcome after so many miles of barren, dry land.

Collin shrugged. "I don't know. It just looked like a straight shot on the map to me."

"It seems pretty desolate up here."

"There'll be more towns once we get over this pass," Collin assured her. Then he pointed to a sign. "See, it says, 'Christmas Valley, eleven miles.'"

"Oh, I got a free pamphlet about that town at the last gas station," she said suddenly, reaching for her oversized bag. She foraged until she found the dog-eared brochure. "Here it is." And then she began to read. "'Tucked into a protected niche of the eastern Cascades lies the sleepy little town of Christmas Valley. This quaint little hamlet received its name two centuries ago when a pair of stranded fur trappers sought refuge during the Christmas blizzard of 1847.'" She stopped reading and looked out the window again, shuddering as she peered up at the heavy-looking gray clouds overhead. "Do you think it's going to snow, Collin?"

"Hope not." He kept his focus on the road, and she turned her attention back to the brochure.

"'Since that frosty winter,'" she read, "'the town has gone from a spot on the map to an unimpressive trading post, to a rather insignificant mining settlement, to a thriving logging community with a working railroad. Then the recession of the eighties arrived, and the logging industry diminished due to environmental concerns that listed the spotted owl as endangered and, not long after that, the boreal toad as well.'"

Collin laughed. "What is a boreal toad?"

She shook her head. "I don't know, but it sounds like it was trouble for Christmas Valley."

"So then what happened?"

"It says that the railroad was rerouted and that Christmas Valley was forced to reinvent itself or disappear." She skimmed the words, worried that she might be getting carsick again. "It basically sounds like the town decided to capitalize on its name—Christmas Valley—and it turned into a tourist town where everything is all about Christmas."

"Interesting . . ."

Amy looked out at the pine trees. It was getting dusky now. "I guess it does look kind of Christmassy up here. But it would be better with snow." And even as she said this, almost like magic, fluffy snowflakes started to fall, spinning from the sky, hitting the windshield in big white splotches. "Look, Collin!" she cried out with childlike happiness. "It *is* snowing! It's really snowing."

But Collin just groaned as he turned on the wipers. Snow was the last thing he needed right now.

"It's going to be a white Christmas for someone!" she exclaimed.

Collin just muttered, "Uh-huh," and tried to shift into a lower gear. He didn't know a lot about engines or mechanical things, but he knew that the grinding sounds coming out of Queenie seemed to be getting worse and worse. He also knew that they were probably not going to make it over the mountain pass tonight.

"Maybe we should check out this town," he said as another sign appeared, this one announcing that the exit to Christmas Valley was only a mile away.

"Could we?" she exclaimed.

"Why not."

And so it was that a rather large and brightly painted bus rolled into the quiet little hamlet of Christmas Valley.

"'Population of 2,142,'" announced Amy as she read the welcome sign on the edge of town. It was after five o'clock now, and it appeared that most of the businesses, which weren't many, primarily a grocery store, hardware store, and barbershop, as well as about a dozen or so small retail shops that seemed to be specifically related to Christmas, were already closed.

"Oh, look," said Amy, "there's the North Pole Coffee Shop." She laughed and pointed across the street. "And there's Mrs. Santa's Diner. This is so cute!"

Collin parked on the main street, right in front of the diner, and they both got out and looked up and down the mostly deserted street. The snow was falling harder now, but Amy seemed happier than she'd been for the entire trip as she pointed out all the various Christmas decorations and shops. It was as if she were her old happy self again, and Collin decided to make the best of it.

"Let's get something to eat," he told her. They went into Mrs. Santa's Diner, sat down, and ordered Blitzen burgers (all the main food items were named after Santa's eight reindeer).

"You folks just passing through?" asked a woman wearing a Santa cap and a red-and-white-striped apron with "Mrs. Santa" embroidered across the front, although Collin had heard someone else calling her "Gloria."

"Yeah," said Collin as he dug out enough cash to pay the bill, along with a very meager tip. "But I think we'll probably spend the night in town."

"That your bus out there?" asked a voice from behind him. Collin turned to see a uniformed policeman. He seemed to be studying the couple with an expression that appeared not too welcoming, not to mention un-Christmassy.

"Yes," Collin nodded politely. He didn't want trouble.

"Well, you'll have to move it."

"But I didn't see any 'No Parking' signs."

"That may be so, but you can't leave it out there on the street. We have ordinances against camping in town. And didn't I hear you say you were planning to spend the night?"

Collin glanced over at Amy, who looked hopeful. "Yes, my wife is pregnant, and this long trip has been hard on her. I thought we might spend a night here." Of course, he didn't want to mention his possible mechanical problems being a concern as well. He didn't want to upset Amy.

"Well, there's a nice bed and breakfast," said Gloria as she wiped down the countertop. "It's called the Shepherd's Inn and is within walking distance from town. It's small, but nice. They only have about five or six rooms, but last I heard they weren't all rented out yet."

"Thank you," said Collin. He listened as she gave specific directions.

"That sounds easy enough," said Amy, smiling up at the policeman. He nodded, as if this plan met with his approval, and then wished them a somewhat restrained "Merry Christmas."

The snow was coming down even harder as Collin and Amy went back out onto the street. "It's going to be cold tonight," said Amy as they hurried to the bus.

"We'll be okay," said Collin with false confidence, but he quickly shut the door to keep the chill out. He forced a smile as he climbed into the driver's seat. "Well, let's go find this little inn."

But instead of going directly to the inn, Collin took them on a full tour of the little town. Of course, there wasn't much to see, but he stretched it out as long as he could, going by the post office and the grade school and through the surrounding neighborhoods until he was going down Main Street again.

"It seems like you're stalling," Amy finally said in tired exasperation. "Why don't we just go to the inn now?"

"Yeah . . ." he said slowly. "The thing is, Amy, we don't really have enough money to stay there, at the inn I mean. It would probably take the rest of our gas money for just one night."

Amy laughed. "I didn't think we were actually going to stay in the bed and breakfast, Collin. As nice as that sounds, I figured we were just going to park there to keep the policeman happy."

Collin chuckled as he turned the big bus up the street that led to the Shepherd's Inn. "Hey, then you figured right."

1

||||||||||||||

December 14

It'd been nearly twenty-five years since Christmas Valley's discouraged business owners had first gathered to determine the fate of their faltering economy. That's when they decided it was high time to capitalize on the town's seasonal name.

"Christmas Valley to become the Christmas capital of the Pacific Northwest," the headlines in their little weekly paper had read back in 1980, and that's when the CVA (Christmas Valley Association) had been established. It started out simply enough, things like raising funds to purchase Christmas lights and basic decorations as well as scheduling some civic activities during the month of December, but over the years it had evolved into something of a Christmastime three-ring circus, which now launched itself shortly after Halloween.

"Gotta make the most of the season," Mayor Drummel (aka Santa Claus) would tell the CVA at their annual planning session in late March. And make the most of it they did. But by early December, some of the townsfolk, weary of this never-ending holiday, could be overheard murmuring things like, "I'm sick of Christmas," or "One more chorus of Jingle Bells and I'll . . ." And some less festive folks had adopted the snowbird way of life, flocking down to Phoenix or Palm Springs at the first sight of a candy cane.

But that was never the case with Edith Ryan, the optimistic owner and operator of the Shepherd's Inn. Edith always looked forward to this time of year with unbridled enthusiasm. "I wouldn't mind if Christmas lasted forever," she'd been known to tell friends and neighbors as she happily prepared for the holiday, cooking and decorating for her family (which now consisted of four grown children and their various spouses plus five grandchildren between the ages of one and nine). She always looked forward to these gatherings in their spacious and gracious family home—the same home that also doubled as the town's only bed and breakfast for the remainder of the year.

Edith's husband, Charles Ryan, was the pastor of the only remaining church in town, and some people figured that Edith had no choice but to maintain her positive outlook on life for his sake. And considering that church membership was down more than usual, even for this time of year, it probably made sense that Edith would look for the brighter side, if only to bolster her husband's spirits. This was fortunate, since some members of his congregation seemed determined to do just the opposite.

"Have you noticed that Pastor Charlie seems to be slowing down?" Olive Peters said, totally out of the blue, during quilting circle that week. Of course, the only reason she dared to make this comment was because the pastor's good wife had been unable to attend that day. "It just occurred to me that he's getting up there in years."

"Goodness knows, he's been here forever," said her best friend, retired army nurse Helen Johnson. Accustomed to these two rather dominating women, the other quilters simply sewed and listened without commenting.

"I think we should encourage the poor old guy to retire," added Olive, who was pushing sixty herself.

"For his own sake, of course," Helen said.

"And then maybe we could hire someone *more hip*," said Olive as she tried to see well enough to thread her needle. Not that either of these women were very hip, although Helen had recently had a hip replacement. "A younger man might breathe some new life into the pulpit." She squinted her eyes and attempted, for the third time, to thread the pesky needle. "Help the church to grow."

"Yes," agreed Helen. "We need someone who could get the young people more involved."

"And the community too," added Olive. "There are plenty of folks who don't go to church around here. We should be getting them to come to our church. Membership is way down this year."

"Maybe if we found someone with a more contemporary world-view," inserted Helen. "We all know that Pastor Charlie is a good man, but he can be a bit old-fashioned, don't you think?"

Naturally, Edith's good friend Polly Emery, also present at the quilting circle, kept her thoughts to herself, since she knew that speaking out would only have resulted in an argument. Then the quilt would never get finished in time for Christmas, and it was meant to be a gift for a needy family in town. But she did inform Edith about the dissenters when the two of them met at the North Pole for coffee the following day.

"I really do hate repeating things like this," she said apologetically after spilling her proverbial beans. "But I just thought you should be aware of the talk, Edith. For Charles's sake, you know, so you two can watch your backsides, if you know what I mean."

Edith considered Polly's words as strains of "Silver Bells" played over the tinny sound system in the small café. "Well, Charles does turn sixty-five this year," she admitted with a bit of amazement. Sometimes Edith forgot that her husband was nearly ten years her senior. "But I don't see that as so terribly old, not really. And he does seem to get along with the young people . . . don't you think?"

"Of course he does, Edith. And you're right, Charles seems much younger than his age. Besides, it's not his fault that the young people can't stick around to go to church here. Everyone knows that most of them are forced to leave town to find *real* work. It's not as if we have great career opportunities here in Christmas Valley."

Edith sighed. "Speaking of young people . . . I just found out that not a single one of our kids will be coming home for Christmas this year."

Polly looked shocked. "Really? How can that be? I mean, I realize that Tommy and Alicia and their kids wouldn't be able to make it since they just got stationed in Germany. And you did mention that Katie and her family might not be able to make the trip from Florida this year. But what about Jack and his new wife—what's her name?"

16

"Constance."

"Right. What about them? I thought they were coming."

"Constance just decided that they should spend Christmas with her parents this year. And, really, that seems only fair. After all, Jack brought her here last Christmas when they got engaged. Remember?"

"What about Krista then? I happen to know that teachers get nearly two weeks off this year, and she only lives in Seattle—she could easily drive here in just a few hours. What's her excuse?"

"Well, that's the thing. She just called this morning, and it seems that she and some teacher friends got the chance to share a condo in Hawaii during the holidays—an opportunity of a lifetime for her. . . . Of course, she had to go."

"Oh . . ." Polly appeared stumped now.

"So it's just Charles and me this year."

"I'd invite you to join us, but we promised Candy and Bill that we'd come to their house this year. We plan to be gone for a whole week."

Edith reached over and patted her friend's hand. "Don't you worry about us, Polly. We'll be just fine."

But as Edith walked home, she wasn't so sure. How could it possibly be Christmas with no kids, no grandkids, no happy voices, no pitter-patter of feet going up and down the stairs, no sticky fingerprints to wipe from the big bay window, no wide-eyed expectations as the little ones tried to guess what Santa might be bringing them this year? How could it be Christmas with nothing but quiet emptiness filling up their big old Victorian house? Why, it just didn't seem possible. It just wasn't right!

So, despite the tall, fully decorated tree in the center of town and the big red-and-white candy cane decorations on every street lamp . . . despite the life-size Santa's-sleigh-and-reindeer stage in the parking lot next to the Oh, Christmas Tree gift shop and despite all the evergreen wreaths and garlands and strings of little white lights around every shop window and roofline . . . well, it just didn't feel one bit like Christmas knowing that her family wouldn't be coming home this year.

Edith glanced up at the cloudless blue sky overhead and realized that the temperature must be approaching the sixties today, and the weather didn't feel one bit like Christmas either. And with Christmas less than two weeks away . . . Edith sighed. It was just all wrong.

2

Tonight was midweek service, and as usual, Edith prepared a light meal for Charles and herself. But as they sat at the large dining room table, just the two of them at opposite ends, she decided she could not, or rather she *should* not, inform him that not even one of their children would be coming for Christmas this year. She would have to save that unfortunate news for later. Nor would she tell him, not now and not ever, about what Polly had mentioned earlier today. No, there was just no sense in repeating something like that. Instead she made pleasant small talk about a radio program that she'd listened to this afternoon while baking six loaves of cranberry nut bread— one, still warm, that they were enjoying along with their dinner, the rest to go into the freezer for later use or to give away to those who expected company for the holidays.

"It's hard to believe that it's December already," Charles said as he wiped his mouth with a green-and-red-checked napkin. "I think each year passes more quickly than the last."

"It probably comes with age," she said as she began clearing the table. "They say the older you get the faster the days go."

"Need any help?" he offered, just like usual.

And, just like usual—for a Wednesday, that is—she said, "Not tonight, dear. You just go to your study and relax a bit . . . get yourself into the right state of mind for your sermon tonight."

He pecked her on the cheek and thanked her for dinner, then went off on his way while she rinsed the dishes and loaded them into the dishwasher. With its red gingham wallpaper and golden wood floors topped with colorful braided rugs, her kitchen was quite a cheerful place—her own private retreat—and she never minded spending time there. Whether it was baking or cleaning or sitting at her little maple desk in the corner, this was her territory, and everyone knew it. She even had a sign posted over the door, politely warning guests that this area was "off-limits."

Not that it would be much of a problem during the next two weeks, for as usual, Edith had been careful not to book guests during the weeks before and following Christmas—those were always reserved for family members. And also as usual, the first two weeks of December had been fairly quiet as well. Other than the nice elderly couple who'd just left yesterday, she had no bookings lined up. She figured this was because people were too absorbed with their own holiday preparations to plan an overnight getaway during this busy time.

In the past, she'd always welcomed this quiet lull, kind of like a little reprieve before things got too frantic and chaotic with all the family members arriving, combined with the comings and goings of Christmas in town and at church. But not this year. This year there would be nothing but quiet, quiet, quiet, at least around this house. And as Edith dried her hands on a hand towel embroidered with bright sprigs of holly and berries, she just wasn't sure that she could handle that much quiet.

She heard the front door open and close, the sign that Charles was heading over to the church now, just across the street from their house. He always went over early to turn on the lights and adjust the fussy furnace and, of course, to pray for the service as well as his congregation. Charles had always been a firm believer in prayer. As was Edith, and despite her heavy heart, she took a few minutes to sit down at her desk and bow her head and earnestly pray, first of all for Charles's sermon—that God would bless his words as well as the listeners who heard them—and second that God would remind people like Olive and Helen to watch their words a bit more closely.

Certainly, she wanted to say more about that, but she knew it was up to God to decide whether or not to dish out any vengeance for their careless tongues. Then she pulled on her favorite wool sweater—no need for a coat on this unseasonably warm evening—and headed over to the church herself. Now this was the truth: although she was completely devoted to Charles and never missed a service without an extremely good excuse, there were times, like tonight, when she might've opted to stay home—if that were an option. Which it was not. And perhaps that was a good thing too. Perhaps an encouraging pre-Christmas sermon was just what she needed tonight. Something to help her get back into the *real* spirit of Christmas.

She paused on the sidewalk in front of their house, smiling with satisfaction as she looked across the street and admired the church's colorful stained glass windows glowing so warmly, so invitingly in the velvety night. She remembered the time when the windows were so badly deteriorated that the board had voted to have them completely removed and replaced with pastel-colored bubble glass, the same kind that was used in shower doors! Well, Edith couldn't bear to see that happen, and so she had rallied some women into a fund-raising frenzy, with bake sales and silent auctions until finally, contributing the difference secretly from her own personal savings, enough funds were collected to preserve those dear old windows. *Such a pretty little church*, she thought as she crossed the street. *Such a nice addition to their town.*

She thought back to when she and Charles had arrived at Christmas Valley, back in the sixties. It had been his first assignment after becoming ordained. They were so young and full of hope. Of course, things didn't always go smoothly, and living in a small town could certainly be a challenge. They quickly discovered how a church could easily be split open by things like gossip or jealousy or greed. They had gone through their own congregational trials and had also sadly witnessed other churches that floundered and eventually failed. But there was little to be done about it. As a result, they had wholeheartedly invested themselves in their church, as well as their family and their community—and all things considered, it had paid off well, since there was no place on earth where either of them would rather live out the rest of their days than right here.

Still, it got her goat when people like Helen and Olive went around saying that Charles was "getting too old." *Lord knows those women*

21

aren't exactly spring chickens themselves, she thought as she walked up the stone stairs and reached for the bronze handle on the big wooden door.

"Hello, Edith," trilled a familiar voice from behind her. Edith turned in time to see her old friend Mrs. Fish standing at the bottom of the stairs. Mrs. Fish had taught fifth grade to both Tommy and Jack before retiring years ago, and now Edith estimated she must be in her nineties, although she kept her exact age secret.

"Hello," Edith called back as she retraced her steps down the stairs and, gently placing her hand under the elderly woman's elbow, helped her to slowly ascend the stairs. "Isn't it a lovely evening tonight?"

"Feels like springtime to these old bones."

Edith laughed. "Not very Christmas-like though."

"Who could know for sure?" said Mrs. Fish when they reached the top step. "Perhaps the good Lord saw fit to warm up the Holy Lands when his son was born that night."

Edith considered this as she held the door open. "You could be right, Mrs. Fish. I guess I never thought of it like that."

Mrs. Fish removed her gloves, daintily placed them in her smooth leather purse, and looked back up. "That's probably because so many people assume that Christmas and snow are one and the same, Edith. But the Bible doesn't specify what sort of weather they actually had on that night when our Savior was born, now does it?"

Edith nodded. "Now that I think about it, I'm sure that you must be right, Mrs. Fish."

Mrs. Fish smiled back. She was accustomed to being right. "Just the same, I *do* enjoy a white Christmas," she said.

"A *white* Christmas?" said Helen Johnson, coming from the vestibule on the right. "I hardly think so. The ten-day forecast was for fair skies and sunshine."

"Well, you never know," said Edith, although she wasn't sure that she much cared one way or another, now that her family wouldn't be around to enjoy it. Oh, how the children, even the grown ones, loved going to One Tree Hill for sledding! They would bundle up in layers of scarves, mittens, and hats, and she would make several thermoses of hot cocoa along with a large tin of sugar cookies, and Charles would build a big bonfire down at the bottom of the hill to warm up by. It was such fun. Well, perhaps it would be just as well if no snow flew this year.

Edith found her regular seat, second row on the left, next to the aisle, and sat down, waiting for the service to begin. The midweek service was always rather small, generally not more than twenty people in all—only the most devout or those who wished to appear so. Edith watched as Marie Williams made her way to the organ. Marie had shown up in Christmas Valley nearly twenty years ago, after her husband had suddenly died while they were on the road looking for work. Broke and in need of employment, Marie was hired by Edith to help with housework, but when Edith discovered that Marie played the organ, she enticed Charles to hire her on as the church organist. Of course, they couldn't afford to pay her much, but Marie said she would've gladly played for free. Still a young and attractive woman (she had been in her twenties back then), it wasn't long before Marie married one of the town's most eligible bachelors, Arnie Williams. And although she no longer needed the job as church organist, she continued to play for all these years out of pure love and loyalty.

Edith leaned back into the pew, relaxing as she listened to the soothing sound of Marie's gifted fingers moving gracefully over the keyboard. Ah, what would they do without her? It wasn't long before Charles made his way to the front of the church and up to the pulpit. As usual, he greeted everyone, made a comment on the warmer than normal weather, and then repeated a humorous story that he'd read in *Reader's Digest* (his favorite source for jokes and anecdotes). The congregation laughed politely, and then he led them in a song and began his sermon. Just like usual.

But, not a bit like usual, Edith was distracted with her own dismal thoughts about how Christmas would not be the same, and how, without her children, it would be bleak and sad. Consequently, she missed the entire first half of her husband's sermon—something she hadn't done since the time when Krista, at the age of six, had pulled out her loose front tooth and bled all over Edith's best blue suit in the middle of a midweek service.

However, when Edith realized that she hadn't been listening to a single word her good husband had been saying, feeling like a child who'd been caught sleeping during mathematics, she sat up straighter and adjusted her gaze directly ahead and even smiled, ever so slightly. Hopefully, Charles hadn't noticed her little faux pas. He certainly had her undivided attention now!

"Our Lord reminded his disciples to show hospitality. He said there could be times when they might help or bless a stranger and in reality be blessing him. Be mindful of this as so many of you open your homes to family and loved ones and life becomes somewhat hectic. Perhaps it is in those moments, when all is not going smoothly and well, perhaps that is the very moment when you might discover the Lord is right there in your midst."

Edith leaned forward just slightly, a bit dismayed at the irony of her husband speaking of hospitality and opening up one's home while their own home would be noticeably empty this year. Of course, he wasn't aware of this yet.

"But will you be ready?" he said now, looking earnestly over his listeners. "Will your heart be ready to greet our Lord? Let me read a passage from Hebrews 13:1–2," he continued as he opened his new leather Bible. Charles had recently purchased a somewhat nontraditional Bible version and had even started using it during his sermons. Edith wasn't sure what church members would think of this modern translation since they were more accustomed to the old-fashioned and traditional Bibles, but so far no one had commented or complained. Perhaps no one had even noticed.

"'Stay on good terms with each other,'" he read slowly, putting emphasis on each word, "'held together by love.'" He paused, adjusted his bifocals, and smiled at the congregation. "Isn't that just beautiful? *Held together by love.*" Then he continued to read. "And then it says, 'Be ready with a meal or a bed when it's needed. Why, some have extended hospitality to angels without ever knowing it!'"

Edith listened as he continued to expound on this idea of getting along with each other, encouraging the congregation to outdo each other in the areas of love and hospitality. It really was a perfect pre-Christmas theme, especially in regard to some of the less than loving and slightly divisive comments that Olive and Helen had made earlier this week. Now Edith wondered if Charles hadn't been aware of this all along. Naturally, he wouldn't have mentioned it.

But Edith put thoughts of Olive and Helen aside as she listened to his words. And then, just as she normally did, she began to apply those meaningful words to the state of her own heart, and by the time he finished his sermon and Marie was back at the organ, Edith had tears running down both cheeks. So it was that Edith knew exactly what needed to be done!

3

After the service ended, Edith made an effort at congeniality with fellow parishioners, but all she could think was that she wanted to get home as quickly as possible. Or as her old grandmother might've once said, Edith had a bee in her bonnet.

"Yes, Olive," she said with as much patience as she could muster, "the nativity costumes are still up in the attic." She wanted to add "just like they always have been," but instead she said, "Come on over and get them anytime you like." Olive had taken it upon herself to head up the church's annual nativity play this year. For the past ten years her daughter Judy had managed this challenging task, but Judy and her husband had relocated to Portland last year, and Olive had promised to handle the program for her. Edith just hoped, for the sake of the church, that Olive was up to it.

"I'll give you a call this week," said Olive as she jotted down something in a little black notebook.

"You're certainly organized," observed Edith.

Olive smiled, perhaps a bit smugly. "Judy explained her whole system to me. It's really quite brilliant, if I do say so myself."

Edith patted Olive on the arm. "I sure do miss Judy. She did such a great job with the children and Sunday school. How does she like Portland?"

Olive made a face. "Not very much, I'm afraid. She says the traffic is horrible. If it weren't for Ron's job, I'm sure they'd be back here in no time. But at least they'll all be here for Christmas. And I don't want her to be disappointed in the nativity play. Goodness gracious, but I've got a lot to do!"

Edith considered offering to help, but only for a second or two. She knew that Olive had certain ways of doing things, and in all likelihood Edith would only get in her way. Besides that, Edith was still not completely over Olive's less than kind comments about Charles's age. Maybe managing the nativity play on her own would remind her that they were all getting up there in years, and that it didn't hurt to lean on each other a bit, or to cut each other a bit of grace from time to time—something like tonight's sermon. Edith simply smiled and said she'd better be getting home now.

She waved a little good-bye to Charles, who was caught in what looked like an interesting conversation between Mrs. Fish and Peter Simpson. Peter had gone to school with their boys but somehow managed to eke out a living as an artist and part-time handyman here in town. If memory served her right, he'd also been in Mrs. Fish's class before she retired. Edith was slightly curious as to what the three of them were talking about in such an animated fashion, but she was also eager to get home.

She hurried across the street and into the house, heading straight for her little desk in the kitchen. Without even taking off her sweater, she turned on her computer and sat down, waiting for the screen to come to life. Funny, how she'd fought against the idea of owning a computer—so technical and impersonal—but eventually her children got to her. "How will we keep in touch?" demanded Katie after having her first baby several years ago. "If you had a computer, we could email each other every day, and I'd even send photos of the baby that you could see immediately."

Well, that settled it. And the next time Tommy had a couple of days to spare, he helped his mother to set up a computer and even gave her some beginner lessons—mostly how to turn it off and on and how to play Spider Solitaire, which still probably occupied far too much of her time. But after a while, she had the good sense to get some serious computer tutoring from Jared Renwick, a local teen who was also a computer whiz. She eventually got the hang of it, and now, thanks to Jared, who had recently started his own small computer business, she even had a website for the bed and breakfast that could be accessed by people from all over the world. Amazing, really.

She emailed Jared now. "Dear Jared," she carefully typed, still using the formal and, according to her children, "old-fashioned" greeting. They usually just wrote "Hey Mom" or sometimes launched right into their latest news without a proper heading. But she still liked to start all email correspondence with "Dear"—it just seemed polite.

> Dear Jared,
>
> I've just come up with a promotion idea that I'd like you to display on my website, that is if you're not too busy. I want to announce that for the first time in the seventeen years of its operation, the Shepherd's Inn will be open throughout the entire month of December. And also that, as a Christmas special, I will be offering a 25 percent discount to all guests. Plus, all guests will be included in all the Christmas activities at no additional cost, including the Christmas Eve party and Christmas dinner and so on. Can you please take care of this for me?
>
> Sincerely,
>
> Edith Ryan

Then Edith hit the magical "send" button and returned to her currently empty email inbox and waited expectantly. Well, she didn't really think he'd get back to her immediately, but sometimes he was a regular Johnny-on-the-spot. Still, when he didn't respond after a couple of minutes, she decided to distract herself with a quick game of Spider Solitaire. What could it hurt? But before she'd even dealt the second row of cards, she heard the familiar little *bing-bing* sound, announcing that new mail had arrived. And sure enough, it was from Jared.

> no problem, E. done deal. jr

She smiled to herself as she signed off, then shut down her computer. Despite his computer "shorthand," Edith knew that Jared had taken care of everything. Just like that. Now, didn't they live in an amazing era! Hopefully, she'd get some responses to her Christmas special by the end of the week. Guests, as instructed on the website, emailed or called Edith directly to book rooms, and she hoped that they'd have all five rooms booked by the weekend. Or at least some of them—perhaps it wasn't imperative to have a full house, although that would be her preference. And who knew what kind of interesting guests they might have during the holidays. Perhaps like Charles had said tonight, they might even entertain angels or the Lord himself without ever knowing it.

She hummed to herself as she puttered in the kitchen, putting on the kettle for their nightly cup of tea, and as she measured the tea she imagined the sorts of people who might book rooms during the holidays. Perhaps there would be some older couples who, like Edith and Charles, didn't have family to gather with this year. Or maybe a young family who'd recently relocated from the East Coast, finding themselves without relatives nearby. Well, Edith and Charles could become their temporary family! And they would show their guests the best sort of hospitality that a place like Christmas Valley had to offer. Really, it would be such fun! Perhaps it truly was a blessing in disguise that her children were unable to come this year. It would give her the opportunity to really reach out to people who might otherwise have a sad and lonely Christmas. A chance to practice real hospitality—just the way the good Lord intended. She couldn't wait to tell Charles about her plan!

The kettle was just beginning to sing when Charles came into the kitchen. Edith turned and smiled at her husband. "I have a surprise for you!"

At first Charles, like she had been, was dismayed to hear that none of their children would be coming home for Christmas, but she quickly moved into the second part of her surprise, and before long his eyes lit up too.

"That's wonderful, dear," he said as he set his mug of orange pekoe tea down on the small kitchen table. "You may be the only one who actually took my little sermon seriously."

"What do you mean?"

He waved his hand in a dismissive way. "Oh, nothing, really."

"What?" she insisted, leaning forward to listen.

"Oh, I think that some members of our congregation may think that angels are an antiquated old fairy tale."

She frowned. "That's too bad."

He nodded. "Yes. Mrs. Fish is certain that angels only visited the biblical characters, not modern-day people like us." He shook his head. "And Peter Simpson believes that angels are simply metaphorical, symbols of God's attempt to reach mankind, or something to that effect."

"Oh . . ."

Charles shrugged. "I was beginning to feel that I'm a bit out of touch with my parishioners."

Edith didn't speak, but she was considering what Polly had told her about Helen and Olive and their concern that Charles was getting old.

Then her husband smiled. "But now I come home to discover that my own dear wife has taken my words to heart." He reached over and put his hand on hers. "That is a great comfort."

"It's a comfort to me too," she said. "I was so discouraged to think that our kids weren't coming. It just didn't seem like Christmas."

"I wonder who the Lord will bring to our home," he mused. "Perhaps we should take a few minutes to pray about this, Edith, to invite our Lord to direct the right people to us—the ones who need a bit of Christmas Valley cheer and hospitality to warm their hearts. Do you think?"

She nodded and bowed her head, and together they asked God to guide the perfect people to the Shepherd's Inn for the holidays.

"Isn't it exciting?" she said when they finished.

He squeezed her hand and nodded. "Yes, dear, it is!"

But the next day came, and not one phone call, not one email had arrived by the afternoon. Even so, Edith busied herself with the same sort of preparations she would do when expecting her family to fill the house. She even called Polly to tell her of the plan.

"What a great idea," said Polly, who had missed Charles's midweek sermon the night before. Edith explained where the inspiration came from, and Polly said she wished she could be around to watch what happened.

"I'll tell you all about it when you get back," said Edith.

"So have you had any bites yet?"

"Not yet," said Edith in her optimistic way. "But it hasn't even been twenty-four hours since Jared changed my website. I'm sure they will come."

"Yes, of course," said Polly, but Edith thought she heard a tinge of doubt in her friend's voice.

"And if they don't," said Edith, "well, I'll just do like the good Lord says. I'll go out to the streets and invite strangers to come in."

"Really?" Polly sounded a bit shocked now.

"Well, I don't know for sure, Polly. I can't imagine there would be many strangers roaming the streets of Christmas Valley right at Christmastime." She laughed. "But you just never know!"

4

On Friday morning the phone rang, and it turned out to be a woman named Carmen Fields from Redding, California. She had just found the Shepherd's Inn website.

"Do you still have rooms available?" she asked hopefully.

"Yes, we do," said Edith, not wanting to admit that *all* the rooms were currently available.

"Well, my husband and I decided that we'd like to do something different for Christmas this year," she said. "And it seems that everyone else in our family has plans." She cleared her throat. "Plans that don't include us."

"Well, we would love to *include* you with us," said Edith happily. Then she took down the pertinent information and booked the room. "And there's a nice website for the town," she informed Carmen. "It tells a bit about us and some of the activities that happen around here at Christmastime."

"Sounds perfect," said Carmen. "We plan to drive up, take our time, and spend a night somewhere along the way. So I guess we'll see you on Monday then."

Edith smiled to herself as she hung up the phone. It was starting to happen. *A real beginning!* And, remembering her wise husband's suggestion on Wednesday night, Edith took a few moments to ask God, once again, to send just the right people to their home. She also thanked him for choosing Carmen and Jim Fields and even asked his blessing on their travels as they made their way up here by car.

By noon on Saturday, Edith had booked two more rooms. One was for a single man named Albert Benson. Judging by his voice, he was older and, Edith guessed, sad. Although she had no reason why. No matter, they would do whatever possible to cheer him up during his stay. The next booking was done online. A couple from Spokane by the name of Lauren and Michael Thomas, just the two of them. No children yet. Oh, well, Edith assured herself, God was in control of the guest list, and it wasn't for her to question.

But later in the afternoon she received a call from a woman named Leslie. "I have a child," she began tentatively, "a five-year-old daughter. . . . I hope that's okay."

"That's wonderful!" said Edith. "I was just hoping that someone would have children. It just feels more like Christmas with little ones around."

"Her name is Megan, and she's still having a hard time adjusting to the fact that her daddy left us more than a year ago. . . ."

"Oh, I'm so sorry."

"Don't be. The guy was a total jerk. The only good thing he ever did for me was Megan. But for some reason she still thinks he's the greatest and doesn't understand why he can't come spend Christmas with us. Anyway, I needed someplace to go . . . to get away from here, you know what I mean?"

"Well, you and Megan are more than welcome to make yourselves at home here," said Edith.

"Great. I'm taking the whole week off, so I plan to drive over on Tuesday. Is that okay?"

"No problem."

And so it was that all but one room was booked. Edith was busier than ever now, but it was just the way she liked it. Naturally, she'd sent her Christmas cards weeks ago and had, just last week, finished wrapping and shipping her children's Christmas presents, but she still had plenty to do to make her guests feel completely welcome and at home here. She was just carrying a load of clean towels upstairs when she heard the doorbell ring. Setting the basket on a chair, she turned and hurried back down. Too early for guests to be arriving, thank goodness. She opened the door to see Olive Peters standing there.

"I tried to call, but your line was busy," she explained. "I came to collect the costumes. We're going to do a fitting this afternoon."

Feeling more generous than the last time they'd talked, Edith offered to help her carry the boxes over to the church.

"Oh, I don't want to bother you," said Olive, impatiently looking at her watch. "And Helen promised to help me, but as usual, she's late."

"Why don't I give you a hand?"

"Oh, I'm sure you've got your hands full. Aren't you busy getting ready for all those kids of yours to arrive?"

So Edith explained how things were going to be different this year.

"You've got to be kidding!" exclaimed Olive. "You and Charles must've lost your minds."

Edith blinked. "Why—what do you mean?"

"Inviting a bunch of perfect strangers into your home during Christmas?"

"Well, I do run a bed and breakfast," said Edith. "We're accustomed to having strangers as guests—"

"But for Christmas, Edith?" Olive firmly shook her head. "It just sounds a little odd. Christmas is a time for friends and family. If you and Charles were going to be alone during the holidays, you should've told us. We would've gladly invited you over to our home. You shouldn't be stuck here with a bunch of strangers."

Edith forced what she hoped was a believable smile. "But that's just it, Olive, we *want* to do this. Don't you remember Charles's midweek sermon about being hospitable? We wanted to open our home to people who don't have a place to go during this time. We thought it would be fun."

Olive pressed her lips together and studied Edith for a long moment. "Well, all I can say is that you two have a very strange idea of what constitutes *fun*. And I certainly hope that this whole crazy plan doesn't backfire and blow up in your face."

Just then Helen drove up, and Edith was relieved that she was now off the hook for helping Olive with the costumes. She led the two women up the two flights of stairs, then turned around in concern to Helen. "Oh, my, I hope this doesn't hurt your hip," she said. "I forgot all about your surgery."

"No problem," huffed Helen, clearly out of breath. "That replacement hip," *gasp gasp*, "is as good as new."

"But I might need one now," said Olive just as breathlessly. It seemed that she too was trying to recover from climbing the two flights of stairs. "Or maybe I should focus on my knees first. They've been giving me trouble lately."

Edith opened the door to the attic and turned on the light. "I'll warn you that it's very dusty up here," she said as she led them over to the corner where the cardboard boxes of costumes were stored.

"All *six* of these?" exclaimed Olive when she saw the clearly marked boxes. "For one little nativity play?"

"That means more trips," said Helen with a frown. "You didn't warn me that I was signing up for hard labor today, Olive."

Olive went over and picked up a box. "Well, at least they're not terribly heavy." Without commenting, Helen followed her lead. Edith, deciding not to waste a trip down the stairs, picked up a box herself, the largest one as it turned out, and it was a bit on the heavy side.

By the time they were all downstairs, both Helen and Olive looked thoroughly winded, but they somehow managed to get out the door and were slowly making their way over to the church when Charles poked his head out of his study. "What's going on?"

Edith explained about the costume boxes, and before the two women had a chance to return, Charles had retrieved the other three from the attic and was already carrying two of the boxes across the street. Edith smiled as she watched him. Maybe this would give Helen and Olive something to think about. Maybe witnessing Charles's ability to carry the boxes without being the least bit out of breath, since, regardless of the weather, he regularly walked two miles every morning, would show those ladies that he wasn't exactly over the hill yet.

"Those two," he said when he came back into the house. "I'll be surprised if the pageant doesn't turn into a complete fiasco."

"Really?" Edith looked at him with concern. "Do you think they're going to make a mess of it?"

He laughed. "Oh, probably not. After all, as Olive assured me, she does have her little notebook, her attack plan . . . that should keep the affair somewhat on target. But the way those two were arguing just now, about who was boss and who was going to do what, well, I just hope they don't set too bad of an example for the children."

"I do miss Judy," said Edith.

"We all do."

"And I know this sounds terrible, but sometimes it's difficult to believe that Judy and Olive are actually related."

He laughed again. "Hopefully, Judy won't be too disappointed when they get here and see what's become of her pageant."

"Maybe she'll be able to save the day."

Just then the doorbell rang again.

"This place is like Grand Central Station today," observed Charles. "I hope I'll be able to get my sermon finished."

"Don't worry," she assured him. "It's probably just Olive and Helen again. Anyway, whatever it is, I'll take care of it. You get back to your work, dear."

But it wasn't Olive or Helen. Instead, Edith found a short and rather squat woman standing at her door. The woman's hair was gray and fluffy, and she appeared to be quite elderly. At least eighty or ninety, Edith suspected.

"Can I help you?" she asked the woman, who didn't look one bit happy to be there.

"I suppose you can. My friend just dropped me off here." She looked over her shoulder and scowled. "You got any room in your inn?"

Edith blinked. "Someone dropped you off? Right here? And you need a room?"

"That's what I said, isn't it? You got a room or not?" The old woman shifted her shabby-looking overnight bag to the other hand and sighed in clear exasperation. "You're not deaf, are you?"

"No, of course not." Edith opened the door wider. "Please, come in."

"Well, that's better." The woman shoved the overnight bag toward Edith as if she were a bellboy.

Without questioning this, Edith took the bag and led the woman over to the long oak table that she used as a registration area, setting the bag down on the chair beside it. She wasn't quite sure what to say now.

"Come on," said the old woman impatiently. "Cat got your tongue?"

"No . . ." Edith studied the woman. Something about her reminded Edith of Ulysses, a bulldog that had belonged to her grandfather when she was a little girl. Maybe it was the square, flat face, or the loose jowls, or perhaps it was something in those intense, slightly beady eyes. But Edith had never quite trusted that dog.

"Well, then . . . what's the problem?"

Still, Edith didn't like to judge people on appearances. "I'm sorry, but people usually call ahead first, to get reservations, and I'm just caught a little off—"

"Look, if you're booked up just tell me, and I'll get out of your hair."

"No," Edith said quickly. Perhaps a bit too quickly. "We do actually have an available room."

"Fine," snapped the woman. "I'll take it."

"Right," said Edith, still trying to grasp what was going on. She hated to be rude, but she really wanted to know why this woman had decided to come here of all places. It wasn't as if they were exactly on the beaten path. Just the same, she slid the information form toward the woman. "You'll just need to fill this out for me."

"You mind if I sit down?" demanded the woman. "My feet are killing me."

"No, not at all," said Edith, removing the bag from the chair and offering the woman a seat. "I'm curious as to how you heard about us."

"My friend knew where you were located. It was his idea to drop me here. I s'pect he didn't want me around during the holidays." She made a disgusted sigh. "Nice friend, huh?"

Just then the doorbell rang again. "Excuse me," said Edith as she went to get it.

It was Olive, and her face looked a bit stricken. "I need your help,

Edith. Helen slipped on a wet spot on the floor in the kitchen, and she can't get up."

"Oh, my goodness," said Edith. "Is she badly hurt?"

"I don't think so. She told me not to call 911. But I'm not strong enough to get her up by myself. As you know, Helen is a rather bulky gal."

Edith looked back at the old woman. "If you'll excuse me for just a few minutes, I need to—"

"I heard the whole stupid thing," snapped the woman without even turning to see them. "I'll be perfectly fine on my own. It's not as if I'm not used to it, for Pete's sake."

Olive's brows lifted curiously at this.

"I'll be right back," called Edith as she headed for the door. "Come on, Olive."

"Who is *that*?" demanded Olive as soon as the door was shut behind them.

"I'm not exactly sure," said Edith. "Well, she's a guest, of course, but I didn't get her name yet."

"There you go," said Olive as if making a point. "Letting a perfect stranger into your house, you don't even know her name, on top of that she's ruder than all get-out. . . . The next thing you know she'll be making off with the family silver."

Edith laughed. "We don't have much silver, Olive. And I seriously doubt that she could carry much with her. She looks like she's about a hundred years old. Someone just dumped her here, poor thing."

"*Dumped* her?"

"Well, dropped her. She said it was a friend."

"Some friend."

"That's what she said too."

They were in the church now, and the sounds of moaning made Edith hasten her pace. There in the small church kitchen, just like Olive had said, was Helen Johnson lying flat as a pancake with arms and legs sprawled out like a beached starfish.

"Are you okay?" asked Edith as she knelt down beside her and attempted to remember what she'd learned at her first aid class, more than twenty years ago.

"You mean other than being in severe pain and humiliating embarrassment?" said Helen.

"Can you move everything?" asked Edith, recalling that you weren't supposed to attempt transporting someone with a spinal injury.

"What would you suggest that I move?"

"You know," said Edith. "Your arms and your legs, does everything work okay?"

Now Helen waved her arms and legs as if she were making a snow angel.

"Okay," said Edith, satisfied. "It looks like you're pretty much in one piece. Can you sit up?"

"Perhaps with a little help."

Neither Edith nor Olive was particularly large or muscular, so Edith took one hand and Olive took the other, and together they pulled Helen to a sitting position.

"How's that?" asked Edith.

"Better." Helen rubbed her knee. "Although I do feel a bit foolish."

Edith went for a wooden chair now. She thought it might be a better way to help Helen to her feet.

"You shouldn't feel bad, Helen," said Olive. "It's that ding-dong janitor who's to blame. He shouldn't have left a wet spot on the floor like that. A person could get killed taking a fall like that."

"He probably didn't realize anyone was going to be here today," said Edith as she set the chair next to Helen.

"What's that for?" asked Helen.

"I thought we could use it to help you get up," suggested Edith. "Olive and I can each lift you from the sides, and maybe you can help to hoist yourself up with the chair."

"Well, as long as you can keep the chair from slipping," said Helen a bit skeptically. So they all got into place, and before long they had Helen on her feet, then sitting in the chair.

"Thank you, girls," said Helen. "I suppose it's time to consider having some work done on these old knees of mine. This right one is really howling now."

"That's what I keep telling you," said Olive. "Get yourself fixed up while you can. We're not getting any younger, you know."

"Are you going to be okay?" asked Edith.

Helen attempted standing now, holding on to each of them as she did. "My hip is okay, but my knee's a bit sore. I'm sure that's partly due to going up and down all those stairs earlier. But I doubt that I'm going to be much help to you today," she told Olive.

"Why don't we help you to your car," suggested Edith. "Do you think you can drive okay?"

"Of course," said Helen, ever the stalwart army nurse. "And if someone calls ahead, Clarence can help me into the house when I get there."

"I'll do that," said Edith.

So the three of them slowly hobbled off toward Helen's Crown Victoria, which was parked close to the side exit from the church kitchen. Thankfully, that meant no stairs. They finally had Helen in her car, and she thanked them once again.

"I'm sorry I can't help you," she told Olive.

"It's quite all right, dear," said Olive, glancing at her watch. "Goodness, the kids will be here any minute. I better get moving."

"Take care," said Edith. "And I'll give Clarence a call right now."

"Appreciate it."

"Let me know if you need a hand today," Edith called to Olive as she was hurrying back to the church.

"I think you have your hands full with grandma over there," said Olive. Then she paused. "But thanks anyway. I think I can handle this on my own."

Edith was relieved to hear this, and as a matter of fact, she was a bit concerned, not to mention curious, about the old woman whom she'd left behind at the registration table. But when she got inside the house, there was no one to be seen. Everything was quiet, and for a moment she wondered if perhaps she'd imagined the whole thing. But then why would Olive have mentioned it?

She decided to peek her head into Charles's study to see if he knew anything. "Sorry to disturb you, dear," she began.

He looked up from where he was intently writing. "Yes?"

"Uh, did you happen to see an old woman anywhere about—"

He adjusted his glasses and peered at her. "You mean *Myrtle*?"

"Well, I'm not totally sure." Edith held out her hand to about four and a half feet high. "She was about this tall"—now she spread her arms—"and about this wide."

He kind of smiled. "I think you must mean our guest. Myrtle Pinkerton."

She nodded. "Our guest?"

"She filled out her paperwork and paid for two full weeks in advance—with cash, by the way; I put it in your little zipper bag—so I could see no reason not to take her to a room. I gave her the Green Meadow Room. Is that okay?" All the guest rooms had names related to shepherds, all taken from the twenty-third psalm. There was, of course, the Good Shepherd Room, the Lamb Room, the Staff and Rod Room (which usually had to be explained), the Cool Water Room, and the Green Meadow Room.

Edith smiled. "That's fine, dear. And thank you for helping out when I know you're busy."

"And is everyone okay over at the church?"

"Yes." She wanted to let him get back to his work now. "Everyone's just fine."

"Myrtle mentioned that someone had fallen down and couldn't get up." His eyes twinkled with curiosity. "But she didn't seem to think it was an actual emergency."

"Yes, that was Helen." Edith decided to give him the sweet, condensed version for the time being. "She slipped, but she's okay. Olive and I got her up and into her car. Don't worry about it. I'll try not to disturb you again."

He smiled. "I can hardly blame you for Helen's fall, dear."

She nodded and quietly pulled the door closed.

Goodness, how did this day get so busy?

5

"I thought this was a bed and *breakfast*."

Edith looked up from where she was sitting at the kitchen table. Her normal routine was to get up early enough to read from her morning devotional book and enjoy a quiet cup of peppermint tea. Her private time. But Myrtle Pinkerton, ignoring the sign above the door, had just stepped over an invisible line and was now standing with a bulldoggish expression as she surveyed Edith's kitchen.

Edith slowly closed her book, glanced at the apple-shaped clock above the stove to see that it wasn't yet 6:00 a.m., then cleared her throat and stood.

"Good morning, Mrs. Pinkerton," she said in a formal voice. "Perhaps my husband didn't give you our brochure yesterday, but breakfast isn't served until seven. I'm sorry for any inconvenience."

"Hmmph. Inconvenience is right. I'm an old woman. I didn't have any dinner last night, and I am *starving*."

Despite her resolve to maintain her normal professional and cool facade right now (her means for dealing with the occasional cantankerous guest), Edith did feel her sympathetic side taking over once again. Edith's family and friends had often warned her that she was a softie and that if she wasn't careful, everyone would walk all over her. But, for goodness' sake, this poor old woman was virtually stranded at the inn, and although there were a couple of eating establishments in town, they were also several blocks away, and who knew what kind of walking shape Myrtle Pinkerton was in.

"Why don't you make yourself comfortable in the dining room," suggested Edith in a kind voice. "And I'll bring you something out. Do you like tea, Mrs. Pinkerton?"

"No. I only drink coffee. Cream and sugar. And call me Myrtle. I don't go in for formalities." She turned around, made a *harrumph* sound as if she were reluctant to leave, then returned to the dining room.

Edith suppressed feelings of guilt now. Was she being too rigid with this guest? Really, what harm would come from inviting Myrtle to join her in the kitchen just this once? "Don't compromise yourself," she could just hear her children warning her. Or even Polly. "Don't give in, Edith. Stay firm or you'll regret it." Of course, they were probably right.

Edith considered asking Myrtle whether or not she had any special dietary needs but then decided the best course might be to start brewing coffee first. Besides, Charles would be down before long, and he would be pleased to see that the coffee was already made. After a few minutes, she carried a tray with a cup of steaming coffee, along with cream and sugar, to the dining room. But no one was there.

"Myrtle?" she called out, thinking perhaps the guest had wandered into the living room or maybe the sunroom, but no one answered. So she set the tray on the table and returned to the kitchen to begin cutting up some fruit for a small fruit plate. Surely fresh fruit would be a safe choice to start with. She also set out a couple of pitchers of fruit juice. Then she neatly arranged a small plate of sliced cranberry nut bread along with the pumpkin bread she had baked only yesterday. She made toast, got out some jelly, and finally set out a selection of yogurts and cereals to choose from—her usual fare when they had only one or two guests in the house. Of course, guests were welcome to order eggs and other cooked items if they liked, and Edith was always more than happy to turn on the stove, but this lighter fare usually suited most guests just fine.

Still there was no sign of Myrtle. And even when Edith did a quick search of the first-floor rooms, she never found her. Perhaps Myrtle had gone back to her room for something. She waited a bit, but eventually it was only her and Charles, sitting down to breakfast just the two of them. A rather grand breakfast too, since they were accustomed to eating much lighter when no guests were about, often simply oatmeal and juice.

"Did you see Myrtle this morning?" she asked as she took a slice of pumpkin bread and broke it in half.

"No, I expect she'd be sleeping in. She mentioned that she was worn out from her trip yesterday."

So Edith explained how Myrtle had been up before six and had claimed to be ravenous. She waved at the nicely arranged table. "Otherwise, I wouldn't have gone to such trouble."

"She's a funny old bird, isn't she?"

Edith nodded, then lowered her voice. "I have a feeling she's going to test my patience a bit. Did you really say that she planned to be here for two whole weeks?"

He smiled. "It'll be better when the other guests arrive. Besides, I suspect that poor old Myrtle just needs to be loved."

"Well, perhaps you can take care of that end of things," she suggested. "And I'll take care of the practical things."

He set down his empty coffee cup. "Oh, you can't fool me, Edith. I know you have just as much love to give as I do."

"Well, it didn't feel like that this morning when she was standing in my kitchen and reminding me that this was a bed and *breakfast*."

He laughed. "This should be an interesting Christmas for everyone."

"Did you invite Myrtle to church when you talked to her yesterday?"

"As a matter of fact, I did."

"And?"

"It sounded as if she plans to come." He wiped his mouth with the napkin. "Speaking of church, I promised Hal Berry that I'd have a short meeting with the ushers this morning. Seems they have some new idea to make things go more smoothly."

"I thought things usually went pretty smoothly." She refilled her cup with tea.

He winked at her. "Well, you know Hal. He's always got some new trick up his sleeve. Remember when he wanted to put the offering plates on sticks so the ushers would have complete control of them at all times?"

She laughed. "Yes, as if there's anyone in our congregation with sticky fingers."

"Well, old Hal isn't quite as trusting as you are, my dear." He bent down and pecked her on the cheek. "See you later."

Edith was just clearing the dining room table when Myrtle made an appearance. She had on a gray woolen coat with an ancient-looking purse slung over one arm. Her cheeks were flushed, and she looked slightly winded.

"Oh, there you are," said Edith as she set the tray back down. "Are you still hungry?"

Myrtle waved one hand and grasped the back of a chair with the other. "No," she puffed. "I just walked all the way to town and back."

"Did you get something to eat?"

She nodded. "I went to that silly café, the one with all the Santa Claus paraphernalia all over the place."

"Mrs. Santa's Diner."

"That's the one. Even the napkins had Santa heads printed all over them. Land sakes, I'd think people would get sick and tired of that Santa stuff day in, day out, year round."

Edith smiled. "Oh, I suppose it gets old for some folks. But I think it's rather charming."

Myrtle released the back of the chair and stood up straighter and said, "Charming? Humph," rolling her eyes for added emphasis.

Edith almost expected her to add a "Bah, humbug" next. But fortunately, Myrtle did not. Instead she turned and began to leave the room.

"I'm going to my room to rest some," she called over her shoulder. "That long walk wore me out something fierce."

"Church is at ten thirty," Edith called out.

Myrtle turned around and tossed her an exasperated look. "I know that," she snapped.

Edith tried not to show her relief as Myrtle slowly made her way toward the staircase. Hopefully, the old woman would enjoy a nice long rest this morning, allowing Edith to get a few more things done without interruption. More guests would begin to arrive tomorrow, and it wouldn't be long before the whole house would be filled. Edith wanted to have everything just perfect for them.

She managed to mix up a batch of sugar cookie dough, which needed to chill, as well as eight pie crusts that she wrapped and stacked in the freezer. She planned to have an assortment of desserts available to her guests throughout the days preceding Christmas. Sweets to cheer the spirits.

Finally it was nearly ten thirty, and Edith knew that it was time to head over to the church. She had neither heard nor seen Myrtle and suspected that the tired old woman might still be soundly sleeping. And perhaps it was for the best. But as Edith made her way down the center aisle, toward her regular seat up front, she was surprised to see that someone was already sitting there. And she suspected, by the gray coat and frazzled-looking hair, not to mention the width that took up a fair portion of pew, that it was indeed Myrtle. Of course, Myrtle would have no idea that she was sitting in the seat that was reserved for the pastor's wife. But Edith could see that the ushers were concerned. She simply smiled at Hal Berry, nodding as if to show him that all was well, before she squeezed past Myrtle, taking the seat to her left. It did feel odd to be sitting in a different spot, even if it was only a few feet different. Funny how people can get accustomed to certain things. Even so, she didn't let on that she was troubled by being bumped from her regular seat. It was silly, really.

After the singing was finished, Charles took a few moments to welcome newcomers. Today that meant Myrtle. He gave a brief introduction, mentioning that she would be staying at the inn throughout the holidays. And then, to Edith's complete surprise and probably everyone else's too, Myrtle stood up.

"Thank you," she said in a loud voice, turning toward the congregation as if preparing to give a speech. "You have an interesting little town here," she continued. "Although I do think you people take this whole Christmas business way too far. Good grief, I actually wiped my mug with Santa faces this morning." A few titters were heard, although Edith suspected that Myrtle wasn't trying to be funny. "What bothers me is that you people are going to forget what Christmas is really about." She shook her finger at them. "It's not about 'Jingle Bells' and candy canes and Santa head toilet-seat covers. It's not about making a few extra bucks or impressing your friends with the way your place is all lit up. And if this is all that Christmas Valley has to offer, well, I'd just as soon spend my Christmas someplace else!" Then she turned and sat down with a *thump*.

The church was so quiet you could have heard a snowflake fall. Not that there was any chance of that today, since it was still quite balmy. Edith, almost afraid to breathe, looked up at the pulpit, where Charles's eyes were wide and his mouth was actually partway open. But he quickly regained composure and even acknowledged Myrtle's stern reprimand.

"I think our guest makes a valid point," he said slowly. "It is important that we not lose sight of the true meaning of Christmas." He smiled. "And I'm sure that's why all of you are here this morning." Then he launched into his sermon.

Unfortunately, Edith was so distracted by Myrtle's strong words, not to mention being deposed from her regular seat, that she was unable to really focus. All she could think of was that this Myrtle had a lot of nerve to dress down the entire congregation. Good grief, she'd been here for less than twenty-four hours, and she was already telling people how to act. It was just a bit much. And, although it wasn't Edith's fault, she felt personally responsible for her guest's less than thoughtful behavior. She couldn't imagine how she was going to make up for it—especially to someone like Olive Peters, and Edith could feel Olive's eyes peering at her from across the church right now.

Finally the service was over, they were singing the anthem, and Edith was considering making a swift exit out the side door in the kitchen. But before she had a chance to make her getaway, someone tapped her on the shoulder from behind.

Edith turned in the pew to see Mrs. Fish. And her old wrinkled face looked concerned.

"I'd like to be introduced to your guest," she said.

But by then Myrtle had already turned around. "I'm Myrtle," she said without fanfare.

Mrs. Fish nodded with a stiff smile.

"This is my friend Mrs. Fish," said Edith quickly. "She's a retired schoolteacher."

Myrtle stuck out her hand. "Nice to meet you."

"I was interested in your comments this morning," began Mrs. Fish.

Then before another word was said, Edith hastily excused herself and made her exit. Oh, she was curious as to what Mrs. Fish was going to say to Myrtle. But not curious enough to stick around. Who knew what might happen with two opinionated women like that. Of course, the ever courteous Mrs. Fish would probably practice perfect self-control. But Myrtle seemed to be a bit of a loose cannon, and Edith didn't care to be around to witness any fireworks. Instead she made her quick getaway as planned, getting all the way to the kitchen before Olive caught up with her.

"Where on earth did that woman come from?" demanded Olive in quiet tones.

Edith smiled. "I'm not sure." Then changing the subject, "How is Helen doing?"

"Helen's fine," Olive said quickly. "But seriously, Edith, what is wrong with that woman? I thought she was going to start preaching fire and brimstone at us. You and Pastor Charles better make sure you keep her in check."

Edith wasn't sure how to respond, but apparently that didn't matter, because now Mrs. Fish and Myrtle were coming into the kitchen.

"I want you to meet Olive Peters," said Mrs. Fish. "Olive?"

Olive looked over with a confused expression. "Yes?"

"Well, Myrtle and I were just discussing the real meaning of Christmas, and she was telling me how she's something of an expert when it comes to nativity productions and such. And I told her that you're managing the pageant this year, and about Helen's fall and how she hurt her knee and won't be of much help." Mrs. Fish smiled. "And it seems you're in luck, Olive. Myrtle just volunteered to give you a hand."

Olive tossed a warning look to Edith, almost as if she expected

Edith to remedy this perplexing situation. But Edith was at a complete loss for words at the moment. She just wanted to get back to her kitchen and baking and to forget all about this unpredictable Myrtle Pinkerton.

"When do we start?" asked Myrtle, as if it were all settled.

Olive's lips were pinched tightly together, and Edith actually felt sorry for her.

"I—uh—we're having a rehearsal today," Olive finally said in a flat voice. "It starts at one."

"Maybe we should spend some time planning first," suggested Myrtle. "During lunch works for me." She frowned. "Although I can't say much for the choices of eateries in this town."

Olive cleared her throat. "Well, if you want to come home with me . . . I could warm us up some beef stew that I made last night."

Myrtle nodded. "What are we waiting for?"

Edith smiled to herself as she crossed the street. Olive might've met her match in Myrtle. Hopefully, it wouldn't ruin the Christmas pageant or do any other sort of permanent damage to Christmas or Christmas Valley in general. And it might keep Myrtle occupied and, consequently, out of trouble.

6

||||||||||||||||||

"Are you going over to the church to help Olive with the pageant today?" Edith asked Myrtle on Monday morning, hoping that perhaps she'd get a short reprieve from Myrtle's nonstop prattle, most of it focused on how Edith was or was not preparing a recipe correctly. Despite the sign above the kitchen door that clearly stated, Edith had previously believed, that this area was strictly off-limits to guests, Myrtle persisted in coming in and making herself at home. Not only that, she persisted in giving Edith culinary suggestions like, "Shouldn't you add some anise to that batter?" And then when Edith's back was turned, Myrtle took the liberty to add it, generously. Perhaps it would make the cookies taste better, but it irritated Edith just the same.

"The rehearsal isn't until this afternoon," said Myrtle as she poured herself another cup of coffee and watched Edith stirring the dough.

Edith considered reminding Myrtle about her kitchen rule again, but since the past two attempts had clearly fallen upon deaf ears, why waste her breath?

"When are the other Christmas guests coming?" asked Myrtle as she watched Edith starting to roll out cookie dough. Edith had already explained to Myrtle about her children and how they'd been unable to come home for Christmas, and thus her plan for opening her home during the holidays.

"Some are supposed to arrive in the afternoon."

"Here," said Myrtle, suddenly reaching for the rolling pin and actually taking it right from Edith's hands. "Let me show you how it's *supposed* to be done."

Edith watched helplessly as Myrtle took over the menial task that anyone else would've gladly relinquished. But instead Edith felt irritated. And something else too. Another emotion stirred within her—a feeling she couldn't even name. But something about this whole kitchen scene felt very familiar to her. She just couldn't put her finger on it.

"Have you always lived in Christmas Valley?" asked Myrtle as she skillfully worked the rolling pin over the dough.

Edith decided it probably wouldn't hurt to tell Myrtle the nutshell version of how she and Charles relocated from Iowa after he finished seminary. The whole while she watched, almost mesmerized, as the rolling pin moved steadily back and forth across the dough.

"What about *your* family?"

"You mean my children?"

"No. I mean your parents."

Edith considered this for a long moment, unsure as to how much she wished to disclose to this almost complete stranger, but finally said, "I was raised by my grandparents. They both passed on several years ago."

Myrtle nodded. "Any brothers or sisters?"

"No."

"That must've been pretty lonely for you, growing up . . ."

Edith nodded, somewhat surprised at what seemed a compassionate response from Myrtle. "Yes, I suppose that's one of the reasons that I like having my children around me at Christmastime. It helps to make up for all those quiet Christmases when it was just my grandparents and me."

"You ready?" asked Myrtle, holding up the rolling pin like a torch or maybe a club.

"For what?" Edith felt confused.

"The dough. It's time to cut the cookies."

"Oh."

As Edith and Myrtle proceeded to cut out cookies in the shapes of trees, stars, angels . . . placing them one by one on the buttered cookie sheet, Edith found herself thinking about her childhood. And that's when it occurred to her that Myrtle reminded her a bit of her grandmother. Fairly bossy, pushy, and rather outspoken. Her grandmother had been one of those women who knew it all and wanted everyone around her to know that she did. Oh, Edith had always been grateful to her grandmother. But she often felt overwhelmed by the woman's strong opinions. So when the opportunity arose to leave home at eighteen, via a marriage that her grandmother had severely questioned, Edith leaped at the chance. Of course, her grandmother thought it was a huge mistake, that Charles was too old for her and that Edith should finish college before marrying. And most disturbing to her grandmother was that Charles wanted to relocate them to Christmas Valley. "A foolish move that you'll one day regret," her grandmother had warned her.

But Edith had never regretted it. Oh, she regretted that the gulf between her and her grandparents had grown wider with each passing year. But with the birth of her first child and the other three so shortly thereafter, she was so distracted with motherhood, her husband's ministry, and all the daily demands of life that contact with her grandparents steadily decreased until it was little more than Christmas and birthday cards.

And then after her children became adults and left home, Edith opened up the bed and breakfast, and her life was just as busy as ever. Her grandfather had died about ten years ago, and her grandmother died the following year. Naturally, she had been saddened to lose them, but then they'd both been in their nineties, so it hadn't been a great surprise. Of course, she did regret that they'd never come out to visit. Even when she specifically invited them to come stay at the newly remodeled B and B, they had declined on account of "health" issues. But she suspected it was merely an excuse.

Myrtle was gathering up the remnants of dough now, slapping them together into a small ball that she proceeded to roll out, back and forth, as if she had done this many a time in the past. Edith no longer cared that Myrtle had taken over. Mostly she felt an overwhelming sense of sadness. She wasn't even sure why.

"You seem to have everything under control here," she told Myrtle as she removed her apron and hung it on the hook by the back door. "Do you mind taking the cookies out of the oven when they're done?"

"Not at all." Myrtle didn't even look up. "Go ahead and do what you need to do. I can handle this by myself. Besides, I'm sure you have a lot to get done before the other guests get here."

"Yes . . ." Edith nodded. But as she walked out of the kitchen, she couldn't think of a single thing that needed doing. Oh, certainly there was plenty to do, but it was as if her usual well-organized mind had been wiped completely clean.

She went up to the room that she and Charles shared. They had remodeled this space for themselves before transforming their home into the Shepherd's Inn. By combining two smaller bedrooms and a bath, they had created a large and comfortable suite that provided a tranquil getaway, a private retreat. And since Charles was visiting a parishioner who was in the hospital in a nearby town, the orderly room was quiet and peaceful now. Edith went inside and closed the door behind her. Then, sitting down in her padded rocking chair, she began to cry. Tears from long ago poured down her cheeks, and she let them. She wasn't quite sure what she was specifically crying for—oh, it had to do with her grandparents, of course, her childhood, their passing . . . but it was all rather vague. Perhaps she was simply grieving.

She wasn't sure just how long she actually cried, but after she'd blown her nose and splashed cold water on her face, it was nearly two o'clock. And she knew it was only a matter of time until the new guests would begin arriving. She *must* pull herself together.

The house was quiet when Edith went back downstairs. She figured that Myrtle was over at the church either helping or harassing Olive. But at least it gave Edith a chance to regroup and get a few things done. To her relief, the cookies looked okay. Perhaps a bit thinner than she would've made them, but at least they hadn't burned. She picked up a lopsided star and took a bite. To be perfectly honest, the anise did make them taste more interesting. She wished there was time to brew a pot of tea, but Edith figured she'd better get busy before the guests started coming. She still needed to put fresh linens in the Good Shepherd Room, where she planned to put Albert Benson, since he was alone and the room was a bit smaller than the others. She also wanted to put the special Christmas mints on the pillows. She'd just picked them up at the Candy Cane Shoppe yesterday afternoon.

"You're going to have your hands full with your new guest," Betty Gordon had told her in a conspirator's tone. Betty was the owner of the candy shop as well as a member of their congregation.

"So you heard her this morning?" ventured Edith.

Betty laughed. "I can imagine she'll really spice things up at the inn."

Edith nodded without commenting.

"Between you and me, I heard that she made a similar scene at Mrs. Santa's Diner."

"Oh, dear . . ."

Betty slipped the package of specialty mints into a red-and-white-striped bag. "It's not my place to say this, but the less time that woman spends in town, the better it will be for everyone, Edith."

"Well, she's helping Olive with the Christmas pageant," said Edith as she put her change into her purse. "That should keep her busy."

"Poor Olive."

Edith nodded. She had been tempted to apologize, but then it wasn't really her fault if a guest behaved badly. Was it?

Edith placed the final mint on the pillow in the Cool Water Room. This room was one of her favorites. All in shades of blue, it was so soothing and peaceful. This was where she planned to put the Thomases. Something the wife had said suggested in her email that the couple had been under a lot of stress lately. Hopefully, this would help.

Edith was just going down the stairs when she heard voices below.

"Hello," she called as she spied a couple standing in the foyer. They looked to be about her age, or maybe younger. "You must be the Fieldses," she said as she shook their hands and introduced herself.

"I'm Carmen," said the woman, then with a slight frown, "and this is Jim."

Jim didn't look too happy.

"We would've been here sooner, but Jim got lost. I begged him to stop and ask directions . . . but you know how men can be."

Edith smiled. "Christmas Valley is a bit off the beaten path."

Then she gave them a brief tour, explained how things worked, gave them some brochures from town, and finally showed them to their room.

"Staff and Rod?" questioned Jim.

"All the rooms are named after portions of the twenty-third psalm," she explained quickly. But still they didn't seem to get it.

"Because this is the Shepherd Inn," she continued. "And the shepherd uses a staff and rod to keep his sheep safe."

"It sounds more like something he'd use to beat them with," said Carmen.

Edith laughed. "No, no," she said. "A good shepherd would never do that."

She was only a couple steps away when she heard the couple starting to argue. She couldn't discern the words, but she could hear the anger in their voices. Surely they would resolve their differences over their trip and start enjoying their visit before long. At least she hoped so.

Edith was just cleaning up the cookie-making mess when Myrtle came into the kitchen. Tempted to point at the sign above the door, Edith decided it was useless. This woman, not unlike her grandmother, would do just as she pleased.

"I thought I'd find you in here," said Myrtle. "I'm just going to town to get something to eat."

Edith nodded. "That's nice."

"Yes, I thought I should let someone know just in case I have a heart attack on the way." Myrtle frowned.

"Are you feeling unwell?" inquired Edith with a bit of concern.

"No, but it is a bit of a walk, and I'm not as young as I used to be."

Just then Charles came in through the back door. Edith knew he was surprised to see Myrtle in the kitchen, but you couldn't tell by his expression. Of course, this was a trick he'd learned after all his years of pastoring.

"Hello, Myrtle," he said pleasantly. "How are you today?"

She scowled. "I was just telling Edith that having to walk to town for meals is inconvenient for someone like me."

"Can I offer you a ride?" he said with a smile.

She brightened. "Well, now, that'd be just fine."

"Can I pick up anything for you while I'm out?" he asked Edith.

So she gave him a short list, then thanked him. Of course, she was thanking him for transporting Myrtle and getting her out of the inn for a bit.

They had barely left before another guest arrived. This time it was Albert Benson, an elderly man who said very little. Edith tried to be friendly as she guided him to his room, but he kept the conversation short and curt.

Edith couldn't help but feel dismayed as she went back downstairs. So far her Christmas guests consisted of a cantankerous old woman, a couple who didn't seem to get along too well, and now a moody old man. Oh, she knew that these were probably people who just needed to be loved. But she had so hoped that Christmas would be fun and fulfilling for everyone, and now she was worried that it was going to be stressful and difficult at best.

So Edith did what she usually did whenever she felt worried about something. She sat down at her little desk, bowed her head, and prayed. She asked God to help her and Charles to help each one of her guests, specifically laying their problems out in the same way that she might arrange bath linens, and finally she imagined herself putting all this into God's capable hands as she said "amen."

Then Edith arranged a tempting selection of breads, cookies, and goodies on the dining room table. She also made fresh pots of tea and coffee, then turned on the Christmas music and watered the tall evergreen tree that stood in the corner of the living room. She paused for a moment to savor the comforting ambience of Christmas—the sights and sounds and smells. Yes, she told herself, this Christmas would indeed be different, but it would also be good. And perhaps next year her children would be gathered around her again.

7

By Tuesday afternoon, the Shepherd's Inn was full. Lauren and Michael Thomas, a pleasant thirtysomething couple from Seattle, had arrived just past noon and were settled nicely into the Cool Water Room. And Leslie, the young and recently divorced mother, and her adorable daughter, Megan, had shown up in time for tea.

"Ooh," said Megan with wide eyes when she gazed up at the twelve-foot tree. "Look how big it is, Mommy!"

"This is beautiful," said Leslie as she looked at the various Christmas decorations and admired the setup for afternoon tea. "Much nicer than I expected."

Edith had to admit to herself that it was a great relief to have some guests who truly seemed to appreciate the inn's humble offerings. Perhaps the week wouldn't be so bad after all.

"Would you like to get situated in your room?" suggested Edith. "Then come back down for tea."

"That sounds great," said Leslie as she removed her thick down coat and hung it over her arm. "You know, the forecast said there was no chance of snow, but it's getting so cold outside that I'm not so sure now."

"Snow!" exclaimed Megan, looking at Edith hopefully. "Do you think it could snow in time for Christmas?"

Edith laughed. "Well, you just never know. And it wouldn't be the first time the weatherman was wrong."

As they walked through the foyer, Megan stopped to look at a delicate porcelain sculpture that was situated on a side table, something Edith had had for years. "Ooh, Mommy, look," she said, tugging on her mother's arm. "*An angel*." She reached for it.

"Don't touch, Megan." Leslie gently pulled her back. "It looks very breakable."

"It's managed to survive all my grandchildren so far," said Edith as she escorted them upstairs. She smiled to herself as she opened the door to their room, the Lamb's Room, pausing long enough to hear Megan exclaiming over the small collection of pictures and statues that depicted lambs throughout the room. Clearly, the little girl was pleased. Well, that was something! Edith was feeling more and more hopeful.

After going back downstairs, she poured herself a cup of tea and gazed out the front window as she sipped. It was definitely getting colder out, but the sky was still crisp and clear with not a single cloud in sight. Of course, that could all change quickly enough. That's how it was here in the mountains. In fact, according to the town's historians, that's exactly how it happened back when the original trappers got stuck here so long ago. The weather had started out mild and unseasonably warm before it snapped and turned into one of the biggest blizzards in recorded history. Not that Edith cared to see a snowstorm of that proportion this year, but a nice layer of white for little Megan . . . well, that would be lovely.

The phone in the kitchen rang, jarring Edith back to the present. And when she answered it, the male voice on the other end sounded rather angry. "We have a little problem down here at the North Pole Coffee Shop."

"Who is this calling?"

"This is Mayor Drummel, Edith. And you have a rather eccentric guest who is making a bit of a scene down here," he told her. "Seems she has a problem with Santa Claus."

"Oh, dear." Edith took in a quick breath. "That must be Myrtle . . . and I'm guessing you must be playing Santa today?"

"You got that right. Can you please come down here and get this woman, or do I have to call in the police?"

"Of course," said Edith. "I'll be right there."

Lauren and Michael were just coming in to get tea as Edith was leaving. "I'm terribly sorry," she told them, "but I have to run to town to pick up a guest. Do you mind helping yourselves?"

"Not at all," said Lauren. "This looks yummy."

Edith nodded. "Thank you. I should be right back."

As usual during the week preceding Christmas, Mayor Drummel was outfitted in a very authentic-looking Santa suit, and a line of young children were waiting to sit on his lap. However, Santa was not seated, and the children looked rather unhappy.

"She's in the coffee shop," said the mayor when he spotted Edith. "I told her to either go in there and shut up, or risk going to jail."

"I'm so sorry," began Edith.

"Just take her away," demanded the mayor in a hushed voice. "She's ruining everything. Do you know that she actually told the children that I was a fake and that there is no such thing as Santa Claus?"

Edith just shook her head. "I am so terribly sorry."

"Just get her out of here," he said as he turned and headed back to his big velvet-covered chair. "Everything's going to be okay now, children," he said in a big, dramatic Santa-style voice. "*Ho-ho-ho!* That poor old woman was very naughty when she was a little girl, and all I ever put in her stocking was lumps of coal and switches."

The children's eyes grew wide with worry, as if they too might've been naughty a time or two.

"But don't fret," he told them in a reassuring tone. "You're all good children, and I'm sure that I'll be bringing you something much better."

Edith hurried into the North Pole Coffee Shop, unsure as to what she might find. Perhaps Myrtle would be standing on a chair and telling the customers to repent of all Christmas folly lest they be doomed forever.

Fortunately, that was not the case. Myrtle was quietly sitting at the counter, sipping a cup of coffee.

"I heard there was a problem . . ." Edith spoke in a quiet voice as she took the empty stool next to Myrtle. She was well aware of the eyes that were watching her now. And she felt certain that they wanted her to get the crazy woman out of here, the sooner the better. Still, she didn't want to do anything to rock Myrtle's boat. That would probably just make things worse.

"Wasn't much of a problem," said Myrtle in a matter-of-fact voice. "I just wanted to set the children straight. Grown-ups shouldn't be lying to children."

"It's just for fun," explained Edith.

"Well, I told those kids that they should come to church and see the Christmas pageant if they wanted to know what Christmas was really about."

"*You didn't?*" Edith was horrified. What a terrible way to invite people to their church! Good grief, Myrtle might as well have been carrying a gun. No wonder Mayor Drummel was so upset. As far as Edith knew, that poor man had never set foot in church in his entire life. And this would probably set him back light-years.

"I did," retorted Myrtle. "And I'd do it again if necessary."

"Please, don't."

"Well, it's a shame letting children think that Christmas is nothing but Santa Claus and ho-ho-ho. Someone should tell them the truth."

"In due time, Myrtle," said Edith. "I'm sure the children will all hear the truth in due time."

Finally, Myrtle was done with her coffee, and Edith quietly escorted her out a side door and to her car that was parked in back.

"It's cold out here," said Myrtle as she climbed in the car. "I can feel snow in my old bones."

"I hope so," said Edith, thankful to change the subject from Santa to snow. "We've got a sweet little girl at the inn who is praying for snow." She looked up toward the mountains and noticed a thick layer of clouds that was accumulating there.

"*Praying* for snow?" Myrtle shook her head in obvious disapproval as she made a *tsk-tsk* sound.

Edith decided not to engage. "All the guests have arrived now. The inn is full."

"No room at the inn, eh?"

Edith smiled. "Yes, I guess you could say that." Of course, she was also thinking that it would be nice if a certain room, a room that was occupied by a certain cantankerous woman, would suddenly vacate. However, she could never admit such an ungracious thing to a single soul. Besides, she reminded herself, this Christmas was about being hospitable to strangers. And she'd certainly never had a guest who was any stranger than Myrtle Pinkerton!

All the guests, except Albert Benson, were having tea in the dining room when Edith and Myrtle walked in. It was nice to see they'd introduced themselves and were now comfortably chatting with each other. To her relief, Charles had emerged from his study to join them and was currently talking to Jim Fields about Australia. It seemed that the Fieldses had spent their last Christmas down under. And Lauren and Michael were visiting with little Megan, telling her that they too thought it might snow for Christmas. In many ways, it wasn't so unlike one big happy family.

Edith introduced Myrtle to the other guests, hoping that this unpredictable woman wouldn't do something to immediately alienate herself from the rest of the group, but to her surprise, Myrtle seemed in good spirits now. And soon she was visiting with Leslie, examining her knitted vest, and giving her tips on how Leslie could've done it even better. Oh, well.

Edith went to the kitchen to make a fresh pot of tea. As she turned on the teakettle, she wondered about Myrtle and what they would do about her. Perhaps it would be best if they restricted her from going to town at all. Edith could offer to fix her simple meals to eat in the kitchen, since she spent half her time in there anyway. But how could they force her to comply? It wasn't as if they were her legal guardians. Perhaps Charles would have some ideas.

The afternoon tea party slowly broke up, with some people going to town, others to their rooms. Charles joined Edith in the kitchen. "Everything going okay?" he asked, and she suspected that her face, as usual, was giving away her concerns.

So she told him about the little fiasco in town with Myrtle. Of course, this only made him laugh. "I can just imagine the look on poor Drummel's face," he said after he'd recovered.

"That's not all," she continued, telling him how Myrtle had "invited" everyone to the church's Christmas pageant.

He shook his head. "Well, don't worry, Edith, I doubt that it'll make a difference one way or another. And, besides, I'm sure she meant well."

"Just the same, I think we should have a talk with her," said Edith.

"Meaning, *I* should have a talk with her?"

"Well, you're better at these things . . .

"Perhaps we can make it seem as if she's our special guest," said Edith suddenly. "We can tell her that since she doesn't have a car and it's difficult for her to get to town . . . that we'd like her to share meals with us. Would that be okay?"

He nodded. "That sounds like a wise plan."

So they put it to her, and to Edith's great surprise and relief, Myrtle seemed perfectly fine with this idea. When the three of them sat down to a humble meal of black-bean soup and cornbread, Edith looked out the kitchen window. She saw that fluffy white snowflakes, illuminated by the back-porch light, were tumbling down.

"It's snowing," she said with childlike enthusiasm. "Perhaps it'll be a white Christmas after all."

Charles nodded. "The weatherman is wrong again."

"They should hire weathermen with old bones like mine," commented Myrtle. "Then they'd know for sure if it was going to rain or snow. My joints have been aching something fierce all day."

"Well, I'm sure that it didn't help to walk back and forth to town," said Edith. "Fortunately, you won't have to do that anymore."

Myrtle just nodded without commenting, and for some reason Edith wasn't so sure she was going to be able to keep Myrtle from her anti-Christmas antics. She might have to keep a special eye on this woman during the next few days.

It had been a long day, but it finally seemed as if things were settling down at the Shepherd's Inn. The guests were all back from their various dinner places. Even the somber Albert Benson had ventured out. Now everyone was in their rooms, and Edith and Charles were turning off the downstairs lights when they heard a knock at the door.

"Who could that be at this hour?" asked Edith.

"We'll soon find out," said Charles as he went to open the door. A blast of chilly winter air mixed with snow burst in, and there on the porch stood a young couple.

Edith blinked as she looked over Charles's shoulder to see them better. These people looked as if they'd stepped right out of time. The tall, narrow-faced man had long brown hair and a full beard, and the shoulders of his dark woolen coat were dusted with snow. But it was the young woman who got Edith's attention with her sad dark eyes and a cascade of curls beneath a plaid woven scarf that was wrapped around her head.

"Do you have a room for the night?" asked the young man.

Charles looked at Edith, then back at the couple. "I'm sorry, but the inn is full until after Christmas."

The woman sadly nodded. "I told you they'd be full up, Collin," she said.

"Why don't you come in," suggested Charles. "That way we can close the door and keep the heat inside."

So the couple stepped into the foyer and, shaking powdery snow from their clothes, they looked around the inn and seemed impressed.

"This is a real nice place you got," said the man.

"It's so pretty," said the woman.

"Where are you two from?" asked Charles.

"Montana," said the woman. "We're heading to California."

"California?" echoed Edith. "Aren't you a little off course?"

The woman made a half smile. "Well, Collin picked the straightest route going west. Then we planned to head due south to San Diego where his brother lives."

"But we were having some engine troubles," explained Collin.

"And then the weather hit," she added. "It's a real blizzard out there."

"And so we thought we'd treat ourselves to a room for just one night," said Collin. "Just to get cleaned up, you know. But that's okay, we're pretty low on funds anyway, we can stay in our bus."

"Your bus?" queried Charles.

Collin nodded toward the big picture window that looked out over the street. "Yeah, it's all set up to live in with a bed and everything. Not the Ritz or anything. But comfy enough."

Edith went over to peer out onto the street, but all she could see was dark shadows and snow flurries.

"Do you mind if we leave it parked there?" asked the woman. "On the street I mean? Just for the night, you know?"

"Or until I have time to tweak on the engine a little," Collin added. "It's running pretty badly right now."

Charles looked at Edith, and she just shrugged. "I don't see that it's a problem," she said.

"You wouldn't think so," said Charles. "Not for just one night."

"Do you need anything?" asked Edith. "Food or anything?"

The woman's eyes lit up. "We're low on water. And, hey, if you want to share some food . . . that'd be cool. We're pretty broke. Just trying to get down to San Diego so that Collin can find work, you know."

"Come on in the kitchen," said Edith, forgetting her sign again. "We've got some leftovers from dinner that you can have if you like. By the way, my name is Edith, and my husband is Charles."

"Oh, I'm sorry," said the woman. "We didn't even introduce ourselves. I'm Amy and," she jerked her thumb over a shoulder, "that's Collin."

In the brighter light of the kitchen, Edith could see that Amy was quite young. Probably early twenties at the most. And she also appeared to be quite pregnant.

"You're expecting?" said Edith as she put the bean soup into the microwave to heat.

"Yeah. My due date is actually the first week of January. But my back's been aching, and I feel as big as a house right now. I wouldn't mind if it came tonight."

"Tonight?" Edith felt her brows shooting up. "But what would you do? The hospital is nearly an hour away, and that's in good weather."

"Oh, I plan to have it naturally, at home." She laughed. "Or in the bus."

"Really?" Edith wrapped a generous chunk of cornbread in plastic wrap and put this into a grocery sack, along with several pieces of fruit.

"You mind if I fill this up in here?" asked Collin as he appeared with a large water jug.

"That's fine," said Edith. "Or if it's easier, go ahead and use the laundry sink out on the back porch."

Now Charles was in the kitchen too.

"Amy is expecting a baby soon," said Edith in what she hoped sounded like a calm voice.

"Yeah," said Amy. "The sooner the better. Although I suppose it might be easier to have it in San Diego. Not to mention warmer."

"It must be hard on you to travel," said Charles.

"Not really," she said. "If my back starts hurting, I just go lie down on the bed. But the bouncing gets to me sometimes. Do you have any idea how bouncy a bus can be?"

Charles just shook his head.

"Here you go," said Edith as she handed Amy the bag of food. "And you two feel free to come in and get some breakfast in the morning. There'll be plenty to go around."

"Seriously?" Amy looked truly surprised.

"Of course," said Edith. "You're more than welcome."

Now Collin emerged with his full water jug. "You guys are way cool," he said with a bright smile. "I told Amy that there were still a few good people left in this world."

Charles smiled at them. "Well, let's hope so."

They walked the couple to the door and told them good night. "Sleep well," called Edith as they went back out into the snow. She wanted to add "and don't go into labor," but that didn't sound quite right. Still, she really hoped that the baby would wait until the parents had safely made their destination in sunny Southern California.

"Wasn't that something?" said Charles as he locked the door.

"They seemed nice," said Edith. "I wish we had an available room. I'd let them have it for free."

He put his arm around her shoulder. "I know you would, dear. That's just one of the many things I love about you."

And then they went up to bed.

8

"What on earth is *that*?" exclaimed Myrtle when she came into Edith's kitchen.

"What?" Edith looked up from her daily devotions, trying not to seem as aggravated as she felt. Myrtle was such an early riser that Edith would have to start getting up a lot earlier if she expected to have a decent quiet time these days. As it was, she was already tiptoeing downstairs long before daylight.

"That hideous contraption that's parked in front of your inn is what."

Edith went to the living room and looked out the big picture window in front. "Oh, my . . ." Her hand flew up to her mouth as she remembered their late-night visitors. "That's, uh, very interesting."

"It's atrocious!"

"Well, it's certainly colorful." Edith smiled to herself as she studied the wild-colored stripes and flowers and geometric designs. "It looks like a hippie bus—straight out of the sixties."

"I'll say," said Myrtle with a look of disgust. "How in the world do you think it got here?"

So Edith explained about the young couple's unexpected arrival the night before. "We told them it was okay to park there for the night." She chuckled. "But we hadn't actually seen their bus since it was dark out."

"Well, you sure can't miss it now."

Even with the thick white cap of snow on top, you couldn't miss the brightly colored bus. In fact, the clean blanket of snow all around only made the bus stand out more. "Well, don't worry," said Edith. "They'll probably be gone by noon." Then she returned to the kitchen, dismayed to see that Myrtle was right on her heels. "They're just a couple of young people, on their way to California, hopefully in time for the baby."

"Baby?" Myrtle frowned. "You mean people are traveling in that old dilapidated thing and they're about to have a baby? That sounds plum crazy to me." She lowered her voice. "Do you think they're drug people?"

Edith sighed. "I don't think so."

"Well, I remember when the kids who lived in vehicles like that were all a bunch of druggies. A bunch of social outcasts who wanted to turn on or drop out or something to that effect. Horrible way to raise a baby, if you ask me."

Edith wanted to remind Myrtle that no one had asked her, but instead she asked her to stir the pancake batter.

Breakfast came and went without an appearance of the mysterious young couple who inhabited the colorful bus on the street. At first Edith felt relieved, as it alleviated the need to explain exactly who these people were to her paying guests. But then, as she was clearing the table and cleaning up, she began to feel some strong twinges of guilt. What if something was wrong? What if they had frozen to death out there? Or what if they'd had a gas leak and were asphyxiated? Or what if Amy had gone into labor and needed medical help?

Finally, Edith was so distraught that she couldn't concentrate on rinsing the plates, so she pulled on her fleece-lined snow boots and her heavy coat and hurried outside to check on them. Oh, certainly, she felt a bit intrusive as she knocked on the door, but really, what if something was seriously wrong? How could she not check?

After she knocked loudly several times and called out their names, a sleepy-looking Collin appeared at the window and opened the door. He was shirtless and blinking, almost as if he wasn't sure where he was. "Yeah?" he said in a gruff voice. "Something wrong?"

"No, I, uh," Edith stammered, "I—uh—I was just worried that something might be wrong out here. Were you warm enough?"

He nodded, realization coming to his face. "Yeah, no problem. It's pretty cozy in here. You don't need to worry."

"Well, come on into the inn if you want breakfast," she told him. "I've put aside some things for you and Amy."

"Sure, thanks." He smiled and closed the door.

Edith felt a bit silly and neurotic as she hurried back into the inn. Of course, they were perfectly fine. Why wouldn't they be? Probably just tired from their long journey yesterday. And she had forgotten that all young people seemed to enjoy sleeping in. Certainly her own children had been late risers. Still, that bit that Myrtle had tossed in about possible drug use did raise a smidgen of doubt in her mind. But, surely, a pregnant mother would have better sense than that. Wouldn't she?

It was nearly eleven when Collin and Amy came in for breakfast, but Edith tried to appear as if this were perfectly normal. She even poured herself a cup of tea and sat down with them, attempting to make light conversation.

"Do you know what's wrong with your engine?" she finally asked, hoping that it didn't sound too rude, as if she were hinting that these two should be on their way.

"Not exactly," said Collin. "I'm not real mechanical, if you know what I mean."

"Charles knows a bit about engines," she said absently.

"Do you suppose he could take a look?" asked Amy hopefully.

"Oh, I forgot this is Wednesday," Edith said. "Not a very good day for Charles to help."

"What does he do on Wednesdays?" asked Collin.

"He's a pastor," she told them. "The church across the street. He usually does the final revision of his midweek service on Wednesdays."

"Oh." Amy sighed and rubbed her large belly.

Seeing their disappointment, Edith quickly said, "But I can certainly ask him if he has some spare time." Also, she realized, if someone didn't get that engine running, the strange-looking bus wouldn't be going anywhere.

After the young couple finished their breakfast, Edith went and tapped on the door to Charles's study. "Sorry to disturb you," she began, then launched into the need for someone with mechanical expertise to help with the bus.

He set down his pen and closed his Bible. "That's quite a bus."

She made a half smile. "Anyway, I thought about calling Hal Berry," she continued, "but I wasn't sure that was such a good idea. I know his arthritis has been acting up lately."

Charles smiled. "I'll take a look at it, Edith. I think my sermon is in good shape, and I'm happy to lend a hand—if I can, that is."

"And it might help to get them on their way. You know, before anyone from town starts to make a fuss. I have to admit that their bus really does look a bit out of place out there."

Just then the phone rang, and Charles answered it. "It's Polly, Edith," he told her. "Want to take it in here while I go see what can be done?"

So Edith sank down into his big leather chair and said, "Hello, Polly."

"What is going on over at the inn?" asked Polly.

Edith laughed. "You mean our hippie bus?"

"Yes. Herb told me about it this morning. He'd seen it on his way into town when he got gas for our trip. But it sounded so outrageous that I actually thought he was making it up. As we were leaving town a bit ago, I made him drive by just so I could see it for myself. I'm calling you on my cell phone. Now I can't stand to leave town without knowing what's up over there."

So Edith explained about the young couple, even the part about the soon-to-be-born baby.

"Good grief!" said Polly. "I wish I could stick around and see what happens next. First it's that crazy Myrtle who seems determined to convert Christmas Valley to something—I don't even know what. And then it's a hippie bus straight out of the blue. Why, the next thing we know, you'll probably be out there helping to deliver a baby on Christmas day."

"Goodness, I hope not. I've never been very good in that situation. I had to be practically knocked out to deliver my own children. If Amy needed help, I suppose I could call up Helen—that's assuming she can remember anything about nursing since she's been retired for years."

"That'd be something else with Helen's bad knees and fading eyesight. I can just see it. Well, keep me informed, Edith. If it gets any more interesting, that is."

"Travel safely," said Edith. "The roads looked pretty slick this morning."

"Right. And have a merry Christmas, Edith. You and all your crazy guests and those hippie bus people too." Then she laughed and hung up.

Edith set the phone down. She supposed they must look a bit crazy to anyone from the outside looking in. But, really, Collin and Amy seemed like nice people, just a little down on their luck perhaps. Even Myrtle in her own way wasn't so bad. Sure, perhaps a bit eccentric and even obnoxious at times, but underneath that Edith thought she had a good heart.

"Leave me alone!" she heard a man's voice yelling and then the loud banging of a door. It seemed to be coming from the second floor, so Edith jumped up and dashed up the stairs to see.

"What's wrong?" she breathlessly asked Myrtle when she saw her standing in front of the Good Shepherd Room, the room where old Albert Benson was staying. "What happened?"

Myrtle shrugged with big innocent eyes. "I don't know."

"But I heard yelling up here," she continued. "Was it Mr. Benson? Is he okay? What's wrong?"

"He's a very moody man," said Myrtle as she turned and headed back toward her room on the other side of the hallway.

Just then Mr. Benson opened the door and stuck his head out. "I'm not moody," he said in a defensive voice. "I just don't wish to be bothered."

"Then why did you come here?" demanded Myrtle. "Why come to a bed and breakfast?"

Edith blinked. "Perhaps it was for some peace and quiet," she said. And normally that would be exactly what her guests could expect to find.

"During Christmas?" Myrtle looked skeptical.

"It's none of your business," he retorted. Edith hoped that was meant for Myrtle.

"That's right," Edith said in a soothing voice. "It's not our business. I just wanted to make sure you were okay, Mr. Benson."

"I'll be perfectly fine as long as *that woman* leaves me alone."

"Did you hear him, Myrtle?" asked Edith, suddenly feeling as if she had gone about twenty years back in time and was now talking to her own bickering children. "Mr. Benson would like you to leave him alone."

Myrtle shrugged again. "That's what he says . . . but if he wanted to be left alone, he should've just stayed home."

And at that, Mr. Benson slammed his door shut again.

Edith couldn't help but roll her eyes. "Please, Myrtle," she said, struggling to keep her voice calm and even. "Leave the poor man alone. I'm begging you."

"Fine," said Myrtle. "But you'll be sorry."

"*I'll* be sorry?"

Myrtle nodded without saying anything, then scuffled off to her room.

Edith sighed and walked away. More and more she was wondering whether she was running an inn or a nuthouse.

Hopefully, they'd all make it through Christmas without killing each other. She had to chuckle as she went down the stairs. In some ways this was a lot more like having her family there than she'd ever imagined possible. Suddenly she remembered how Katie and Krista usually got into at least one little, or sometimes big, snit before the holidays were over. Or how Tommy and Jack could get so competitive that they would bore everyone to tears by trying to one-up each other in their accomplishments. Well, what families always got along perfectly, anyway? Just as long as no one got hurt.

"I'm afraid that bus is in no condition to travel," announced Charles as he came into the kitchen and washed his hands in the sink. "Not without some serious mechanical work, not to mention expense."

"Do they have any money to fix it?"

"Not to speak of . . . and we, I mean the church, could probably help them. But I'd have to call an emergency board meeting first . . . and it's not the best time of year for that . . . I'm not sure . . ." He shook his head. "Besides the engine, the tires are bald, and they don't even have chains to get over the mountain pass. Kids these days."

"Well, you know what the Good Book says . . ." Edith smiled.

"I do and I don't. What do you mean?"

"That God watches out for fools and children."

He nodded. "Well, I think they could fit into both categories." He scratched his head. "Collin told me that Amy is only nineteen. *Nineteen?* Can you believe it? I mean, our baby Krista is seven years older than that, and I couldn't imagine her in this position."

"Well, she would never put herself in this position, dear."

"And Collin is only twenty-one. They really aren't much more than children, Edith."

"Yes. But don't forget that I was even younger when we got married, Charles. And not even twenty-one when we had Tommy."

"But you were mature," he argued. "You were old for your age."

She laughed. "Thanks. I guess."

He sighed. "I just don't know what to do about them."

"Well, it's not as if you have to figure it all out today," she said. "Besides, if they spend another night, they might come to church tonight. And that might be a good thing for them, don't you think?"

He smiled now. "Perhaps you're right, my dear. Perhaps it would."

And as it turned out, Edith was right. Not only were they willing, but the young couple was happy to come to church with her.

"We're only going because of you guys," said Amy after Edith invited the two of them to come. "You and your husband have been so kind that it's making us rethink some of our opinions about church and religion and stuff."

It was after seven when Edith walked across the freshly plowed street to the church. She knew she was running late, but there'd been so many distractions at the inn this afternoon. Mainly because of Myrtle. It seemed that woman had gotten some kind of a bee in her bonnet about poor Albert Benson. But Edith wasn't sure what her real motives were—was she flirting with the old man or just trying to drive him batty? Edith finally had to plead with Charles to step in and intervene. Fortunately, Mr. Benson seemed to appreciate this, and he didn't even mind heading over to the church thirty minutes early so that he could help Charles with a stubborn lock, since they'd just learned that Mr. Benson was a retired locksmith.

Of course, this left Myrtle at loose ends again, and as a result she had started offering "marriage counseling" tips to the Fieldses. Not that they didn't need some help in that regard, for it was plain to see that this couple had some real issues. But Myrtle hardly seemed the answer. Finally Edith persuaded Myrtle to head over to church herself, and after the meddling old woman was gone, Edith tried to smooth things over with the feuding Fieldses.

"Myrtle's one of those people who likes to have her finger in every pie," offered Edith. "I hope you won't take her words too seriously."

Carmen Fields, sitting on the sofa with arms crossed tightly across her front, still looked upset. "Well, she made a good point. Jim *does* seem to take me for granted."

"Who takes *who* for granted?" he shot back at her.

"You do!" snapped Carmen. "We've been married almost thirty years, and I'll bet I can count on one hand how many times you've told me that you appreciate me."

"That's not true!"

And on they went until the rest of the guests quietly slipped away, either to church or to the Christmas play that the town was putting on tonight. Finally, Edith excused herself too. And consequently, she was late to church.

9

||||||||||||||||

When she got to church, Edith wasn't terribly surprised to see that Myrtle was, once again, in her seat. And since she was late, Edith decided to sit in the back. Sure it felt strange, but in light of everything else it seemed fitting. It was as if her world were getting turned upside down, or perhaps tilting sideways. Hopefully, things would improve by Christmas. The idea of having a houseful of bickering guests over the holidays made Edith want to run away from home.

She scanned the backs of heads, recognizing old friends and neighbors as well as a few of their guests. She was just late enough to have missed introductions, and she desperately hoped that Myrtle hadn't done anything to upset anyone's applecart, specifically Mr. Benson's. But all seemed calm and normal. And the church was fuller than usual, although that still meant that more than half the seats were vacant.

She noticed Collin and Amy, only a couple of rows ahead of her, and she might have imagined it, but it seemed that when Charles came to the challenging part of his sermon, Collin leaned forward just a bit as if trying to soak the words in. That was encouraging. Perhaps the delay of their departure really was for a good reason. Maybe these two young people would take away something good— perhaps even something life changing—before they left Christmas Valley for good.

Just three days until Christmas Eve, she told herself as the service wound down and they stood to sing the anthem. *So much to be done.* And, she wondered, was it really worth all the work and effort? Oh, it was one thing to stretch herself this thin for her own family and loved ones, but what had she been thinking to go to this much trouble for a bunch of strangers? Somewhat cantankerous strangers at that. Just then some of the words from Charles's sermon last week drifted through her mind. *Showing hospitality to strangers . . . perhaps entertaining angels unaware . . .*

She looked again at the young couple standing just ahead of her. Collin had his arm draped protectively over Amy's shoulders as he gave her a little squeeze. So seemingly vulnerable and in such a desperate state of need, and to think these two were about to become parents! It must be overwhelming. Would these young people be able to make it? Goodness knows they barely had a roof over their heads.

And that's when something hit her—almost as if God himself had whacked her over the head with a hymnal. She actually jumped. Why hadn't she considered this before? This struggling young couple wasn't so different from sweet Mary and Joseph so long ago! And, not unlike Jesus's parents, Collin and Amy had found no room at the inn as well! How interestingly ironic! In fact, here she'd been thinking about hospitality and angels and, well . . . but the song ended, and she was quickly brought back to the here and now by her husband's voice. He was making an announcement.

"There will be an unscheduled board meeting tonight," Charles was telling the congregation. "We'll meet in the conference room, and it, hopefully, won't take too long."

Edith assumed this must be the "emergency meeting" he'd mentioned earlier. He was probably going to try to convince the board to help this young couple. Feeling reassured, she smiled brightly at her husband. He was such a good man. And then the church began to empty to the soft tones of Marie's organ playing.

"What is going on at the inn?" demanded Olive before Edith even had a chance to slip into her coat.

Edith blinked. "What do you mean?"

"That bus."

"Oh, that . . ." Edith forced a smile. "It's temporarily stranded,

Olive. But I think you'll hear more about that at the board meeting tonight."

"Well, hopefully, it won't be there for long. It looks perfectly terrible, Edith. And don't you forget that the pageant is only two nights away. It had better be gone by then, or I'll want to know the reason why."

Now Helen limped over to join them. She was using a shiny black cane to help her walk. Edith hoped that Helen didn't have any lawsuit plans in mind—that would surely send the church insurance sky-high. "Are you talking about that monstrosity out in front of the inn?" she asked.

Edith glanced over to the aisle to see if Collin and Amy were close enough to overhear any of this. Fortunately, it looked like they weren't. But it also looked as if no one in the entire congregation was speaking to them either. Edith longed to go over and join them, make them feel welcome, but she was completely blocked in her pew by Olive and Helen as they discussed the inappropriateness of the colorful bus parked across the street.

"Not only that," continued Helen, now turning her attention to Edith, "but Clarence said that Mayor Drummel plans to give you a call. He's not the least bit happy with this. Especially at Christmas."

"Oh . . ." Edith was distracted by the young couple. They were slipping out the front door mostly unnoticed, probably going back to their bus, which was likely cold. She was just about to rush over and stop them. She didn't know what she'd say or do, but somehow she had to—

"Did you hear me?" demanded Helen. "The mayor is going to call you on this, Edith Ryan. Aren't you the least bit concerned?"

Edith watched the door close behind the couple, then looked at her watch in dismay. "Are you ladies planning to attend the board meeting?" she asked suddenly.

"That's right," said Olive crisply as she took Helen by the arm that wasn't attached to the cane. "Let's go."

Now, although Edith, being the pastor's wife, was welcome to sit in on board meetings, she rarely did. She found the conversations not only dull, but usually rather frustrating. It seemed that some people, particularly board member types, liked hearing the sounds of their own voices more than they did resolving issues. And often they would end up in a big argument, and the meeting would adjourn, and everyone would go home disgruntled. Then they would talk among themselves during the week, some holding a grudge, others just hurt. Finally, they would meet again, and worn out from the battle, they would work out some sort of compromise. She hoped that wouldn't be the case tonight, since the plight of Collin and Amy seemed rather urgent.

And so she decided that perhaps this was a good night for her to sit in. With people like Olive and Helen already so worked up about the presence of the bus, who knew what might happen tonight. The board members might emerge from the church with torches, storm across the street, and beat on the bus as they demanded that the "hippies leave town!" Oh, she knew she was being overly dramatic, but at the same time she might not be too far off either. So, filled with trepidation, she headed for the conference room, and hoping to be inconspicuous, she took a seat by the door.

In his usual formal way, Hal Berry called the meeting to order. "As you know, this is an emergency board meeting," he said, "requested by Pastor Charles, and being that it's the holidays, our good pastor has promised to keep it short."

Then Charles stood up. "I'm sure you've all seen the bus across the street. . . ."

Several sarcastic twitters and indistinguishable comments assured Edith that she'd been right to come. And as her husband made his plea, she could tell by their expressions that most of the board members were not feeling sympathetic to Charles's straightforward request for assistance.

"Why should we help *them*?" asked Olive after he sat down. "They don't even live here."

"That's right," added Helen. "If we're going to help someone, why not start in our own town. We have young families who are struggling to make ends meet right here in Christmas Valley, and they're just as needy as those—those *bus people*."

"I don't know about that," said Peter Simpson, the youngest member of the board. "We don't have anyone in town who's actually living in a bus."

"And who lives in a bus?" demanded Olive. "For all we know, these people could be drug dealers. They do have that sort of look about them."

"Maybe we should let the law intervene," suggested Hal. "They might be better suited to handle something like this."

And on they went, back and forth and getting nowhere fast. As was her custom, Edith just sat and listened, until finally she did something she'd never done before. "May I say something?" she asked.

The room got quiet, and everyone looked at her.

"I know I'm not an official member of the board, but I really would like to say something."

"Go right ahead, Edith," said Hal in a kind voice. Charles smiled at her.

She stood up, feeling slightly light-headed and more than a little self-conscious, unsure if she could even continue. Speaking in front of a group, even one as small as this, had never been her strong suit. She hoped she was really up to the task. "I understand your concerns about our, uh, our *visitors*. And I realize their accommodations are a bit, well, shall I say unconventional?" More twitters. "But as I was sitting in church tonight, I was remembering what Charles had preached on just last week . . . about showing kindness and hospitality to strangers . . . and how sometimes we might be actually entertaining angels or our Lord without even knowing it. And as I was looking at this young couple, Collin and Amy, it occurred to me that they are in very similar straits as another couple . . . it occurred to me that more than two thousand years ago, Mary and Joseph were strangers in town too. They were looking for a place to stay . . . and, well, I just thought perhaps this is the Lord's doing. Perhaps he has sent Collin and Amy to remind us of something. Or maybe it's simply our opportunity to show kindness and hospitality. Or . . ." She lowered her voice now, almost afraid to actually put to words what was really on her mind. "Or is it possible that they might be angels or even our Lord himself in disguise? How could we ever know this for sure? But even if that's not the case, don't you think that our Lord would want us to open our hearts to them? To welcome them as if they were sent down from heaven above?"

Now the room got very silent for a long moment, and Edith, with nothing more to say, was almost afraid to breathe.

"Oh, that's ridiculous," said Olive finally. "They're obviously *not* angels."

"Of course not," agreed Helen. "And the Lord?" She shook her head.

"Arriving in that hideous bus?" added Olive.

"And yet," said Helen, with a thoughtful expression across her brow, "and yet . . . I think I am starting to see Edith's point."

And just like that, the attitude in the room began to shift and transform until not only was the board willing to pay for all the mechanical expenses *and* new tires, but Helen was talking about giving an impromptu baby shower for Amy.

"But they'll be leaving soon," protested Olive. "There'll be no reason for them to stick around once their bus is running."

"Then we'll have to jump right on it," said Helen with excitement. "I'll bet you that they don't have a single thing for that baby. Do they, Edith?"

Edith held up her hands. "I really don't know. But I guess I could find out."

"Right," said Helen. "You find out and call me first thing in the morning. Don't worry, I'll take care of the rest."

Edith's heart and heels were happy as she and Charles walked across the street later on that night. "It's just so amazing," she told him. "I don't ever remember the board being so generous, so quickly, before."

He squeezed her hand. "Well, you made a beautiful plea, dear. I don't know how they could've turned their backs after what you said."

"Do you think it sounded crazy?" she ventured. "I mean the part about them possibly being angels or even our Lord? Goodness, I don't want everyone to think that I'm losing my marbles."

"No, I think it sounded very tenderhearted and compassionate. And who knows? Maybe they are angels unaware."

Snowflakes were starting to fall again as Edith paused on the sidewalk to look over to where the bus was parked. For a few seconds she just stared and wondered. Wouldn't it be like God to send angels in a funny old vehicle like that—so quirky and unexpected? So unlike anything that humans would think of doing. But hadn't it been like that when the Lord Jesus was born in a humble barn? And as she went to sleep that night, she felt a deep and comforting sense of peace, as if she really was on the right track after all.

The next morning, Edith was happily puttering in her kitchen, getting cinnamon rolls into the oven and just starting up a pot of coffee, when the phone rang. "Shepherd's Inn," she sang out cheerfully.

"Edith Ryan?" said a male voice.

"Yes?"

"This is Mayor Drummel. I'm sorry to call so early, but I hadn't really planned to be in my office today, and I wanted to take care of this as soon as possible." He cleared his throat. "There's been concern expressed over the rather outlandish vehicle that's been parked in front of your inn."

"Yes?" Edith didn't know what to say.

"Well, I wanted to let you know that they'll need to leave as soon as possible. City ordinances do not allow for this type of vehicle to be parked in town. This morning won't be a bit too soon."

"But that might not be possible, Mayor Drummel. You see, they're broken down, and although our church is going to help them with mechanics and whatnot, I seriously doubt that the bus will be up and running anytime this morning."

"So they are leaving, then?"

"Of course. I'm sure they'll leave as soon as it's possible."

"Because it doesn't look good, Edith. I mean, we're a town that prides ourselves on appearances, especially at Christmastime. I'm sure you must understand the importance of this since you run a very nice inn and Charles oversees the town's only church—a rundown old bus that's broken down in the street doesn't reflect well on you folks either. If necessary, we could probably have them towed away."

Now, this rubbed Edith wrong. And while she didn't care to take the mayor to task, she thought perhaps a gentle reminder might be in order. "I can respect your concern," she began, "but you must remember that these are *real* people with *real* problems, and you can't simply brush them away as if they were garbage—especially at Christmas. If we're a town that really cares about Christmas, I'd think that we'd all want to reach out in the spirit of charity and help them out."

The mayor didn't respond to this.

"We'll do whatever we can to get their vehicle up and running," said Edith in a firm voice. "I just can't make any promises as to how soon that will be."

"But what about your church's pageant tomorrow night?"

"A bus on the street will hardly stop a Christmas pageant."

"But it won't look good, Edith."

Edith was looking out the window now, staring at the brightly painted bus, which suddenly reminded her of a giant Christmas ornament. "Beauty is in the eyes of the beholder," she said simply enough.

"*What?* What do you mean by that?"

"I mean that we are a town that loves to celebrate Christmas, and this year it seems that we are also the lucky recipients of a *Christmas bus*, and I happen to think it's rather beautiful."

"Oh."

After telling the mayor "Good day," Edith put on her coat and boots and hurried outside to check on Amy and Collin. She was surprised to see that about four more inches of snow had fallen during the night, bringing the accumulation to the top of her boots. Edith trudged through the snow and then knocked on the bus's door. This time Amy answered, but it looked as if they were already awake and dressed. Collin was sitting in the driver's seat, hunched over as he studied a worn map with a rather dismal expression.

"Sorry to bother you," Edith began.

"No bother." Amy held the door open. "Want to come in?"

Edith hesitated, then quickly said, "Yes, that'd be nice."

The interior of the bus was crowded with all manner of boxes and bags and, Edith's nose suspected, a fair amount of dirty laundry too. But Amy cleared a spot on a wooden crate and pointed for Edith to sit down. "It's not much," Amy apologized. "But, hey, it's better than nothing."

Edith nodded, glancing to the back of the bus where a mattress, heaped with quilts and blankets, was wedged. "It is cozy."

"You can say that again," said Amy. "And the bigger I get with this baby, the cozier it seems to get. I can't wait to get out of here. Collin's going to get work when we get settled, and then we'll rent something. Even a one-bedroom apartment will feel like a mansion compared to this."

"Speaking of the baby," began Edith, "I, uh, *we* were wondering if you have everything you need for it."

Amy shrugged. "I have a few things. Like some sleepers and blankets that I got at Salvation Army back home. And Collin got some newborn-sized disposable diapers that are in here . . ." She looked around. "Somewhere."

Edith nodded. "Yes, and that's a good start. But some of the women at church got this idea last night . . . they thought it would be fun to have a baby shower—"

"*A baby shower!*" Amy's eyes lit up. "Oh, man, I've been wishing for a baby shower. But we didn't really have anyone who wanted to do it. I mean, my family is, well, you know, a little dysfunctional. And Collin's family, well, they live all over the country."

Edith could feel Collin watching her now, and she wasn't sure what he was thinking, but she turned to him. "And that's not all, Collin. Our church would like to help you with your engine troubles, and even with some new tires . . ."

"Really?" He seemed a bit skeptical.

"Really," she said with a smile. "We had a special meeting last night. And everyone is behind this."

"Wow." He looked at Amy now. "I guess you were right after all."

"Right?" Edith wasn't sure what he meant.

"Oh, Amy kept telling me that you guys were good people. But after church last night, well, I just wasn't so sure."

Edith frowned slightly. "Well, some of our congregation can be a bit old-fashioned and hard to convince at times, but they basically have good hearts."

"That's just what I told Collin," said Amy. "I said we can't judge these people by appearances and that they probably thought we were pretty weird showing up in our bus like this—like from out of nowhere."

Edith smiled. "Yes, you've got that about right. In fact, I am curious as to where you came from and how you got this bus in the first place. It's not the sort of thing that one sees every day. At least not in Christmas Valley."

"The bus belonged to my dad," said Amy in a matter-of-fact tone. "But he didn't need it anymore. And we did." She held up her hand as if to say, "End of story."

"Oh." Edith looked around their cramped quarters again. "Well, come on in for breakfast whenever. You're welcome to use my laundry room if you'd like."

"That'd be great," said Amy. "I'm totally out of clean underwear." She laughed. "I'm actually wearing a pair of Collin's today. The funny thing is that they actually fit."

Edith wasn't quite sure how to respond to that, so she simply stood up and told them she had to get back before her cinnamon rolls burned.

10

At ten o'clock, after the last of the guests had finished breakfast, Edith called and informed Helen that the shower was a go.

"It sounds like they don't have much of anything," said Edith. "And living in the bus like that, without laundry facilities, well, I'm sure some extra clothes and blankets will come in handy."

"This is going to be fun," said Helen. "And I have all these decorations and plates and napkins and things that I'd wanted to use when Angie had her baby, and then her sister-in-law went and beat me to the punch."

"But that was more than twenty years ago, Helen."

"I know. But they were so cute that I hung on to them, and I plan to use them tomorrow."

"So you really think you can pull this off by tomorrow?"

"I don't see why not. People will come or they won't. But we *will* have a shower."

Not for the first time, Edith was reminded that Helen had once been a military nurse and that she was used to giving orders.

"Is ten o'clock all right with you?"

"It's fine."

"Great. I'll be there by 8:30 to set up."

"Be where?" Edith felt worried now.

"At the inn, of course. You didn't think I'd have it here, did you, Edith? Goodness knows, you've got far more room than I. And if you're not too busy, could you bake something yummy? You're such a good cook."

84

What could Edith say?

"And it might be easier if you made the punch too. Maybe something pink, since the decorations are blue and pink."

"Cake and punch," said Edith. "Anything else?"

"Well, do you happen to have mixed nuts and those little pastel mints on hand?"

"No, but I can get some."

"Oh, good. I think that should do it."

"How many people do you think we can count on, Helen?"

"Hmm . . ." Edith imagined her counting on her fingers. "I'd say at least twenty."

"Twenty?" Edith was surprised. "On such short notice? And just two days before Christmas?"

"Maybe even thirty."

Edith was not so sure. "Okay, well, I'll just make sure we have plenty, and if there are leftovers, I can use them during the holidays."

"Of course."

They said good-bye and hung up, and Edith just shook her head and sighed.

"What's wrong?" asked Charles as he came in to refill his coffee mug.

"Oh, nothing much. But it now looks as if I'm the one hosting the baby shower tomorrow."

"I thought Helen was taking care of everything."

"So did I. But it seems her way of taking care of it is to have it here."

He put a hand on her shoulder. "Poor Edith, you'll be ready for a vacation by New Year's."

She forced a smile. "Actually, I should be thankful. I'm very happy for Amy. And Helen has the hardest task anyway."

"What's that?"

She laughed. "Lining up guests who are willing to come to a shower for a girl they might not have met, who doesn't live here, and whose bright-colored bus is causing a bit of a fuss in town." Then she told him what the mayor had said.

"Don't worry about it, Edith. I'll talk to him. And I was just about to get Collin to come with me to get parts. We'll probably have to go out of town for them."

"Well, he's out shoveling snow," said Edith.

Charles smiled. "Good for him. Did you ask him, or did he just offer?"

"He just found the shovel and started doing it."

"And you think Amy will be okay here without him?" asked Charles with a slight frown. "I mean, if she should suddenly decide to go into labor and have her baby or need help or anything."

Edith laughed. "You sound just like an anxious father-to-be."

"Well, these kids seem a little helpless . . ."

"I know. And don't you worry. Amy's downstairs at the moment, doing several loads of laundry. I'll be here. She should be just fine. And if she should go into labor, there is always Helen."

He nodded. "Then I guess you're all in good hands." He reached for his plaid wool coat and went out the back door. Edith watched him going out to speak to Collin, who had nearly finished shoveling the sidewalk by now.

"Edith?" called a familiar voice. "Where are you?"

"In the kitchen, Myrtle," Edith called back.

"Edith," said Myrtle as she came into the kitchen, "you have a problem."

"And that would be?"

"There's a loose board on the stairs, and I nearly fell and broke my neck just now."

Edith reached out and put a hand on Myrtle's fleshy forearm. "Are you okay?"

Myrtle, looking slightly indignant, pursed her lips and said, "I think so. But it was quite a scare."

"Oh, dear. I'm so sorry. Do you recall which board it was?" Edith had come down the stairs herself this morning but hadn't noticed anything. Of course, Myrtle was quite a bit heavier, so it was possible that her weight had helped to loosen it.

"Second one from the top."

Edith looked out the window in time to see Charles and Collin driving away in the car. "Oh, dear," she said again. "I wonder if I could fix it myself."

Myrtle shook her head. "Not likely. You'll need to call in a handyman."

Edith considered this. Usually, she and Charles liked to do as much as possible for themselves, to spare their finances, but then again, if the board was really loose, she couldn't risk having a guest take a fall. "I'd better go look at it," she said suddenly. "And perhaps keep people off the stairs until it's fixed."

She saw Leslie and Megan just coming down the stairs now. "Did you notice a loose board up there?" she asked.

"As a matter of fact, I did," said Leslie. "It must've just happened, because I don't recall it wobbling like that before."

"Oh, dear. I better call a handyman right away." So Edith got on the phone and dialed Peter Simpson's number. Peter had occasionally helped them with bigger projects at the inn. As it turned out, Peter was not busy and promised to come right over. Edith hung up the phone and felt better.

"And what are you two doing today?" she asked Leslie and Megan. So far she'd been so busy with the other guests that she'd barely had a chance to talk to these two.

"I'm not sure," said Leslie, and Megan just shrugged. "We've already been to town to see Santa . . . and it's awfully cold out there today . . ."

"I have an idea," said Edith, leaning down to look into Megan's big blue eyes. "Do you like to decorate cookies?"

"With frosting and stuff?" Megan looked hopeful.

Edith nodded. "Yes, with frosting and stuff."

"Can I, Mommy?"

Leslie looked at Edith. "Are you sure? I mean, Megan hasn't had much experience with—"

"I'm sure by the time she finishes, Megan will be an expert. I have about eight dozen sugar cookies in the freezer, all ready to be decorated." Edith laughed. "Not that I expect Megan to do all of them."

Leslie smiled. "And if it's okay, maybe I could help her. I love doing creative things like that."

"Oh, it's better than okay. It would help me immensely. In fact,

I was just about to invite you, as well as all the female guests at the inn, to come to a rather impromptu baby shower that I'm hosting tomorrow morning."

"*A baby shower*?" Megan clapped her hands and danced around. "I've always wanted to go to a baby shower. Can we, Mommy? Can we?"

Leslie just smiled. "I don't see why not." Then she looked at Edith. "But we'll have to get something for the baby. And I have no idea what to get. Is there a place in town with baby things?"

So Edith explained who the shower was for and that Rudolph's Five and Dime had a limited selection of baby things and Amy could probably use just about anything. "And can you come too, Myrtle?" she asked the older woman.

"I don't know . . . I still have a lot to do for the Christmas pageant. And besides," Myrtle frowned now, "I don't really like baby showers."

Megan looked at the old woman in disbelief. "You *don't* like baby showers? Why not?"

"Too many women in one room, and everyone yakking their heads off, all at once. Just gets on my nerves."

Edith tried not to look too relieved as she patted her on the shoulder. "Don't worry about it, Myrtle. I understand completely."

"I guess I could pick up something for the baby though." She grimly shook her head. "Poor child . . ."

"How about if Megan and I make a quick run to town now?" said Leslie with excitement in her voice. "We'll find something for the baby, then get back here to do cookies."

"Sounds like a great plan."

Edith posted a sign warning guests about the second stair tread and then went into the kitchen to get things ready for cookie decorating. She would cover the dining room table with waxed paper and just leave all the frostings and other tempting goodies out there in case any other guests wished to participate. It was the way she'd always done it with her own children, and usually, by the end of the day, the cookies were all decorated, although at final head count there were always quite a few missing in action.

After getting things ready for cookie decorating, Edith turned on her computer. She'd learned how to make cards at her last computer class, and so she found the right program, picked a baby graphic, and wrote out a very simple invitation that she neatly folded and addressed and slipped under the doors of all the women at the inn. Silly perhaps, since she'd already informed more than half of them. But it made the shower seem more special to go to this little bit of extra trouble. Amy emerged from the basement just as Edith was returning to the kitchen.

"Oh, do you need help?" offered Edith when she saw how off balance the very pregnant Amy looked while carrying a full basket of clean and folded clothes.

"I'm okay," said Amy. "But maybe you could get the door for me."

So Edith went ahead of Amy, opening and closing doors until they reached the bus, and this time it was not quite as laborious since Collin had made a clean path right up to the bus's door.

"Oh, yes," said Edith as she opened the door. "Charles and Collin went to get parts for the engine. I hope you don't mind."

"That's great." Amy smiled. "You guys are great. And I totally love your laundry room. You have so much counter space and stuff," she held the basket up proudly, "that I actually folded our clothes for a change. Collin will be surprised."

"That's nice."

"I still have one more load down there in the dryer, but my back was starting to ache so—"

"Don't worry about it. You go in there and have a little rest. We don't want you wearing yourself out, or going into labor, especially since your baby shower is scheduled for tomorrow morning."

Amy let out a happy squeal. "That is so totally cool!"

Edith nodded. "I'd better get back now." But as she walked back to the inn, heading for the front door to make sure that the steps had been properly de-iced, she couldn't help but agree with Amy. It was *so totally cool*!

Before Edith reached the front porch, she heard loud female voices arguing. They sounded as if they were coming from the direction of the church. She turned to see Myrtle and Olive, face-to-face, near the side door that led to the church kitchen, in what appeared to be some kind of standoff. She paused to watch them for a moment, and as the volume of their voices elevated, she grew seriously concerned that this argument might actually come to blows. She hurried across the street to see if she could help.

"You are not going to bring a bunch of stinking farm animals into this church!" shouted Olive. "I forbid it."

"Who died and made you God?" spat Myrtle.

"Edith!" exclaimed Olive when she saw her approaching. "Help me out with this lunatic."

"What's wrong?" asked Edith, fearing that she was already in over her head.

"This woman," said Olive dramatically, "wants to bring *live* animals into our church, the house of God—chickens and pigs and—"

"I *never* said pigs!" argued Myrtle. "I only thought it would make the pageant more interesting to have live animals, and I talked to a fellow on the phone this morning who said—"

"We are not going to have animals in church!" shouted Olive. "And the sooner you get that into your thick head, the better!"

"What makes you think that *you* get to make all the decisions?" demanded Myrtle with her feet spread apart and hands on hips.

"Because I'm the one in charge."

"Says who?"

Olive let out an exasperated groan and turned to Edith. "Please, Edith, do something! Or do I need to call Pastor Charles? This is really your fault, you know. Myrtle is your guest, and you've allowed her to help."

"So, she's been helping you?" asked Edith weakly.

"Helping me?" Olive practically shrieked. "With help like this, I might as well go out and hang myself."

"Oh, Olive . . ." Edith sighed. "There must be some way to resolve this."

"Yes!" said Olive. "And that's to tell her *no* farm animals." Then she turned and marched into the kitchen, slamming the door behind her.

"Are the children around?" asked Edith in a quiet voice.

"No," said Myrtle, still clearly unhappy. "They won't be here for another twenty minutes." Now she looked at Edith. "And how do you think the children would react to having live animals?" she asked. "Do you think they would enjoy feeling the nose of a fuzzy donkey or rubbing their hands through the thick curly wool of a sheep?"

Edith considered this. "Well, yes, I'd have to agree with you there, Myrtle. Kids love animals."

Myrtle smiled as if she had the upper hand now. "And if having animals around was good enough for the baby Jesus, I can't see how they could do much harm to a church, can you?"

"Well, no. Not actually . . . but then there's Olive . . . and she's dead set against it, Myrtle. And, really, she's the one who's supposed to be in charge. You're only supposed to be helping her." Edith was actually wringing her hands, something she hadn't done since childhood. "Please, Myrtle, can't you try to get along with her—for the sake of the children?"

Myrtle nodded. "This whole pageant is for the children, Edith. I won't do anything to ruin it for them."

"You won't?" Edith felt a smidgen of hope.

"Of course not. I want them to enjoy this time—and to remember it always."

"Oh, good." Edith glanced back to the inn just in time to see a small pickup parking in front. "I think my handyman is here now. I better go."

11

Within minutes, Peter had repaired the loose step and then headed off to the kitchen in search of Edith.

"All done," he announced.

Edith had just put in the last ingredients for tomorrow's shower cake. She'd decided to make it lemon with cream cheese frosting. And she would decorate it with pink and blue. Not terribly clever, but this was fairly last minute, and sometimes one just had to make do.

"Already?" she said as she turned on her big mixer and moved toward her little desk. "What do I owe you?"

Peter glanced around the kitchen, then grinned as his eyes spied something. "Are those cinnamon rolls?"

"Want one?" she offered.

"Got any coffee?"

"I do for you," she said. "Why don't you sit down and make yourself comfy."

"I can't believe that none of your kids came home for the holidays," said Peter. "If my parents' place was as great as this, I'd sure make the effort to go see them."

"How are your folks doing?" she asked as she set not one but two cinnamon rolls before him. "Do they like Arizona?"

"I guess. But I don't get it."

"Well, your mom said the winters here were getting to her. And then there was your dad's bypass surgery. You can't really blame them, Peter." She filled the coffeemaker with water.

"Maybe not. But when I get old, I don't plan on leaving. Christmas Valley is my home."

She smiled to herself as she imagined Peter old and gray but still tromping around town. "But you have to admit, it's not easy."

"Easy isn't always best," he said.

She turned on the coffeemaker and turned off the mixer, glad to be rid of the extra noise. "Speaking of best, when are you going to start dating again, young man?"

He groaned. "You sound just like my mom."

"Well, it's a pitiful waste if you ask me, Peter. Just because your first wife didn't have the good sense to see that she got a great guy doesn't mean there's not someone else out there who would appreciate you."

"Not a whole lot of single women to pick from around here."

She considered this. At one time, she'd even tried to match Peter up with Krista, but that had turned into a disaster. "It was like going out with my own brother," Krista had told Edith afterward.

"Christmas Valley has its share of single women," she told Peter, trying to think of a single one that might appeal to him. "But perhaps none that are right for you."

"You got that right."

"How about some of those online matchmaking services? I get pop-ups and email ads from things like that all the time. Not that I need anything like that."

He laughed. "Somehow I just don't see myself as an online dating kind of guy."

She sneaked the still-brewing pot out and filled a mug, then set it down in front of him. "Well, maybe you should give it a try." She sat down across from him. "You're not getting any younger, you know, and it's awfully nice, as one gets older, to have someone beside you."

He nodded wistfully. "Can't disagree with you on that."

"Look, Mommy!" called a child's voice in the dining room. Edith was certain it was Megan. "Everything's all ready!"

"Let me put our stuff away first," called Leslie. "And you go wash your hands."

"Cookie day?" said Peter.

"Yes. Remember when you used to come over and help?"

"Those were good times."

"And sledding," she said with a sigh. "You kids had such fun at One Tree Hill."

"Yeah, and if your kids had had the good sense to come home, we'd be out there doing it again."

"Plenty of snow for it too." She stood up and went back to her desk now. "Seriously, Peter, what do I owe you for that stair?"

"You already paid me." He grinned at her. "And then some."

"Well, you take your time and finish up in here. I need to go out there and help them get all set. They're really doing me a big favor since I'm so busy just now. Those poor cookies probably never would've gotten decorated at all."

"And Christmas wouldn't be Christmas without Mrs. Ryan's famous Christmas cookies."

She laughed and went out to the dining room. Before long, she had Leslie and Megan all set, and it looked as if Leslie really knew what she was doing too. "I've got to go put a cake in the oven," she told them, "for the shower tomorrow." But before she could get back to the kitchen, she heard voices in the foyer, one that was definitely Myrtle's, and worried that Myrtle might be stirring up more trouble or getting into a flap with poor Mr. Benson, Edith decided to go see.

"Come on," Myrtle was saying, as it turned out, to Michael Thomas. "You won't be sorry."

"But I, uh . . ." Michael looked slightly helpless.

"Myrtle?" said Edith with a bit of a warning tone in her voice. "What are you doing?"

Myrtle turned around and gave Edith a sheepish expression. "Nothing . . ."

"Are you pestering Michael about—"

"She's fine," he said quickly, tossing Edith an assuring smile. "She's just trying to talk me into taking her somewhere in my car."

"Myrtle, please, don't be bothering the other guests."

"This is between me and Michael."

"I guess it couldn't hurt," he said now. "Lauren walked to town and won't be back for a while. I was just going to read and maybe catch a nap."

"You can nap anytime," said Myrtle.

Michael laughed. "I guess you're right."

Edith frowned. She didn't like the idea of Myrtle bullying the guests around. And she suspected that Myrtle had seen Michael's sporty little Porsche and just wanted to get him to take her for a joyride. Although how Myrtle was going to get her portly self in and out of that little car was a bit of a mystery.

"Have fun," said Edith, imagining Michael using a giant shoehorn to pry Myrtle from his car after they were done.

When Edith came back through the dining room, she was surprised to see that Peter had joined Leslie and Megan. He was bent over a toy soldier cookie and frosting him in what Edith could only imagine must be camouflage.

"Decided to help out?" she said.

"Do you mind?" he asked without looking up.

"Not at all. Did you introduce yourself to the ladies?"

He looked up now. "Of course. I told them that your kids and I used to do this every year, and Megan invited me to join them."

"And he's making G.I. Joe," said Megan, giggling.

"An untraditional Christmas cookie," he admitted, "but in honor of our armed forces."

"I think it's nice," said Leslie as she admired his work. "And it looks like real camouflage too."

"Peter is our local artist," Edith informed them.

"A real artist?" said Megan with big eyes.

"That's right," said Edith. "And he usually decorated the most interesting cookies too." Then she went into the kitchen to finish her cake making. Hopefully, the batter hadn't set too long. But it looked okay when she put the pans into the oven and even better when she took them out. Nice golden brown.

She set them on the counter to cool, then went upstairs to search for something. At least, she hoped she still had it. It was a baby quilt that she'd sewn for Tom and Alicia's last baby. Made from an adorable fabric that was covered with farm animals, the colors had been bright and bold. But then she'd heard that Alicia had chosen pastels for the nursery, and so Edith had put together a completely different quilt. She figured she'd have this one on hand for the next baby, and wasn't there always a next?

As far as she could remember, she hadn't given it away yet. After several minutes of intense hunting, she finally unearthed it in a plastic crate, along with a few other baby items. Things she'd probably gotten on sale for her own grandchildren, thinking that she would send them, or have them on hand when they came to visit her . . . and then, of course, she forgot all about them. Oh, well.

Since all seemed calm and quiet, for a refreshing change, Edith decided to take the time to wrap the baby gift, as well as to put up her feet. Already it seemed to have been a long day, or maybe the years were starting to catch up with her. Before she knew it, she had dozed off.

She awoke to what sounded like an urgent knocking on her door. "Edith?" called a female voice. "Are you in there?"

Thinking perhaps the inn was on fire, or worse, she stumbled to the door and opened it to see Lauren, Michael's wife, standing there. And she was clearly upset. "What's wrong?" asked Edith with a racing heart.

"It's Michael!" said Lauren breathlessly. "I went to town to get a gift for the baby shower, and he was going to have a nap while I was out, but now I get back and he's not in our room. And then I went downstairs and he's not down there, and his car's not here, and I'm just so—"

"It's okay," said Edith soothingly. "Michael simply took Myrtle for a little drive."

Lauren blinked. "A little drive?"

"That's right. Of course, it was all Myrtle's idea, but somehow she talked him into going. I'm sure she just wanted to have a ride in that pretty little car—"

Now Lauren burst into tears.

"It's okay," said Edith again. "Really, you don't need to be worried."

But Lauren just continued to sob, until Edith didn't know what to do, other than to guide her into the bedroom, something she had *never* done with a guest before. She sat Lauren down in the rocker, then sat herself down in Charles's recliner and waited for Lauren to recover. At first impression, Lauren had seemed a very together and controlled sort of person. A career woman, Edith had imagined, due to the classy business suit and leather briefcase. And certainly not the sort of woman who was given over to hysterics. Why should Lauren be so upset over Michael having gone somewhere with Myrtle—surely she couldn't be jealous of the heavyset woman who was old enough to be Lauren's grandmother? Finally, Lauren's sobs softened some, and Edith handed her a box of Kleenex.

"I'm so sorry," Lauren said as she blotted her face with a tissue. "I didn't mean to fall apart like that. It's just that I got so scared—it's like I knew that I'd lost him."

"You're a beautiful young woman," said Edith, still feeling confused. "I'm sure your husband would never leave you, and especially for someone, well, like Myrtle."

Lauren looked directly at Edith now, first with a shocked expression, but then she began to smile, and finally she actually laughed. Edith wondered what the joke was, but she didn't ask. She was just relieved to see Lauren happy.

"No, no . . ." said Lauren. "I didn't think that Michael had run off with—" she chuckled, "*Myrtle*, of all people. But, well, you see, the reason we came here for Christmas, rather than being with our families . . . oh, it's a long story."

"Well, you've aroused my curiosity," said Edith. "And I have time."

"And after all I've subjected you to, you probably deserve an explanation. Let me give you the short version. You see, Michael was diagnosed with and treated for cancer not long after we got married, about five years ago. And after all that time in remission and no symptoms, we believed that he was cancer free. We were even beginning to think about starting a family—" Her voice broke, and she looked down at her lap.

"But it came back?"

She nodded without speaking.

"And it's serious?"

She looked up. "Yes. They said there's no point in doing surgery and that they could try doing chemo, but it might just subject him to a lot of discomfort for no good reason. We just found this out a couple weeks ago, and we couldn't bear to be around family just yet. We didn't want to ruin everyone's Christmas, you know?"

"That was very selfless of you," said Edith. "But to be honest, if one of my children were sick, I would rather know."

"And we will tell them. We just wanted to wait until after Christmas. We also wanted to have this time together, just the two of us, to talk and think and sort it all out, you know?"

"And then Myrtle whisked your man away." Edith shook her head. "That woman!"

"Oh, it's okay. I mean, I know Michael wouldn't have gone with her if he didn't want to. Although why he would want to . . . well, I just can't imagine."

"I'm sure they'll be back soon."

"I'm sorry to burden you with this . . ."

"Please," said Edith, "don't be. You know, when we learned our kids weren't coming home, and when we decided to open the inn during Christmas, well, I just believed that the good Lord had a plan. And I'm sure you're part of that."

"Well, we really appreciate being here. And it's so great having a church so nearby. It's a real blessing." Lauren stood. "I'm going to go clean up my face before Michael gets back. Please, don't let him know that I fell apart on you."

"Of course not."

"Or that I told you about it."

"These lips are sealed."

"Thank you."

Of course, Edith felt like she could strangle Myrtle for enticing poor Michael to take her for a ride. And who knew when they'd be back. By now Myrtle could've convinced the poor man to take her, well, who knew where. And they were driving on snowy roads too. *Dear Lord, watch over them*, Edith prayed as she put on her shoes and went back downstairs.

98

At least Charles and Collin had gotten back. And, it appeared, with parts, since they were both outside, along with Peter now, looking into the engine of the bus.

"Peter knows how to fix cars," said Megan when she noticed Edith looking out the window.

"He sure does," said Edith. "He's good at fixing all kinds of things." She walked over to the table. "And how are our cookies coming?"

"Great," said Leslie, looking up from an angel-shaped cookie that she was transforming into something exquisitely celestial.

"Oh, my!" said Edith, examining the cookies that were already decorated. "I don't think we've ever had cookies this beautiful before. Are you an artist too?"

"Not exactly," Leslie admitted. "I mean, I like to dabble, but I'd never be able to support myself. But this," she held up the cookie, "is excellent therapy."

Edith smiled. "Well, I'm so glad you think so." Then she went in the kitchen to see if the cake layers had cooled yet.

"Hello there," called Charles as he came into the kitchen. "Sure smells good in here."

"Did you find everything you needed for the engine?" she asked as she mixed some frosting for the cake.

"For the engine. But we had to order the tires, and they won't be in until next week, after Christmas."

"Oh . . ."

"Now, don't worry, Edith. Hal Berry and I plan to do damage control in town this afternoon. We're going to talk to the mayor, during his Santa break, and try to make him understand that this is just a temporary problem. We'll also remind him that it wouldn't look good if the newspapers heard that we forced those poor kids to hit the road with bald tires on packed snow."

She smiled. "No, that wouldn't look good."

"And Hal has connections, you know." He winked at her. Hal's wife wrote the food column in their little weekly paper, and occasionally she sold a piece to one of the larger papers too.

"Sounds like you and Hal have it all taken care of."

"Peter offered to help Collin finish up out there." Charles was washing his hands in the sink now. "It gets a bit crowded with three heads under the hood. Besides, I was getting awfully cold. I think the temperature is dropping."

"Oh, I hope that Collin and Amy are warm enough in there."

"He said their noses get cold, but mostly they're fine."

"I'll take them out an extra comforter just in case."

"Yes, I figured you would, dear." He dried his hands. "I'm heading to town now. Anything you need?"

She gave him her short list of mints, nuts, and punch mix for the shower. Then, thinking twice, she took it back and wrote very specifically what kinds of mints, nuts, and punch mix.

"You know me well," he said as she handed it back.

That was true enough. Edith had learned from experience that if you simply wrote "mints," he might return with a small box of Junior Mints or mint-flavored gum. He was a smart man when it came to books and sermons, but he was at a complete loss in a grocery store.

It was getting dusky out when Collin and Peter came into the house by way of the kitchen, which was feeling more and more like Grand Central Station. Edith looked up from her task of trying to make the cake look like something fit for a baby shower.

"I think we got it," said Peter.

"Yeah," said Collin. "Peter's a genius."

Peter nodded. "Thank you, my man. It's nice that someone has finally noticed."

"Amy asked me to get a load of laundry for her," Collin said to Edith, and she directed him to the basement.

Now Peter seemed to be examining Edith's cake. "What is *that*?"

She frowned. "It was supposed to be a bassinet."

Peter laughed. "Looks more like a Volkswagen."

"Thanks a lot."

"You have any more of that pink and blue frosting?"

"Sure." She studied him. "You want to take a stab at it? I know you're more artistic than I am, but I don't want to see any soldiers in camouflage."

"I was thinking you should ask Leslie to help. She has a real knack."

Edith held her hands up. "Now, why on earth didn't I think of that? Go see if they're still out there. It's been so quiet, I think they might've finished."

Then Edith took her metal spatula and proceeded to scrape off the mess of blue and pink that she had created. Thank goodness she'd made plenty of frosting.

"I hear you need help?" said Leslie, standing in the doorway to the kitchen.

"That's right." Edith nodded toward the white-frosted cake.

But Leslie didn't make a move. Instead she pointed over her head. "The sign."

Edith laughed. "Goodness, I'd almost forgotten about that. Seems that no one's been paying attention to it lately anyway. Come on in."

Leslie came over and looked at the blank cake. "Peter's helping Megan to finish up the cookies. There's about a dozen left. So what did you have in mind for this?"

Edith shrugged. "Something babyish. I only mixed blue and pink frostings. I attempted a bassinet, but Peter said it looked like a Volkswagen. I think it looked more like a big blob. Anyway, I removed it. Do whatever you like with it. Judging by your cookie skills, I'm sure you'll have no problem."

12

"Seems quiet around here tonight," said Charles as he took a seat at the kitchen table.

"It's really settled down." Edith put the lid back on the boiling rice and turned the burner down to simmer. "It was getting pretty crazy earlier."

"I see only two places set," he observed. "Where's our friend Myrtle tonight?"

Edith just shook her head. "You're not going to believe it."

"Try me."

"Well, Leslie and little Megan had been helping me to decorate cookies, and then Leslie even did the decoration on the cake for the shower tomorrow—and what a beautiful job she did! But anyway, we were just finishing things up, and Myrtle walked in and asked Leslie and Megan what they were doing for dinner. At first I thought maybe she was going to invite them to join us, which would've been okay, actually, they'd been so helpful and all."

"So Myrtle went to dinner with Leslie and Megan?"

"Yes, she pretty much invited herself, and then she even invited Peter."

"Peter?" Charles looked confused.

"Peter had been helping with the cookies too, and he was still here. So the four of them went to dinner together."

"Interesting . . ." Charles smiled.

"Oh, yes, and Peter told me to tell you that the engine is running just fine now. Collin called him a genius."

"And how is our little mother-to-be?"

"I think she wore herself out doing laundry today. Her back's been hurting, and she's been resting. I took them out a comforter and some dinner. And they were very sweet and grateful." She sadly shook her head. "But that bus! Oh, it may look bright and cheery on the outside—in fact, I've started calling it the Christmas bus—but on the inside it's downright depressing. And not very warm either, especially with the temperature dropping. They have this little heater that they run off a battery, but it can only be on for short periods of time."

"I wonder if we could run an extension cord out there," mused Charles. "Plug it in the outlet on the front porch."

"That might work, well, as long as no one tripped over it. That Myrtle gave me a good scare today when she said she tripped on the loose step. I thought this could turn into a lawsuit for sure. And wouldn't Myrtle be the one to do it?"

"Oh, I don't know . . ."

Edith knew this was his gentle way of defending Myrtle. But that's just how he was. Charles never liked to say a bad word about anyone. And normally, she didn't either. She checked on the poached fish and decided it was done.

Then she decided to tell him about Lauren's emotional breakdown and confession after Myrtle hijacked Michael earlier that day, not so much to shine a negative light on Myrtle as to bring Michael's illness to Charles's attention.

"That's too bad."

"I have absolutely no idea what Myrtle was up to, but it really upset poor Lauren."

"But he made it back okay?"

"Yes, he actually seemed in really good spirits, and he and Lauren went off to dinner and the Christmas play tonight. They were having a double date with the Fieldses, if you can imagine. Unfortunately, the Fieldses got into another argument just as they were leaving. Hopefully, they'll settle down."

"Might help Lauren and Michael to be thankful for what they have . . ." Charles said, "even if it is going to be cut short."

She smiled at him as she set the rice on the table. "You know, I'd rather have a few wonderful years with love than a long life with animosity."

"Well said, my dear."

She put the rest of the food on the table and removed her apron. "And how about Mr. Benson?"

"He told me that he'd had an early dinner in town and wanted to just stay in and read."

"Poor old guy. This is his first year without his wife, and he's feeling very lost."

"So that's why he's so sad," she said as she sat down. "And then he's got Myrtle pestering him almost nonstop. I just don't understand that woman. It's as if she cannot keep her nose out of everyone's business."

"Takes all kinds, my dear."

"I just hope she doesn't spoil dinner for those kids tonight."

Then Charles bowed his head and asked a blessing. He also took a few moments to pray that their guests might have a good evening. Despite her concerns for the young people subjected to Myrtle's unpredictable prattle, Edith couldn't help but relish this quiet dinner with just Charles and her. And as they ate, he filled her in on the details in town today. It seemed that he and Hal had made some headway.

"I think Mayor Drummel is softening up about the bus," he finally said. "In the spirit of Christmas."

"Oh, and I almost forgot to tell you. The strangest thing . . . people have been stopping by to look at the bus. Can you imagine it? As if it's some kind of sideshow attraction. Peter said that at one point there were at least half a dozen out there just looking at it."

Charles laughed. "This is a small town, Edith. Word gets around."

"You'd think people would have more to do, just three days before Christmas, than to stand around gaping at an old bus."

After cleaning up the dinner things, Charles went off to his study, and Edith went down to put a load of linens into the washing machine. She normally did this in the morning, but what with the baby shower and all, she figured she might as well get ahead of the game. She was pleased to see that her laundry room was in good shape. Amy had even cleaned the lint out of the lint trap, something her own children usually forgot to do. Edith didn't like to admit it, but she was meticulous about laundry and her laundry room. Normally, like her kitchen, it was off-limits to guests. But then rules were made to be broken. And perhaps it was good for Edith to bend a bit.

When Edith came up from the basement, she heard voices in the dining room. As usual, she had put out refreshments for guests to help themselves to—well, even more so since it was the holidays. And she wasn't surprised that people were out there, but she was surprised that it sounded like Myrtle.

"Don't you know that'll send your cholesterol sky-high?" she was saying in that know-it-all tone she so often used.

Edith paused on the other side of the door, not exactly eavesdropping since this was her own home, after all, but she was curious as to who Myrtle was talking to.

"My cholesterol is *my* business," said a voice that sounded like Mr. Benson's.

"And coffee before bed?" she said. "Do you know what caffeine can do to your blood pressure?"

"It's *my* blood pressure."

"It won't be for long if that's the best you can take care of yourself."

Edith was just about to break it up, but his next sentence stopped her.

"Look, woman." His voice grew louder. "Maybe I don't care about *that*. Maybe I don't *want* to be here for long."

"Tsk, tsk. That's no way to talk, Mr. Benson. It was the good Lord who put you on this planet, and it's up to the good Lord to decide when it's time for you to go. Don't you know that much by now?"

"All I know is that you're the most exasperating human being I've ever run across, and I wish you'd mind your own business!"

"How do you know that it isn't my business? People are supposed to help people. What kind of a world would it be if everyone just turned their backs and walked away?"

"It would be a much happier world for me!"

Edith couldn't take any more. She pushed open the door and walked out, pretending that she'd heard nothing. With a forced smile, she turned her attention to Myrtle, asking how dinner with the young people had gone.

"It was fine," she answered quickly, still appearing to have her sights set on poor Mr. Benson. Edith was surprised that he was even still here, but he was standing by the table, his face flushed and brows drawn tightly together. He had a plate with a large slice of pumpkin pie and whipped cream in one hand and a cup of coffee in the other. He reminded Edith of a trapped animal.

"Would you like to sit down?" offered Edith.

"Thank you." He seemed relieved to have someone else in the room.

"Where are Leslie and Megan?" Edith asked Myrtle, hoping she might distract her from this relentless attack on Mr. Benson.

"They decided to go see the play."

"Good for them." Edith cut herself a thin slice of pumpkin pie and topped it with a dollop of whipped cream. She wasn't all that fond of pumpkin pie, but after Myrtle's comments about cholesterol, she wanted to do this as an alliance with Mr. Benson. Then she poured a cup of tea and went over to sit across from him, keeping an eye on Myrtle as she did.

"Aren't you having anything, Myrtle?" she asked.

"I can't decide."

Edith made light conversation with Mr. Benson as she watched Myrtle standing by the dessert table. She spoke of the weather, town happenings, and the Christmas pageant that would take place the next night, and after a bit she sensed the old man was beginning to relax.

"I haven't seen a Christmas pageant in years," he said wistfully. "I remember when I was a boy and I got to play the shepherd once."

"Myrtle is helping with the pageant," Edith told him, feeling a bit guilty, not to mention inhospitable, for not including her in the conversation as well.

"That's right," said Myrtle as she finally poured herself a cup of herbal tea and placed two small pieces of divinity on a plate. Edith had to smile to herself at this healthy choice, since she already knew that Myrtle ate things loaded with fats and sugar.

Myrtle sat down at the end of the table. "And tomorrow will be a very busy day. I wish I could talk someone into driving me to town. There are a few props that I still need to pick up at the hardware store."

"I'm pretty busy with the baby shower," Edith said.

Now Myrtle looked hopefully at Mr. Benson. "I don't suppose you'd want to help out . . . especially after I gave you such a bad time about taking care of yourself." She looked down at her plate now. "I'm sorry."

Edith blinked in surprise. This was the first apology she'd heard from Myrtle.

Mr. Benson cleared his throat. "I guess I shouldn't be so touchy."

"And I shouldn't be so bossy. People tell me that all the time. But it's just my nature."

"The truth is, you're right about the cholesterol and the high blood pressure."

Myrtle gave a little victory nod that made her double chins wobble.

"My wife always tried to get me to watch what I ate. And I did just fine while she was around. But after she died last year . . . well, it's just not easy."

"And how do you think your wife would feel to know that you've thrown your diet to the wind?"

He sighed.

"So how about giving me a ride to town tomorrow?" she said. "It can be your contribution to the Christmas pageant."

And to Edith's flabbergasted surprise, Mr. Benson actually agreed. Whether this was a calculated and well-executed plan in Myrtle's strange mind or just a crazy fluke, Edith wasn't sure. But she couldn't help but think that Myrtle was a bit of a manipulator.

"If you'll excuse me, I need to go put some things in the dryer,"

Edith said, standing. She figured her job as referee was over. Surely these two wouldn't kill each other now.

"That's some good pie," said Mr. Benson as he set his fork on his now-empty plate. "But if you'll excuse me," he nodded to both of them, "I'd like to say good night."

"Thank you and good night." Edith was gathering a few empty dishes from the table to take with her to the kitchen.

But Mr. Benson was barely out of sight before Myrtle got up and helped herself to a generous piece of pumpkin pie and whipped cream. When she saw Edith watching, she just smiled sheepishly. "Just trying to set a good example for the old guy," she said as she sat down and began to eat.

Edith chuckled as she went into the kitchen and set the small stack of dessert plates in the sink. Of course, she had to wonder about Myrtle's cholesterol levels and blood pressure. Not that she would dare mention it!

By the time Edith finished with the laundry, the house was quiet. She put the perishable foods into the refrigerator but left a nice selection of cookies and treats on the table, in case any guests were in need of a midnight snack. Then she unplugged the Christmas tree lights and blew out the candles that she had lit earlier in the evening. But as she bent over to blow out the large white pillar candle in the foyer, something gave her pause. Something wasn't right.

She studied the shiny holly with its red berries that gracefully wreathed around the candle, reflected in the glossy finish of the smooth mahogany tabletop, and finally she knew what was wrong— her porcelain angel was gone. She searched around the foyer, by the registration area, then in the living room, and finally she stopped at Charles's study. The light was showing beneath the door, so she suspected he was in there.

"Hello?" she said quietly as she opened the door.

He looked up and sort of blinked, almost as if he'd been asleep, but she suspected he'd simply been immersed in his book. Charles loved reading old-fashioned western novels. Of course, he'd read every one he could get his hands on over the years, but claiming his memory was fading with age, he had started reading them all over again. If he ever got Alzheimer's, God forbid, he would probably be happy just reading the same one over and over again.

"Sorry to bother you."

He smiled and closed the paperback. "You know that's never the case."

"Have you seen my angel?"

He looked puzzled.

She smiled. "The porcelain angel that I keep in the foyer. It seems to be missing."

He scratched his head. "I do remember that angel. Very pretty. But I have no idea where she may have flown off to."

Edith frowned. "Do you think someone might've accidentally bumped into it and broken it?" She remembered how taken Megan had been with the pretty sculpture, how she had almost touched it until her mother stopped her.

"Without mentioning it?"

"That does seem unlikely." She thought about it for a moment. "You don't think anyone took it, do you?"

"I can't imagine why."

"Well, it actually is a fairly valuable piece."

"Really?"

She kind of shrugged now, sorry that she'd even said that. "Not that anyone would be aware of its value . . . besides me."

He leaned forward with interest now. "I suppose I've never asked you—it just seems it's always been around—but where did the angel come from, Edith?"

She sat down in a chair across from him. "My grandmother."

"Oh . . ."

Now, Charles knew as well as anyone that Edith still had some regrets about her grandparents. But he never pried. "She gave it to me for my sixteenth birthday," Edith told him. "Of course, she also informed me that it was an expensive piece that would get more valuable with time. And she told me not to break it." Edith made a meek smile. "I was rather clumsy as a kid."

"Because you were tall for your age."

"Yes."

109

"So where do you think your angel is, Edith?"

She shook her head. "I have no idea. This has been such a busy day with people coming and going. But I think if someone had accidentally broken it, I would've heard something, don't you think?"

He nodded.

"Do you think someone has taken it?" She hoped this was not the case.

"I sure wouldn't like to think that."

"No, no . . ." she said quickly. "Neither would I."

"Maybe it will turn up."

"Yes. I'm sure it will."

Just the same, Edith felt a gnawing concern growing inside of her. Could it be that someone had actually stolen her angel? And, if so, who? A lot of people had been in and out of the inn today. Of course, she knew that most people would point their fingers at someone like Collin or Amy—they were virtual strangers and obviously in financial need. But Edith couldn't believe that they would do that, not after all the kindness Edith and Charles had shown them. She refused to believe it.

13

Edith rose early on Friday morning. There was so much to be done that she needed a head start. She'd already started composing a detailed list in her head, and hopefully, she could get it all down onto paper before she forgot anything. But as she walked through the foyer, she paused by the mahogany table. Last night, while in bed, she had wondered if perhaps she had imagined the whole thing, if she would get up in the morning and the angel would be in its proper place. But it was not there. She even took a moment to look closely at the wooden floor, actually running her fingers over the surface just in case there was a fragment of broken porcelain. But other than a day's worth of dust, the floor was clean.

She tried not to let it get to her as she went into the kitchen, sat down at her desk, and made out her list of tasks. And she tried not to think about it while she sat and read her daily devotional. But as she went around doing her regular morning chores, she thought not only about the missing angel, but also about her grandmother. She wasn't having the usual memories about her grandmother, the negative ones. Instead she was remembering some of the good things. It was her grandmother who had first taught her to rise early. And to make lists. And even as Edith measured the ingredients for Belgian waffles, she remembered that it was her grandmother who had taught her to cook and sew and keep house. Although her grandparents had been wealthy enough to pay someone else to do those things, her grandmother had always been very thrifty and frugal and insisted on doing them for herself. "It's from

111

my childhood," she had told Edith once. "My mother was from the old country, and she taught us to make do."

And as Edith went about her daily tasks, she realized more and more how much her grandmother had influenced her—and she realized how much of it was good.

For the first time that she could remember, Edith realized that she really did love and appreciate her grandmother. And her soft-spoken grandfather too. And she truly was thankful that they had taken her in after her parents were killed in a car wreck when Edith was just a toddler. Certainly they were old-fashioned and a bit set in their ways, but then they were old, probably too old to have been raising a child. But, she now knew, they had always had her best interests at heart. Why hadn't she seen that sooner?

Goodness, she hoped no tears had fallen into the batter while she stirred. She set the big bowl aside and went to wipe her wet face on a dish towel. Even as she did this, she knew that these were not bitter tears. They were simply tears of release. Letting go. Accepting things for what they were and finding something to be thankful for in the process.

By the time she had breakfast ready to serve, she felt as if the tears had cleansed something in her. And even if she never saw that porcelain angel again, she knew that it had done its work.

"Need any help?" asked Charles as he came in from his walk and hung up his coat and scarf.

She was already pouring him a cup of coffee. "No, I think it's all under control." She wanted to tell him about her little epiphany in regard to her grandmother but figured that could come later. When life wasn't so busy. For now she just needed to stay on track, get breakfast served and cleaned up, and then help Helen set up things for the shower.

Edith had suspected that Mr. Benson would have second thoughts about playing chauffeur to Myrtle today. After all, she'd sort of bullied him into it last night. Edith wasn't surprised to hear them talking about it as she set a platter of fruit on the table.

"I'm sorry, but I don't think it's a good idea," he was telling Myrtle.

"You're not backing out on me, are you?" Her bulldog face was set.

"I just think—"

"I would've taken you as a man of your word," she said.

"Oh, well, fine," he huffed. "I'll drive you, then."

Edith tried not to laugh as she went back to the kitchen for more waffles. Poor Mr. Benson. He didn't have a chance against the likes of Myrtle Pinkerton.

Edith tried not to act as if she was hurrying her guests, but to her great relief the last of them departed the dining room before nine o'clock, giving her just enough time to whisk the breakfast things off into the kitchen. She'd already sent Helen to the living room, where they would have the shower, to decorate or rearrange chairs or whatever it was she felt needed to be done.

The inn's male guests, probably sensing that they were not particularly welcome at a baby shower, made themselves scarce. And the female guests actually offered to help. Little Megan was literally dancing with joy as she watched streamers of blue and pink crepe paper being hung in the doorway.

By ten o'clock the shower guests began to arrive. Mostly ladies from church, but also a few from Helen's bridge group, and even the mayor's wife made a showing. Along with the guests from the inn (excluding Myrtle, who was noticeably absent—at least to Edith, who had simply breathed a sigh of relief), there was a grand total of twenty-three women present! Not bad, thought Edith as she placed another gift on the impressive pile, especially considering how Amy was a complete stranger to most of them and it was only two days until Christmas. Of course, Edith suspected that some of these women had come out of plain old curiosity. They'd probably heard talk in town and wanted to see what kind of people inhabit a wild-looking bus like the one parked in front of the inn. And others, possibly pressured by Helen, one of the town's leading socialites, had probably been afraid to say no.

Helen, limping around with her cane in hand, played the gracious hostess by greeting everyone, introducing them to Amy, and finally coaching the women through some familiar shower games, complete with prizes. The napkins and plates and things, older than Amy, were old-fashioned but sweet. And everyone thought the cake decorating was outstanding—a frilly pink and blue bassinet that looked nothing like a Volkswagen. Edith told them it was Leslie's doing.

"You should stick around," said Betty Gordon, owner of the Candy Cane Shoppe. "I could use someone like you in my business." Leslie laughed and said she couldn't imagine living anywhere as charming as Christmas Valley. Of course, this pleased the ladies, especially the mayor's wife, who took any compliment to their town as personal praise.

Amy, Edith felt certain, was overwhelmed when it was time to open the gifts. But she kept a sunny smile on her face and said thank you about a hundred times. She did get some nice and much-needed baby things, especially considering the short notice. But it wasn't long, barely an hour, before women began to excuse themselves, saying, "I still have gifts to wrap . . ." or "I'm not done baking . . ." Edith began to think that having a baby shower just days before Christmas was actually rather brilliant as she handed women their coats and thanked them for coming.

Olive was standing next to her, reminding everyone about the Christmas pageant as they went out the door. "The children have been working so hard," she said. "You all be sure to come."

Edith felt bad for Olive. Local interest in the Christmas pageant had been in a steady decline for the past several years, and that was when Judy had been managing it. She just hoped Olive wouldn't be too disappointed if the church was only half full tonight.

Finally the last of them left, including Helen, still leaning on her cane as she carefully made her way down the porch steps, with Edith steadying her from the other side. The last thing Edith wanted was for Helen to take another spill on the slippery path.

"Thanks for doing this for Amy," Edith said as they walked. "It was really wonderful."

Helen smiled. "It was, wasn't it?"

"And now Amy is all ready to have her baby."

"Well, let's just hope she's not too ready. But if anything happens, you make sure you call me."

"Do you really mean that, Helen? I mean, you've got your bad knees and all. Not that I think Amy is going to go into labor. Hopefully, the baby will wait until they get to California."

They were at Helen's car now, and Helen turned to look at her. "I do mean it, Edith. You know that Dr. Martin is out of town, and I've delivered babies before. Although why Amy wants to do a home birth, or should I say *bus birth*, is beyond me."

"They don't have insurance," Edith reminded her. "Plus they're nearly broke."

"I know that. But everyone knows how lots of uninsured people take advantage of hospitals without the wherewithal to pay for it. Not that I approve of that, mind you."

"Maybe Collin and Amy have more scruples than that."

Helen laughed. "You wouldn't know that to look at them, now would you?"

"Do you think that's what folks might've said about Mary and Joseph when they came to town, road weary and dusty, looking for a place to stay?"

"I don't know about that, but you can tell our little Amy to get plenty of rest. I think the festivities might've worn her out. And knowing she hasn't had proper prenatal care is a big concern to me. Insurance or no insurance, that young woman should see an obstetrician before the baby comes."

"I don't know what we can do about that. But I'll encourage her to rest and take it easy."

But Edith didn't need to tell Amy to rest. Collin had already come in to collect Amy along with all the baby things, and they were heading out to the bus as Edith came in.

"That was fun," Amy told Edith. "But my back's killing me. I'm going to go lie down for a while."

"Good for you."

"Thanks again for everything," Amy called as she and Collin slowly made their way out the back door.

Edith was surprised that Collin didn't say anything to her. Not even a thank-you for the baby things, which were for his child. And suddenly thoughts of the missing angel flashed through her mind again, but as quickly as they came she dismissed them. It would do no good to dwell on it or to wrongly blame someone like Collin. Like Charles had said, the missing angel would probably show up in time.

By midafternoon, Edith realized that she was actually ahead of herself today. Things from the shower were all cleaned up, daily chores at the inn were complete, and she even had a roast in the Crock-Pot. So she decided to take this time to write her kids a short note on email. She usually did this every other day or so, but due to the busyness at the inn, she was a few days behind. To her delight, she had correspondence from each of them—including Krista, in Maui. All of them expressed sadness about not being home for Christmas. But they had all received their packages, except Krista since she'd already left the mainland, although, Edith suspected by Krista's ebullient email, being in Maui probably made up for it.

She took her time reading each letter and even printed out the pictures that some of them had sent to show to Charles. Edith still marveled at this new age of technology. But she was thankful to have photos of nine-year-old Jessica's Christmas recital; Jameson dressed up like Santa, with a lopsided beard, for his kindergarten Christmas program; and baby Allison in her red velvet dress. And, of course, there was Krista standing by a palm tree, looking cute as a button in her bright-colored sundress. Edith hoped she remembered to use sunblock. Krista always burned so easily.

Edith heard voices in the inn as she hit the send button on a rather long letter that she'd written to all four of her kids, telling of the comings and goings at the inn, promising to write more later, and ending the letter with, "It's not exactly like having my own dear children home with me at Christmas, but it has been interesting. Love always, Mom." Then she turned off the computer and went out to see who was here.

"Oh, there you are," said Myrtle. "Didn't you hear me calling you?" She was setting two large bags from the hardware store on the dining room table.

Mr. Benson put two more beside them. He glanced at Edith and made a slight eye-rolling gesture, as if he'd had it with Myrtle. "Now, if you ladies will excuse me," he said in a tightly controlled voice, "I'd like to go have a rest in my room."

"Of course," said Edith, feeling sorry for the beleaguered man.

Myrtle just shook her head. "Good grief, I didn't force him to go."

Edith decided not to tackle that one. "What are these?" She nodded to the bags cluttering her pretty dining room table.

"For the pageant," Myrtle said as if that explained everything.

"Why don't you leave them at the church?"

"Olive might not like it."

Now Edith was curious. "Mind if I take a look?"

"No. It's only to make it more realistic. You know they didn't have electricity two thousand years ago."

Edith peeked in a bag to see that it contained some kerosene lanterns and a bottle of kerosene. She frowned as she imagined young children burning their fingers, or the church possibly going up in flames. "Don't you think this might be a little dangerous in the church?"

"They're not for in the church. It's for later."

"Later?"

"Yes, *later*."

"Meaning you're not going to let the children use these in the church during the Christmas pageant tonight?" Edith wanted to be perfectly clear.

"Right."

"So, why did you get them?"

Myrtle just waved her hand. "Oh, you'll see. Look, I've still got lots to do before the day is over, and my feet are killing me. I need to go put them up for a while." And she walked away, leaving the four hardware store bags on the table.

Edith just shook her head, then stowed the bags in a small storage closet beneath the stairs. Perhaps Myrtle would forget about the lanterns, since it didn't seem that she had much use for them, and something that hazardous certainly wasn't going to be allowed in the church. What was that woman thinking anyway?

14

"Edith?" His voice had a sound of urgency in it.

"In here, Charles," she called from the kitchen, where she was packaging up some cookies for the pageant.

"Have you seen *this*?" he said as he came through the door.

"What?" She turned to see what he was talking about, and it seemed he had some sort of flyer in his hand.

"This!" He thrust the flyer at her, then ran his hands through his hair, a gesture he reserved for only the most frustrating of times. Usually it had to do with their children getting into mischief or something that had gone seriously wrong at church. It'd been a while since she'd seen him do it.

She studied the pale green paper with handwritten letters. Not very professional looking, almost as if a child had done it. It seemed to be an announcement in regard to the pageant tonight. But it also said that live animals would be involved and that they were having a live nativity afterward and everyone was invited. At the bottom of the flyer was a rough-looking sketch of what appeared to be a manger scene, although the donkey looked more like a miniature elephant. Or maybe it was supposed to be an ox.

"A live nativity?" he said. "Live animals? No one told me."

"Well, Olive and Myrtle had been arguing about some such thing, but I'm fairly certain that Olive has this under control."

"Then where did these come from?"

"I don't know." Of course, she had a pretty good idea. "It looks as if a child may have done it . . . or perhaps Myrtle."

"Where is that woman?"

Unused to him using that tone, she felt slightly alarmed. "Now, Charles, we can't go blaming her if we don't even know that she's responsible."

He sank down into a kitchen chair. "I know, dear. You're right. It's just that everyone in town is talking about this and the bus, and then, of course, there's Myrtle. I'm sure they think we're all crazy. What am I going to do?"

She put her hand on his shoulder. "I'm sure you'll think of something."

"You know Olive has been hinting that I'm getting too old to pastor a church," he said in dismay. "She's insinuating that I'm losing it, out of touch . . . and now this. I'm afraid she may be right."

"No, dear, she's not right. It's just that, well, things have been a little odd lately." She kind of laughed. "And it all seemed to shift right after you did your wonderful sermon about showing hospitality."

He nodded. "Well, maybe the good Lord has a hand in this. But, seriously, what do you think I should do?"

She considered this. "Well, if you ask Olive about it, she might just get upset. I think Myrtle's up in her room. Maybe we should start there." So they went upstairs and knocked on Myrtle's door, but no one answered. Edith looked at her watch. It was nearly four. "Well, Myrtle did tell me she had a lot to do today. I'm not sure what that means, but—"

"Anything wrong?" asked Michael as he and Lauren came up the stairs.

"No," said Edith. "We're just looking for Myrtle."

Michael nodded and smiled as if perhaps he knew something, but he didn't say anything.

"Do you know where she is?" asked Charles.

Michael kind of grimaced now. "Well, I do . . . but I'm not supposed to tell."

"Michael?" said Lauren. "What are you talking about?"

"It has to do with that little car trip we took yesterday."

"Yeah?" Lauren continued the questioning.

"Well, she made me promise not to tell."

Charles held up the green flyer. "Does it have anything to do with this?"

Michael made a funny little smile that seemed to confirm this. "But don't worry, she's got everything all worked out. We actually had a lot of fun setting things up and, well, I really can't say anything more, but it should be a great evening—if all goes well."

"If all goes well?" repeated Charles in a weak voice. "Meaning that it might not?"

"Really, Pastor Charles," Michael assured him. "It's like you said in church Wednesday night. It's all just a matter of trust."

Charles nodded. "Yes, I suppose you're right."

But Edith wasn't so sure. Oh, it wasn't that she didn't trust God. She did. It was just Myrtle who worried her. She considered telling Charles about the lanterns but thought better of it. Poor man had enough on his mind already.

As they went downstairs, he just shook his head. "Well, maybe I need to just take my hands off this," he said. "It's not as though I'm the one responsible for the pageant. That's why I delegate things . . . but sometimes . . . ." He turned and looked at Edith. "And as soon as I call Hal Berry and ask him to go remove all these flyers from town, I think I will remain in my study to pray about this matter."

She smiled. "That sounds like a wise plan. Dinner will be ready around five so that we'll have plenty of time to, uh, help with the pageant—just in case it's needed." Edith hadn't "helped" with the pageant in years. It had been such a relief when her children were too old for it and she was able to pass the responsibility to another. Then Judy got involved, and Edith had never really given it a second thought, until this year.

Thinking of Judy gave Edith an idea. Surely Judy and her family would be in Christmas Valley by now. Hadn't Olive said they were coming in time to see the pageant? Perhaps she could give Judy a call and give her a little heads-up about what might or might not happen tonight. She dialed Olive's number, and to her relief, Judy answered. After dispensing with cordialities, Edith got right to the point. "Judy, I wanted to let you know that there could be a slight problem at the pageant tonight."

"Does this have to do with the animals?"

"How did you know?"

"Mother and I were in town, and she saw a flyer and went ballistic. She's on her way to the church now. I'm sure you'll see her in a few minutes. She's looking for some crazy lady named Myrtle. But, honestly, it sounded so weird that I thought maybe she was making it up or getting senile. Who is this Myrtle person?"

Edith tried to explain but saw the futility. "The main reason I called, Judy, was to ask for your help tonight, I mean if things should get a little, well, you know . . ."

"Crazy?"

"Yes. I spoke to another guest, and he seems to have some inside information that it is entirely possible that Myrtle has arranged for real animals to be involved tonight. How she managed this, God only knows. But I hate the idea of seeing your mother being, well, stressed out—and then there are the children, and well . . ."

"I understand, Edith. And I do plan to be on hand. And if you want to know the truth, I think the idea of having live animals is rather charming. I even considered it myself one year, but it was so overwhelming that I finally gave up. If your Myrtle can pull this off, I'm happy to do what I can to keep things running smoothly."

"You're a saint!"

Judy laughed. "I'm glad you think so. My mother may have a fit if she finds out I'm in support of this."

"Well, it's more about being in support of the children, don't you think? This is their night, really. I just don't want it spoiled for them."

"I understand."

Edith felt much better after she hung up. She would reassure Charles whenever he emerged from his study. No sense in interrupting his prayer, since she was certain they'd all need it before this night was over.

"Edith?"

She knew it was Olive. Taking a deep breath, she went out to meet her.

Olive had a flyer in her hand and a look of rage on her face. And before Edith could get out a word, Olive began. "What is going on? Is this Myrtle's doing? Where is that woman?"

"Olive," Edith said in her best calming voice. "Come into the kitchen and sit down. I just made a pot of peppermint tea, and I think you could use a cup." She reached for her coat. "Let me take that for you."

"Edith!" Olive exclaimed as Edith wrestled her for her coat. "This is serious."

"Come sit down." They were in the kitchen now, and while Olive continued to rant about what a total catastrophe this evening would be, Edith busied herself with tea and a plate of goodies.

"I swear, unless someone arrests Mad Myrtle and puts her safely in jail, we are all doomed tonight."

"Oh, Olive." Edith set the cookie plate and tea in front of her. "I think you're overreacting."

"Overreacting?"

"Look, if it makes you feel any better, Charles and I both plan to be on hand to help out, to keep things under control. And I've even lined up some other helpers." Edith didn't want to mention the phone call to Judy. It might make Olive feel badly, as if she were unable to keep this thing under control herself. "And I'm sure it's going to be just fine."

"But what about this flyer?" Olive said, waving the paper in the air like a surrender flag. "What about everyone in town who's seen these?"

"First of all, Hal Berry is probably down there right now, taking them all down. But second of all, you know how much attention people pay to flyers, especially this time of year. And these don't even look like anything official. I doubt that anyone even took them seriously."

"You really think so?" Olive looked slightly hopeful as she picked up her teacup.

"Yes, I do. Furthermore, Charles is in his study right now praying for this whole evening to go well."

"Hmm." Olive didn't seem particularly moved by this. "Might do more good if he came out and put Mad Myrtle in her place."

Edith wanted to ask Olive to refrain from calling their guest Mad Myrtle, but sometimes one had to choose one's battles. "Myrtle isn't here."

"Oh?"

"I don't know where she is."

"Well, she wasn't at church. I checked there first. Do you think she's left? Perhaps gotten scared that she stepped over the line and just taken off with her tail between her legs?"

Edith shrugged. "I have no idea."

They finished their tea, and Olive, somewhat subdued, said she had things to get ready at the church.

"I'm bringing cookies over," said Edith. "Do you want me to stay and help?"

Olive waved her hand. "No, barring any visits from Mad Myrtle, I should be just fine. But if you hear screaming from across the street . . ."

"Olive!" Edith gave her a warning look.

"Kidding."

Charles and Edith had just finished dinner when Edith noticed a large truck parked across the street. Other than Collin and Amy's bus, which was strange enough, or the occasional moving van, she was unaccustomed to seeing large trucks in this neighborhood. Edith went into the living room to look out the big picture window.

"It could be a farm truck," she told Charles, seeing that he was coming too.

"Can you see anything else?" he asked as he joined her.

"Not really. The truck is pretty much blocking everything."

"I'm going over," he told her.

"Do you want me to come?"

"No, you finish up in the kitchen. If I need backup, I'll call some of the men."

Edith nodded and returned to the kitchen, thinking that it sounded as if Charles were going off to war. She certainly hoped not. But as she cleaned up, she did pray—very earnestly—that God would keep things under control tonight. Finally, she could stand the suspense no longer. She freshened up, pulled on her coat, scarf, and boots, and trudged on over to the church.

Expecting to see Charles ordering these people, whoever they were, off the church property, she was surprised to see that he was holding one end of a rope with a donkey attached to the other end.

"Come here," he said to her. "Feel this guy's nose."

She walked over and, removing her glove, put her hand on the donkey's warm muzzle. "Very soft." She looked curiously at Charles. "So, what does this mean? Are you letting them stay?"

"I met the owner, George Brown. He owns that little farm just south of here."

"Brown's Eggs?"

"Yes, and other things too. Anyway, he's a really nice guy, and it seems he knows Myrtle—God only knows how that happened. But he's gone to so much trouble first loading and then bringing these animals, and in the snow. Also, Myrtle promised his little girl that she could be an angel tonight. And he's brought bales of straw and pens for the animals . . . and, well, I just don't have the heart to turn him away. This is Buster, by the way," he said, nodding to the donkey. "He belongs to April, the little girl." He pointed over to the large side yard next to the church where Myrtle and a little girl were trying to get a sheep into a pen.

"Need any help?" called a voice from behind. And they looked to see Michael and Lauren approaching.

"Welcome to the petting zoo," said Edith.

"She really pulled it off," said Michael as he looked around at the animals in various stages of unloading.

"Well, not actually," said Edith, perhaps a bit too skeptically. "The night isn't over yet. All manner of chaos could still occur."

"Looks like George could use a hand," said Michael, leaving them to go assist George as he urged another sheep out of the truck. Charles followed, leading the donkey as he went.

"Michael told me about visiting George's farm," Lauren said to Edith. "He really enjoyed it. He said George is a really nice guy."

"He's certainly gone to a lot of work," said Edith, trying to get in the spirit of what was feeling more and more like a three-ring circus.

"I think I'll go help Myrtle with the sheep," said Lauren, leaving Edith to stand by herself on the sidelines.

"Dear Lord," she prayed quietly. "Please, help this to work out."

"What's going on?" said a woman's voice. Edith turned to see Leslie and Megan approaching now. Illuminated by the truck's brake lights, they trekked through the snow with curious expressions. Edith gave them a brief explanation, and Megan begged to go and pet the animals.

"I'm sure that it's fine," said Edith. "I just wish it weren't so dark out here." Then she remembered Myrtle's lanterns. Of course, that's what they were for. "I'll be right back," she told them.

Back at the inn, she discovered Mr. Benson pouring himself a cup of coffee. "How are you doing this evening?" she asked.

"I'm all right."

"Did you see what's going on across the street?" she asked, glancing nervously up at the mantel clock, worried that Olive could get here any minute, and then things could get messy.

He looked out the window and shook his head. "So, she wasn't making it all up?"

"Making it up?"

"About the live nativity at the church. She had me drive her all over town to put up those flyers, but when I actually saw what they said, I got mad at her. I told her she was nuts."

"Oh, don't worry, you're not the only one who thinks that. I just came over to get the kerosene lanterns. They could use some light over there."

He set down his cup. "That was supposed to be my job."

So, feeling relieved of her duties as well as a bit tired, Edith went up to her room and put her feet up. Oh, she was a little worried about all the details and how Olive was going to react, but as was her usual way, she brought those concerns to the Lord. And then she fell asleep.

When she awoke, it was a little after seven. Oh, dear, she hoped she hadn't missed anything. She threw on her coat and boots and rushed out the door. To her surprise there were cars lined up for as far as she could see, up and down both sides of the street, which meant the small parking lot was probably full too. Feeling as excited as a child, she hurried up to the church to find that the doors were open and people were crowded into the foyer. The church was packed! And the pageant was just starting. Edith just stood there and watched with wonder. Of course, it wasn't perfect. Benjamin Craig, a shepherd, forgot his lines, and little Maggie Turner's angel wings fell off. But how they got those animals to behave during the performance was a mystery to her.

When it was all said and done, the audience clapped and cheered, and Charles stepped forward to announce that the living nativity and refreshments would continue outside. "At least for a while," he told them. "As long as the children and animals can handle the cold. But while they're setting things up, let's all join together for some Christmas carols."

Edith, being in the back of the church, was one of the first ones out when the singing ended. Relieved to be out of the stuffy foyer and in the fresh air, she wasn't prepared for what she saw. It was like a Christmas card. Someone, the men probably, had moved the stable structure outside, and it was flanked by straw bales and illuminated with the kerosene lanterns that Mr. Benson had brought over. Children and animals were in their places, and the effect was amazing. Edith spied Olive and Judy off to one side, quietly coaching the children, but Myrtle didn't seem to be around. Hopefully, they hadn't had fireworks . . . Edith was sure she'd hear all the details later. And, really, Olive should be happy—this was the best Christmas pageant ever, and the turnout was incredible. Not only that, Edith noticed that some people who hadn't even been in the church were already outside, standing on the sidewalk and looking on. It was really something!

15

Edith had a lot to do today. But even as she went about her chores, she felt a general spirit of lightness—a joy that had been missing earlier in the week. She knew that it was because of the pageant last night. It was as if the pageant had put things into perspective.

Unfortunately, it hadn't gone off without a hitch. Later that night Charles had told her that when Olive arrived, she and Myrtle did get into a terrible squabble. "Fortunately, the children were already inside putting on their costumes by then. Judy had gone in to help them, but Olive was absolutely livid that Myrtle had gone behind her back to bring in the livestock. And she didn't care who heard her say so. Of course, our Myrtle didn't do anything to help the situation either. I finally had to step in and tell them both to stop their fighting or leave."

As it turned out, Charles's warning had worked. Edith was just glad that she hadn't had to give it. She wasn't sure that she could've made that kind of an impression on two such strong-willed women.

As usual, Edith had invited a few friends from church, those without family and such, to come to the inn for their annual Christmas Eve party, and she expected up to thirty to attend. Although she'd done a lot of the preparations in advance, there was still much to do, and she spent most of her day in the kitchen. Not that she minded, since her kitchen was her domain, and surprisingly enough, no one was pushing their way into her territory today.

Knowing that some restaurants in town weren't open on Christmas

Eve, she had made sure to put a small luncheon buffet out on the dining room table at noon for her guests. And judging by what was left, it appeared they had enjoyed it. All in all, it had been a quiet day at the inn. Peter had invited some of the guests to go sledding on One Tree Hill, and Charles had even gone up there to build a big bonfire. She expected they'd all come home by dusk, if not sooner. They'd be cold and tired and hungry. But she would be ready for them. The party, officially slated to begin at six, could start earlier for the guests at the inn.

Later in the afternoon, she went around the house, putting on Christmas music, turning on the tree lights, lighting candles. She paused where the missing angel once had been, then just sadly shook her head. Perhaps she'd never get to the bottom of it. Maybe little Megan had accidentally broken it, cleaned it up, and hidden the pieces. Her children had been known to do such things without meaning to. Although, if that was the case, for Megan's sake, Edith wished she'd come clean. Guilt like that could stick with a child for years and years to come. *Don't worry about it*, Edith told herself as she turned on the outside lights and looked out at the snow. It was a small thing, really.

Soon the house was bustling with people. It started with those who had been sledding, cold, tired, and hungry, just as she'd expected. But they were in good spirits, and her table full of scrumptious foods hit the spot. Even the Fieldses, who had indulged in sledding too, seemed to have set aside their arguing for a pleasant change. And Michael and Lauren, taken with little Megan, had officially "adopted" her as their new niece. But perhaps most surprising and exciting, at least to Edith, was that Peter and Leslie seemed to have established some sort of bond. She mentioned her suspicions to Charles, and he just winked at her.

Collin and Amy came in at a little before six. Edith hadn't seen them since the night before at the pageant, and then only briefly. She hoped they were doing okay. But they also seemed in good spirits and had even taken some care with their appearance. Collin had on a shirt, slightly wrinkled, with a tie, and Amy had on a long green dress that was very pretty with her eyes.

"How are you feeling?" Edith asked Amy as she led them to the buffet table.

"Okay, I guess. My back hasn't been hurting so much . . ." Then she looked around to see if anyone was listening. "But I'm wondering about these things . . ."

"Things?" Edith looked curiously at Amy.

"Can we go in there?" Amy nodded to the kitchen, and Edith led her through the swinging doors.

"What is it?" asked Edith, concerned.

"I don't think I'm having contractions," Amy explained, "because it doesn't hurt, and aren't contractions supposed to hurt?"

Edith nodded, then reconsidered. "Well, not always so much at first. First it just gets tight around your abdomen, like the muscles are clenching."

"Yes, it feels kind of like that."

"But, of course, there are Braxton Hicks too. They feel like that. Goodness, I had Braxton Hicks for weeks before Katie was born. It almost made me crazy."

"Maybe that's what this is," said Amy hopefully. "I really don't want to have this baby until we're in California."

Edith patted her on the shoulder. "And you probably won't. I've heard that it's unusual for first babies to come early. Mine was two weeks late."

"Oh, good."

So they went back out and joined the others. Mr. Benson had come down now, wearing a white shirt and red bow tie. "You look very festive," Edith told him as she handed him a plate for the buffet table.

"And so does this!" he said as he began to fill it.

Soon other friends began to arrive, and it wasn't long until the house was filled with people and laughter and visiting. Almost the same as when her children were home, Edith thought as she went to the kitchen to refill a cheese tray. But not quite. Still, it was certainly better than being alone, and she thought that her guests would probably agree with her. But as she considered this, it occurred to her that she hadn't seen much of Myrtle. Of course, Myrtle, with her quirky ways, could be waiting for just the right moment before she came out and made some kind of entrance, perhaps even with a speech about the true meaning of Christmas. No need to hurry that up. Edith took the tray out and discovered that the cheese puffs needed replenishing.

Peter, a good piano player, had made himself comfortable playing Christmas carols in the living room with a jolly little circle gathered around him doing their best to sing, although only a few seemed to know all the words. Others had broken into various groups and were visiting comfortably, and as far as Edith could see, everyone was engaged and having a pretty good time. But for the second time tonight, she didn't see Myrtle anywhere. Finally, she decided to ask if Charles had seen her. It was entirely possible that Myrtle had come down while Edith was busy in the kitchen and gotten into some kind of a fracas with someone, perhaps even Mr. Benson, although he seemed to be enjoying himself as he looked at Millie Mortenson's pictures of grandchildren.

"I haven't seen her," Charles told Edith after she inquired.

"Not at all?"

"No. Come to think of it, I haven't seen her since last night."

"Not even at breakfast?" asked Edith. "I was so busy in the kitchen that I didn't really pay close attention to who came and went."

"I was only there for about thirty minutes, but Myrtle didn't come down during that time. That's probably why I had such a pleasant breakfast." He smiled a bit sheepishly. "Sorry, that wasn't very gracious of me. But, if you think about it, things are going rather well this evening. Why push Myrtle into being social if she'd rather keep to herself?"

She considered this. "Yes, she may be using this time to think about things. But I do hope that she's not feeling badly about last night. Do you think that's the problem?"

He patted her on the back. "My guess is that she's simply worn out from all the activities yesterday. She probably grabbed a quick breakfast when neither of us were looking . . . and don't forget that you left all those luncheon goodies out, which I'm sure she helped herself to . . . and perhaps after that she took a little afternoon nap. Don't worry. I'm sure she'll be down here before you know it."

"You're probably right."

After that, Edith had her hands full just keeping the food coming as well as taking time to visit with her guests, so much so that she hardly noticed that nearly two hours had passed and Myrtle still hadn't come down.

"Has anyone seen Myrtle today?" she finally asked a few guests. But no one seemed to have seen her.

"I haven't seen her since yesterday." Mr. Benson chuckled. "Not that I mind so much."

"She's probably tired out from yesterday," Edith told him, echoing Charles's earlier explanation, although she wasn't so sure anymore.

Finally, it was getting late, the party was dwindling to an end, and Myrtle still hadn't made an appearance. Charles still felt certain that the old woman was simply catching up on her rest. "She had a very busy few days," he reminded Edith. "And she's not exactly a young woman. Besides, tomorrow's Christmas, and I'm sure she'll be up bright and early to interrupt your quiet morning time. Just wait and see."

Edith thought he was right, but she still felt a bit concerned when she went to bed. What if something *was* wrong? Perhaps she should've checked on the old woman earlier just to be sure, but now it was so late that she didn't like the idea of disturbing her. Edith had done that with an elderly guest once before, waking the poor old fellow out of a perfectly good sleep, only to get scolded for her intrusion. And she certainly didn't wish to be reproached by Myrtle of all people. Charles was probably right. She'd see Myrtle soon enough in the morning.

16

Christmas morning came, and Edith got all the way through her devotional reading without being interrupted. She fixed a festive Christmas breakfast, with Charles's help, and still no Myrtle. Even the other guests noticed the old woman's absence. And finally Edith couldn't stand it any longer. Goodness, what if Myrtle had died in her sleep?

"I'm going to go check on her," she announced, then glancing at Charles, she considered asking him to join her. But that might alarm the other guests. And this was, after all, Christmas. Edith was probably just blowing this thing all out of proportion.

"I'll come with you," said Charles, standing. Edith wanted to hug him and say thanks, but she simply nodded.

"I'm sure she's fine," Charles said as they went up the stairs. "But I do understand your concern."

"She's normally such an early riser," said Edith weakly, trying not to fear the worst.

Now they were standing in front of the door to the Green Meadow Room, the room where Myrtle was staying. Edith tapped on the door, first lightly, then louder. But there was no response. "Myrtle?" she called, waiting. Nothing but silence.

"It's probably locked," said Edith, reaching into her pocket for the master key. But before she got it out, Charles had already tried the door, and it opened. Edith took in a quick breath, bracing herself for whatever might be in there, but when the door swung open they

132

could see the neatly made bed, and as they went inside, everything seemed in perfect order. Almost as if Myrtle had never been there at all. And she certainly wasn't there now. Everything was just as tidy as it had been after Edith straightened and replaced linens yesterday.

"Where is she?" said Edith, feeling a bit lost.

"Where are her things?" asked Charles as he continued looking around the orderly room as if he expected to find a clue.

Edith didn't know what to think. "I have no idea."

"Look," said Charles, pointing at something on the bureau.

Edith came over to see that it was her porcelain angel. "My angel!" she exclaimed. "What is it—"

"There's something underneath it," said Charles as he carefully lifted the angel and picked up the small white envelope with the picture of a shepherd and lamb on one side, stationery provided by their inn.

"To the innkeepers." Edith read the front of the envelope as Charles handed it to her. She slowly opened it, and the first thing she noticed was the money inside. "What is this?" She handed the bills to Charles, then proceeded to read the juvenile-looking handwriting out loud.

"Thanks for your hospitality. You got a nice place here. Sorry I couldn't stick around to say good-bye, but it's time for me to go. Collin and Amy can use my room now that I'm gone. I have one more week paid up, and the money enclosed is for any extra days or in case they need gas money. I know you'll take care of it for me. Sincerely, Myrtle."

"So she's really gone." Edith looked around the room one more time, almost in disbelief. "I was prepared to have her around for another week."

Charles just shook his head. "But how did she leave? She had no car. Did you see anyone coming to pick her up yesterday?"

"No . . ."

"Do you think someone might've picked her up on Friday night, during the Christmas pageant? There were so many people there, it's possible that she arranged to be quietly picked up and we just didn't notice."

"I suppose . . ." Still, Edith thought it was odd. "But I don't know why she would be so secretive. Myrtle wasn't exactly a private person, you know. She didn't really seem to care what people thought of her. Why would she leave so quietly?"

"I don't know." Charles frowned. "I hope I didn't offend her when I told her and Olive to stop arguing. But I didn't single her out. I addressed Olive in the same manner."

"Oh, I don't think Myrtle was easily offended," said Edith, even though she'd had a similar concern earlier. She just didn't want Charles to feel guilty.

"You don't think she would've tried to make it out of here on foot, do you?" said Charles uncertainly.

"Oh, I don't think so . . ."

"Just the same, maybe I should drive around a bit, check around town, just in case. I'd feel horrible to think that old woman is out on the road, in the snow, and on Christmas."

"Yes, that's a good idea. I know I'd appreciate it. But before you leave, let me go take a look at her registration form. Maybe I can give her home a call and see if she's arrived safely."

"Yes. That's a good plan."

They hurried downstairs, and Edith searched in her file until she found Myrtle's registration form. But other than her name, the form was blank. "I thought you said she filled this out," she said to Charles.

He adjusted his glasses to look at it. "Well, I thought she did." He scratched his head now. "But then I remember she wanted to pay in cash, and so I was more focused on doing the math and making her change, and I suppose I just dropped the form into your file and never really looked at it."

"This is very weird, Charles. Someone drops this eccentric woman off, she pays for two weeks' lodging in cash, and then she disappears after one week. It could almost make someone think that she's some deranged patient who escaped from some institution."

"Or an angel."

She turned and looked at Charles. "You don't really think?"

He kind of laughed. "Well, certainly an odd angel."

"Very odd."

"Edith?"

She turned to see Collin, and his face looked frightened. "What is it?" she asked.

"Amy!" he exclaimed. "She's in labor. What should I do?"

By now several of the guests had gathered around, witnessing this little spectacle.

"Oh!" Edith looked at Charles. "Should we drive them to the hospital?"

"No," said Collin. "Amy refuses to go to the hospital. I already asked her, and she got really mad at me. I promised her that she wouldn't have to go, but now I'm not so sure. What should I do?"

"Can you get her into the house?" asked Edith. "Can she make it up the stairs?"

"Up the stairs?" Collin looked confused now.

"Myrtle left. She wanted you kids to have her room."

Collin brightened a bit. "Really?"

"Yeah, but can Amy get in here okay?"

"I'll go see."

"I'll come help," said Charles.

Then Edith got on the phone. She hated to disturb Helen on Christmas Day, but Helen had made her promise. And as it turned out, Helen sounded quite pleased. "No, it's not a problem, Edith. We're not really doing anything at all. It's just Clarence and me. I'll have him drive me right over, well, as soon as I get some things together first."

It was quite amazing how the other guests stepped in to help. Leslie, the person who had most recently given birth, took it on herself to help coach Amy through labor. Meanwhile Lauren and Michael entertained little Megan with games and books. Edith, distracted in trying to help Helen and Leslie and making sure they had what they needed for Amy, was forced to let her regular chores go, but Carmen and Jim Fields jumped right in, actually putting away all the breakfast things and cleaning the kitchen. And Mr. Benson and Helen's husband, Clarence, enjoyed several games of chess.

During this hectic time at the bed and breakfast, Charles was out scouring the town of Christmas Valley. He even called Peter and asked him to look around a bit too. But finally the two of them met on a deserted Main Street and, certain that Myrtle wasn't out shivering in an alley somewhere, decided to return to the inn.

Amy's labor intensified in the afternoon, and everyone continued to pitch in to help, taking turns running things upstairs and helping to get Christmas dinner ready in the kitchen. All the guests offered to straighten their own rooms and replenish their own linens. Edith was actually able to sit down and put her feet up for a few minutes.

Angela Myrtle was born at 3:45 p.m. After helping Helen to clean off the squirming wet infant and wrapping her into a snug flannel blanket, Edith went down to fetch her kitchen scales. Little Angela weighed in at seven pounds and four ounces.

"Angela *Myrtle*?" Edith queried as she adjusted the pillow beneath the tired mother's head.

Amy smiled. "Angela is for Collin's grandmother. Myrtle is for the kind woman who allowed us to stay in this amazing room." She looked around the room, with its soothing green colors and peaceful pastoral pictures adorning the walls, and smiled. "I feel like I'm in heaven right now. I never dreamed I'd have my baby in such a beautiful place."

"Myrtle's timing couldn't have been better," said Edith as she gathered up some linens.

"Where did she go, anyway?" asked Collin. He was sitting at the end of Amy's bed now, cradling his brand-new daughter in his arms.

"We don't really know," admitted Edith. "But it seemed her mission here was done."

"Mission?"

Edith smiled. "I think God gives us all some kind of mission."

Somehow the turkey and dressing and all the rest of the Christmas dinner made its way to the big dining room table on time. And as Charles and Edith and all their houseguests, minus the new little family upstairs and plus Helen and Clarence and Peter, gathered together, Charles invited them to all bow their heads in a Christmas blessing. Before Charles said "amen," he specifically thanked God for sending them Myrtle.

"So, do you really believe that God sent Myrtle?" queried Mr. Benson with a somewhat skeptical expression across his brow.

Charles nodded solemnly. "Yes, I do. I'm just sorry that I didn't notice sooner."

That's when everyone at the table began to share their own personal experiences and exchanges with the peculiar woman. And most had to agree that Myrtle had indeed rubbed them wrongly, at least to begin with, but at the same time she had touched them at some level—some deep level where they all needed a touch.

Certainly, not everyone was convinced that Myrtle had literally been sent by God via a direct route from heaven. But some weren't so sure she hadn't.

"Perhaps it's not so important that we know where Myrtle came from for certain," Charles finally said. "As long as we believe that God can use someone as unexpected and unconventional as Myrtle to touch our lives. Maybe that's what really matters."

But Edith felt certain that Myrtle was indeed an angel. Only, like her husband, she wished that she'd come to this realization sooner. She also wished that she'd treated Myrtle with a bit more love and respect. Although that might've spoiled things for the strange old woman, blowing her cover, so to speak—because, Edith suspected, Myrtle's mission may not have been accomplished if she hadn't performed it incognito.

The GIFT of CHRISTMAS PRESENT

Christmas Past: the gift we keep with us forever
Christmas Future: the gift that is yet to come
Christmas Present: the gift we open today

1

Christine studied the tall brick house from the sidewalk. Not unlike the other prestigious homes in this dignified university neighborhood, and yet somehow this one seemed different. She glanced down the tree-lined street to survey the other houses. Obviously, these were old and established residences, not anything like the houses in the neighborhood she'd grown up in, where houses popped up almost overnight, like mushrooms, her father liked to say, and where landscaping was minimal and trees were immature and spindly at best. No, this influential neighborhood appeared well established in both history and wealth. And for some reason that irked her.

But why did this house feel different than the others that lined the street? Was it an aura of heaviness? A feeling of sadness? Or perhaps it was simply the lack of Christmas decorations. No bright evergreen wreath hung on its stark black door. And no cheerful lights helped to relieve the foggy gloom of the late afternoon dusk. She walked up the neat brick walk and rang the doorbell, afraid that to hesitate one more moment might compel her to turn back and abandon this crazy stunt altogether.

After what seemed several minutes, the door slowly opened and the face of an older woman with steely blue eyes and silver hair peered through the slit of the open door.

"Yes?" Her voice had the sound of gravel in it, like someone who had smoked for many years.

"Hello . . . Mrs. Daniels? I'm . . . I'm Christine Bradley—"

"You're late," the woman snapped as she leaned forward on an aluminum crutch to see Christine better. Then she opened the door a little wider to reveal a foot wrapped in elastic bandage. She glared at the girl. "And you may as well know right from the start that I absolutely will not tolerate lateness."

"Late?" Christine said, feeling slightly off balance but curious just the same.

"Yes, the agency said you'd be here an hour ago. And I was just about ready to give up on you completely."

"Oh, I'm terribly sorry." Christine tried her best to smile, deciding to go along with this strange woman's charade, for the moment anyway. At least it delayed the inevitable, which suddenly seemed a good thing, especially since Mrs. Daniels appeared rather abrupt and foreboding, not to mention rude.

"Well, come in here, and close that dang door behind you. I can't afford to heat the entire neighborhood. Despite what some people may think, I have to live within my means."

Christine quickly shut the door, careful not to slam it lest she be chided for that as well. "I'm sorry, Mrs. Daniels, but I have to explain—"

"Look, don't waste my time on apologies or explanations, you're probably not right for the job anyway. Just hang your coat there and then come into the living room and we'll get this over with as quickly as possible." Mrs. Daniels hobbled on her crutches toward a leather club chair, then eased herself down with a loud sigh. "This ankle! I don't know how I could've been so clumsy as to sprain it."

"How did you—"

"Never mind that! I'm the one asking the questions here." She stared openly at Christine as if she were summing her up and finding her lacking. Then she waved her hand as if to dismiss her altogether. "First of all, you're much too young. How old are you, anyway? Sixteen?"

"I'm nineteen, almost twenty."

Mrs. Daniels shook her head. "Well, I wanted an older woman. Someone more responsible. You do understand this is a full-time position, don't you? And it's going to include some evenings as well.

I don't want some flighty young thing who thinks she can come and go as she pleases or take off early just because she has a date. I simply won't tolerate it."

You don't tolerate much, Christine thought, but instead she said, "To be honest, I really don't go out much. The Wednesday night worship service, occasionally. But that's about it."

"You're a church girl, then?" Mrs. Daniels's brows lifted with a faint flicker of interest, but her cold blue eyes still looked at Christine as if she could see right through this impromptu deception.

Christine shifted uncomfortably in her chair. What in the world was she doing here? And why on earth had she allowed their conversation to reach this weird place. "Uh, Mrs. Daniels, I need to tell—"

"Just where are your references?" It sounded like an accusation.

"References?" Christine studied this woman's soured expression and decided to continue with the charade.

Mrs. Daniels ran her hand through her short-cropped hair and rolled her eyes in irritation. "Don't they teach you young people anything these days? When you come for a job interview, you're supposed to bring references. I suppose you don't have any. Have you ever held a job before?"

"Actually, I did work at McDonald's during high school, for nearly two years."

Mrs. Daniels laughed but with no mirth. "Now, that's real handy. Maybe you could go into the kitchen there and whip me up a Big Mac for dinner. Good grief, girl, do you know anything about house-keeping?"

"Housekeeping?"

"Oh, I don't know why I'm even bothering with you, Miss . . . Miss—what was your name again?"

"Christine. Christine Bradley."

"Right." Her eyes narrowed. "Well, Miss Bradley, tell me, do you even know the difference between a mop and a broom?"

Christine nodded slowly. "I did keep house for my father dur-ing the last six years." A lump grew in her throat as she suddenly realized how much she missed him as well as the familiarity of her previous home.

Mrs. Daniels looked skeptical. "And what did your mother do?"

"My mother died," Christine said quietly. *Twice*, she thought.

"Oh, well, that's too bad." Mrs. Daniels seemed to soften just a little. "But at least it seems you do know how to keep house, then?"

Christine nodded again, ready to end this ludicrous interview, but not quite ready to divulge her true identity to this antagonistic woman. How could someone this cold, this calculating, actually be her genetic grandmother? Perhaps she'd made a mistake somewhere, gotten it all wrong. But she knew that was impossible. Without a doubt this must be the right woman. It was the right address, the right town, the right name. But just the same it was all wrong. Terribly wrong!

"Mrs. Daniels," Christine began again. "I really need to—"

"Well, I really need you to write down those references for me, and if they meet my satisfaction, and if no one better shows up, well, then you can start work right away. My daughter-in-law is wearing on my nerves these days. And she said just today that she can't keep this up forever, especially during the holidays, which is perfectly fine by me. The less I see of that woman, the happier I'll be. For the life of me, I still can't see why my stepson ever married someone like her to begin with."

That must be my uncle, Christine thought. Although her father had never mentioned anything about Lenore's other siblings. But then maybe he was a stepuncle. She wasn't sure. And her father hadn't really known much about her birth family in the first place, other than the name and the town, and that had been discovered only recently and quite by coincidence.

"And those grandkids aren't anything to brag about either. A couple of spoiled brats, if you ask me, always whining and complaining and getting underfoot."

"But how fortunate you are to have family that—"

"Fortunate?" Mrs. Daniels scowled. "Why, they're just waiting for me to croak so they can inherit all this." She waved her hand around, then laughed in a sharp, cynical way. "But what they don't know won't hurt them. And, just so you'll know, Miss Bradley, just in case you're thinking you can sneak in here and steal from the old broad, well, you'd better think again. I may be pushing eighty, but I've still got all my marbles up here." She pointed to her head. "Not that my family thinks so. I'm sure they'd love to declare me senile and have me committed to some old folks home to whither away and die." She leaned forward and peered at Christine. "Felicity didn't send you here, did she?"

"Felicity?" Christine said, feeling more and more like she'd just stepped into the twilight zone.

"My daughter-in-law," Mrs. Daniels said with a frown. "That girl is out to get me. I just know it."

"But why?" Despite her reservations and a longing to escape this cantankerous woman, Christine felt herself being reeled in. She sensed there was a reason that Mrs. Daniels was so bitter and jaded. And she wanted to know what it was.

"Like I said, they're after my money." She got a sly smile, as if she were keeping a secret. "And that's perfectly fine with me. I plan to keep stringing them along just to ensure that they show me a bit of respect during my final years. I'm sure that's the only reason they even attempt to be nice to me—thinking I'm going to leave my *vast* fortune to them." She laughed again, only this time the hollow sound seemed to echo with sadness as it reverberated through the impeccably decorated rooms of the large, quiet house.

Inexplicably, and to her own irritation, Christine felt a real wave of pity for this embittered woman. And although it seemed impossible to think they were actual blood relatives, she felt some strange kind of connection.

"Okay, Mrs. Daniels, I'll write down my references for you. I can give you my pastor's name and number, and my manager at McDonald's. I could give you my father's phone number too, but he recently left the country to teach at a mission base down in Brazil. Will just two names be enough?"

"I guess it'll have to do. But mark my word, young lady, in the future if you should ever apply for a job again, you had better bring your references along with you!" With a loud groan, she pulled herself to her feet and then struggled for her crutches. "Young people nowadays!"

Christine stood too. "So when do you want me to come?"

"Well, Felicity is coming back today. Why don't you come tomorrow at eight o'clock sharp, but not a minute before since I don't get up until eight. And if you can promise to come tomorrow, I can tell Felicity that she no longer needs to bother herself with me. Actually, I've been telling them both that since I got home from the emergency room last Saturday, but do they listen to me? Ha! Not on your life." The woman arranged her crutches beneath her arms, then hobbled away without even saying good-bye or seeing Christine to the door.

Christine pulled a small notebook out of her purse, neatly wrote down the references, and left them on the gleaming mahogany table in the foyer. Then quietly she slipped on her parka and let herself out the front door. It was already getting dark outside, and she shivered against the cooling temperature. She hurried down the walk and questioned what she was getting herself into. But then again she had wondered what she'd do with herself during Christmas break. Surely this would be a holiday she'd never forget.

2

"You're sure you'll be okay on your own during the holidays?" Christine's roommate asked as she shoved her dirty clothes into a laundry sack. "We've got a full house, but you're welcome to come home with me if you don't mind sleeping on the floor."

Christine picked up a dirty sock and tossed it into Brianna's rapidly filling bag. "Thanks anyway, but I've taken a job during the holidays."

"You're going to work during Christmas?"

She nodded. "It should be pretty interesting too."

Brianna frowned as she attempted to tie the bulging bag closed. "Sounds like a drag to me. But then I've never found work to be terribly engaging."

Christine didn't say anything, but she knew firsthand this was true. She'd only just met Brianna at the beginning of fall term, when they'd been paired off to share a room, but in the past few months she'd witnessed up close and personal how this less-than-motivated girl allowed her side of the room to pile up until she practically needed a snow shovel to unearth her bed.

"Well, you have fun now," Brianna said with a bright smile.

"Thanks," Christine said, although *fun* hardly seemed the appropriate word to describe her new housekeeping job for the demanding Mrs. Daniels. "And you have a good Christmas with your family," she called as Brianna struggled to get out the door, loaded down with her backpack and laundry bag.

Christine lingered in the unusually quiet hallway for a few moments. It was amazing how quickly the place had evacuated following finals. She wouldn't be surprised if she was the only one left on this floor by now. Finally she went back into her room, closed the door, and locked it. She glanced around the small space and told herself that she should appreciate these next few weeks of peace and quiet. And yet somehow she knew it wouldn't be quite that simple.

She sat down at her desk and reopened her father's latest letter. He was writing only weekly now, if that. When he'd first arrived down there, she'd gotten letters from him almost every other day. She thumbed through the recent photos he'd sent. His tanned face looked years younger and more relaxed than it had in ages. In fact, he hardly appeared to be sixty-four. She felt certain this must be the result of his new teaching position down at the mission in Brazil.

"It's always been a lifetime dream of mine," he'd confessed to her last year. "Long ago, back when I was still in college, back before I met your mother, I seriously considered becoming a foreign missionary. For some reason I fancied the idea of South America. I suppose it was because of all those missionary books I'd been reading. But I'd sent for the mission information and had even begun filling out an application."

"And then you met Mom and decided to get married instead?" Christine had asked.

"It didn't seem like such a difficult decision at the time. Once I met your mother, I knew she was all I'd ever wanted. It felt as if she brought everything I'd ever missed into my world." He'd smiled. "And she made my life seem more alive and happy and full."

"You were really in love, weren't you."

Christine had always enjoyed hearing her dad talk about their romance—how he had just been starting out in his teaching profession and her mother had been a registered nurse, how they'd met at church and fallen in love almost instantly. It was straight out of a storybook. And she still hoped that someday she'd have a similar experience herself. Although so far it didn't seem terribly likely.

"I was so completely smitten," he'd confessed last year, "that I forgot all about wanting to be a foreign missionary. I was just happy to have a good job at the local elementary school, to marry your sweet little mother, and to live happily ever after."

"But are you happy now?" she'd asked. "In your work, I mean."

He'd frowned slightly. "Oh, I don't know . . ."

"Then why don't you do it?" she'd said suddenly. "Why don't you just go for it, Dad? Revive your old dream and just do it. I mean, lots of people your age take off to do something different. And you've been saying you're going to take early retirement ever since Mom died, but you keep putting it off."

"I just wanted to make sure you were settled," he'd said. "I wanted to be here for you during your first years of college."

"And you've done that, Dad. But you know I'll be transferring to the university for my junior year. I won't even be living at home after next summer." She'd looked around the familiar kitchen, memorizing the cheerful yellow and white checked wallpaper her mother had hung back when Christine was still in grade school. "You know, Dad, you could even sell the house if you wanted. I mean, I'd totally understand."

"Oh, no, no." He'd waved his hand. "I wouldn't do that, Christine. Where would you come home to during your vacation times?"

But, as it turned out, he'd leased the house, for just two years, but there'd also been talk of signing an option to buy, although Christine wasn't sure about that. Still, it had seemed the sensible thing to do at the time, what with her off at college and him planning to be out of the country. And Christine had assured him that she would be perfectly fine on her own. She'd had a part-time job, a partial scholarship, and faith that God would see her through. So far so good.

She stared at the recent photos of her father amidst the smiling brown faces of schoolchildren until her eyes became too blurry to focus and she feared that her tears would ruin the pictures completely. "Oh, how I miss you, Daddy," she said as she carefully stacked the pictures and placed them back in the envelope.

Of course, she knew he wasn't her "real" father. Or, more accurately, her biological father. And she knew the only mother she'd ever known wasn't her birth mother. But they'd both been her *real* parents, and she'd loved them as much, perhaps even more, than if they'd shared the same gene pool. And now that she was completely alone and on her own, she missed them both more than ever.

She picked up the family portrait on her desk. It had been taken just about a year before her mother had suffered the brain aneurysm that had so unexpectedly taken her life. Christine remembered the day as if it were yesterday. She'd just started her freshman year in high school. It had been the first week and her mother had dropped her off at the front entrance.

"Have a good day, honey," she'd said, just like always. Then she'd added rather unexpectedly, "And don't forget that God's always watching out for you."

Christine had nodded, then uttered a quick good-bye before she dashed from the car. It wasn't that she was embarrassed, exactly, to be seen emerging from a seventeen-year-old peach-colored sedan with a dented front fender, or even to be seen with a slightly frumpy mother who was quite a bit older than most of her friends' parents, but the truth was she wasn't eager to be seen like that either. And certainly not during the first week of school, especially when she'd been trying extra hard to make a good impression. At the time it had seemed incredibly important to look cool, and Christine's parents, home, and car didn't fall anywhere close to the cool category. But then life and values can change in a heartbeat. And by the end of that day, Christine couldn't have cared less about appearances. All she wanted was her mother back. But that wasn't going to happen.

She and her father had grieved together, helping each other along like the blind leading the blind. Her first year of high school passed almost without notice. But eventually their lives fell into something of a pattern. Something that vaguely resembled normal. Not that it was anything like when her mother was alive. But they got by. And Christine slowly learned a bit about housekeeping and grocery shopping and how to do laundry without turning her father's jockey shorts pink. She had never fully realized or even appreciated all that her stay-at-home mother had done to make their lives pleasant and comfortable and easy.

It was midway through this year of grieving and getting by that her father had broken the news to her. As life turned out, Christine had lost not just one mother but two.

150

"Your mother wanted to tell you several years ago," he'd said one evening in late winter. "But I thought it was unimportant. I thought we were all the parents you'd ever need, the only ones you've ever known. But now that Marie is gone, well, I think maybe it's time you knew the truth."

"The truth?" Christine had felt as if her world was suddenly shifting again. She'd felt the need to grab on to something before she went totally sideways.

"This isn't easy for me, honey. I've always thought of you as our very own. And, believe me, you are. But not completely." He'd paused to take a deep breath. "The fact of the matter is we adopted you at birth."

Christine had blinked. How could this be? "I'm adopted?"

He'd nodded. "Marie and I had always wanted to have children, but the good Lord just never saw fit to give us any—until you, that is. You were our little miracle child."

Christine had tried to take in his story, but at the time she'd been in such a state of shock that much of it went right past her. She'd had him retell the story days later, more slowly and carefully, so that she could begin to put the pieces together in her own mind. Her birth mother was Lenore Blackstone, an eighteen-year-old who had left home because of an unwanted pregnancy.

"Lenore's parents were unsympathetic," her father had explained. "Her condition was an embarrassment to them. So Lenore moved from her hometown to Larchwood and got a job at Buddy's Café. Marie and I were regulars there and knew all the waitresses by name. So, naturally, we noticed whenever a new girl came along. We quickly befriended Lenore and learned that she was on her own and lonely and frightened. She was renting a room above the hardware store but was barely able to make ends meet. When Marie learned that Lenore was pregnant, she invited her to come to church with us, and eventually we offered her a room in our home. We both loved Lenore and felt right off the bat that she was like family. As the end of her pregnancy drew near, she began to suggest that we might want to adopt her baby. We were a bit stunned at first, but the more we thought about it, the more it seemed to make sense. Most of all, Lenore wanted to ensure that her baby had a good home."

Christine had patted her father's hand. "And you and Mom saw to that."

He'd nodded. "We did our best. Your mom even gave up her job as a nurse just so she could be a full-time mother to you. We didn't mind the extra scrimping, not one bit. You were worth it."

"But what happened to my birth mother?"

"It was only about a month after you were born. We could both see that Lenore was an intelligent girl, and we encouraged her to register for classes at the community college. We even offered to pay her tuition, since she had no intention of going back to her family just then. It was a freezing day in January, and she'd just gotten off the bus near campus, when she was struck down by a car that had skidded across the icy pavement. She went into a coma and died two days later."

Christine had felt her eyes filling with tears for a woman she'd never even really known.

"Marie and I were just devastated." Her dad had sadly shaken his head. "We made arrangements for her funeral and desperately tried to locate her family in the town she'd said she'd come from, but there wasn't a single Blackstone listed in the phone book. That's when Marie wondered if perhaps Lenore had made up the name to distance herself from her family."

"Maybe she didn't want to be found," Christine had suggested.

But, as it turned out, Lenore hadn't made up the name at all. Only last summer while getting his traveling shots at the county health department, Christine's dad had met a man named Blackstone, and out of curiosity he'd inquired further. The man told him about a second cousin, Allen Blackstone, who had lived in the same town Lenore had come from and who had also had a daughter by that name. Unfortunately, Allen had died of a heart attack when Lenore was still a young teenager, and her mother had remarried only a year or so later. The man wasn't absolutely certain, but he thought the second husband's name was Daniels and that he was some bigwig at the university.

"Isn't it ironic," her father had said as they sat at the kitchen table, eating the chicken casserole she'd prepared that afternoon, "that you're already enrolled to go to college in that very same town. It's possible that you could have a grandmother there."

"I don't care if I do," Christine had said as she refilled her water glass.

Her father's brows had raised slightly. "Wouldn't you like to meet her?"

"Not if she was that horrible to my birth mother. Really, Dad, why would I want to have anything to do with someone like that?"

"I don't know . . ." Her father had taken another bite and then smiled. "Good dinner tonight, Christine. Your mother would be proud."

Which mother? Christine had wondered. But, of course, she knew who he meant. Naturally, he could only be speaking of Marie, the only mother Christine had ever known. Still, it bothered her that she'd begun to wonder about this other mother, the one who had died at an even younger age than Christine was now. What was Lenore Blackstone really like, anyway? And what was wrong with her family that they would abandon her like that?

Well, starting tomorrow, Christine would find out. The big question was, Would she spill the beans to her biological grandmother? Or would she simply play along in the housekeeper role and discover these things for herself? She wondered what her father would recommend, but, of course, she knew. He would be quick to quote something like "Honesty is the best policy." And under normal circumstances she would agree with him completely. But this was anything but normal.

3

Esther Daniels cursed as she attempted to shove herself up from the low-seated chair where she'd fallen asleep in the living room. She wondered why she bothered to put up with these blasted wingback chairs anymore. It wasn't as if they were comfortable. And at her age she should be sitting in a recliner, maybe even one with vibrating massage or a heater or one of those lift-seat contraptions she'd seen on television commercials. Oh, sure, they were ugly as sin, but they did the trick, didn't they? Who cared about looks at her age? She looked around her impeccably decorated living room and rolled her eyes. "Hang those decorators, anyway!" she muttered as she finally managed to prop her crutches beneath her arms and steady herself. "What do they know about comfort?"

She'd been speaking to herself more and more as the years passed. At first she'd questioned this odd behavior a bit, but after a while she'd decided it was better than the lonely silence that always prevailed in the large, empty house. Besides, what did she care if some people thought she was batty? Let them live all by themselves in a big old house and see how they liked it. Oh, she'd considered selling her home several times, but at the last moment she'd always reneged. Perhaps it was a matter of pride, or maybe it was just plain old laziness, but Esther had decided to remain here until her last days. They'd have to carry her out feet first.

"What about checking out some of those nice retirement homes?" Jimmy had suggested to her just recently.

"You're not putting me in some old folks home," she'd told him. "Not as long as I'm able to walk and talk and breathe."

Of course, it wasn't long after she'd spoken those words that she'd slipped on her patio and sprained her right ankle. But even if she couldn't walk, she could still talk and breathe, and she had absolutely no intention of being locked up in one of those smelly old folks homes like she'd taken her own mother to live in. Of course, her mother had been without funds at the time and her choices limited. Esther had told herself that she was doing the poor old woman a favor. Now she wasn't too sure. But there was no going back. Only forward. And the prospects of that weren't terribly encouraging.

"Growing old is for the birds," she said as she opened her large double-wide refrigerator and peered in. "Orange juice, one-percent milk, Fuji apples, cottage cheese . . ." She rattled off the contents as if she were reading a menu, then picked up the cottage cheese carton and shook her head. That obtuse Felicity! Wouldn't she know by now to get the low-fat kind? Was she trying to give her mother-in-law a heart attack? Esther put the carton back into the refrigerator and slammed the door. "Maybe I'm not hungry after all."

Just then the phone rang, causing her to jump. "Who could that be?" she grumbled as she hobbled over to answer the wall phone next to the granite-covered breakfast bar.

"Hello?" she said, more of a growl than a greeting.

"Mom?"

"Hello, Jimmy. Did you know that harebrained wife of yours got me the wrong kind of cottage cheese again? I think she's just doing this to spite me. I have half a mind to—"

"Oh, that's probably my fault," Jimmy said. "I don't like the low-fat kind myself, and she probably got confused."

"Well." Not for the first time she wondered why he was protecting that woman. Furthermore, she wondered what exactly it was about that woman that had attracted him in the first place. Esther had always considered her stepson to be a fairly sensible young man. Well, until he'd gone and married that flibbertigibbet. Oh, she wasn't blind; she could admit that Felicity was beautiful and could occasionally even be charming. But most of the time Esther thought the young woman's head was just stuffed with fluff.

"I wanted to check and see how you were doing, Mom," Jimmy said. "Can we get you anything? Felicity and I got a sitter and are going to a Christmas party tonight, but we could stop by and bring you something first."

"I don't need anything," she said sharply. "Well, other than some low-fat cottage cheese, that is."

"We'll drop some by."

"Oh, don't bother." She sighed. "Don't go to the trouble."

"It's no trouble, Mom. The party is near your house anyway."

"Whose party is it?" Suddenly she felt interested. She remembered the days when she'd been invited to the best university parties. Back when James was alive.

"It's at the Stanleys'," Jimmy said.

"Oh," Esther said in a flat voice. "Well, they aren't so terribly smart. Don't even know how they can afford a home over here in the first place."

"They're nice people, Mom."

"So say you."

She heard him sigh over the phone and knew that was the signal that his patience was wearing thin. Well, what did it matter to her? Her patience was worn thin too. And, besides that, he was the one who had called her.

"Anything else you need?"

"No," she snapped. "As a matter of fact, I don't need anything. Don't bother yourselves to stop by—"

"It's no bother, Mom."

"No, no . . . ," she said, regretting that she was using such a sharp tone on Jimmy. Sometimes she wondered what made her so cranky and mean. "Don't bother yourselves with me, Jimmy. I'll have my girl go out and get me whatever I need tomorrow."

"Your girl?"

"Yes. I've hired a housekeeper."

"A housekeeper? Are you sure about this?"

"Of course I'm sure. Good grief, Jimmy, do you think I'm going senile on you? Or getting Alzheimer's? Or just plain decrepit and helpless? I've hired a girl, and I will be perfectly fine. Please tell Felicity there's no need for her to stop by anymore."

"Are you sure?"

"Jimmy!"

"Okay. Fine, Mom. Just let us know if you need anything, will you?"

"If I need anything, I'll have my girl go get it for me."

"All right. Then have a good evening, Mom."

She laughed in her customary way. It was her way of showing that someone had said something completely ludicrous. "Oh, sure, Jimmy. I'll have a wonderful evening. Thank you so very much!" Then she hung up the phone with a loud bang.

Oh, she knew she was a mean old crow, and sometimes she even regretted it. But she'd spent most of her life acting gracious and courteous and nice—the way the wife of an important man should act. But things had changed. She was old and alone now. Why continue the act? Besides, she told herself as she hobbled back to the refrigerator, if a person couldn't get ornery when she was old, what was the use of getting on in years?

She stood before the open refrigerator, peering in to see the exact same contents as before. Finally she took an apple, stuck it into the pocket of her oversize sweater, and tottered off toward her bedroom, turning off the lights as she went. No sense wasting electricity. She was careful not to catch her crutch on edges of the Oriental rug that ran down the length of the hardwood floor. Another fall could be her undoing.

She turned on the bedroom light to reveal tall walls of pale blue and ivory. The striped wallpaper had an elegant moiré pattern that had been popular during the eighties. Along the walls stood a few pieces of gleaming cherry furniture, all very expensive and all in the Queen Anne style, including her king-size four-poster bed. It was centered between two tall windows, and beneath it was a large Persian rug in shades of blue and ivory. Some might think the room overly formal and cool, but it suited Esther. Or so she liked to tell herself. She occasionally considered changing the ivory satin bedspread to something a little softer and cozier, but somehow she never got around to it.

157

She removed the apple from her pocket and set it on the bedside table, then struggled to balance herself on one foot as she attempted to remove her clothing without toppling over. Finally she gave up and climbed into bed still half dressed. She turned off the light and waited in the darkness for sleep to come and rescue her. Sleep and dreams seemed her only respite from this ongoing endurance race called life. Sometimes, especially lately, she wondered why she even bothered to participate at all. What was there to live for, anyway? Her doctor had prescribed some powerful pain pills when she'd sprained her ankle, but she'd taken only a couple, and those on the first day. She thought the rest might come in handy some other day. She just wasn't sure which day that would be. She considered taking one now, but at the moment she was simply too exhausted to climb out of bed and get them. Like so many other things in her life, it would have to wait.

4

Christine pushed the doorbell again. It was ten minutes after eight, and, as she recalled, Mrs. Daniels (she couldn't bring herself to call her Grandmother, not even in her mind) had said not to arrive before eight. She hadn't specified exactly when to come, or maybe Christine had been too flustered to listen correctly. But 8:10 seemed a safe time to show up for her "job." During her twenty-minute walk across campus, on her way to Mrs. Daniels's home, she had attempted to convince herself that was all this was. A job. Suddenly she wasn't so sure.

The door opened a crack. "Who is it?" demanded a voice that sounded like Mrs. Daniels's, only huskier than before.

Christine peered through the two-inch crack. "It's me, Christine Bradley," she said. "Your . . . your housekeeper."

The door opened wide enough to show that Mrs. Daniels had a pale blue bathrobe draped over her.

"I'm sorry," Christine said. "Did I get you up?"

"No." Mrs. Daniels stepped back and waved her inside. "Get in here before my house gets cold."

Christine stepped inside and quickly closed the door behind her. She stared at the frazzled old woman, unsure if this was actually the same Mrs. Daniels she'd met yesterday. Her short silver hair was sticking out in every direction, and she had on some wrinkled tan slacks with a pink pajama top beneath the robe that appeared to be half on and half off.

159

"Well, don't just stand there gaping at me," Mrs. Daniels snapped. "I know I look a fright. I didn't sleep well last night, and I need some help getting dressed right now. You are able to do that, aren't you?"

"Of course."

"Then follow me."

Christine followed the old woman down the long hallway. In the dim light she could see that several works of art hung on the walls. Even her inexperienced eye could tell they were originals and probably valuable. She would've liked to have taken time to examine them more closely, but Mrs. Daniels had already made it to the room at the end of the hall.

"Come on, come on," the old woman called. "Don't dawdle."

Christine hurried along and followed her into a very elegant bedroom suite. The room was about twice the size of the living room Christine had grown up with and was decorated like something out of a magazine. Other than the unmade bed, only one side actually, and a few articles of clothing on the floor, everything was absolute perfection.

"This is a beautiful room," Christine said as she watched Mrs. Daniels easing herself into a pale blue velvet chair by the window.

"Yes, yes." Mrs. Daniels frowned. "I hope never to catch you snooping around in my things, Miss . . . Miss . . . What is your name again?"

"Christine." She tried to smile. "Christine Bradley."

"Yes, that's right." She nodded. "Miss Bradley. Anyway, I won't put up with any snooping . . . or stealing either, for that matter." She peered up at Christine. "You say you're a churchgoing girl, right?"

"That's right."

"Well, I expect that means you should be honest. At least that's what it used to mean. Not too sure what it means anymore. But I will not put up with any shenanigans, you understand?"

Christine swallowed and nodded, still incredulous that this woman was a flesh and blood relative. She studied the old woman's long, straight nose and wondered if it didn't look a bit like her own. Or perhaps she was imagining things.

"Fine. Now help me get these ridiculous trousers off. I don't know what got into my crazy daughter-in-law's head yesterday, helping me put these confounded things on. I told her I should stick to loose, stretchy garments until my ankle heals up. But, oh no, she thought I should dress up nicely. She's a ridiculous young woman!"

Christine felt a bit embarrassed as she helped the old woman slip out of the lined wool trousers, carefully slipping the narrow pant leg past the oversize, bandaged foot. She couldn't help but notice the pale, scrawny legs. *How awful to grow old*, she thought as she turned away and laid the trousers on the bed.

"Don't leave those pants on the bed," the woman chided as she pulled the bathrobe around her. "There." She pointed to the wall with two doors. "The closet is on the right. Find a pants hanger and hang them up. Then find me a jogging suit." She cackled. "Not that I plan to do any jogging. Get the blue velour one, please. Those pants have extra-wide legs as I recall."

Christine walked into the large closet. It was about the size of her dorm room, only completely outfitted with shelves and drawers and rods full of beautiful clothes. Expensive clothes. And shoes! She'd never seen so many shoes—that weren't in a store, anyway. She quickly located what appeared to be the more casual section of the closet and found not one but two blue velour jogging suits.

"Do you mean the dark blue or the light blue?" she called from the closet.

"The darker one, I think."

Christine emerged with a jogging suit. "This one?"

"Yes, that's it. I don't care much for that color on me, but at least it will be comfortable." Mrs. Daniels was attempting to stand now, struggling to get the crutches in place. "However, I've decided I want to take a shower after all. I'll need you to help me with the bandage."

So Christine followed her into a large bathroom where everything was white. White marble tiles, white fixtures, and white towels. Mrs. Daniels lowered herself onto a metal bench topped with a white velvet cushion. She stuck out her bad foot and groaned slightly. "Be careful when you unwrap it," she warned. "It's still very tender."

Christine knelt down and gently untwined the layers of elastic bandage until she exposed a very swollen and odd-colored foot. It was shades of yellow, purple, and black. "Oh, my," she said as she laid the bandage on the counter. "That looks like it hurts."

"Of course it hurts," Mrs. Daniels snapped, her brows drawn tightly together.

"I'm sorry."

"Well, it's not your fault." Mrs. Daniels seemed to soften just a bit. "And I suppose the pain is making me a little grouchier than usual."

Christine took some comfort in the old woman's confession. "That's understandable."

"Besides that, I'm old," Mrs. Daniels said. "I've earned the right to be a curmudgeon if I feel like."

Christine smiled. "That's not a word you hear every day."

"Well, I used to teach English. Back in the days when students were expected to have an actual vocabulary."

Christine stood, feeling a bit overwhelmed at the idea of helping this old woman bathe. How on earth had she gotten herself into this crazy mess, anyway? "Do you want me to start the water in the shower for you?"

"Yes."

So Christine turned on the water and adjusted it to what felt like the right temperature, then stepped back. "That's nice that you've got a place to sit down in there," she said. "That should make it easier for you."

"That's the whole point," Mrs. Daniels said. "Now turn your back while I get into the shower, but don't leave. I may need your help getting out. I haven't actually attempted this yet."

"All right." Christine waited until she heard the shower door close. Then she picked up the bathrobe and pajama top and wondered what to do next. She decided to move the bench close to the shower for when Mrs. Daniels got out. She also set a couple of thick white towels on the edge of it. Next, she located a thick white bath mat, which she placed right next to the shower entrance.

"Okay, I'm done now," Mrs. Daniels called from inside the shower stall. "Hand me a towel."

Much to her relief, Christine managed to open the shower door and hand the old woman a towel without seeing too much old, wrinkly flesh.

"Now give me a hand," Mrs. Daniels said. She was wrapped in the towel and struggling to balance on one foot. "And hurry it up, my ankle is starting to throb."

Christine prayed as she helped the old woman out of the shower and eased her onto the bench, amazingly without a mishap.

Mrs. Daniels groaned. "Maybe I should've skipped the shower after all."

Christine got a smaller towel, and without asking she began to blot the dripping silver hair. Fortunately, Mrs. Daniels didn't protest.

"Let's get you dried and bandaged up again," Christine said with a bit more authority. She wrapped another towel around Mrs. Daniels's shoulders before she stooped down to help dry her legs and feet. Then, kneeling on the hard marble floor, she carefully rewrapped the ankle as closely as she could to the way it had been before she'd unwound it.

"Have you done this before?"

She shook her head. "No, but I had considered going to nursing school for a while."

"Whatever for?"

"To become a nurse." Christine stood.

"Well, of course. But why on earth would anyone want to become a nurse, of all things? Changing bedpans and caring for sick people. Good grief."

"As it turned out, I wasn't really suited for it." Christine handed her a white terry bathrobe that was hanging on a hook by the shower.

"You could've fooled me." Mrs. Daniels pushed the bathrobe back at her. "No, just go and get me my clothes. I believe I'll just get dressed in here. You'll find my underthings in one of the top drawers in the closet. And while you're at it, bring me a sturdy tennis shoe for my good foot."

After about twenty minutes and a bit of cursing on Mrs. Daniels's part, they managed to get her adequately dressed and seated on the pale yellow leather couch in the living room.

"I think you should put your foot up," Christine advised.

"Yes, I'm sure you're right."

"And I think you should have some breakfast." Christine adjusted the tapestry pillow beneath the injured foot. "What do you usually have?"

"I'll start with some orange juice." Mrs. Daniels leaned back and closed her eyes and sighed. "Do you know how to make coffee?"

"Yes. How do you like it?"

"Strong and with cream."

"What else would you like?"

"I would like a poached egg and a piece of lightly buttered toast." Mrs. Daniels opened her eyes. "Do you know how to do that?"

Christine nodded. "My dad likes poached eggs too."

Mrs. Daniels closed her eyes again. "Good."

Christine wandered through a spacious dining room with a long, dark table large enough to seat at least twelve. Along one wall of this room was a bank of French doors that looked out onto a perfectly landscaped backyard and what appeared to be an inground pool. Christine wondered if Mrs. Daniels actually used the pool, or was it just for looks? Then she went through a set of double swinging doors and found what she'd hoped for—a kitchen. And to Christine's surprise, it was a sunny-looking kitchen with walls the color of butter and light wood cabinets with glass doors. She ran her hand across the sleek granite countertops. A bit cool perhaps, but at least they were a pleasant color, a nice sandy tone that resembled the beach on a summer's day. She decided that so far this was her favorite room in the house.

She quickly located a juice glass, filled it, and took it to Mrs. Daniels. "Here," she said, worried that the old woman had fallen asleep. "You should probably drink this now. It's good for your blood sugar level."

Mrs. Daniels frowned. "What do you know about blood sugar levels?"

"My mother was a diabetic."

"Was? Oh yes, I do seem to remember that you mentioned she had passed on. When was that?"

"A few years ago." Christine looked away. This wasn't a subject she particularly cared to discuss with this woman.

"Yes, well, I'm sorry."

She nodded. "I'll get back to your breakfast now."

Christine was relieved to be back in the kitchen. Before long she had a poached egg, a slice of wheat toast, lightly buttered, and a hot cup of strong coffee, with cream. She placed these on a tray with silverware and a napkin, then took them to the living room.

"Did you want to eat in here?" she asked.

Mrs. Daniels shrugged. "I might as well. Although, normally, I frown upon such practices." She pointed to the glass-topped coffee table. "Put it there."

Christine returned to the kitchen to begin cleaning up. As she finished washing out the saucepan, she paused to look out the window over the sink and found herself staring at the large oak tree on the left side of the backyard. Something about its bare branches silhouetted against the pale gray sky held her attention in an almost haunting way. Then suddenly she realized that this house might have once been her biological mother's home. She wasn't sure how long Mrs. Daniels had lived here, but it seemed entirely possible that Lenore might have once stood right here at this very window, perhaps as a teen, and actually stared out at this very same tree.

She went back into the living room to see that Mrs. Daniels was finished. "More coffee?" she asked.

"Yes, please. And for future reference, you don't have to make it *that* strong."

"Sorry."

"Usually people make it too weak, so I always say strong. That was, however, too strong."

"Right." Christine picked up the tray and wondered if she would ever do anything to this woman's satisfaction.

"Everything else was all right."

"Thank you." Christine paused for a moment. "This is a lovely home, Mrs. Daniels. How long have you lived here?"

Mrs. Daniels frowned. "Oh, I'm not really sure. Let's see, James and I got married in 1980, and we moved in here shortly after that. You do the math."

Christine nodded and smiled. "A long time ago, anyway."

But as she walked back to the kitchen, it hit her full force that her mother had indeed lived here, walked upon these very floors, looked out of these actual windows. She wondered which room might have been Lenore's bedroom and if she might get to see it at some point. Also, she wondered about photos. So far she'd seen nothing. But why not? Oh, the questions that tumbled through her head as she refilled Mrs. Daniels's coffee cup. If only there was a way to get this cantankerous old woman to talk without revealing her true identity. Because, like it or not, the more Christine played this game and the deeper she got into it, the more she realized it would be difficult to step out of. Perhaps she would never be able to divulge the truth to her grandmother.

By noon Christine had done two loads of laundry and cleaned the downstairs bathrooms, Mrs. Daniels's bedroom, and the kitchen. She'd vacuumed and dusted the den and emptied all the trash receptacles. She continued to search for photos and clues while she worked, but so far she'd found nothing that seemed relevant to Lenore. Christine's chores were regularly interrupted by Mrs. Daniels, who was always asking for things like books, the newspaper, reading glasses, another cup of coffee, whatever seemed to strike her fancy at the moment. Plus, Christine was responsible for answering the phone and the door. And, for an older woman who lived alone, Mrs. Daniels seemed to have a lot of callers. Some of the phone calls were invitations to various luncheons and Christmas gatherings, all of which were declined, and the callers at the door were usually seeking donations or selling Christmas wreaths or delivering packages.

"This just came," Christine said as she handed Mrs. Daniels a box that was marked "Perishable."

"You can open any packages that come," Mrs. Daniels instructed. "Make sure you give me the card, then make a note of what's inside." She shook her head. "Christmas gifts can be such a bother."

Christine decided not to respond to that.

"Do you drive?" Mrs. Daniels asked suddenly.

"Drive?" Christine removed a fruit basket from the box. "A car, you mean?"

"Well, I wasn't referring to a golf cart."

Christine nodded. "Yes. My dad taught me to drive, but I don't have a car, if that's what you mean?"

"But you do have a driver's license?"

"Yes, of course."

"Good. I want you to take me somewhere."

"Do you want me to fix you some lunch first?"

"No, don't bother. We'll get something along the way."

Christine wondered what this woman was planning as she helped Mrs. Daniels get her coat and purse. But she knew better than to ask. Mrs. Daniels did not like to be questioned. Particularly by the hired help. Christine followed her out to the large three-car garage and helped her down the step, preparing herself to catch her if she started to fall.

"Wow," Christine said as she spotted the single car in the large garage. "You have a Jaguar."

Mrs. Daniels made a "humph" sound. "Not a very sensible choice either. I regret that I didn't keep the Mercedes instead. This car has been nothing but trouble."

"Trouble?" Christine ran her hand over its sleek silver surface.

"Mechanically speaking." Mrs. Daniels handed her the keys. "Of course, my mechanic loves me. Why, he even sends me a Christmas card each year. But then he could afford to send me fine jewelry for what he charges to fix this thing."

Christine opened the door for Mrs. Daniels and waited for the old woman to slowly arrange herself in the passenger seat before she closed the door. As Christine slid into the driver's seat, she noticed the faint smell of stale cigarette smoke. "Do you smoke?" she asked as she slid the key into the ignition. She instantly regretted her question and prepared herself to be chided again. To her surprise, Mrs. Daniels simply answered.

"Once in a while, but only when I'm feeling particularly stressed." She fumbled to fasten her seat belt. "But I've never smoked in the house. Can't abide the smell of smoke in a house, and it ruins the furniture and carpets. Unfortunately, I used to smoke in the car. Quite a lot, as a matter of fact. I can't seem to get rid of the smell." She took a deep breath. "But I actually rather like it."

Christine thought that was a bit strange, but then a lot about this woman seemed strange. "Where are we going?"

"To the La-Z-Boy store. I want a comfortable chair."

Christine smiled to herself as she waited for the garage door to go up. It was interesting to imagine how a bulky recliner would fit into Mrs. Daniels's perfectly attired home with its fine Oriental carpets, valuable antiques, and original artwork. But it was plain to see this old woman was craving a little comfort in her old age. So despite what appeared to be Mrs. Daniels's style-dictated ways, Christine wondered if it might actually be possible to teach an old dog new tricks. And, if so, maybe the day would come when Christine could divulge her true identity.

5

"Where would you stop for a quick bite of lunch?" Mrs. Daniels asked as she peered out at the traffic zipping around town.

"Me?" Christine felt surprised. "Well, that would depend."

"On what?"

"A lot of things. Like whether I was alone or with a friend, or whether I was feeling flush or almost broke, or what I felt like eating. Remember, I'm a college student. I'm not above getting a buck burger when I'm starving and low on cash."

"What's a buck burger?"

"You know," Christine waited for the light to turn, "Whoppers for ninety-nine cents at Burger King. They're not bad, really."

"I thought you had worked for McDonald's. I'd think you'd be loyal to that establishment."

"Just because you work someplace doesn't mean you like it." Christine hadn't meant it to sound like that. She glanced uneasily at Mrs. Daniels, worried that she'd make the connection, but it seemed to have floated right past her.

"Does this Burger King place have one of those windows where you can place an order without getting out?"

"Sure."

"Well, let's go there, then. I don't want to get out of the car." She slumped down into the seat.

"Are you all right?"

"Yes. I just don't want anyone I know to recognize me."

Christine laughed as she turned down the street toward Burger King. It took Mrs. Daniels a while to read the menu and decide on what she wanted, but finally they placed their order.

"That'll be seven forty-eight," said a grumpy voice through the intercom.

"Seven dollars and forty-eight cents?" Mrs. Daniels peered at Christine. "Can that possibly be right?"

"It sounds about right to me." Christine pulled the sleek car forward, careful to avoid the sign that seemed to stick right out into their lane. "Is it too much?"

Mrs. Daniels laughed. Only this time it didn't sound quite as cynical as it had yesterday. "Goodness, think of all the money I could've saved over the years if I'd eaten here. Of course, their food probably tastes like cardboard and glue."

To Christine's relief, Mrs. Daniels seemed to like her lunch. Although, when they were finished, she complained at the amount of cholesterol she'd just consumed.

"Oh, I suppose I shouldn't worry. I'm not long for this world anyway."

Christine glanced uneasily at the old woman. "Are you having health problems? Besides your ankle, I mean?"

She waved her hand. "Oh, nothing out of the ordinary. It's just that everything starts to go once you begin getting old. Don't know why people have to grow old, anyway. My two husbands certainly didn't bother with it."

At the La-Z-Boy store they were greeted with Christmas music, and a young blond woman dressed like an elf offered them store-bought cookies.

"Merry Christmas, it's our Holiday Blowout week," she told them in a chirpy voice. "Everything in the store is marked down, some up to 50 percent off, and ready to be delivered by Christmas."

"By Christmas?" Mrs. Daniels harped. "I need a chair and I need it now. Can't I have one delivered today?"

"Oh, I don't know," the woman said. "I—uh—"

"Hello, there," said a man in a khaki suit. "I'm Leon Myers. Now, what can I do for you today, ma'am?"

"I want a recliner chair," Mrs. Daniels said. "But I want it delivered before Christmas. I'd like it delivered today, if possible, or tomorrow at the latest."

He smiled. "No problem. If we have it in stock, we can deliver it by tomorrow."

"Fine, if that's the best you can do." She adjusted her crutches and moved forward. "Show me what you have."

"Looks like you've hurt your foot," the man said.

"Obviously," she snapped. "Why else would I want a recliner?"

He chuckled. "Oh, some people find our chairs to be quite comfortable. Now, tell me, ma'am, will this chair be for you or for your husband?"

She rolled her eyes at Christine, as if to say, *This man is a complete idiot*. "It's for me. I need it to keep my foot elevated."

"Yes, yes, that's just what I thought." He paused by a pink velvet chair. "Now, how about this little number—"

"I can't stand pink," she snapped. "Show me something in an earth tone, please. And nothing too sleazy."

He chuckled again. "Oh, don't worry, ma'am. We have some real beauties." He led them over to a section of better-looking chairs, which also wore some more expensive price tags, Christine noticed.

However, Mrs. Daniels didn't seem to care. She pointed to a nice-looking tan chair by the wall. "I'll take that one," she said.

The salesman laughed. "Without even trying it out?"

"Why do I need to try it? Aren't they all the same?"

"No, no, they're all different. They're made to fit various body types and needs. I recommend you sit in it before you make up your mind."

"Fine." She hobbled around the maze of chairs until she reached the tan one. Then, holding her crutches out to the sides, she slowly leaned back and sat down with an "oomph." She reached for the small wooden handle on the side and after a bit of pulling finally managed to release the footrest. Then she put her head back and sighed. "This one suits me just fine. I'll take it."

The salesman grinned, and Christine suspected that, despite Mrs.

Daniels's demanding ways, this had been one of his easiest transactions of the season. And Christine didn't disagree with the choice either. Of all the chairs, this one looked the least like a recliner. In fact, the sand-colored chenille fabric was rather soft and attractive. Christine wished she had enough money to get something like that for her father someday. She could imagine him putting his feet up after a long day. Maybe when he was finished with his missions work and she was done with school and had a real job, maybe then she could get him one.

Mrs. Daniels wrote out a check and inquired again as to the delivery.

"It's our busiest time of year," the woman behind the counter told her.

"I was promised that I would have it by tomorrow," she insisted.

The woman checked on the computer again. "We don't have anyone scheduled to deliver in your area until the end of the week."

"Well, if I can't have it by tomorrow, I simply won't purchase it today," Mrs. Daniels said firmly. "I'll just go to another store where—"

"Something wrong here?" Leon asked as he returned to the counter and looked at the woman who had written up the purchase.

"She wants it delivered by tomorrow," the woman said in a tired voice. "We don't have a truck going—"

"I told her it would be delivered tomorrow," Leon said, flashing a smile toward Mrs. Daniels. "And we expect it to be delivered tomorrow. Figure out a way to make it happen, Donna."

The woman scowled at him, then pushed some more keys on her computer keyboard. "Fine. It'll be delivered by tomorrow. Do you plan to be home all day, ma'am?"

"I'm not exactly gadding about town with this bum foot," Mrs. Daniels said. "Of course I plan to be home. And if the chair's not delivered by tomorrow, I'll put a stop payment on my check."

"And a Merry Christmas to you too," the woman said as she wearily handed Mrs. Daniels the receipt.

Christine couldn't help but feel sorry for the woman as they headed for the exit.

"Happy Holidays!" the elf girl chirped.

"Yeah," Christine said as she opened the door for Mrs. Daniels. "To you too."

"Bah humbug," Mrs. Daniels said when they were out in the parking lot.

Christine glanced at the heavy clouds now filling the sky as she unlocked the car. "Do you think it's going to snow this year?" she asked once they were inside. "I'd love to see a white Christmas."

"Good grief! I certainly hope not. I already ruined my ankle from slipping on my wet patio. Now all I need is snow on the ground with these crutches and I could probably end up in a body cast for the entire holidays."

Christine noticed a Christmas tree lot as she pulled into traffic. "Do you plan to get a Christmas tree?"

"Of course not. What on earth would I do with a Christmas tree? Do you expect me to hobble around and decorate it?"

"I could decorate it."

"I don't put up a tree anymore. I haven't since the kids left. That's when my husband and I began going down to Palm Springs for the holidays. This will be the first year I've been forced to stay at home."

"So why don't you have your stepson or grandchildren over for Christmas?"

She harrumphed. "Not if I can help it."

"What do you do, then?"

Christine could feel Mrs. Daniels glaring at her, and she suspected she'd pushed her too far by asking way too many questions. The old woman cleared her throat, then spoke in a sharp voice. "I plan to do as little as possible for the holidays. I suppose someone like you would think I was a real Ebenezer Scrooge. And maybe I am. But then that's my business."

Christine nodded and continued driving in silence until they reached Mrs. Daniels's home.

"Furthermore," Mrs. Daniels remained in the car as she continued speaking, as if they'd still been in the midst of a conversation. "I have hired you to be my housekeeper and errand girl. I do not expect you to be my companion."

Christine felt tears burning in her eyes, but she was determined not to show this thoughtless woman how her words were able to cut. She opened the passenger door and helped her get out of the low car and then into the house.

After getting Mrs. Daniels settled comfortably on the couch for an afternoon nap, Christine busied herself by washing the windows in the kitchen. It looked as if they hadn't been washed in ages. And as she washed them she wondered about her birth mother. Had Lenore ever washed these windows? Or had they always been the kind of family to hire out their household chores? Christine couldn't imagine having enough money to pay other people to do things like this. And even if she did, she couldn't imagine wanting to. Something about manual labor and taking something that was once dirty and making it clean appealed to her. She always felt better when it was done. She realized that this work ethic probably wasn't genetic, but rather a trait she'd been taught by her hardworking parents. More than ever she felt thankful for them now. And more than ever she missed her father's warmth and kind, loving support.

6

||||||||||||||||

By the second day "on the job," Christine felt she was falling into something of a rhythm. At least it seemed so to her. Mrs. Daniels, on the other hand, seemed to enjoy stirring things up a bit by changing her mind about things like how she liked her coffee or the best way to dust the antique furniture. Still, Christine was trying to be patient. But by four o'clock, two things happened that just about undid her. First the deliveryman arrived with the recliner. And that was not so bad, but just as he was setting the rather bulky chair in the center of the living room, Mrs. Daniels's daughter-in-law, Felicity, showed up quite unexpectedly.

"Why is there a La-Z-Boy truck in your driveway?" she demanded as soon as she was in the door.

Mrs. Daniels turned and stared at her. "Well, hello to you too, Felicity."

"What's going on?" Felicity asked when she saw the deliveryman removing the plastic wrappings from the chair.

"What does it look like?" Mrs. Daniels asked in an exasperated voice. "I've purchased a recliner."

"A recliner?"

"That's what they call them." Mrs. Daniels glanced over to where Christine was looking on without speaking. "And I'd like you to meet my new housekeeper, Christine Bradley. Christine, this is my stepson's wife, Felicity Daniels."

Felicity moved her attention from the recliner to Christine. "Aren't you a little young to be a housekeeper?"

"I'm nearly twenty."

"Oh. Well, do you have much experience doing—"

"Felicity," Mrs. Daniels interrupted. "I am the one who hired Christine, and she works for me. I am perfectly capable of ascertaining her qualifications, thank you very much."

"Well, I—"

"And what brings you here this time of day, anyway? Shouldn't you be picking up the children or something?"

"They're at my mother's."

Mrs. Daniels seemed to stiffen a bit. "Of course."

"Well, that's it," the deliveryman said as he gathered up a bundle of plastic. "You wanna try her out before I leave?"

Mrs. Daniels frowned at him, then seemed to think better of his suggestion. "Yes, as a matter of fact, I will." She hobbled over and eased herself down, tested the leg rest, then leaned back and nodded. "It's just fine. Thank you."

"Merry Christmas, ma'am," the man said. He hesitated for a moment, and Christine wondered if he expected a tip or something. But finally he just backed out and left.

"Is that where you're going to leave it?" Felicity asked. "Right in the middle of the room like that?"

"Maybe." Mrs. Daniels smiled smugly. It was plain that she enjoyed irritating her daughter-in-law. Then she turned to Christine. "I'd like a cup of tea, please. The same kind you made for me yesterday will be fine."

Christine glanced at Felicity. "Would you like a cup too?"

Felicity flopped down on the couch across from her mother-in-law. "Sure, why not."

Mrs. Daniels didn't look pleased. "So what brings you by today, Felicity?"

Christine couldn't hear the rest of their conversation from the kitchen, but she hurried to make the tea and returned quickly with a tray, complete with a small dish of some chocolate mint cookies she'd spied in the pantry. She set it down on the glass coffee table between them. Then she took her time handing Mrs. Daniels her tea and offering her the cookies.

"I already told you that I have no plans for the holidays," Mrs. Daniels said. "What's so unusual about that?"

"I just don't understand it," Felicity said. "You have this big, beautiful home. And it would be so lovely to decorate it for Christmas." She pointed toward the staircase. "I can just imagine that banister strewn with evergreen garlands—"

"I do not want my banister strewn with evergreen garlands, thank you very much."

"What about a tree over by the fireplace. Your ceilings are so tall that you could have a ten-foot—"

"I do not want a ten-foot tree, Felicity, any more than I want a ten-inch tree. What is it about no that you don't understand?"

Felicity frowned and set her cup down with a clink. "I would think you'd do it, at least for your grandchildren. Give them some memories—"

"Felicity," Mrs. Daniels began in a very stern voice. "I know you well enough to know that it's not for the children. If I opened my home to a Christmas party, as you call it, it would only be to impress your family and friends. If you want to have a Christmas party, have it at your own house."

"But I would do all the work—"

"And I would foot the bill."

Felicity's face puckered up now. Whether she was going to cry or explode was anyone's guess, but Christine suspected by the way she was glaring at her that she'd already overstayed her welcome.

"Can I get you anything else?" she asked as she prepared to make a hasty exit.

"No, thank you, Christine, this is fine," Mrs. Daniels said in a surprisingly polite voice.

Christine returned to the kitchen but lingered by the door, hoping to hear a few more snippets of conversation. And to her pleased surprise, the long dining room worked almost like an echo chamber. Sure, she felt a bit guilty for eavesdropping, but then, whether they knew it or not, she was actually part of this family. Didn't she have some right to know about the goings-on here?

"Well, fine," Felicity said in a sharp voice. "If that's the way you're going to be about it."

"That's right."

"Well, I suppose you won't want to trouble yourself to come over for Jamie's birthday either? Poor kid, it's bad enough having a birthday in December, but I suppose you're going to let your injury keep you from—"

"I still plan to come over for Jamie's birthday. Isn't the party on Friday?"

A few more words were said, and then it sounded like Felicity was leaving. After a bit Christine returned to the living room to pick up the tray of tea things.

"Looks like we'll need to do a little shopping tomorrow," Mrs. Daniels said as Christine loaded up the tray.

"Shopping?"

"Yes. My grandson is having his seventh birthday on Friday. Do you have any idea what a seven-year-old might like?"

"I used to baby-sit for a couple of little boys who just loved Legos. And they collected all these amazing sets, like clipper ships and space shuttles. They'd play with them for hours."

"Legos?" She nodded. "Might be just the trick."

So, on the following morning, after the basic routine was completed, Christine drove Mrs. Daniels to the toy store at the mall. Of course, the parking lot was packed, and after driving around several times, Christine finally decided to drop Mrs. Daniels at the door.

"I don't see why you don't just park in the handicapped space," Mrs. Daniels complained as Christine helped her out of the car.

"You don't have a permit," Christine said for the third time.

"Permit shermit."

"I'll be back in a few minutes."

Christine found Mrs. Daniels waiting at the door, clearly aggravated by the potbellied man clanging a bell as he solicited donations.

"Do they think they'll make money by irritating the shoppers?" she asked as Christine held the door open for her.

They circumvented the crowded "Take Your Photo with Santa" display, complete with stuffed reindeer, elves, and fake snow, as they made their way toward the nearby toy store. The sounds of children laughing and shouting, and some even crying, mixed with the tinny sound of Christmas music being played over the PA system. After working their way through the holiday shoppers crowding the toy store, which was naturally having a big holiday sale, they finally located the right section. And after examining the various sets of Legos, Mrs. Daniels decided on the Extreme Tower building set. It had been Christine's recommendation, although she hadn't realized it was so expensive, but Mrs. Daniels seemed happy to think it was her own idea. And Christine didn't mind. She was just thankful to get out of there before Mrs. Daniels's mood or energy level deteriorated.

"Do you mind waiting while I bring the car around?" Christine asked.

"I suppose I could sit on this bench in here," she grumbled. "That way I can avoid the neurotic bell ringer outside."

Christine smiled. "That's a good idea." Then, carrying the bulky package, she jogged across the parking lot to the car.

"I don't know what I'll do about Christmas shopping this year," Mrs. Daniels said after she was seated comfortably back in the car.

"You buy Christmas presents?" Christine felt mildly surprised.

Mrs. Daniels cackled. "Well, I may be a Scrooge about all the trappings and trimmings, but I'm not cheap when it comes to gifts. I certainly don't want my grandchildren growing up thinking I was stingy."

"You could shop online," Christine suggested.

"You mean on a computer?"

"Yeah. It's really pretty convenient. You can find anything."

"Anything?"

"Pretty much." Christine waited in a long line of traffic trying to get out of the parking lot.

"Even people?"

"Huh?" Christine glanced over at Mrs. Daniels, who seemed to be deep in thought. "You want to buy your grandkids some people?"

"No, of course not. But I've heard you can use the Internet to locate people. Is that correct?"

"Sure. There are all kinds of ways to search."

"And you know how to use a computer?"

"Yeah. I've been using one for years."

"But I don't have a computer."

"You could get one," Christine suggested as she finally made her way onto the street.

"I suppose I could. Of course, I wouldn't have any idea of what to look for or where to go. Would you?"

Christine pointed across the street to Computer World. "That's a pretty good place right there. My roommate just got a great deal on a laptop."

"What's that?"

Before Christine could even finish her explanation, Mrs. Daniels interrupted. "That's what I want too, Christine. Stop in there and let's get one."

Christine grinned as she put on her turn signal. This woman might be a little grumpy, but she was certainly entertaining. Fortunately, Computer World was not as busy as the mall, and Christine found a space right in front.

Mrs. Daniels leaned back her head and sighed. "The problem is that I'm exhausted from our toy shopping."

"Do you want to go home?"

"Not without a computer." Mrs. Daniels opened her purse and removed her Visa card. "Here, you go pick out the one you think will best suit me."

"Are you sure?"

"Of course," she snapped. "Just hurry."

Feeling a bit strange, Christine went in and purchased the same computer that Brianna had bragged about just a month ago. She was all ready for the high-school-age salesclerk to question her signature on Mrs. Daniels's credit card, but he didn't seem to notice or care. He was probably just happy to make such an easy sale. The store didn't appear overly busy, and she suspected the salesclerks worked on commission.

"Merry Christmas!" he yelled as she carried the box out the door.

"Merry Christmas," she called back.

Mrs. Daniels was fast asleep and snoring quietly when Christine opened the car door to let herself in. Saying nothing, Christine started the engine and headed for home. She glanced over at her silent passenger while waiting at a stoplight and noticed how much softer the old woman's face looked when she was sleeping. She almost did look like someone's grandmother. A wave of longing swept over Christine. Suddenly she wished she could tell this woman who she was and why she was here. But then she remembered the old woman's warning about no shenanigans. How would Mrs. Daniels react to the news that she'd been tricked like this, deceived by her own granddaughter?

7

"Do you recall that I said you'll be required to work some evenings?" Mrs. Daniels asked on Friday morning.

"Yes," Christine said as she helped Mrs. Daniels from the shower.

"Well, I need you to drive me over to my stepson's house. It's my grandson Jamie's birthday party this evening, and I promised to come. And, if you don't mind, you could just stick around and then take me home afterward. I know it's an inconvenience for you, but I don't plan to stay late. Naturally, I will pay you extra. I don't expect you to work for nothing."

"It's okay," Christine said as she carefully rebandaged the injured foot. "And you don't need to pay me extra. I'm glad to do it as a favor."

"Nonsense." Mrs. Daniels firmly shook her head. "How do you ever expect to get ahead in this world if you talk like that?"

"Money isn't everything," Christine said as she finished the last wrap and pinned it securely. She stood up and smiled. "But I'm sure you know that."

She frowned. "Goodness, I hope you're not going to preach a sermon at me now."

Christine shrugged as she gathered the wet towels. "Sorry, I'm not much of a preacher."

Due to the festivities planned for the evening, Mrs. Daniels decided they would have a quiet day at home. They'd gone grocery shopping yesterday, and Mrs. Daniels was still learning how to use her new computer. Christine had started her out by teaching her how to play some of the card games so she could get comfortable with the keyboard and mouse, and later on today she'd show her how to cruise the Internet.

"Would you wrap Jamie's gift for me?" Mrs. Daniels said that afternoon. "There are wrapping things in that high cupboard in the laundry room."

"I'd be happy to," Christine said as she picked up the empty teacup from the side table she'd moved next to the new recliner. "I love wrapping gifts."

Mrs. Daniels seemed to consider this as she picked up her book. "I used to enjoy wrapping gifts too. Then my daughter took over for me, and, well, I guess I never really did it much after that."

Christine felt an unexpected tightness across her chest, almost as if someone had wrapped a wide leather belt there and then suddenly cinched it. It was the first time Mrs. Daniels had made any mention of a daughter.

"You have a daughter?" Christine said, hoping to sound only mildly interested.

Mrs. Daniels sighed. "I used to."

"Oh."

Mrs. Daniels pulled out the footrest and leaned back. "I think I'll rest now. You'd better take care of that gift. And see if you can find a birthday card. I keep a box in the second drawer down on my desk."

It was obvious that Christine wasn't going to extract any other information about Lenore just now. So she went on her way and discovered a very nice selection of gift wrap and bows in the cupboard above the dryer. She suspected these items had been there for a long time. Maybe even back when Lenore lived here. Christine selected a blue and white paper with sailboats. It seemed boyish, even if it was a bit old-fashioned. Then she carefully wrapped the box, taking time to neatly fold under the seams and create a large red and white bow to go on top. *Not bad*, she thought as she carried it into the kitchen.

Next she went to the desk where she usually sorted and set the daily mail. She'd never opened a drawer before. To her, a desk seemed a private place, and something a person should never go snooping in. As instructed, she pulled open the second drawer down and saw embossed stationery and envelopes and stamps and even some postcards and pretty note cards. But no box of greeting cards. She decided to try the next drawer down. Surely, this couldn't be considered snooping. But that drawer revealed only some old, yellowed typing paper and notepads with the university logo on them. Maybe the box was in the bottom drawer. She felt slightly guilty as she tried the drawer. She knew she was looking for more than birthday cards now, but she couldn't stop herself. The drawer stuck at first, but with a harder pull it came open.

There, lying face down in the mostly empty drawer, was what appeared to be a framed photo. She knew she should close the drawer immediately, that she had definitely crossed over the line and this would be considered snooping, but it was too late. Glancing over her shoulder once, she picked up the frame, then turned it over and stared in astonishment.

The pretty brunette girl in the picture had to be Lenore. Christine had never seen a picture of her birth mother before (her father had explained that Lenore had claimed to be camera shy and never allowed them to take even one photo). Just the same, Christine instinctively knew this young woman had to be her birth mother. It was probably a high school graduation picture. And it wasn't so much that the woman in the photo looked like Christine, although she sensed a familiarity in the eyes. They were brown and big and had another quality she couldn't even be certain of. But everything else about the two young women seemed to be different. Where Lenore's hair was dark and straight, Christine's was auburn and much too wavy. Their faces were entirely different too. Lenore had a sweetly rounded face with a cute little nose, where Christine's face was more angular and her nose straight and narrow and, in her opinion, slightly too long. Not so unlike Mrs. Daniels's. Christine heard a sound and quickly replaced the photo, closed the stubborn drawer, then stood up with heart pounding fast.

She waited a full minute before she moved. Then, walking casually toward the living room, she prepared herself for Mrs. Daniels's accusations and questions. But the old woman was still asleep in her recliner, snoring peacefully.

Probably as an act of penance, Christine got out the mop and bucket and gave the kitchen floor a good cleaning. She felt guilty and nervous about her snooping, but at the same time she didn't completely regret it. Even though it was unsettling to look into the eyes of the woman who had birthed her, it seemed right too. After all, Lenore was her mother. Didn't she have every right to know what the young woman had looked like? She knew so little about her short and tragic life. Suddenly Christine felt hungry to know more. But how could she find anything out when her grandmother was so reluctant to talk? And how could she go around snooping and still live with herself?

Christine scrubbed hard as she considered ways to find things out and how she might get her grandmother to open up and talk about her daughter. She paused as she rinsed out the mop. When had she quit thinking of that old woman in there as "Mrs. Daniels" and begun considering her a grandmother? Perhaps it had to do with seeing the photo of Lenore. Or maybe Christine was actually becoming fond of the cranky old woman. Whatever it was, she decided not to think about it too much. She poured out the dirty mop water and turned to see the tile floor gleaming as a result of her energetic scrub down. Perhaps this would help cleanse her conscience a bit too.

It was almost five now and the time when she usually set out her grandmother's dinner and then said good-night and headed back to her dorm. But since she was taking Mrs. Daniels to the birthday party, she was unsure as to what she should do. After her mopping spree, she suddenly felt as if she really should run back to her dorm and change before the party, but then she wasn't sure what time they needed to leave, or even how far away the house was. Why hadn't she thought of this sooner?

"What are you doing in there?" Mrs. Daniels called from the dining room.

Christine poked her head out of the swinging doors. "I just finished some mopping. Don't come in here though, the floor's still damp, you might slip." She put the mop and bucket back in the laundry room closet and went back to check on her grandmother.

"Mopping?" the old woman said as she sat up straight in her chair.

"It looked like it needed it."

"I suppose it did."

"Do you want me to fix you a bite to eat before I leave?"

"Leave?" she looked alarmed. "Where are you going?"

"I thought maybe I could run back to my dorm and change before it's time to go."

"But we should be leaving for the party in about twenty minutes, and I need you to help me change."

"Well, do you want me to fix you something to eat, then?"

"Didn't I tell you it's a dinner party?"

"A dinner party for a seven-year-old?"

"Well, they had the kiddy party this afternoon," she explained. "They always invite their grown-up friends and relatives over in the evening for another party." She laughed in that cynical way. "Ensures the kids get more gifts that way."

"Oh."

So Christine stayed and helped Mrs. Daniels get dressed in a pair of black knit pants and a burgundy velvet jacket. "You look really nice," she told her when they were finally done.

Mrs. Daniels patted her hair. "Best I can do under the circumstances." She frowned at Christine. "Is that what you're wearing?"

Christine looked down at her gray sweatshirt and jeans. "Well, I thought maybe I'd have time to go home and change, but then the party was earlier than I thought . . ."

"Well, it just won't do. Felicity is, shall we say, a bit of a snob." She rolled her eyes. "She likes for people to dress and act right. Especially at her little parties. Now go in there and look in my closet. I'm sure my trousers would be too big for you, but see if you can find a different shirt to wear. Something that looks respectable. Choose whatever you like, I don't care."

Christine tried not to show her displeasure at this task. The last thing she wanted to do right now was to don some fuddy-duddy old lady shirt. But she felt bad that she hadn't planned ahead better and decided that she should at least be cooperative. She hunted for a bit until she found a rust-colored turtleneck sweater that wasn't too bad. She held it out to show Mrs. Daniels, who was waiting comfortably in the easy chair by the window.

"How about this?"

"That should look good on you. Will go nicely with your hair."

Christine went back into the closet and slipped it on to discover it was quite soft and cozy. She emerged with a self-conscious smile. "It fits okay."

"Better than it fits me, I suspect." Mrs. Daniels pushed herself up from the chair and fumbled for her crutches. "In fact, you should just keep it. That color makes me look too sallow anyway. Something I don't need at this stage of life." She chuckled. "I will say this for you though. For a girl without money, you certainly have good taste."

"Huh?" Christine was walking behind her down the hallway.

"Cashmere," Mrs. Daniels said. "Imported from France."

Suddenly Christine felt terrible. "Oh, I'm sorry. You should've told me. I can't keep this, I'll go—"

"No. Like I said, the color does nothing for me. My late husband got that for me for Christmas one year when rust was all the rage."

"Are you sure?"

"Positive."

Mrs. Daniels stopped by the large coat closet by the door. "And while we're at it, there's a coat in there that you might like to have too. As I recall it went nicely with the sweater. Go ahead and open it. It's a suede jacket in a brownish gold tone that looks awful on me."

Christine looked in the mostly empty coat closet, then spied a caramel-colored suede jacket behind a hooded rain parka. She pulled it out. "Is this it?"

"Yes. I've been meaning to give it away. Can't stand how it makes me look. Go ahead, try it on."

Christine slipped on the jacket. The suede was so smooth that it felt like butter. And she suspected by the luxurious satin lining and fancy label that it must've been very expensive. "It's beautiful."

"It's yours." She looked at her watch. "We better go. Doesn't do to keep Felicity waiting."

Christine almost felt like a princess as she drove Mrs. Daniels's Jaguar, dressed in the cashmere sweater and suede jacket. She wondered what Brianna, or even her dad, would think of her right now.

"That's the housing development," Mrs. Daniels said. "Aspen Grove."

Christine didn't say anything, but she was surprised. This didn't seem like a very impressive neighborhood for the way her grandmother had described Felicity. It was nice, of course, and probably much more expensive than the neighborhood Christine had grown up in. But even in the night, with only the streetlights to illuminate, all the houses appeared to look alike, and they were so close together it seemed like neighbors could reach out their windows and hold hands. Of course, she didn't mention this.

"You're here," said a tall man as he opened the door wider. "Come on in, Mom. Is that your caregiver with you?"

"Housekeeper," Mrs. Daniels corrected him in a stern voice.

"Let me help you," he said as he tried to usher her inside.

"No, you just stay back, Jimmy. I can do this better on my own."

"Getting pretty feisty with those crutches, aren't you?" He turned and winked at Christine. "She's a handful, isn't she?"

Christine wasn't quite sure how to respond. So she stuck out her hand and said, "Hi, I'm Christine Bradley." She stopped herself from saying, *Lenore's long lost daughter.*

"Well, welcome to our humble abode, Christine. I'm Jimmy. I hear that you've already met my wife, Felicity, and—"

"Who's that?" asked a little boy peering out from behind his dad. He had curly red hair and was eyeing the large gift in Christine's hands.

"This is Christine," Jimmy said. "And this is the birthday boy, Jamie."

She smiled. "Hello, Jamie. Happy birthday. Kind of a bummer having a birthday so close to Christmas, isn't it?"

He grinned to reveal a missing tooth. "Yeah. Some people give you only one present and say that it's for both."

188

"Well, this is for you from your grandma," Christine said as she handed him the large box.

His eyes grew wide. "Cool."

Soon she met the other child, a little girl named Casey. And despite their grandmother's less than favorable description, Christine thought they were sweet kids, even if they were fairly rambunctious. Casey had blond hair and blue eyes like her mother, while Jamie resembled his dad. And both children insisted on showing Christine their rooms. Maybe it was because she was the closest to their age group, or maybe they just assumed she was the babysitter. As it turned out, she spent more time with the kids than the adults, which was perfectly fine with her.

She sat next to Casey at dinner. The other guests consisted of Felicity's parents, Janet and George, and her newly married sister, Amber, and Amber's husband, Rick.

"Do you go to college here?" Amber asked.

"Yes. I'm a junior," Christine said.

"I graduated from here," Amber said. Then, more proudly, "But Rick went to Stanford."

"I went to school here too," Jimmy said. "It's a great place to go."

"What was your major?" Christine asked, only because it seemed the conversation had come to a lull.

"Secondary education," he said. "I'm a P.E. teacher at Edison High."

"And a coach," Felicity added.

"I'm majoring in education too," Christine said. "Elementary ed."

"Good grief," Mrs. Daniels said with a frown. "You seemed like you were smarter than that to me. What's wrong with these young people wanting to waste their lives being teachers?" She seemed to direct this comment to Felicity's parents. "Don't young people care about making a good living anymore?"

"Thanks a lot, Mom," Jimmy said. "But don't forget that my dad was in education and so were you."

"*Upper* education," Mrs. Daniels corrected him. "I was an English professor, and the head of my department before I retired. And don't forget that your father had his doctorate. As did my first husband."

"And I'm sure they're terribly thankful about that now," Jimmy teased.

Christine thought she saw her grandmother wince slightly at that.

"Sorry, Mom," Jimmy said quickly. "I guess I'm just saying that everyone's got to do what makes them happy. Life isn't just about making money, you know."

"My father's a teacher too," Christine said quickly, hoping to smooth over whatever had just transpired. "Actually, he retired from public school last spring. But he's volunteer teaching down in Brazil right now."

Fortunately, that took the conversation into a whole new realm as Felicity's parents enthusiastically shared their latest trip to Mexico.

Soon dinner was over and it was time for the gifts to be opened. Naturally, all this attention for her older brother was upsetting to Casey, and before long she was in tears.

"It's been a long day," Felicity explained, "and she never got her nap."

"Would you like me to help her get ready for bed?" Christine offered.

Felicity looked surprised then relieved. "Would you?"

"Sure, if she doesn't mind." She turned to look at the little girl's tear-streaked face. "Would you like to show me your room again, Casey? And where you keep your jammies?"

Casey nodded, and Christine took her hand and walked her up the stairs to her bedroom. It didn't take long before she was ready for bed, and although she looked pretty tired, Christine asked her if she'd like to hear a story.

"A book?" Casey's eyes grew wide as if this were a special treat.

"Yeah. Want me to read to you?"

She nodded and leaned back into her pillow, tugging a stuffed bunny closer to her. Christine took the bunny as a cue and picked out a rabbit story. Casey listened happily but was fast asleep before the story was half finished. Christine set the book down and pushed a stray blond curl off the little girl's forehead. She knew this child was no relation to her, but she felt an inexplicable sense of kinship just now. Maybe it had to do with Christmastime or missing her father. Or maybe she was just longing for a family of her own, people who loved her and really belonged to her.

"How'd it go?" a male voice whispered from the hallway.

She looked up to see Jimmy with his son in his arms. "Good," she told him. "Poor thing, she really was tired."

"So's the birthday boy."

Christine smiled. "Do you want me to put him to bed too?"

Jimmy shook his head. "I got it covered. Thanks though."

So Christine went back downstairs to where the adults had gathered in the small living room.

"We're getting our Christmas tree tomorrow," Felicity announced. "Jimmy doesn't like getting it before Jamie's birthday. But it always feels late with only a week left until Christmas. Most people have had their trees up for ages by now."

"And you're still planning on having everyone over for Christmas Eve?" Janet asked. "It'll be quite a full house for you."

Felicity sighed. "Well, you guys don't have much space since you scaled down to the condo and motor home. And Amber and Rick's apartment is pretty tiny. So I guess it's up to me."

"Is Jimmy's aunt still planning to come?" Janet asked.

"What?" Mrs. Daniels looked somewhat shocked.

Christine studied her grandmother, curious as to why she would be upset by this news.

"Aunt Hattie," Jimmy explained. "She wants to come visit during the holidays. She hasn't seen the kids in a couple of years."

Mrs. Daniels groaned. "My, how time flies."

Christine noticed Felicity nudging Jimmy with her elbow. It was a small gesture and probably not noticed by anyone else. But the expression on Felicity's face looked urgent.

Jimmy cleared his throat. "In fact . . . ," he said, "we were wondering if you might be able to put the old girl up for a couple of days—"

191

"What?" Mrs. Daniels demanded.

Jimmy smiled hopefully. "Otherwise she'll have to sleep on the couch, and that's not very comfortable. You have so much room, Mom. Surely you could let bygones be bygones this one time. You know, you ladies aren't getting any younger. Besides that, it's Christmas."

"You honestly think Hattie would be willing to stay at *my* house?" Mrs. Daniels narrowed her eyes. "You know that the last time we spoke was at your father's funeral."

"People often say things they don't mean during times of grief," Janet offered, obviously trying to smooth things over.

"I suppose Jimmy has told you the Aunt Hattie story," Mrs. Daniels said in a droll tone. "I suppose the whole town knows the Aunt Hattie story."

Christine wanted to raise her hand and say, *I don't.* But she wisely kept her peace, knowing it would look suspicious for Mrs. Daniels's housekeeper to be curious about some estranged aunt. Just the same, she did wonder if this woman might be related to her.

"I told Felicity's family only so they could be prepared for any fireworks between you two." Jimmy smiled at Christine now. "You probably wonder what on earth we're talking about, don't you?"

She shrugged. "Oh, that's all right."

"Aunt Hattie is my dad's sister. And she said some things to my stepmom at his funeral that Mom's never forgiven her for."

"That's enough," Mrs. Daniels snapped.

"Please, Mom," Jimmy pleaded. "Couldn't you consider having Aunt Hattie for a few days? I mean, she is Dad's sister. Doesn't she deserve a little respect for that?"

Mrs. Daniels rolled her eyes. "Fine. She can stay at my house. But she better not expect me to cater to her. I'm not exactly in tip-top form, you know."

"But you have Christine," Felicity said hopefully. "I'm sure she can do whatever it takes to help make Aunt Hattie feel welcome."

"Of course," Christine said. "That's no problem at all."

"Any other surprise visitors you'd like to spring on me?" Mrs. Daniels glared at Jimmy.

He laughed. "No, Mom, that's it."

"Now if I can just figure where we'll put everyone for the Christmas party," Felicity said. It seemed an obvious hint.

Janet frowned. "That's too bad about your foot, Esther. Otherwise, you might want to have been able to host the gathering at your house."

Christine glanced at Mrs. Daniels in time to see her bristle.

"Yes, it's a shame. But as you can see, I have difficulty doing much of anything these days. A Christmas get-together would be completely out of the question."

"That is, unless you wanted to put me to work," Christine offered. She instantly wondered what on earth had prompted her to make such a bold offer. She saw her grandmother's eyebrows lifting and knew she'd stepped way over the line this time. But after seeing how small Felicity and Jimmy's house was, she could almost understand their dilemma. "It was just an idea," she said quietly.

"It's a great idea," Felicity said with a bright smile. "And I would help with everything too."

"Well, there you go," Janet said with a twinkle in her eye. "Looks like you're fresh out of excuses, Esther."

Mrs. Daniels scowled at Christine, but then to everyone's surprise she said, "Oh, I suppose I might as well give in. You're all ganging up against me anyway. But don't expect me to lift a finger."

"Oh, you won't have to, Mom," Felicity gushed. "Christine and I will handle everything. Won't we, Christine?"

Christine nodded, wondering what she'd gotten herself into. She hadn't really intended to coerce the old woman into opening up her home for the holidays. She knew it could totally backfire on her. But perhaps it had simply been her subconscious mind at work, making sure that she was included in this odd family during the holidays. Of course, she had no idea if they would even want her around. It seemed more than likely that they would simply expect her to play the role of housekeeper and then make herself scarce. Well, whatever, she'd already stuck her foot in her mouth.

"I hope you know what you've gotten yourself into," her grandmother said as they drove home.

"I'm so sorry, Mrs. Daniels," she began. "It just slipped out. And if it makes you feel any better, I don't want you to pay me for anything I do to get ready for Felicity's party. I want it to be my gift."

"First of all, I don't want you to keep calling me *Mrs.* Daniels. My students always called me *Professor* Daniels, and my friends just call me Esther. I've never been too fond of *Mrs.* Daniels, it sounds so matronly. Please, just call me Esther."

"Well, okay."

"And the second thing. I don't like hearing all this talk about not being paid. I am not a charity case, Christine. And I've never cheated anyone out of what is their just due. If you do a job well, you should be paid well."

"What if I mess it up?"

Esther laughed, but it was her cynical laugh. "Then I suppose you'll get what you deserve."

"That's what I'm afraid of," Christine said in a quiet voice. So quiet that she suspected her grandmother hadn't even heard.

8

To her own surprise, Esther wished Christine was around to help her prepare for bed. Not that she'd had too much trouble with that lately. It had helped a great deal when Christine had started laying out her bed things, everything right where she could reach it after she sat down. Why, the girl even went to the effort of placing a glass of ice water on her bedside table, along with a pain pill on a little china saucer, just in case she needed it. Which she usually did not. Not only that, but the girl had even begun turning down her bed for her lately. Just like in a nice hotel. Next thing, she'd probably be putting a chocolate on her pillow. Esther chuckled to herself as she pulled on her pajama top.

And yet, despite all this good service, there was something about the girl that disturbed Esther. She couldn't quite put her finger on it. But something just didn't feel right. It was like the old adage "If it sounds too good to be true . . ." Somehow Esther suspected this might be the case with this Christine Bradley. If that was her real name. One couldn't be too careful these days. She had just read about an elderly woman getting swindled in a bank deal. The old lady had been befriended by a young handyman who had worked for her a few days. After gaining her trust, he'd told her that his father was trying to transfer some money to him so he could rent an apartment, but the bank wouldn't accept the transfer unless he opened an account and deposited enough money to cover the transfer. Naturally, "enough money" had amounted to several thousand dollars. Several thousand dollars the poor old woman would never see again. People prey on the elderly, Esther reminded herself as she eased into bed.

Still, Christine didn't exactly seem like a scam artist to her. Although you can never be too sure, she told herself. Kids were sharp these days, and everyone has an angle. She just wished she could figure out what Christine's was. She seemed too smart of a girl to be stuck living in a college dorm during the holidays, then working as a housekeeper, of all things. Why, other kids her age were probably off doing exciting things like skiing in the mountains or sunning down in Florida or whatever it was that college kids did these days. More and more it seemed that young people had become a bit of a foreign commodity to her. The last young person to live in her home had been Lenore. And even she'd been something of a mystery. Then, to make matters worse, just consider what her own daughter had done to her. Well, maybe she'd better watch out for herself with Christine. Maybe she just shouldn't trust young people at all.

She laid her head back on the pillow and sighed. Still, she had to admit she liked the girl. And despite her misgivings and suspicions, this particular girl had a way of growing on a person. But perhaps that was simply the result of Esther's temporary handicap. She'd read accounts of victims, people who had been kidnapped by hoodlums, but after a while they learned to love and actually trust their ruthless captors. She thought it was called Stockholm syndrome, but she wasn't positive. Perhaps that was happening to her with this caregiver or housekeeper or whatever it was she'd been trying to classify Christine as.

It was hard being needy like this. But, in reality, it wasn't going to get any better in the coming years. Good grief, she'd be eighty soon. She'd never intended to live this long, to outlive two husbands and wind up all alone like this. She didn't like feeling so vulnerable and defenseless. And to be so dependent, and to have to rely on a perfect stranger like this. Well, it was downright discomfiting, and she'd be highly relieved when this nonsense was all over and done and she could be back on her own two feet again. Although her doctor had said that wouldn't be until after New Year's.

Despite her worries, Esther smiled to herself in the darkness. She'd been surprised at how easily Christine had interacted with Jimmy's kids. It was rather sweet, really, and perhaps a sign that the girl wasn't of a criminal character after all. Didn't they say that children and animals had good instincts about people? Of course, Esther had never had a knack for children herself and it didn't mean that she was a bad person. Surely, it was simply the result of growing up as an only child. But then if she remembered correctly, it seemed that Christine had been an only child too. But then Christine was majoring in elementary education, so of course she'd be comfortable around children. She obviously just had a natural affinity for them. Well, some people were like that. Some were not. She definitely was not.

Christine, Christine, Christine. She should have something better to think about than that silly girl. It was as if she was becoming obsessed with this young woman. And what was the sense in that? This was a temporary arrangement at best. Good grief, for all she knew the girl might not even show up tomorrow. And even so, Christine would return to her classes after the New Year, and that would be the end of that. Isn't that the way young people were nowadays? They draw you into their lives and immerse you into their problems; then, just when you feel that you know them, they whip the rug right out from under you by doing something totally out of character. Or else they simply leave and you never hear from them again.

Esther pressed her hand against her forehead. Now who was she really thinking about here? Christine or her own daughter, Lenore? And why was she getting so confused? Perhaps Felicity was right. Perhaps she was getting a bit senile, or maybe it was even the onset of Alzheimer's. Good grief, she hoped not. She'd watched her best friend Barbara Winfield deteriorate from that dreadful disease until they'd finally put her in an awful nursing home. Esther had gone to visit a couple of times, but her friend had never recognized her, and after a while she'd quit going altogether. It had been something of a relief to everyone when the poor woman finally passed away. Esther would rather take a bottle of pills than end up like that. No, certainly, this wasn't Alzheimer's.

Maybe it was simply that Christine was about the same age Lenore had been.

197

Oh, she knew Christine was a year older and probably much more mature, but she still looked young. She had that youthful innocence about her. Not so unlike Lenore back before she went away. Esther sighed. For so many years she'd tried not to think about Lenore. She'd trained her mind to move on quickly whenever a memory sneaked in uninvited. She'd become an expert at distracting herself from thinking about the things that hurt.

But being laid up like this, with too much time and emptiness on her hands, made it more difficult than ever. Or maybe it was Christine's fault. Perhaps it was the presence of that silly girl that had placed Lenore on Esther's mind more than ever lately. But, in all fairness, she'd been thinking about her missing daughter even before she'd slipped and ruined her ankle. Perhaps that was even what had caused her to fall. Perhaps she hadn't been paying attention. Her mind might've been wandering down memory lane, wondering about all the what-ifs and whys about their lives, and as a result she'd stumbled. Who knew?

She'd confessed her troubles to her psychologist friend, May Ferrer, a couple months earlier. May had told her that it was only because she was growing older and naturally regretting some of her choices in life. And maybe that was true. But there seemed to be little to be done about it now. She'd always thought Lenore would come back home one day. She'd been certain of it. Many times Esther had imagined her pretty brown-haired daughter standing at the front door, sad-eyed and repentant, saying that she was sorry, that she'd been wrong, asking for her mother and stepfather to forgive her and allow her to return to her home and make a fresh start. And, naturally, Esther would've taken her back—in a heartbeat. She would've completely forgiven her only daughter. Oh, perhaps she would've given her a stern lecture first, about how she'd made bad choices but how we can all learn from our mistakes . . . But Lenore could've returned to her home, attended college, and gotten on with her life. She'd be close to forty by now. Forty? It seemed impossible. Esther couldn't imagine her sweet young daughter being forty. But then Esther had been a young forty herself. She'd gotten pregnant for the first time when she was all of thirty-nine. Perhaps forty wasn't so old after all.

Esther knew she'd be just as happy to see her daughter at forty as she would've been when she was still nineteen. She wondered if Lenore had finished her schooling. Had she married? Were there children?

She'd always figured Lenore had the kind of beauty and intelligence to marry quite well. Esther had, in fact, already been scouting out available young men in the local community when Lenore was only eighteen. Not that she'd wanted her to marry young, but there seemed no harm in looking. And, naturally, she'd always considered those well-bred young men, always the sons of her closest friends, and coming from families of influence. In the early years, back when she expected her daughter to come home like a prodigal, she'd imagined the sort of wedding she'd give her. Something quiet and discreet, but certainly elegant. Perhaps with a reception in the backyard with a small orchestra from the music department. Oh, she knew Lenore wouldn't have been able to wear white. No sense being hypocrites. But then Lenore had always looked good in ecru. Esther had always imagined her lovely daughter going down the aisle in a beautiful lace gown of ecru.

She felt tears rolling down her cheeks and scolded herself for allowing her mind to run away with her. Goodness, she knew better than to dwell on Lenore like this. It only broke her heart. Again and again and again. Oh, why hadn't that foolish girl come home? Why had she been so stubborn? Why had she stayed away so long? Never called, never written, never looked back? How could anyone be so cruel and coldhearted?

9

It was after ten that night when Christine returned to her dorm. She'd never been a girl to be easily spooked, but after walking across the silent, empty campus, and then hearing the sound of her footsteps echoing down the hallway of the mostly vacant dorm, she suddenly imagined herself being followed, envisioned someone breaking into her room.

"Stop it!" she chided herself as she locked and dead-bolted the door to her room behind her. She knew she was being ridiculous. But still the idea of spending the holidays alone in the dorm did feel a bit daunting just now. Of course, she had her grandmother's holiday party to plan and possibly, if she were lucky, to attend. Although she shouldn't assume too much. For all they knew she was simply the hired help. Certainly, they'd expect her to make herself scarce when it was actually time to celebrate Christmas. After all, she had no doubts that people like her grandmother and Felicity weren't the sort to invite the housekeeper to a social event. Of course, tonight had been an exception since the old woman had needed a ride. And even then Christine had mostly felt on the outside of things. Of course, she'd enjoyed the children and felt a real connection with them. But that would probably be a one-time thing.

That is, unless she decided to end this game of deception and break the news to her grandmother. Grandmother. It still sounded so foreign and unbelievable. She couldn't even believe she'd already been using that title for the cranky old woman. Especially since the only grandmother she'd previously known was her father's mother. Talk about your opposites. That grandmother had been tiny and soft-spoken, with curly white hair and soft, rosy cheeks. But she'd died a few years ago at the age of eighty-seven. But besides the physical differences, this grandmother hardly seemed like a grandmother at all. Not even to her two sweet little grandchildren. Even if they were her stepson's children, they seemed to have accepted her as their own.

But that was all beside the point, she told herself as she hurriedly prepared for bed. The dorm was colder than usual, and she'd been bundling up at night to stay warm. She layered on flannel pajamas, fuzzy socks, sweats, and even a knitted hat. The point was, she re-minded herself, that she was suffering from a terribly guilty conscience for the way she was deceiving not only her grandmother but also her stepuncle, Jimmy, and his family. It was wrong, wrong, wrong, and she knew it. Even more than that, she knew she hadn't been brought up this way. And she knew her father would be disappointed in her. But perhaps worse than that, she knew God expected more from her too. Like honesty. As a result of all this guilt, she'd had difficulty praying this past week. And that was starting to take its toll on her in many ways. She felt more stressed and worried than ever, and she was actually starting to feel somewhat depressed too. And that was completely unlike her.

Tears of frustration began spilling down her cheeks, and she knew she had to make this right somehow. But that would mean blowing her cover and revealing her true identity. And she just wasn't sure she could do that. Not without risking everything. And, for some reason, it seemed more important than ever to find out about her birth mother and her family before they threw her out on her ear for tricking them. This need to know made her feel that no sacrifice would be too much.

She wished she could pray about it, to lay it all out there and simply ask God to help her, but she knew that was wrong. You can't very well ask God to help you deceive someone. Finally she settled for a quick "I'm sorry" and "Please help me" kind of prayer. It wasn't much, but it was more than she'd managed all week. And at least it was honest, or sort of honest. Maybe she'd wake up in the morning and everything would make sense again. And she'd know the perfect way to clear up this little misunderstanding. And everyone would be perfectly fine and happy. At least that's what she tried to make herself believe as she fell asleep.

As she walked to her grandmother's home the following morning, she didn't feel so hopeful or confident. The dense, wet fog seemed only to add to her feelings of heaviness and gloom. At least Saturday was supposed to be a half day for her, and then she had Sunday off. And so she firmly told herself, *You have until noon to figure a way to tell your grandmother the truth.*

But by eleven thirty, the opportunity still hadn't arisen. Or perhaps she'd missed it completely. It didn't help matters that her grandmother had been in a foul mood all morning. Christine wasn't sure if this was because of the impending unwanted Christmas party or simply a result of being laid up with a bum ankle. Even so, Christine did her best to make the old woman comfortable and happy, but nothing seemed to help.

"My coffee is cold," her grandmother complained.

Christine considered telling her that it was cold because it had been sitting there too long, but she held her tongue. "I'll get you some more."

"Make it a fresh pot. I don't want any stale stuff."

So Christine made a fresh pot. But on the morning went, and nothing seemed to satisfy this cantankerous old woman. By the time it was noon and Christine had set a nice lunch tray next to her grandmother, she was emotionally exhausted.

"I put some dinner things on the shelf in the fridge," she said as she slipped on her parka. "Can I get you anything else?"

"No. I'm fine."

Christine frowned. "And you're sure you don't need me to come by tomorrow? I could come after church, you know."

"Jimmy promised to come by." She didn't even look up from her soup. "I'll be fine. I'm not a baby, you know. I can do some things for myself."

Christine nodded. "Right. Well, you have the number to my dorm room if you should change your mind."

"I won't."

Christine walked slowly across campus. She wondered if she'd done something to upset her grandmother. She knew the woman wasn't the most congenial person, but it had seemed, up until today, that they'd been getting closer. She'd actually thought her grandmother liked her, at least a little bit. Or maybe she just tolerated her better than back in the beginning. But today had felt like a real setback. And Christine felt more frustrated and disappointed than ever. She'd wanted to sit down with the old woman, to look her right in the eyes and explain everything today. But there just never seemed an appropriate moment. And as grumpy as her grandmother was, she probably would've reacted quite badly. She most likely would've been seriously angry to hear the truth. Who knows, it might've totally ruined all possibilities of a relationship at all.

"What possibilities?" she had to ask herself as she crossed the street toward the dorm. When her grandmother found out she'd been deceived, she'd probably throw Christine out on the streets. And who could blame her? Maybe Christine should put the whole thing off until after Christmas. Perhaps that would be the kindest thing to do. Why should she risk upsetting the entire family?

Yes, she would wait until after the Christmas Eve party. Of course, that meant four more days of continuing this charade. But if Felicity was anything like Christine suspected, those would be four very busy and demanding days. Perhaps it was just as well that she was getting Sunday off. She felt fairly sure she'd need a day of rest just to prepare herself for all the work and preparation, not to mention the continued playacting, that was coming.

When Christine reported for work on Monday morning, she quickly discovered that Felicity had already made a complete list of things for her to do.

"Jimmy brought it by yesterday," her grandmother announced. "I hope you know what you've gotten yourself in for, young lady."

She glanced at the list, then smiled, purely for her grandmother's sake. "No problem. I can handle this," she said.

The old woman's brows lifted. "And keep up the quality of work you've been doing for me as well?"

She nodded. "You'll see."

Her grandmother rolled her eyes. "Yes, I suppose I will."

After lunch they sat down together to work on the computer. "I want you to show me how to search for a person," her grandmother said.

"There are a lot of ways," Christine explained. "First we choose a search engine."

"What?"

"Oh, it's like a service that works as a directory. Here, let me show you." She went to her favorite search site and pointed out the empty box. "We'll start by putting the name of the person in here and see if it pulls anything up. Is this person living or dead?"

"Living."

"Okay. Go ahead and type in the full name, and then we'll hit enter and see what comes up."

Christine stepped back and waited as her grandmother began to type. But she felt herself take in a fast breath when she saw the name. *Lenore Louise Blackstone.* In that same instant her stomach tied itself in a knot and her hands began to tremble.

"Okay, now what?"

Christine's mouth felt too dry to speak. And even if it hadn't, she still had no idea what to say. She felt slightly faint. She sat down on the chair across from the couch and took a deep breath, trying to regain some sense of composure.

"What's wrong?" her grandmother asked as she looked over at Christine. "Goodness, you look pale. Aren't you feeling well?"

Christine shook her head.

"Good grief, I hope you haven't picked up that horrible flu bug. That's all I need right now. Maybe you'd better run along home until you know what it is that's ailing you. I certainly can't afford to get that flu with my ankle still bummed up. I can barely get around as it is. That would land me in the hospital for certain. I mean it, Christine, you'd better get out of here right now."

Christine stood up and walked to the closet, retrieved her parka, and left. She knew it was stupid. She didn't have the flu. But, at the same time, she didn't know if she could tell her grandmother the truth right now.

"Oh, what tangled webs we weave . . . ," she said to herself as she started heading back toward her dorm. Then, instead of going to her dorm, she decided to stop by her church. It was only a few blocks out of the way, and she hoped she might be able to get a word with the pastor. She felt she was in deep need of some wise counsel. How had she gotten herself into this mess, anyway? By lying, of course. That was simple enough. But now she needed to find a way to get out.

"What brings you here?" Pastor Reinhart asked. "Coming to complain about yesterday's sermon?"

She shook her head. "Actually, I just needed someone to talk to."

His brow creased. "Have a chair. Is everything okay with your father? I hear bits and pieces of news about South America, but, to be honest, I don't pay that much attention. Everything going all right down there?"

She nodded. "That's not what's troubling me."

He sat down behind his desk, then leaned forward. "Well, that's a relief. So, tell me, what's making you look so glum?"

She poured out her story, and he listened, making careful comments here and there, until she was completely finished.

"Wow. That's quite a story," he said. "I know of the Daniels family. James Daniels used to be the president of the university. Quite a powerful and respected man in the community. He passed away a few years ago. They had a big memorial service."

She nodded.

"I've never met Mrs. Daniels, but I know she used to be quite involved in community affairs. Her name would appear in the paper quite frequently."

She nodded again.

"Of course, that's not what you came to talk about. Is it?"

"What should I do now?" she implored. "I need help."

He pressed his lips together. "Well . . . I think you know what you need to do, Christine."

205

"I know."

"And, the way I see it, the sooner is usually the better. Lies don't get smaller over time. You can sweep them under the rug, but they won't stay there for long."

"Do you think she'll be mad?"

He shrugged. "It's hard to say. I'm sure she's a fairly proud woman, and most people don't like being deceived."

"That's true."

"But, on the other hand, she should be happy to learn that she has a granddaughter." He smiled warmly. "Especially someone like you, Christine. Did I tell you that Beth Maxwell said you did an absolutely brilliant job with her third graders while she was on vacation last month? She thinks you should take a class of your own whenever one opens up."

Christine smiled weakly.

"I know. I know. That's not what you need to hear right now." He folded his hands. "Sometimes the truth is hard to hear, but I think you knew it before you came in here."

Christine looked down at her lap. "What about her daughter, Pastor Reinhart? I mean my mother . . . My grandmother doesn't even know Lenore is dead."

"Unfortunately, you're going to have to tell her." He shook his head. "It's very sad. But you need to remember that it's not your fault. You're just the messenger."

"The messenger who messed up."

He chuckled. "Well, it'll probably smooth out. Just go and tell her the truth. I can tell it's eating you up inside. You don't need that, especially at Christmastime. Besides, I have a feeling it's all going to work out just fine. I think your grandmother is going to be really happy to realize she's got a granddaughter."

"Do you think we could really have a relationship like that?" She stood and made her way to the door, as she realized her pastor must have other things to do. "Do you think that's really possible?"

"All things are possible with God. Just put it in his hands."

As she walked back toward the Daniels home, she did just that. She put the whole thing into God's hands.

When she rang the doorbell to the house, she felt stronger and braver than she'd felt in days. That is, until she saw her grandmother's face.

"What on earth are you doing back here?" she demanded. "I thought you were sick."

"We need to talk," Christine said in a sober voice.

10

Christine prayed silently as she followed her grandmother into the living room. It seemed the old woman was maneuvering her crutches much better these days. Perhaps her ankle was improving and she wasn't in such pain. Maybe it wouldn't be long before she didn't need Christine's help anymore. Christine noticed a dust bunny she'd missed beneath the table in the hallway. She'd have to go over the hardwood floors more carefully later. It was surprising how familiar this home had become to her during the past week. Like she'd known it for years.

"So you don't have the flu after all?" her grandmother asked as she eased herself into the recliner and frowned at Christine. "What is it then?"

Christine sighed and then looked down at her lap.

"Oh, no," her grandmother exclaimed in a horrified voice.

Christine quickly looked up. "What?"

"Don't tell me you've gone and gotten yourself pregnant. And you, supposedly a good church girl."

Christine shook her head. "That's not it."

"Well." Her grandmother leaned back. "That's a relief."

Christine took a deep breath. "This is rather hard to explain."

Her grandmother frowned. "What is it? Are you in some kind of trouble with the law?"

"No. That's not it. But I do have something to tell you that might not be easy to hear."

"What is it?" she demanded.

"Well, it's hard to know the best way to begin . . ."

"Just tell me." She leaned forward and peered at Christine. "At once!"

"All right," Christine said. "But you better brace yourself."

"I am losing my patience!"

"Okay." Christine winced, then quickly said it. "I'm Lenore Blackstone's daughter."

The room grew so silent that Christine could hear her grandmother's breathing coming out in short, ragged puffs. She stared at the stunned woman sitting across from her, watching with fear as the color drained from her grandmother's face. What if she suffered a stroke or heart attack from the shock? Why hadn't Christine thought this through better? Broken it to her more carefully?

"Are you okay?" Christine asked.

Her grandmother said nothing. Just sat there and stared as if seeing a ghost.

"I'm so sorry to tell you like this," Christine said. "I came here originally with the intent of introducing myself to you, but then you assumed I was here for the job, and you just kept talking to me like I was having an interview, and, well, I was so nervous and scared that I just went along with it, and I meant to tell you the next day, but then I got caught up in the job and in helping you, and the more time went on, the harder it became to tell you—"

"Silence!"

Christine blinked, then leaned back into the couch. "Sorry . . . ," she muttered.

Her grandmother shook her head sharply, as if she was trying to shake some sense out of what she'd just heard. "Are you actually telling me that Lenore Blackstone, my only daughter, is your mother?"

Christine nodded.

"My daughter is your mother?" she said it slowly this time, as if it were still sinking in.

"My *birth* mother." Christine added. She still thought of Marie Bradley as her real mother. Lenore was little more than a stranger to her. "My parents adopted me at birth."

209

"And that would've been about twenty years ago?" Her grandmother seemed to be doing some math in her head. "The same year she left home?"

"I guess so."

Her grandmother sighed. "She was pregnant with you when she left."

"That's what I'd heard."

Suddenly her grandmother sat up straight and eagerly looked at Christine with what seemed like an almost childlike hope and expectancy. "So, tell me, do you know anything about Lenore now? Do you know where she lives or whether she's married or has other children? Can you give me her address?"

Christine felt a lump growing in her throat. "I'm—I'm sorry," she began, then choked on the words. "But sh—she's dead."

Her grandmother sank back into her chair like she'd been deflated. She leaned her head back, then closed her eyes and moaned as if she were in great pain.

Christine, worried for the old woman's health, jumped up and went to her side. "Are you okay?"

"Oh no. Oh no. Oh no," she muttered in an almost incoherent way.

"Shall I call someone?" Christine asked. "Do you need help?"

Her grandmother slowly shook her head, eyes still closed, still moaning. Christine wasn't sure what to do now. Was this turning into a medical emergency? Should she call Jimmy and Felicity? She put her hand on her grandmother's shoulder and silently prayed for help and guidance. She begged God to comfort this poor woman in the grief she'd so carelessly poured upon her.

"I'm sorry to be the one to tell you about Lenore," Christine said. "I thought you already knew, but then you wanted to look her up on the computer and I realized—"

"When did she die?" her grandmother said suddenly. She sat up and looked at Christine. "And why wasn't I notified?"

"My parents tried to find you, but they didn't know your name was Daniels back then. Apparently, they attempted to locate a Mr. and Mrs. Blackstone in this town but couldn't. Lenore died nearly twenty years ago, just a month after I was born. She was hit by a car. Since my parents were unable to reach any of her relatives, they just handled the funeral arrangements and everything themselves. They'd been good friends to Lenore. She'd even been living with them for a while. That's about all I know."

"Is there a gravesite?" she asked in a hollow voice.

"Yes, it's in Larchwood, my hometown."

"I'd like to see it."

Christine nodded. "I know where it is. I've been there a few times, and my mother's grave is nearby. I can take you there if you think you're up to it."

She shook her head. "Not today. I don't think I can handle much more today." Then she looked at Christine and frowned. "You were dishonest with me."

"I know. And I'm really sorry." Christine sat back down on the couch, preparing herself for her grandmother's chastening.

"I don't like being tricked by anyone, young lady, even if it is my own granddaughter." She narrowed her eyes. "In fact . . . why should I even believe you now? Perhaps you're *not* my granddaughter. Perhaps you've made all this up, and maybe Lenore is still alive. How do I know you're not lying to me right now?"

Christine considered this. "Why would I do that?"

"Well, you admit to lying to me before, right?"

"Not outright lying," Christine said. "But I guess I didn't tell you the complete truth."

"So how do I know you're not lying now?"

Christine felt confused. "But what reason would I have to lie about something like this?"

"Money." She studied Christine carefully, almost as if she were examining a bug beneath a magnifying glass. "You could be here to scam an old woman into giving you some kind of inheritance." Then she laughed, but it was that old cynical, menacing laugh again. "That is, assuming this old woman has anything to leave anyone. And that's a pretty big assumption."

Christine shook her head. "No, I don't want your money. I only wanted—"

"Well, of course you wouldn't admit to wanting my money. What kind of scam artist would do something as stupid as that? No, you're a clever girl, Christine. First you'd ingratiate yourself to me and to my family. Then you'd reveal your identity, and then you'd wait around for the money."

Christine stood up. "That's not true."

"How do I know what's true and what's not? Everything you've done up until now has been a big, fat lie. Why should I believe anything you have to say?"

Christine felt hot tears burning in her eyes. Tears of anger and indignation. "I'm telling you the truth," she said. "I have absolutely no reason to lie."

"How can I know?"

Tears were streaming down Christine's face now. "Look, I'm sorry I deceived you before. That was stupid and wrong and thoughtless. But I am telling you the truth now. I am Lenore Blackstone's daughter. You can call my father and ask him." She rushed over to the desk and wrote down the phone number of the mission compound in Brazil. "Call him if you don't believe me." Then she turned and ran out the front door and away from the house.

She cried as she walked back to the dorm. Why had she been such an idiot? Why hadn't she just told the truth from the beginning? She wished she could turn back the clock. But if she could, she wouldn't bother going back over the past couple of weeks. Instead she'd turn the clock back to at least six years ago. Back to when both her parents were alive and well. And they were all together and happily enjoying the Christmas holidays the way they were meant to be enjoyed. With warmth and love and family. Something she'd taken so for granted at the time, but something that might never happen again.

11

Christine awoke to the shrill sound of the phone ringing. She reached for the phone, fumbling in the darkness to find it. "Hello?"

"Christine?" It was a male voice but not her father's.

"Yes." She flipped on the light and glanced at the clock. It was only eight thirty, but it felt more like midnight. How long had she been sleeping?

"This is Jimmy. I'm sorry to disturb you, but my mother called a bit ago. And she was very upset and actually sounded a little bit delirious—"

"Is she okay?" Christine asked.

"I think so. Felicity just gave her a pain pill and helped her to bed, but we're feeling concerned . . ." He cleared his throat. "She said some strange things about you. I don't know if she's imagining things or—"

"Did she mention Lenore?"

"Yes. First she said that Lenore was dead, and then she said that it was all just a lie and that you were not to be trusted."

Christine sighed. "It's a long story."

"I've got time."

So Christine attempted to explain it all to him, carefully going over the details she knew, and how she'd never meant to trick his mother, and how she was very sorry.

"And you can call my father down in Brazil to verify everything. I'm sure this information must all be on my birth certificate, which

I think must be in his safety deposit box at the bank. In fact, I have a key, if it would help matters to see it."

"Oh, I don't think that's necessary, Christine. I believe you, myself. I mean, why would you make something like this up?"

"Your mother thought I might be a scam artist trying to con her out of her money."

He laughed. "Yeah, that sounds like something she might say. But don't worry. The truth is you remind me a little bit of Lenore." He grew quieter. "I'm really sad to hear that she's dead. But I'd wondered about that possibility. She just didn't seem like the kind of person who would leave like that and never come back or call or anything. She always seemed a very kind and forgiving person to me."

"That's nice to know," Christine said. "Actually, the main reason I wanted to contact Lenore's family was to learn more about her."

"I didn't know her really well," he explained. "I was already in college when our parents got married, and that was only a few years before Lenore, uh, left."

"Did you know she was pregnant when she left home?"

"I suspected as much. I think it was supposed to be some big secret, but it wasn't hard to guess what was going on."

"Is there anything I can do to help your mother?" she asked. "I wasn't sure whether I should come back and work for her after this. I mean, she was pretty upset with me."

"Well, that's the problem. You see, Aunt Hattie is supposed to arrive tomorrow. And Felicity has her hands full trying to get things ready for Christmas. And we could use your help, if you don't mind, that is."

"I don't mind at all. I just don't want to upset your mother by being around."

"How about this?" he said. "What if I pick you up tomorrow and bring you back over to Mom's, and the three of us can sit and talk this thing out?"

Christine sighed in relief. "Would you?"

"Hey, I'd be happy to. After all, you're family."

She smiled. "I guess you're sort of like my uncle, then. Although I realize you're really a stepuncle."

"Hey, you can call me Uncle Jimmy anytime you like. Suits me just fine."

"Thanks. And thanks for calling. I feel a lot better now."

"See you around eight in the morning, then?"

"Sounds great."

Christine prayed for her grandmother before she went back to bed that night. She asked God to help her adjust to the hard news of losing her only daughter. And then she asked him to help her forgive her granddaughter for lying.

Esther awoke in the darkness with an overwhelming feeling of confusion and sadness. *What's wrong with me?* she wondered as she reached to turn on the lamp on her bedside table. Then she remembered. Lenore. Lenore was dead. Or so said that manipulative girl who had tricked her way into Esther's life and home. She should've known better. If it sounds too good to be true . . .

She swung her legs over the side of the bed, cautiously extending her injured foot lest she bump it against the side rail again. She'd done that enough times to remember to be more careful. Then she frowned as she noticed that her crutches, instead of being right next to her bed where they should've been, were clear across the room.

"That silly Felicity," she muttered as she slowly worked her way to the foot of the bed and then used the bench as a very short walker to enable her to finally reach her crutches. Then, with her crutches beneath her, and nearly out of breath, she managed to locate her robe and slippers. Not thoughtfully laid out like when that girl had been working here. She no longer thought of Christine by name. Instead she had become *that girl* in her mind. That evil, deceptive, selfish, lying girl.

"Can't believe I was such a fool as to be duped like that," she mumbled as she slowly made her way down the hall toward the living room. She knew she wasn't going to be able to fall asleep again. She'd hoped she might be able to simply sit and relax in her recliner, preferably with a hot cup of tea, but that was probably too much to attempt on her own tonight. She'd have to settle for the comfort of the recliner. But before she reached the recliner, she paused at her desk, noticing the writing scrawled across the notepad. "Allen Bradley, CMA compound," followed by a long phone number that appeared to be international. Although that could have just as well been made up too. That girl probably didn't think Esther would call her bluff. But then she just didn't know what a tough broad she was up against either.

Esther sat down at her desk and picked up the phone. But then she looked at the clock. It was a little past three in the morning and probably not the best hour to be dialing what was most likely a wrong number. No sense in disturbing innocent people. She glanced down at the bottom drawer, then shook her head. "It's not true, Esther," she told herself. "It's all a big, fat lie. That girl is just trying to pull one over on you. Don't fall for her tricks."

The contents of the drawer seemed to be pulling her hand down toward it as if it had a magnetic force of its own. Finally she gave in and leaned down and tugged on the stubborn drawer. Once it was open, she slowly reached inside, removed the framed photo, then turned it over to stare at the lovely young woman who seemed to have been captured in time. She sat for a long time just staring at the image of her daughter. She hadn't even noticed the tears that had fallen from her eyes and splattered like raindrops on the glass surface covering the photo. She used the sleeve of her robe to wipe it clean, rubbing it over and over in circles as if to polish it.

"Lenore," she whispered. "Tell me it's not true." But even as she said these words, she knew that it was indeed true. She knew beyond any shadow of doubt that Lenore was dead. Dead and gone and buried just like that girl had said. It was the eyes that told her so. Those big, golden-brown eyes that had the fresh look of youth and innocence, and honesty, in them. The same eyes that Lenore had passed down to her daughter, Christine.

Esther set Lenore's picture on her desk and faced it toward the recliner. Then she slowly made her way across the room and eased herself into the recliner. And there she sat, gazing at the photo through her tears, wishing desperately that she could do it all differently.

12

Christine sat on the cement steps in front of her dorm as she waited for Jimmy to pick her up. As she sat she prayed that God would do something miraculous to salvage the mess she'd created. *I'm sorry that I didn't tell the truth from the beginning. But I do believe you can take our worst failures and turn them into your successes. That's all I'm asking you to do. Just bring something good out of this for my grandmother. Help her through this sadness, and heal her wounded heart.*

Just then she saw the Ford Explorer pull up with Jimmy waving from inside. "Hey," he called as he stuck his head out the window. "Am I late?"

She jogged up to the SUV. "No. I was just early."

"How you doing?" he asked as she buckled her seat belt.

"Okay, I guess. Considering." She sighed. "But I really do feel bad for making such a mess of everything for your stepmother."

"*Your* grandmother."

She nodded. "Yeah. But I doubt she'll ever want me to call her that. In fact, I won't be surprised if she refuses to let me into her house. She was really mad at me yesterday."

"I know. But she can be like that. She might come across as pretty feisty and mean, but underneath everything she has a very tender heart."

Christine studied him in wonder. Of all the members of the Daniels family, Jimmy seemed the most thoughtful and kind. "Can I ask you a question, Jimmy?"

"Sure."

"What makes you so nice?"

He laughed. "Oh, you should see me getting down on the boys' basketball team lately. I'm sure they wouldn't agree with that assessment."

"Well, I appreciate your help in this."

"Hey, we're family now. And I happen to think Mom needs someone like you around right now."

"It's interesting that you call her Mom. I mean, she's really your stepmom, and she's not always exactly nice to you."

He smiled. "Well, she and I have an understanding. Both my parents have passed on, and she's always been there for me. I guess I've pretty much adopted her as *Mom*."

"That's cool."

"Sometimes family isn't so much about whose DNA you're carrying as it is about love. You know?"

"Definitely. I mean, my parents aren't my birth parents, but I love them both more than anything."

"Even so, I think it's important that you get involved in Mom's life. Like I said before, I think she needs you."

"Even after the way I deceived her?"

"Hey, we all make mistakes, Christine. It's the way we deal with them afterward that makes a difference."

"Yeah, I'm sure you're right. But I usually don't make mistakes of this caliber."

"Well, if it makes you feel any better, I can understand how this whole thing might've happened. I know as well as anyone that Mom can be pretty intimidating, and if she gets going in a certain direction, it can be awfully hard to derail her. Besides that, you've been an excellent caregiver to her. That's something."

"I actually really like her. Although I wasn't too sure at first. I mean, she can be, well, like you said, intimidating."

He laughed. "Yeah, and I can think of a few other words people might use to describe her. But they're not very nice words."

"Can I ask you something else?"

"Shoot."

"What's up with her and your Aunt Hattie?"

He blew a long, low whistle. "Funny you should ask . . . since that's a can of worms that has just turned potentially explosive." He laughed. "Wow, talk about mixing your metaphors. You can sure tell I don't teach English."

"What do you mean by explosive?"

"Well, now that Mom knows Lenore is dead, and Aunt Hattie is here . . . Well, it might get interesting or ugly, or who knows . . . maybe they'll fall into each other's arms and forgive each other for everything. Now, wouldn't that be something." He pulled into the driveway.

"But what does Aunt Hattie have to do with Lenore?" Christine asked, eager to get to the bottom of this before they went inside.

"I don't know the full story. I don't think anyone really does. Well, besides Aunt Hattie and Mom, that is. But they got into it at Dad's funeral. All I know is that it had to do with Dad and Lenore and there was a lot of blame and accusation going on. But I never heard exactly why or what, which was probably just as well. But, as you could tell the other night, Mom is still not over it. And I'm not too sure about Aunt Hattie either." He turned off the ignition and got out of the SUV. "Although Aunt Hattie never brings it up, not to me anyway. In fact, she acts as if nothing ever happened. But then she's a sweet little lady. I'm hoping she plans to help Mom to bury the hatchet."

"That'd be good."

"You're going to like Aunt Hattie, Christine. She and Mom are complete opposites." He laughed as they walked up to the front door. "Being so different makes me think these two old gals should actually get along better."

Christine's heart was pounding like a jackhammer as she followed Jimmy down the hallway. Was she making a mistake in coming back here so soon? Perhaps Esther needed more time to recover from her shock.

"Mom," he called in a cheerful voice as they approached her bedroom. "You up yet?"

But her bed was empty. It looked as if there had been some sort of struggle, with the satin comforter half on the floor and the bench overturned against the wall.

"Goodness," Christine said. "I hope she's okay."

They hurried out to the living room to discover her asleep in her recliner, snoring softly.

"She looks fine to me," he whispered to Christine.

"What?" Esther jerked herself awake. "Who is it? What's going on?"

"Hi, Mom," Jimmy said, walking over to her chair. "It's just me, coming to check on you. I brought Christine with me, and before you get yourself all riled up, we'd like to sit down and talk to you, rationally."

She nodded without saying anything.

Jimmy pointed to the couch. "Take a seat, Christine."

She followed his order and sat down across from her grandmother. Then she waited as he pulled up a side chair and sat next to his stepmom. The three of them sat in a triangle, and Jimmy began to speak. "I know that you think Christine is lying about Lenore, but I've talked with her and gone over some things, and I have no reason to think she's not telling the truth." He held up one finger. "For one thing, she can produce a birth certificate from her dad's safety deposit box." He held up two fingers. "And she said you can call her dad and ask him." He put up a third finger. "And she can take you to Lenore's grave and—"

"That's enough, Jimmy," she snapped. "No more fingers."

"But, Mom."

"And no more buts." She glanced at Christine and then back to Jimmy. "I know she's Lenore's daughter. I think that, somewhere inside of me, I knew it from the very first day she showed up at my door." She looked down in her lap and let out a long sigh. "And I also know that Lenore's dead. The truth is I think I've known it all along. I just never wanted to admit it before."

"I wish I'd been bringing you happier news," Christine said.

"Well, it doesn't do any good to beat up the messenger," Jimmy said.

220

"I'm so sorry about everything," Christine told her grandmother. "I hope someday you'll be able to forgive me. But I'll understand if you don't."

"Don't call me Esther anymore," she said.

Christine nodded, feeling certain that she was about to be dismissed for good.

"You can call me Grandmother," she continued. "Or Grandma, I suppose, like Jimmy's kids do. Although I'm not particularly fond of that title." Her lips turned up at the edges just slightly. "And I'm sorry I didn't believe you yesterday, Christine. I guess I just hoped it wasn't true, about Lenore, I mean. No one likes to learn that their child has . . . has died . . ."

"I'm so sorry," Christine said, wishing she could say something else. But nothing else seemed to work.

Her grandmother slowly shook her head. "There should be a law . . . ," she said in a tired voice. "There should be a law that children should never die before their parents do—" She began to choke up again. "But I guess I'm partly to blame for Lenore's death. I—I never should've—" She put her hands over her face and began to sob.

"Oh, Mom," Jimmy said, reaching over to put his hand on her heaving shoulders. "You can't go blaming yourself for Lenore's death."

Christine wasn't sure she could watch this display of emotion without falling apart herself. She felt she was barely holding it together as it was, and so she excused herself and headed off to the kitchen to make some strong coffee and fix breakfast just the way Esther—just the way *Grandmother*—liked it.

Her grandmother seemed nearly recovered when Christine appeared with the breakfast tray. "You should probably eat something," she told her as she set the tray on the table next to her.

"Good thinking," Jimmy said. "Sorry to run off like this, but I promised Felicity I'd watch the kids while she does some quick Christmas shopping. And, by the way, she'll be picking up Aunt Hattie at the train station."

"Speaking of Aunt Hattie," Esther said. "I wonder if Felicity

221

couldn't keep her for a while today." She glanced at Christine. "We have something we need to attend to, if that's okay with you, Christine."

She shrugged. "I'm at your disposal, Grandmother."

Esther smiled. "Good."

"I'm sure that'll be okay with Felicity," Jimmy assured them. "Maybe we could take the old girl out for an early dinner tonight. I wonder if she still likes Chinese food."

"I wouldn't know," Esther said stiffly.

Christine wished she could ask her grandmother about the conflict between her and her sister-in-law, but in light of all the recent emotional upheavals, she felt it unwise.

"Then we can drop Aunt Hattie by the house this evening?" Jimmy asked.

Esther nodded with a grim expression. "That should be fine."

After breakfast Christine helped her grandmother bathe and dress as usual, but perhaps with just a bit more tenderness than before. She didn't say much.

"You're being awfully quiet," her grandmother said as Christine helped her slip her good foot into a loafer.

"Sorry."

"I would think you'd be filled with questions."

Christine looked up at her. "Oh, I am. But I hate to push things too much. You've had a lot to take in. I guess we both have."

She nodded. "You're pretty wise for your age. Well, in most things. I still don't think it was terribly wise to trick me like that. But then I suppose it seemed right at the time."

"What is it we need to take care of today?" Christine asked. "I suppose we need to pick up a few more groceries since we're having company . . ."

"Yes, there's that too. But first we need to drive over to Larchwood."

Christine nodded. "To see her grave."

"Yes. I need to do that."

"Do you want to stop by the bank and see my birth certificate too?" Christine asked.

Esther shook her head. "No, I don't think that's necessary."

"I do have a question that's pestered me more than most," Christine said as she drove toward Larchwood. "It's about my birth father."

Esther looked out the passenger window without answering.

"But it's okay if you'd rather not talk about it now," she said quickly. "I'm just curious, you know."

"The problem is that I'm not too sure, Christine. At the time I really thought it was Lenore's on-again, off-again boyfriend, Peter Summers. I never really approved of the young man and didn't feel he was a good match for Lenore. But when I bumped into him on campus one day, just a few months after she'd left, I confronted him about the pregnancy, and he completely denied everything. Of course, Lenore had insisted from the very beginning that it wasn't Peter's child." Esther turned and looked out the window again. "But I didn't listen."

"Do you have any idea who my father might be?" Christine asked. She didn't like the idea that her birth mother had possibly been the kind of girl to sleep around and not even know who the father of her child was. It didn't fit with the image Christine had built into her head. But then again if it was the truth, it would be best to just get it out in the open.

Without answering, her grandmother opened her Gucci handbag and reached in for a handkerchief to dab her eyes.

"I'm sorry if I'm upsetting you," Christine said. "We can talk about something else."

She nodded. "Yes, I think I'd appreciate that."

But they didn't talk about anything else. They just drove the next forty minutes in silence. But Christine knew what they were both thinking about, or rather whom. Lenore Blackstone was very much on their minds. As they entered Larchwood, Christine broke the silence. "The house I grew up in is down that street." She pointed toward Meadow Lane.

"Drive past it," Esther said.

Christine turned down the street and drove the five blocks to her house. "That's it," she said as she parked on the other side of the street from the small clapboard-sided house. "It was always yellow when we lived there. That was my mother's favorite color. The new renters must've painted it." She felt a tightness in her chest, a longing to go back to her safe childhood world.

"It's awfully small," her grandmother said. "But I think it would've looked better painted yellow."

Christine smiled. "It did."

"And you lived there your whole life?"

She nodded.

"And is that the house where Lenore stayed with your parents?"

"Yes. My parents lived there for more than ten years before I was born. The mortgage is completely paid off, and the rent money is supporting my dad while he's volunteering in the mission school. It was his lifelong dream."

"Well, good for him. Your parents sound like fine people, Christine. I'm thankful for that. For your sake, I mean."

"So am I." Christine began to pull away, resisting the urge to look back. "It used to bother me some, as a child, that my parents were so much older than everyone else's. I guess I was actually embarrassed by them sometimes. I'm ashamed to think of that now."

"Kids always have problems with their parents," her grandmother said. "It's just the way of life."

"But these past couple of years I've really learned to appreciate all my parents have done for me. Unfortunately, it was too late to show it to my mother. But I try to let my dad know."

"I'm sure he knows, Christine. You know, I'd like to write him a letter. To thank him for his kindness to my—my girls."

"Oh, he would love that, Grandmother. And you'll have to meet him when he comes back from Brazil. He's the sweetest person ever."

"Do you have any photos of your family?"

"I do. I even made up a little album last summer. I wish I had a photo of Lenore, but my dad said she was camera shy."

Esther nodded. "That's true, she was. A beautiful girl, but she hated getting her picture taken. So I don't have many photos of her after she became a teenager. I do have quite a few of her as a baby and young child. You can see them when we get back home."

They had reached the edge of town. "Shall I drive to the cemetery now? Or do you think we should stop and get something to eat? It's past lunchtime."

Esther waved her hand. "I'm perfectly fine. Why don't we just keep going. Those thick, gray clouds look like they might have snow in them."

"Oh, I hope so," Christine said. "I'd love to have a white Christmas this year."

Esther just shook her head.

When they reached the cemetery, Christine could feel a silence settling into the car, like a thick blanket of sadness draped around them. "Lenore's grave isn't too far from the road," she said, hoping to alleviate the heaviness. "It's near my mother's. I think you can make it there fairly easily with your crutches."

She parked the car as close as she could to the gravesite, then went around to help her grandmother out of the car. The wind was biting cold, and Christine thought she saw a few snowflakes fluttering through the air.

"It's right next to this path," she said, pointing down the graveled walk. "But be careful with those crutches, this ground isn't terribly even." She stayed near the old woman, keeping her hands ready to support her if she stumbled. But soon they were there, and, thankfully, there was a marble bench directly across from Lenore's grave. It must've been placed there by the people who maintained a family plot just adjacent to hers, but the two of them sat down on it just the same.

Esther pulled her handkerchief from her pocket and dabbed at her eyes as she stared speechlessly at the small granite marker.

LENORE LOUISE BLACKSTONE
1965–1984
SAFE IN HER FATHER'S ARMS
JOHN 3:16

Christine sat in silence for several minutes, then finally said, "My dad told me Lenore had a really good heart, that she was kind and good and gentle. And I don't know if it'll make any difference to you. I mean, I don't know where you stand about these things, but

225

my dad said Lenore gave her heart to God not long before she died. That's always been reassuring to me."

Esther turned away, holding her handkerchief over her face as she sobbed quietly. Christine laid a hand on her shoulder. "I know it's hard, Grandmother, but I really believe she's happy now."

Esther shook her head. "No, this is—all—all my fault. My daughter is dead and gone because I was so—so wrong. So stubborn and wrong." Suddenly she stood, clumsily gathering her crutches beneath her as she began moving closer to the grave. "Oh, Lenore," she sobbed. "I was so wrong—" And then, like a house of cards, she crumbled and fell on the dry brown grass.

"Grandmother!" Christine shrieked as she fell on her knees next to the old woman. "Are you okay?"

But her grandmother's eyes were closed, and though she was breathing, it was coming out in quick little pants. Christine gently shook her, then looked around to see if anyone was nearby. Oh, how she wished she had a cell phone just then.

"What's the problem?" a male voice called.

Christine whipped around to see a man in overalls and a sweatshirt jogging toward them. "It's my grandmother," she said. "She's collapsed. Please, can you call an ambulance?"

The man pulled some sort of radio from his pocket, telling someone on the other end to call for an ambulance. Then he knelt beside Esther and leaned over to see if she was breathing.

"She's still breathing," Christine said.

"Is it her heart?" he asked. "Does she need CPR?"

Christine had already checked her pulse. "She has a heartbeat, but it's not very strong. I'm not sure what to do."

"The ambulance should be here soon." The man whipped off his sweatshirt and used it to cradle Esther's head. "The hospital's only about a mile away."

"That's right," Christine remembered. Then she removed her own parka and laid it over her grandmother to help preserve her body heat. In the same moment, as if to mock her, the snowflakes began to fall faster.

"Oh, hurry," she cried. "Please, please, hurry." Then she began to pray. *Dear God, please take care of Grandmother. Please help her to be all right. And please send the ambulance quickly.*

Just then she heard the siren coming closer. Within minutes the whole crew was there, checking her grandmother's vital signs, putting an oxygen mask on her, and loading her onto the gurney.

"I'll follow you," Christine said as she turned to run back to the car.

As she drove toward the hospital, she continued to pray. But as she parked the car and dashed toward the ER entrance, it hit her. This was where her mother had died only five years ago. And, most likely, though she'd never asked, this was where Lenore had died nearly twenty years ago. Would this be where her grandmother would die today?

Please, God, no, she prayed as she pushed open the doors.

"You'll have to wait out here," the receptionist said after Christine quickly explained the situation. "We'll let you know when Mrs. Daniels is stabilized, and then you can see her."

First Christine paced back and forth, and then it occurred to her that her grandmother had other family that should be notified. She ran to the pay phone and dialed information to get Jimmy and Felicity's number. Jimmy was supposed to be home with his kids today.

"Hello?" His voice sounded as cheerful as ever.

"Jimmy," she gasped. "This is Christine. I'm at the hospital in Larchwood with your mother—"

"Oh no, is she okay? What happened?"

Christine quickly told him about what had happened at the cemetery.

"I guess it was just too much for her." She was crying now. "I should've known better than to take her. But she seemed to be doing so well, and she really wanted to go. And then she just fell apart. Oh, it's all my fault—"

"Easy does it, girl. It's not your fault at all. It's just the way things go sometimes. And, knowing Mom, I'm guessing she's going to be just fine. That woman is really resilient. Just the same, I'll be over just as soon as I can. But I may have to bring the rugrats with me."

"That's okay. I can help watch them," she offered.

Then she went and sat down in a hard vinyl chair. She leaned over and put her head in her hands and just cried. Why did this keep happening to her? And just when she thought she'd gotten a grandmother, it looked like she might lose her. *Maybe it's me,* she thought. *Maybe I'm some kind of jinx to everyone I love or have any connections to. Maybe I should just wear a big caution sign across my chest, warning people to beware—don't get too close.* But, at the same time, she knew she was being ridiculous. Still, she couldn't help but wonder if she'd played the granddaughter-for-a-day game—and lost.

By the time Jimmy and the kids arrived, Christine still hadn't been told anything, and every time she inquired the receptionist grew more exasperated with her, telling her not to worry so much and that she just needed to be more patient. "These things take time."

"You'd think they could tell us *something*," she said to Jimmy. "I mean, is she okay? Was it a heart attack? A stroke? What? Even if we can't see her, they ought to know something by now." She glanced at her watch. "It's been well over an hour."

"Let me go give it a try," he said. "You kids stay with your cousin and I'll be back in a minute."

She smiled at that word. *Cousin.* It sounded comforting.

"Where's Grandma?" Jamie asked as he sat down beside Christine.

"She's in there." Christine pointed toward the big swinging doors. "The doctor is with her now."

"Is she getting a shot?" Casey asked with wide eyes. "I don't like getting shots."

"I don't know," Christine said honestly. "She might be getting a shot."

"We got our Christmas tree," Jamie said as he noticed a small artificial tree on the reception desk.

Casey clapped her hands. "Our tree is so big it touches the ceiling, and Daddy put an angel on top."

"It must be beautiful."

"And we have presents," Jamie said. "We even have one for you."

Christine blinked. "For me?"

He nodded. "Me and Daddy picked it out."

Suddenly she realized that she was part of the family now and that she still needed to get Christmas presents. However, that responsibility seemed to pale in comparison to today's medical emergency. "All things in due time," her father would probably tell her.

"I spoke to the doctor," Jimmy said. "She's okay."

"Really?" Christine wasn't sure whether she could believe this or not. "I mean, is she really okay okay? Or is she just stabilized? Was it her heart or—"

He held up his hand to stop her. "Let me tell you. They checked her heart and everything, and it all looks pretty good. The doctor says it was probably low blood sugar and exhaustion. I told him about visiting the grave, and he said that might've contributed to everything. But the good news is she's just fine."

"Thank God," Christine said as she sank down into a chair. "I thought for sure that I was going to lose her. I mean everyone was going to lose her. But it just didn't seem fair after getting to be her granddaughter for only a day."

He laughed. "Well, don't worry. It looks like the old girl will be around for a good long time. I'd better call Felicity though. I left a somewhat urgent message on her cell phone, and if she got it, she's probably coming a little unglued by now."

"Grandma's okay," Christine reassured Jamie and Casey. Of course, they didn't seem overly concerned. They'd probably assumed she was perfectly fine all along, just getting a shot or a checkup or some everyday sort of thing. But Christine was so happy that she hugged them both. "It looks like we'll be having a Merry Christmas after all."

13

"I can't believe this would happen only two days before the Christmas party." Felicity frowned as she pulled out yet another imitation evergreen garland from her apparently bottomless bag and handed it to Christine. Then she turned back to where she was arranging about a dozen red candles along with porcelain elves and reindeer on the fireplace mantle.

"Oh, Felicity," Aunt Hattie said from her position on the couch, where she was untangling a string of white lights. "These things happen. Let's just be thankful it wasn't more serious."

Christine returned to her current assignment without saying a word. She, for one, was getting a little weary of Felicity's complaints. Would she have been happier if Grandmother had been seriously ill? It seemed Felicity's biggest concern right now was not having anything ruin *her* party.

Christine may have been out of sight, but she was still within hearing distance. Even so, she tried to block out Felicity's words as she attempted to wind another length of that stubborn garland around the staircase banister. It was like wrestling with a long, green monster.

"Well, I don't see why she had to go traipsing off to the cemetery clear over in Larchwood just days before Christmas."

"She just learned that her daughter is dead," Aunt Hattie said in a weary voice.

"I know, I know. And I'm sorry, really, I am, Aunt Hattie. But then

Jimmy said that everyone has suspected as much for years. I think she just needs to let the past go and move on with her life. She has plenty of relatives around here who are alive and well. In fact, she's even got more than she knew she had." Felicity lowered her voice now, but this probably served only to attract more of Christine's attention. "What do you think she came here for, anyway?"

"To meet her family, I suspect."

"But why now?"

"Why not?"

"Well, did you know that she pretended to be someone else when she first came here? She acted like she was taking a job as Mom's caregiver."

Aunt Hattie just laughed. She had a sweet, merry laugh too. It reminded Christine of jingle bells, and probably helped her to suppress the urge to go out there and set Felicity straight. As a result of her frustration, she was probably wrapping the garland too tightly. Felicity had warned her not to do that. "Just gently drape it," she'd instructed. "But make the drapes hang evenly."

Although Christine had known Felicity for only a couple of weeks, she realized that she wasn't mean spirited as much as she was simply thoughtless. But thoughtless people had always aggravated Christine. Besides that, she didn't see why Felicity was so consumed with this party. Wasn't it enough that loved ones were going to gather together? Did every single detail have to be perfect too? Christine really wished Felicity would just lighten up and relax a little.

"You just need to take Felicity with a grain of salt sometimes," Grandmother had quietly told Christine as she had helped get the tired woman ready for bed earlier that evening. Of course, this was only after Felicity had implied that today's emergency trip to the hospital might've been partially Christine's fault.

"We all say things we don't mean sometimes," Grandmother had said sadly. "Goodness knows I've done it enough times." She'd leaned back into the pillows and closed her eyes. "I probably know better than anyone how words are hard to retract."

Christine hadn't known how to respond to that. She knew that Grandmother was still grieving over Lenore, and despite her assurance to everyone that all was well, she still seemed troubled. Deeply troubled. Christine hoped that a good night's rest might help her to get past whatever it was that seemed to be haunting her. Hopefully, she would be able to enjoy the festivities Felicity seemed bound and determined were going to happen.

"I invited twenty people," Felicity had told Christine when she came back out from attending to her grandmother. "And I need all the help I can get to pull this thing off. You promised me you'd help, Christine. I hope you're not backing out now."

And so Christine had stayed late stringing garlands and hanging lights and decorating a tall spruce tree that dominated the entire living room. Felicity had even gone so far as to remove the recliner and stick it in a dark, out of the way corner. Christine wondered what Grandmother would say about all this in the morning. Fortunately, the staircase was Christine's last assignment. Felicity had told her she was free to leave when it was done. *Free to leave!* As if she was the hired help. But then isn't that what she'd been masquerading as? Perhaps she was only getting her just dues now.

Christine had immediately liked Aunt Hattie. Of course, that was only her first impression of the little old woman, but Christine had found that her first impressions were often fairly accurate. Aunt Hattie was short and rotund with an equally round face. She had red tinted hair and sparkling blue eyes along with a quick smile that seemed genuine. She had appeared happy to meet Christine, hugged her warmly, and welcomed her to the family. Naturally, Hattie, like Jimmy and his family, was no actual relation to Christine, but she made her feel loved and accepted just the same.

"I was so sorry to hear about your ordeal with poor Esther today," she had told Christine. "Good land, it must've been terribly stressful for you. I'm so glad she's okay."

But their conversation had been cut short by Felicity's list of chores. Christine thought that Felicity, despite her sweet, blond appearance, would've made a good army sergeant.

At last Christine's portion of the list was completely done, and with only a quick "See you tomorrow," she was out the door and on her way back to the dorm.

But she wasn't prepared for the loveliness that greeted her outside. It had been just starting to snow when she'd driven her grandmother home from the hospital that afternoon, but it had stuck and by now accumulated what looked like almost two inches. Enough to transform their normally attractive college town into a beautiful winter wonderland. Streetlights reflected off the snow and made the night seem much brighter and more cheerful than usual. Christine felt like a little kid as she practically danced through the streets toward the dorm. And she knew just what she was going to do when she got to her room. She had a plan to make her grandmother a special Christmas gift.

It took her a while to locate the right box in her closet. She'd used most of this space to store boxes and items she hadn't wanted to put into storage with her father's things. But she finally found the precious box of old family photos her father had asked her to keep safe while he was out of the country. And she didn't think he'd mind if she shared some of these snapshots with her grandmother since they still had all the negatives for them.

By midnight she'd made a nice little stack of pictures of herself as a baby, a toddler, a young girl, and so on. She made sure that some of these shots included her parents, because it seemed important that her grandmother see and appreciate their role in her life. She wanted to reassure her grandmother that, despite Lenore giving her up for adoption, she'd still had a wonderful life and been loved by a pair of sweet, if slightly old-fashioned, parents. She hoped this would somehow help her grandmother resolve the inner conflict that seemed to be eating at her regarding Lenore. Oh, she knew it wouldn't fix everything. Only God could do something as big as that. But it might help a bit.

Tomorrow she'd go to the campus bookstore and get the perfect little album to contain these photos, and then she'd have something really special to present to Grandmother for Christmas. Of course, she'd still need to find something for Jimmy and his family, and Aunt Hattie too. But that might prove fun. She'd never had many relatives to buy presents for in the past. And she'd already sent her father his gift weeks ago to ensure its arrival. She'd carefully packed a box with some of the local foods, like raspberry jam and Starbucks coffee, things he had mentioned missing. And on top she'd tucked in a video Brianna had made of her before Christmas break. There were shots of her in their messy dorm room and around and about on campus. Christine knew her father would probably love the video even more than the food.

Finally Christine went to bed. She knew that tomorrow would be a demanding day. Felicity would probably have more lists, twice as long as tonight's, for her. But even so, she had a hard time going to sleep. She prayed for her father and then her grandmother and then everyone else she could think of, and finally, after what seemed hours, she drifted to sleep.

14

At last Esther's house was quiet. Felicity must've finally given up on her infernal decorating and gone home, and it sounded like Hattie had finally decided to call it a night too. Oh, why in the world had she ever agreed to let Hattie be her houseguest? It was bad enough that Felicity had insisted on having her ridiculous party here, but Esther was beginning to think that her family was trying to torture her. Just how much could an old woman take?

Knowing that sleep would be avoiding her, Esther pushed herself up into a sitting position on her bed and turned on her bedside light. Thankfully, Christine had left the crutches propped within reach. At least someone seemed to be looking out for her interests. That was something. She struggled to put on her robe, then slowly made her way out into the living room.

"Good heavens!" she exclaimed, then instantly regretted it, since Hattie was sleeping in the room down the hall. All these decorations for a little Christmas party! What went on in Felicity's brain was a total mystery to Esther. Greenery and ribbons and baubles and bangles and every possible Christmas trinket were draped and hung from every pillar and post. She shook her head. Leave it to Felicity to try to take this thing right over the top. Of course, she'd assured her stressed-out daughter-in-law that everything was perfectly fine and that she should go right along with the party as planned, but she'd secretly hoped that Felicity would think better of it, especially considering the circumstances. Or at least tone down her plans a bit.

But, no, Felicity was a headstrong young woman, and she seemed bound and determined to have the party of the year despite how her mother-in-law felt.

Esther went over to her desk. Even it was adorned with candles and greenery, and to her dismay the photograph of Lenore was nowhere to be seen. She checked in the bottom drawer, but it wasn't there either. Frustrated and feeling like a hostage in her own home, which had suddenly turned into Santa's Village, she flopped down in her desk chair, almost causing it to tumble. Well, it might just serve them right if she toppled right over and broke her neck. How would that make Felicity feel? Esther suspected that she'd probably go ahead and host the party without her.

Esther leaned back and tried to remember Lenore's face. Her big, brown eyes, so similar to Christine's, her sweet features. Oh, she'd been such a pretty girl. Perhaps that was what had gotten her into trouble in the first place. Naturally, the boys would be attracted to someone like her. Why hadn't Esther thought to warn her daughter? Why had she saved her motherly counsel until it was too late?

Esther still remembered that hot confrontation, almost as if it had happened today.

"How could you do this to me?" she'd demanded of her daughter all those years ago. It was only a week before high school graduation, and she'd just taken Lenore to the doctor and learned the news that her eighteen-year-old daughter was pregnant.

"To *you*?" Lenore had looked indignant as she slumped down in the passenger seat, arms folded tightly across her chest as if she wanted to shut out the entire world. "What about *me*, Mom? What about *my* life?"

"You should've considered that a few months ago," Esther had shot back at her. "I guess we should just be thankful that you're not showing yet. You can simply graduate as planned, and then we'll tell everyone you're going to tour Europe as a graduation gift." She'd laughed. "But we'll send you out to stay with Aunt Hattie instead. And that way you can just quietly get rid of it out there. No one will be the wiser. And, hopefully, you'll have learned your lesson by the time you get home."

"Get rid of it?" Lenore's expression had been horrified.

"Well, you know what I mean. You'll have an abortion, Lenore. Girls do it all the time. And it's perfectly legal where Aunt Hattie lives. I'm sure she might even know of a good doctor, since her late husband was a physician, you know. It's really quite simple."

"Quite simple?" Lenore had firmly shaken her head. "It might sound quite simple to you, Mother." Lenore called her *Mother* only when she was very angry. "But I refuse to kill another human being just to make my life more comfortable."

"It's not a human being," Esther had assured her daughter. "It's just fetal tissue. And it's easily disposed of."

"Disposed of?" Lenore's voice had gotten louder, and Esther had been thankful to be in the car. "Look, Mother," she'd told her, "I am not the least bit happy to know that I'm pregnant, but like it or not there's another human life involved now. And I am *not* going to just kill it to make everyone feel better." She'd started crying then, turning away from her mother and facing the passenger door. "I couldn't live with myself . . ."

Well, she should've known her daughter might pull something like this. After all, this was the girl who couldn't bear to kill a spider even when it was in the house. No, she would go find a cup, gently scoop it up, then transport it outside to its freedom. This was the girl who had rescued a fallen baby bird and climbed the tree to return it to its nest, nearly breaking her own neck in the process.

"I know this is hard for you, Lenore." Esther had decided to try a more gentle approach. "But maybe you should just trust me with the details for now. Perhaps I can go with you to Aunt Hattie's. We can make it a fun trip if you like. We'll do some shopping and—"

"No." Lenore's normally soft chin had become firm. "I am not going to kill my baby and then go out shopping as my reward. It's just not going to happen, Mom. I don't want to discuss it anymore."

Naturally, Esther hadn't given up. The very next day, she'd stopped by the Planned Parenthood office on campus. She'd discreetly worn dark glasses and had a scarf over her head as she picked up some brochures that explained the simple abortion procedure. She'd left these on the dresser in Lenore's room. Just a subtle hint. And it wouldn't hurt Lenore to read the facts about this simple procedure. She'd even called Hattie and, trusting her sister-in-law's discretion, told her the whole story. Of course, Hattie had been shocked and dismayed to learn of her niece's "promiscuous" behavior, as she had put it, but she'd also promised to keep Lenore at her home as long as needed.

The week before graduation had passed slowly, and Esther had felt that she and Lenore were playing some sort of game as they prepared for and attended various graduation events, both of them pretending that nothing whatsoever was wrong. Naturally, James had been absolutely no help. But then Lenore wasn't his daughter, and Esther had assumed that he was blaming her for her daughter's downfall. As a result, he'd barely spoken to either of them after he'd learned the embarrassing news. And then he'd taken off unexpectedly with the baseball coach to scout some young man with a "fastball in Peoria." He hadn't even attended Lenore's graduation. But that hadn't been such a surprise, considering his stepdaughter's wayward behavior. Esther hadn't held it against him.

It was a couple of days after graduation that the fireworks came out again. Esther had worked it out to take Lenore to Hattie's. They would fly out together the following week on the pretense of a little European vacation. She'd already been telling her friends that this was a plan to surprise her daughter. By the time the two of them returned later in the summer, no one in town would be the wiser. Even James had agreed that it was a good solution to an embarrassing situation. After all, he did have his image to protect.

But when she'd come home from the travel agent's office, airline tickets in hand, she'd discovered Lenore and James engaged in a horrible argument.

"You're a monster!" Lenore had screamed at her stepfather. "You should be thrown into prison and—"

"Listen to reason," he'd said in a loud voice. "You're acting completely foolish, Lenore. Your mother is only trying to help—"

"Help me murder a poor unborn baby?" she'd yelled back. "Clean up this unfortunate mess so the important Dr. Daniels can get back to his life without anyone knowing—"

"Lenore!" Esther had stormed in and scolded her daughter. "How dare you speak to your stepfather in that voice? Apologize to him at once."

But Lenore had turned and glared at her mother. It was an expression Esther had never seen on her daughter's face before, and one that would be forever etched in her memory.

"Apologize to him?" Lenore had shrieked. "That horrible monster should be apologizing to me."

"Lenore!" Esther had been completely shocked.

"That's right, Mother!" Lenore had held up her hands. "Go ahead. Take his side. I knew you would." Then she'd stormed off to her room and slammed the door.

Esther had apologized profusely to James, trying to explain how hormones could set a pregnant woman off, assuring him that everything would be okay once she got Lenore off to Hattie's.

But Lenore was gone the next morning. Naturally, Esther had assumed that she'd be back in time to fly out to Hattie's. After she'd had time to cool off a bit and think things through. She'd return to her mother, sorry and contrite and ready to go take care of this unfortunate business. But the following week passed, and then summer passed, and Lenore never came home.

"She's eighteen going on nineteen," James had reassured Esther when she'd suggested they declare her a missing person. "She doesn't have to come home if she doesn't want to. Maybe it's better like this, Esther. Maybe she needs to deal with this in her own way. You know she'll come back in time, when she's ready."

And Esther had listened to him and believed him. But one year followed the next, and Lenore never came home. At one point Esther had even considered hiring a private detective to search for her daughter, but by then pride and bitterness had begun to set in, and she'd decided to see who had more staying power—her or her daughter?

She sighed and leaned back in her desk chair. Now it was too late. Lenore was never coming home again. Death had separated them forever.

"Would you have returned, Lenore?" Esther asked the question aloud. "Would you have come back home to me if you had lived?"

She felt hot tears running down her cheeks again. How many tears had she cried in the past twenty-four hours? She felt like an old sponge that had been squeezed and wrung dry. How could she possibly have any tears left? Her heart ached as if someone had plucked it from her chest and torn it into pieces. How could a mother endure such pain? It was wrong, wrong, wrong to lose a child like this. But it was even more wrong to lose a child who had been estranged.

"I'm so sorry, Lenore," Esther whispered. "I was wrong and stupid. Please forgive me. I'm sorry . . ."

Her nose was dripping now, and she started jerking open her desk drawers in search of a tissue or handkerchief. But she stopped when she saw the small black book Jimmy had given her when his father died. It was lying on top of some papers in a drawer. Oh, she knew it was a Bible. But what on earth he'd thought she'd ever want with something like that was beyond her. She had no use for such religious relics. In fact, she thought she'd thrown the silly thing away long ago. For some reason, she picked it up now. She ran her finger over the gold embossed lettering of her name. Esther Louise Daniels. She supposed it was a sweet gesture on Jimmy's part. But then he'd always been a good boy. Maybe he wasn't her own flesh and blood, but he'd always treated her with such love and loyalty.

She opened the book, fanning through the delicate pages. Suddenly she remembered the last words on Lenore's gravestone. *John 3:16.* She had suspected at the time that they might be indicative of something from the Bible, but being generally unfamiliar with Bibles, the name and numbers meant nothing to her. Yet, for some unexplainable reason, they had remained in her mind. Perhaps this was meant to be a message for her, a message from beyond the grave, from her beloved daughter.

It took Esther a while before she figured things out and actually discovered where she might find this mysterious message. But finally she put her finger on what had to be it. She read the verse silently at first, and then aloud, pondering over each word.

"For God so loved the world that He gave His only begotten Son, that whoever believes in Him should not perish but have everlasting life."

She pulled out the satin ribbon that was sewn into the Bible and slipped it between the pages to mark the verse. Then she closed the book and leaned back in her chair and wondered. Was it really possible to have everlasting life? Could a person actually live forever? And who would want to? Good grief, she was so tired sometimes, like tonight for instance, that she wished she would simply go to sleep and never wake up again. Not ever.

But what if? What if there really was such a thing as everlasting life? A heaven, even? What if her beautiful Lenore was up there right now, perhaps even looking down and watching her? What if there was a way to see her daughter again, to tell her she was so very, very sorry, to tell her that she loved her, had always loved her? Oh, it was almost too much to imagine, too much to hope for. Too good to be true.

Esther pushed herself to her feet, left the Bible on her desk, and slowly made her way back to her bed. But before she went to sleep, she made a feeble attempt at prayer. Just in case God was really there and actually listening.

"I'm a foolish old woman," she said. "I don't even know how to say a proper prayer. But if what I just read in that black book is true, and if there really is some sort of life that goes on after death, then would you please show me what I must do to have it?" She wondered if she should add anything else, then finally said, "Amen."

Of course, she felt skeptical and slightly childish. But, she reminded herself, it might be better to ask the question and be wrong than to never ask at all.

15

Christine slept later than usual the next morning. Feeling guilty, she jerked on her clothes and then jogged through the snow, hurrying to her grandmother's house. It was close to nine, and she hoped she hadn't been missed yet. Although it seemed unlikely.

She knew Felicity was especially counting on her help today. Not only with the party preparations but also with Aunt Hattie's visit. Christine wondered if her grandmother's activities yesterday might have made her more tired than usual. Perhaps she'd decided to sleep in today. Otherwise, she'd probably be upset that Christine was late.

Christine let herself into the house and hurried into the living room.

"About time you got here," Felicity said as she set a cup of coffee next to her mother-in-law. "I already took care of Mom for you."

"I'm sorry," Christine said as she took off her coat. "I didn't sleep very well last night and I woke up late and—"

"Oh, don't worry about it," her grandmother said. "Felicity is just getting herself too worked up over this confounded Christmas party. She thinks everything has to be picture perfect."

"Not perfect," Felicity said as she jotted something down on her ever-growing list. "Just nice."

"Have you had your breakfast yet, Grandmother?" Christine asked.

"No, she hasn't," Felicity said quickly. "And neither has Aunt Hattie. You take care of that, Christine, and I'll make a quick run to the

242

store. Then I want you to start on that list that I've left for you in the kitchen. Okay?"

Christine nodded and went into the kitchen to discover that Felicity had initiated some sort of major baking project that had left bowls, measuring utensils, and various ingredients strewn across every countertop. Christine located her list in the midst of this mess and, blowing off the flour, read the first chore: "Clean the kitchen."

Christine shook her head as she cleared enough space on the counter to begin fixing breakfast. First things first. She found ham in the refrigerator and cut some slices, then poached enough eggs for the two older women as well as herself. If Felicity planned to work her like a dog today, she would at least fortify herself with a good breakfast.

She decided to serve breakfast in the dining room for a change, and searched until she found three placemats that matched the blue willow dishes she'd admired in the cabinet. When the food was done and the table was set, she went out to announce, "Breakfast is served in the dining room," as if she were an English butler.

Her grandmother chuckled. "Does that mean I have to get out of my chair?"

"Do you mind?" Christine asked tentatively. "I thought since we had a guest . . ."

"I think it would be lovely to eat in the dining room," her grandmother said. Christine blinked in surprise but said nothing.

Aunt Hattie came into the room. "We're eating in the dining room?" she asked in a cheerful voice.

"Yes," Esther said. "My granddaughter thinks we should dine in style this morning."

And so they did. Christine had already opened the drapes to reveal the beautiful white blanket that had turned the backyard into a sparkling winter wonderland.

"This is lovely," Aunt Hattie said. "What a nice treat."

"Christine is a good cook too," Esther said as she leaned her crutches against the table and maneuvered herself into the chair at the head of the table. "She used to cook and clean for her father after her mother passed away."

"And your father?" Aunt Hattie asked. "Is he still alive?"

Christine explained about Brazil, and Aunt Hattie smiled. "Oh, that must be wonderful. I've often wished I could go do something like that."

"Why don't you?" Christine asked.

"Don't you think I'd be too old?"

"My father is sixty-four," Christine said. "You can't be much older than that."

Aunt Hattie laughed. "Well, now, aren't you a sweet thing." She winked at Esther. "If you ever get tired of her, just feel free to send her my way."

"Humph." Esther grunted as she reached for a second piece of toast. "You don't need to worry yourself about that, Hattie. Christine and I get along just fine, thank you very much."

Christine tried to keep the chatter light after that. She didn't like the idea of the two women getting riled up about some old offense during the breakfast she had so carefully prepared. Fortunately, they didn't. Perhaps Jimmy had been right after all. Maybe Aunt Hattie had simply come to help bury the hatchet.

She left the two women to their coffee and returned to her task of cleaning the kitchen. She was just finishing up when Felicity came blasting through the back door with a full load of groceries. "There's more in the car," she told Christine.

Christine restrained herself from saluting her drill sergeant aunt. Instead she turned to dry her hands, then went out to the garage to retrieve several more bags of groceries from the open trunk. How many people was Felicity expecting anyway?

"But why do you need to call your lawyer *today*, Mom?" Felicity was asking when Christine came back inside.

Christine set the bags on the counter and paused to listen. Not that she really wanted to eavesdrop, but Felicity's voice sounded more aggravated than usual.

"I have my reasons," Esther said in a sharp voice. "I only asked you to bring me the phone and my phonebook, Felicity. I didn't expect you to put me through the Spanish Inquisition."

"I just wondered," Felicity said. "Hang on, Mom, I'll go get the cordless for you."

Christine continued unloading the groceries from the bags, taking time to sort things a bit and putting the cold things in the refrigerator.

"Is that it?" Felicity asked when she came back into the kitchen.

Christine nodded. "That was everything in your trunk."

"Did you get that box from the backseat too?"

Christine wondered if Felicity thought she was her personal slave. "No, I didn't know there was any—"

"It's the napkins and plates and things," Felicity said. She glanced over her shoulder to the dining room. "Can you get them right now, please?"

So Christine returned to the garage to retrieve the box. She suspected that Felicity wanted to get rid of her for a minute or two, and when she returned she noticed Felicity standing motionless next to the swinging doors that led to the living room, where Grandmother was talking on the phone, presumably to her attorney. It seemed that Felicity was listening. So Christine dropped the cardboard box on the counter with a loud thud that made Felicity jump.

Christine smiled at her aunt. "Anything else?"

Felicity seemed momentarily stumped, but she quickly recovered. "Yes. We need the walks shoveled. There's nearly three inches of snow out there."

This time Christine actually did salute. "Aye-aye, ma'am," she said in what she hoped would be taken as good humor.

Then she headed to the closet for her parka and to search out a snow shovel. She actually felt relieved to escape the house and Felicity's never-ending list of demands. Outside the air was fresh and brisk, and Christine felt that nothing was more invigorating than shoveling snow on a crisp, sunny day. She took her time to carefully clear all the walks and the sidewalk and driveway before she finally went back into the house. She was just hanging her parka back in the hall closet when she heard voices coming from the guest room where Aunt Hattie was staying.

"I just don't get it, Aunt Hattie," said Felicity in an urgent tone.

"What's that, dear?" Aunt Hattie asked in her usual cheerful voice.

"Why Mom suddenly wants to change her will."

"Most likely it's because she knows she has a granddaughter now."

"But why just two days before Christmas?"

"I don't really know, dear. Perhaps she's worried about her health."

"But we don't even know that Christine is really related. I mean, she hasn't done a blood test or anything."

"Oh, Felicity." Aunt Hattie's voice was an odd mix of frustration layered with patience. "We can all see that Christine is Lenore's daughter. I realize that you never knew Lenore, dear, but believe me, we can all see it plain as day. It's right there in Christine's eyes . . . and in her spirit. Oh, the two of them may not look that much alike, but she is definitely Lenore's flesh and blood. I have absolutely no doubt of that."

"Even so," Felicity persisted, "it just doesn't seem fair."

"What's that, dear?"

"That Mom should suddenly change the will. I mean, everything she has, this house and, well, whatever . . . didn't it all come from Jimmy's dad in the first place? The way I understood it was that the Daniels side had all the money."

"All the money . . ." Aunt Hattie sighed.

Christine suddenly felt guilty for listening in. Why, she'd just gotten irritated after catching Felicity doing the same thing with Grandmother's phone conversation. And here she was doing it herself. Just the same, she couldn't seem to make herself leave.

"I know, I know," Felicity continued. "And I know I probably sound petty and greedy to you. But does it seem fair to you that a perfect stranger should walk in and claim to be a relative and then Mom goes off changing her will?"

"Oh, Felicity," Aunt Hattie said.

Suddenly Christine couldn't take it anymore. Not only did she know that it was wrong to eavesdrop, but she realized it was painful too. She turned and walked toward the living room.

"There you are," Esther said as she hobbled toward her.

"Grandmother," Christine said in surprise, hoping that her face didn't look too guilty.

"You look flushed, Christine. Are you all right?"

She forced a smile. "I've been outside shoveling snow."

"Good for you." Her grandmother struggled to balance on her crutches as she fished around in her sweater pocket for something. Then she held out a closed fist as if she had a surprise in her hand. "Something for you."

Christine held out her open hand and waited as her grandmother dropped a small brass key. "What's this?"

Her grandmother glanced up the staircase. "It's the key to Lenore's room. Second door on the left."

Christine nodded.

"I never changed a single thing after she left. I guess I always thought she'd come back someday, and I wanted it to look just the same as before she left. As if I'd been expecting her to come home. I even had a deadbolt lock installed years ago. Just to make sure no one could go in and disturb anything." She shook her head sadly. "I'd go up there with you now if I could just handle those stairs—"

"Oh, no, you don't need to do that."

"Yes. It's probably better that I don't." She sighed. "Anyway, I thought you might want to see her room and her things, you know, perhaps get a better idea of who she was. I suppose we should eventually clear those old things out. It's not as if I want it to become some sort of shrine or anything. I just wanted it to be there for her . . ."

Christine sensed her grandmother's pain. "Maybe I could help box her things up for you, Grandmother."

"Yes, that would be good."

"Maybe I could do it after Christmas. I know our church is always looking for clothing items for our homeless shelter."

"Good." Her grandmother nodded. "I figured you might have some ideas. And then, Christine, once it's all cleared out . . . Well, I thought maybe you'd like to use it for yourself. I mean, it's really a lovely room, with its own bath and a balcony that overlooks the backyard and pool." She smiled in a sad way. "Of course, I don't expect you to live here. Goodness only knows why anyone would want to stay with a decrepit old woman like me. But I want you to know that you're welcome to use that room anytime you like."

"Thank you." Christine was trying to think of adequate words to describe how she would be perfectly happy, thrilled even, to live in this lovely house with her grandmother, but before she could speak her grandmother turned away.

"Now I've got some business to attend to." She started moving down the hall again. "I'll be in James's study if anyone needs me."

Christine wondered why her grandmother still called that room "James's study." Perhaps it was simply out of respect for her deceased husband. Christine had peeked in to admire the dark-paneled room with its floor-to-ceiling bookcases one day. She'd always thought it would be so lovely to have a library like that. Yet the room had such a rigid formality to it, so much so that she hadn't felt quite welcome in there. She'd also noticed that her grandmother seldom used the room and kept her own desk in a corner of the living room. Perhaps she didn't feel quite welcome in there either.

16

Christine began to climb the stairs, careful not to disturb the evergreen garland she'd so painstakingly draped there the other day. She'd been upstairs a few times before. Just to vacuum and dust, and once to look for an old book her grandmother had thought was in one of the bedrooms up there. She'd noticed that closed door with the deadbolt lock and wondered. But she hadn't asked. Even so, she'd figured it had something to do with Lenore.

She slipped the key into the lock and turned it. Feeling like an intruder, she went inside. She stood by the door, looking around and simply taking it all in. It's not that she believed in ghosts or anything like that, but it was as if she could feel a presence or an aura or something almost tangible. She actually held her breath for a moment as she listened to the silence and tried to imagine an eighteen-year-old Lenore moving through this pretty room.

The spacious room had daintily flowered wallpaper in pastel shades of peach and green that ran up the walls above the wainscoting. Old-fashioned framed prints of fairies playing among flowers and pretty girls in gardens adorned the walls. Very feminine and very sweet. The furnishings all matched and were painted a creamy white that had been made to look old. The bed was covered in a patchwork quilt that reminded Christine of a spring garden just beginning to bloom.

She slowly walked over to the large bureau with a mirror on top. This was the only part of the room that seemed to show any clutter or actual use. Here she found all sorts of high school memorabilia—

all covered in a thick layer of dust. A pair of red and gold pom-poms, a yearbook, several awards, graduation announcements, photos of friends, a gold graduation tassel . . . all the bits and pieces of an eighteen-year-old life. But suddenly Christine's eyes stopped when she came across a brochure. For some reason it seemed completely out of place. The words *unwanted pregnancy* seemed to glare at her in bold black and white. Christine picked up the brochure, shook off about two decades worth of accumulated dust, and read a few lines. It seemed to be a clinical explanation of how an abortion was a "safe and efficient way to terminate an unwanted pregnancy." Christine set the brochure back down, placing it exactly where it had been before, the outline clearly visible in the layers of dust. She knew she was the reason the brochure was on the bureau.

So her birth mother had actually considered an abortion. Christine's hand went up to her throat and her chest tightened as the word *unwanted* seemed to echo through her entire being. Suddenly she realized that she had been and still was a great inconvenience to this family. She considered Felicity's words just moments ago; her attitude toward Christine had seemed to reflect this same attitude. And now as Christine stood there—in her dead birth mother's room, in her grandmother's house, among people who were virtually strangers to her—it seemed quite obvious. Everything about this was all wrong. Why had she even come here in the first place? What was her motive? And why had she forced her way into a world where she clearly did not fit in? A world where she hadn't even been wanted. Not then. Not now.

She started for the door, ready to run, escape from this place. But then she paused. She took a deep breath and attempted to calm and steady herself. Perhaps she was overreacting. And, certainly, she'd been through a lot during the past few weeks. Why not give herself some time to sort this all out? And even if Lenore had been considering an abortion, there obviously had been something that influenced her to change her mind. Christine was here, after all. That proved something.

Christine knew that *something* had caused Lenore to run away from her family home and then to carry her "unwanted" baby to full term. But perhaps that was also what had caused her death in the end. Perhaps if she'd stayed home with her family and gotten the abortion described in that brochure, perhaps Lenore would still be alive today. Not that Christine believed that abortions were right. She pressed her fingers against her forehead and tried to think. But it seemed too much to consider, too hard to understand, too painful, too confusing . . .

"Christine?"

Christine whirled around to see Aunt Hattie standing in the doorway.

Aunt Hattie smiled. "May I come in?"

Christine swallowed and nodded. "Of course."

Aunt Hattie looked around. "It looks just the same in here. Such a pretty room. Lenore picked out everything in here herself, you know. It was while James and Esther were honeymooning in the Bahamas. I stayed here at the house with Lenore while the newlyweds were gone. Lenore was only fifteen at the time, but James had given her permission to decorate the room however she liked. 'Spare no expense,' he'd told her right before the two of them took off." Aunt Hattie sighed happily.

Christine nodded, trying to catch some of the old woman's enthusiasm. "That must've been fun for her."

Aunt Hattie frowned. "I suppose. But it wasn't long before Lenore discovered that money isn't everything."

Christine nodded but said nothing.

"Mind if I sit down?" Aunt Hattie nodded to a white wooden rocking chair next to the bed.

"Sure. But you might want to dust it off first."

But before she sat down Aunt Hattie closed the bedroom door. Then she went over and sat down on the chair without bothering about the dust. Her expression had become troubled, but she didn't say anything. Instead she sat there for what seemed like several minutes, just looking at Christine as if she was studying her. Or perhaps trying to figure her out. Christine felt uncomfortable and wondered again why she had tried to force her way into this family. Why didn't she just leave?

251

Finally Christine couldn't take any more silence. "Is something wrong?" she asked. She sat down on the edge of the bed, directly across from Aunt Hattie, and waited.

"Well, that depends on how you look at it," she said.

Christine suspected this had to do with Felicity. Perhaps she had asked Aunt Hattie to speak to Christine today. Maybe they were going to ask her to get a blood test. Or demand to know why she was here. Or perhaps they wanted to ask her to leave. Christine simply waited.

"I have something to tell you that I feel you have the right to know." She sighed. "But this isn't easy for me."

Christine looked down at her hands folded neatly in her lap, Sunday school hands, her mother used to say, and she continued to wait. Whatever it was, she wished Aunt Hattie would just spit it out. Get it over with.

"As you know, dear, Esther's second husband, James, was my little brother. He was only four years younger than me, but I always babied him as if I were much older. You see, our parents were very busy people. They were quite wealthy, and, as a result, they were always caught up in every social cause and function, and, well, we children were left to our own a lot. I suppose I became something of a mother hen to James. We were very close."

Christine looked curiously at Aunt Hattie. What did any of this have to do with her? But still she didn't say anything. Just waited for the old woman to continue.

"I'm sure you're wondering where I'm going with my little story." Aunt Hattie attempted a meek smile. "Well, as you can imagine, Esther, your grandmother, was very upset when Lenore became pregnant. Her plan was to send her to me for a while so that Lenore could have an abortion and then get on with her life."

Christine nodded. "I saw the brochure on Lenore's dresser." She swallowed. "It's kind of hard to think about your birth mother wanting to—well, you know—abort you."

"Oh, no, no, no. Lenore didn't want an abortion at all. That was all Esther's idea. She felt it was a neat way to clean this whole mess up. Personally, I didn't much care for the idea myself, but then I knew enough to keep quiet."

252

"*Grandmother* wanted Lenore to have an abortion?"

"That's right. She was worried about James's reputation at the college. He was being considered for presidency at this time. And she didn't want anything to hurt his chances."

"Oh." Christine knew this made sense, but it still cut deeply to think that her own grandmother had wanted her life "terminated," as the brochure put it.

"Anyway, all this became moot when Lenore disappeared."

Christine nodded.

"But then something happened . . . ," she continued slowly, as if she wasn't sure how to say whatever it was she wanted to say, "shortly before my brother James died several years ago. Perhaps you've heard by now that he'd been diagnosed with an unusual form of cancer and given less than six months to live . . . Well, it was during that time that he wrote me several letters. At first I thought my little brother was losing his mind due to his terminal illness and the heavy pain medications, because the letters made absolutely no sense whatsoever to me. They were filled with remorse and regret and guilt. And yet, in my opinion, this was a man who had led an exemplary life. It made no sense."

Christine felt like she was getting an informational, not to mention emotional, overload today, and she just wished Aunt Hattie would get to the point. If there was a point. And right now she wasn't too sure.

Aunt Hattie reached in her pocket to remove a pink linen handkerchief with lace trim. "Then the final letter came . . . and in this particular letter James confessed that he'd been the one responsible for Lenore's pregnancy, which resulted in her subsequent disappearance. And he felt certain that his illness was his punishment for this transgression, and he wanted to tell Esther the truth, but he simply couldn't do it. Oh, believe me, it was a very, very sad letter indeed."

Christine just stared at her, too stunned to speak or respond. In fact, she felt her lips growing numb and wondered if she might actually be having some sort of stroke or seizure, although she knew that was probably ridiculous and highly unlikely. But how could she possibly have heard what she thought she'd just heard? Or maybe she'd simply misunderstood. "Wh—what?" she managed to stutter.

"I know it's shocking, dear, but I felt you had the right to know."

"What are you saying?" Christine winced at the words that were about to come from her mouth. "Are you saying that Lenore's stepfather is my birth father?"

Aunt Hattie nodded sadly, then dabbed her moist eyes with the corner of her handkerchief. "I'm sorry, dear, but that's what my brother wrote in his letter."

Christine's stomach twisted and turned, and she felt as if she was going to be sick. How could this be? It was so wrong. So unfair. Not only had this poor girl been judged and misunderstood by her own mother, but she'd been sexually abused by her stepfather as well. It was too painful and hideous to even think about. Christine longed to purge this tale from her mind and to run from this horrible house where such dirty little secrets had been hidden for so many years. What was wrong with these people?

"Oh, I know it's disturbing to hear this, dear. But I think it's best to just get these things out in the open and then move on. James fully admitted his guilt in his last letter to me. Yes, he admitted that he had raped his stepdaughter. And, of course, it was wrong. But you must keep this in perspective, dear. He'd been under enormous stress at work, and Esther had taken off to visit her sick mother and had been gone for weeks."

Christine listened to Aunt Hattie going on and on about how it had been spring break and how "poor James" had been doing some very heavy drinking and missing his wife. As if that excused such inexcusable behavior!

"Apparently the weather had been nice that week," Aunt Hattie rambled as if she was telling a bedtime story, "and Lenore had been swimming in the pool with her friends, and walking around the house in a very provocative bikini. Oh, I know that's no excuse, dear." She pressed her lips together, and Christine controlled herself from saying something very regrettable. *Just get this over with*, she was thinking. *Tell your story and be done with it!*

Finally Aunt Hattie continued. "There's really no easy way to understand these things, dear, but James admitted he was so intoxicated that he barely remembered what had happened that day. He wrote that Lenore had confronted him with it later, when she'd discovered she was pregnant, and that they'd gotten into quite an argument. Naturally, James tried to make himself believe that her accusations weren't true. Maybe he'd even managed to convince himself that it wasn't true over time. But I think that beneath it all, he always knew he'd done it. He knew he'd raped Lenore."

"That's so disgusting." Christine grimaced and tightened her fists. "That's like . . . like *incest*."

Aunt Hattie firmly shook her head. "No, dear, it's not actually incest since they weren't blood relatives."

"Well, my father isn't a blood relative either," Christine said hotly. "But if he ever did that to me—" She shuddered at what she knew was an impossibility. "Ugh, that would be just the same as incest to me."

"I know, I know. It's a horrible thing to hear. And if it makes you feel any better, James was completely heartbroken with regret over it. You can read his letters if you like. He would've done anything to turn back the clock and erase that awful day. And I have a feeling that it really did contribute to his illness and his death in the end."

"And Lenore's death too." Christine shook her head. "What a stupid, stupid waste."

"Not completely," Aunt Hattie said with a hopeful smile. "At least there's you."

Christine felt a large lump filling her throat now, making it hard to breathe, let alone respond. It was one thing to be an illegitimate child, an unwanted pregnancy, an embarrassing inconvenience. Although, in fact, she was still grappling with those unkind labels. But it was something entirely different to be the product of a violent crime, the result of rape that was practically incestuous. How would she ever reconcile herself to something like this? Suddenly she wanted her father more than ever. She wanted to pour out her troubles to him and have him comfort her and then just make everything go away.

"I've got to go." She quickly stood.

255

"Oh, I hope I didn't upset you, dear," Aunt Hattie said. "I only wanted you to know the truth. You seem like such a sensible girl to me. I thought you could handle it. Of course, I plan to tell Esther too, but I wanted to tell you first. I felt you had a right to know. You see, I tried to tell Esther once before and, well, it caused quite a scene."

"At the funeral?"

"Yes. But I think it's important that she knows and accepts the truth now that you're here. And, actually, once you adjust yourself to everything, well, it's not so bad, really."

Aunt Hattie stood and held her arms open wide as if she were expecting a big hug. But Christine was still too stunned to respond. She simply backed away.

"I've got—got to go," she said for the second time as she made her way to the door. "I'm—I'm sorry."

She dashed down the stairs, carelessly tearing a strip of garland loose on her way. She opened the closet and grabbed her parka, then shot out the front door without even closing it behind her. She could hear Felicity calling after her, probably wanting her to stuff a turkey or bake a pie or hang some mistletoe, but Christine was finished with all that Christmas nonsense now. More than that, she wanted to be finished with this crazy family as well.

17

Esther sat and stared blankly at the old letters splayed across James's normally orderly desktop. They looked almost as if the wind had blown them in. Or Hurricane Hattie. She should've known better than to let that crazy old woman into her home. Good grief, hadn't Hattie always been the bearer of bad news?

Oh yes, the letters appeared to have been written in James's handwriting, perhaps not as neatly as his usual smooth and controlled hand, but that was most likely due to his illness or the medications, and, of course, there'd been stress. And there was no doubt they'd been written on his own personal stationery embossed with his own initials, JD. And, of course, he wouldn't have used the college letterhead that he normally reserved for official work correspondence. And, most likely, he'd sat right here, right in this big leather chair, when he'd composed them.

But was the content really true? Poor James had endured some heavy pain medications during the last few months of his life. Perhaps those drugs had affected his mind. Maybe he'd even been hallucinating. These were the excuses she'd given Hattie shortly before she'd closed the door and barricaded herself in James's den with the sternest instructions: "I do not wish to be disturbed."

Once the door was locked and she was alone, she'd sat there and read and reread each letter until she'd nearly memorized each and every painful word. And now, despite her own earlier misgivings and doubts, she realized that the letters relayed the truth. James had indeed raped her only daughter. Oh, it was difficult to form those words in her mind. It sounded so crude and base and immoral. Not at all like the man she'd been happily married to for fifteen years. Just the same, she knew it was true.

Perhaps she'd always known. At least deep down in some hidden corner of her mother's heart. After all, hadn't Lenore tried to tell her without actually saying the words? But mired in her own foolish pride and stubbornness, Esther had refused to listen to her own daughter.

She leaned back into the chair and closed her eyes. Oh, the stupid and senseless messes people make of their lives. One mess leads smack into another and then another and another. It made her weary just thinking of it. It was like the redundancy of the seaside, one wave tumbling into the next. She had always grown tired of the sound of the ocean after a few days. James had never understood this. Maybe it was just her, since most people seemed to love the sound of the ocean, but the endless pounding of wave after wave after wave had always worn on her nerves. Just the way this whole nasty business with James was wearing on her now. His guilt only added more layers to her own guilt, making her feel worse than ever. And just when she'd been hoping for some resolution too. Oh, when would the hurting ever cease?

She looked at the photograph of James that she kept on his desk. It was taken shortly after he'd been selected as the university president. Such a proud day that had been. In fact, it would've been perfect except for the fact that Lenore was missing. She studied his smile and wondered how he'd really felt that day. Was he pleased with himself for the way he'd managed to conceal such a hideous offense? Or was he smiling like that simply to hide the shame?

Oh, she'd always known that James Daniels was a rather self-indulgent man. But then he'd been raised that way. Rich from birth, and always given everything, life had been easy come, easy go for him. And he'd always been the golden boy—the man with the Midas touch. Everyone who knew him had respected him. Even Lenore.

Esther choked back a sob as she remembered the evening, almost a year after she and James had married, when Lenore had come downstairs to tell them good night. Wearing flannel pajamas and a freshly scrubbed face, she'd said, "I don't know how to say this . . ." Lenore had paused then as if this was something very important to her. "But I'm really glad that you guys are married. I know I wasn't so excited at first because I didn't really think anyone could replace my daddy. But I think James is the next best thing, and if it's okay, I'd like to start calling you Dad." Well, James had jumped up from his chair and hugged her, saying that of course she could call him Dad and that he'd be proud to have her for his own daughter. It was a tender moment then, but it burned like hellfire now.

"That beast!" Esther said as she pounded her fist on his desk. "That abominable monster!" She stood up, shaking her fist in the air. "How could you, James Allen Daniels? How dare you?" She hobbled around the desk, ignoring the pain of her throbbing ankle as it knocked against the leg of the chair. With angry sobs, she reached for his shining brass football trophy, the one he'd won in college, and then she threw it to the floor. Like a madwoman, she clung to the bookshelves and struggled her way around his office, taking every single item he'd been proud of, every award and honor he'd ever received, and one by one, she smashed them to the floor. Finally she took his photo, held it high above her head, and brought it down with a loud crash that sent glass flying across the desk. "You demon!"

"What's going on?" Felicity demanded as she loudly knocked on the door. "Are you okay, Mom?"

"I'm fine!" Esther shouted. "Perfectly fine. Just leave me alone!"

Finally, exhausted and in pain from her ankle, Esther collapsed onto the leather couch by the window and just sobbed. *Why, why, why?*

When she awoke, the room had grown dark and it took her a moment to remember where she was, but she thought she heard someone knocking on the door again. "Who is it?" she asked in a voice that sounded like an ancient toad.

"It's me," said an apologetic voice. But before Esther could get up, a key turned in the lock, the door opened, and the light came on. And there stood Hattie looking around the room with an expression of horror. "My word, Esther, whatever has happened in here?"

Esther sat up and rubbed her eyes. "A little temper tantrum."

"Do you feel better now?" Hattie asked with what seemed genuine concern.

"As a matter of fact, I do." Esther looked at the mess, then just shook her head. "Can you hand me my crutches, Hattie?"

Hattie carefully picked her way through the broken glass and debris to retrieve the crutches, then leaned them against the couch beside Esther. "I don't blame you, Esther," she said as she sat down beside her. "You know that James was my only brother and that I loved him dearly, but, believe me, I wanted to kill him myself when I read that last letter."

Esther blinked, then looked at her sister-in-law. "Really?"

Hattie nodded. "Yes, if he hadn't been terminally ill, I might have."

Esther shook her head again.

"And if he hadn't been in such bad shape, I probably wouldn't have forgiven him either."

"But you did?"

She sighed. "I did. It's hard to deny mercy to a dying man. In the end I actually felt rather sorry for him. Oh, I couldn't excuse his behavior, there's no excuse for that. But I do think it's what killed him. I believe the guilt was eating him alive and the cancer was simply his body's way of surrendering to it."

"He said something like that in his letters."

"Poor man."

"Poor Lenore," Esther said.

Hattie patted Esther's hand. "Yes, poor, dear Lenore. She was such a sweet angel of a girl. She certainly didn't deserve that kind of treatment."

"No one does," Esther said sadly.

"Did I ever tell you that your girl won my heart right from the start?" Hattie said. "Why, I still remember the first day I met her, just a few days before the wedding, and she gave me the sweetest little tour of this house. Well, I took her into my heart as if she were my very own niece that very day. She was precious, Esther."

Esther started choking up again. "I—I know."

"And my, but she loved you. I remember how she was slightly

brokenhearted after the two of you left for your honeymoon. Oh, but she missed her mommy."

"Did she?"

"My, yes. I did everything I could think of to cheer her up, including driving to every furniture store in the county until we found the bedroom set of her dreams to distract her."

"You were a good aunt to her, Hattie."

"Well, thank you."

"I feel so guilty," Esther said. "Lenore tried to tell me it was James, but I just wouldn't listen. I told myself she was simply trying to blame us for her making bad choices and getting into trouble. But, beneath it all, I think I suspected something was wrong. Still, it was too horrible to actually believe. I mean, how could he do—" She shook her head as the words choked inside her.

Hattie wrapped her short arms around Esther and squeezed tightly. "I know, I know," she said. "It just makes no sense at all. But life is like that sometimes, Esther. And like I told Christine earlier, we can at least be thankful that we have her now. I think she's our blessing in disguise in this whole unfortunate affair."

"Christine," Esther said suddenly. "She knows about this?"

Hattie nodded. "It seemed only fair to tell her. And since James had written the letter to me, and I am, after all, her blood relative, her aunt, I thought it best I tell her. I figured you'd be enduring a pain all your own today."

Esther nodded. "Yes, perhaps you're right about that. But how did she take the news? Was she shocked or upset?"

"Yes. I think it was unsettling for her. She left here in a hurry." Then Hattie smiled. "But don't worry, she's young. The young have a way of bouncing back from these sorts of things. She probably just needs some time to sort it out."

Esther frowned. "I'm not so sure. She's so much like Lenore. She has a very tender heart, and this might be very disturbing to her."

"Maybe you're right. Should you give her a call and see how she's doing?"

"Yes. That's what I'll do." Esther started to stand.

"Wait," Hattie said as she bent over to pick up the dented football

261

trophy and set it on the side table. "Let me clear you a safe path first. In fact, why don't you go call from another room while I straighten this place up a bit?"

"Oh, you don't need to—"

"Nonsense, dear. I want to."

So Esther hobbled out to the living room and sat down at her desk to search for Christine's number. Finally she found it and dialed. She glanced at her watch as the phone rang several times. It was almost six o'clock and no one was answering. Perhaps Christine had gone out with friends tonight. Maybe to some holiday party. The girl was certainly entitled to her own activities. Esther considered leaving a message, then, unsure of what to say, she simply hung up. Maybe Hattie was right. Maybe the poor girl just needed some time and space to get over this thing. Give her time. Surely, she'd be back by tomorrow.

"Felicity?" Esther called, thinking her daughter-in-law must still be around, probably off in the kitchen fussing with some fruitcake or appetizers for her infernal Christmas party, which, more than ever, Esther wished they could cancel now. But, to her surprise, no one answered, and Esther decided that Felicity must've finally gone home to her husband and children. Well, that was for the best.

Esther had just gotten to her feet and was about to go and see if she could stir up something for her and Hattie to eat for supper when it hit her. If Christine was James's daughter, that meant that she was Jimmy's half sister. Suddenly she realized she had a responsibility to tell him this news. She sat back down and dialed his number, and, thankfully, he answered the phone. She didn't think she could bear to have one more conversation with Felicity today!

"Hello, Jimmy," she said in an uncertain voice. "I have some news for you, but now I'm wondering if I shouldn't tell you face to face."

"Is something wrong, Mom?" His voice sounded concerned. "Felicity said you were acting a bit odd today."

"Not exactly wrong," she told him. "But it is something important. Are you kids in the middle of dinner right now?"

"Actually, I already fed the kids, and Felicity and I were just thinking of sending out for Chinese."

"Well, how about if you order enough for Hattie and me, my treat, of course."

"Sounds great. I felt bad that we didn't get to take Aunt Hattie out for dinner yesterday."

"I'm sure she'll enjoy it tonight just as much."

"How about Christine? Should I bring some for her too?"

"No, she's not here."

"Okay. I'll call it in now, and it'll probably be about seven thirty by the time we pick it up and get there. Is that all right?"

"That'll be fine." Esther hung up the phone and took in a slow breath. She hoped it would be fine. More likely than not, it would turn into a total mess.

18

Hattie and Esther had just finished setting the dining room table, complete with china, silver, cloth napkins, and even candles, which was Hattie's idea, when Jimmy and Felicity arrived with several white bags of food.

"That smells yummy," Hattie said as the two younger people arranged the little white cartons in the center of the table.

"Where are the kids?" Esther asked as she sat down at the head of the table, her usual position.

"My sister took them to a musical at her church," Felicity said.

Esther nodded. That was convenient, since she wasn't quite sure how to make kids understand what she had to say tonight.

The four of them made casual chitchat throughout dinner, but Esther could tell that Felicity was smoldering with curiosity. Esther wondered what Jimmy had told her, if anything. Her guess was that Felicity would be assuming this had to do with the revisions to her will, since she knew her daughter-in-law had been hovering around her for much of the day, most likely trying to eavesdrop on her conversation with her attorney. But all that would have to come later, when Christine was here too.

Jimmy leaned back in his chair and patted what was beginning to look like a slight paunch on his belly. "Mmm, that was good. Thanks, Mom."

Felicity sat straighter in her chair now, a forced smile gracing her pretty pink lips. "Jimmy said you have something to tell us."

Esther glanced at Hattie, who nodded as if to encourage her to begin. "Well, it's something of a long story that I'd prefer to tell in a slightly shorter version."

"Go ahead and shoot," Jimmy said.

"This won't be easy to hear," she began, "and, believe me, it's not easy to tell." She had decided to start this off gently, since James was Jimmy's father. So she began by explaining how James had been under a lot of stress twenty years ago, about how he'd been drinking too much, and so on. But finally she could tell by their bewildered faces that she might as well just cut to the chase.

"What I'm trying to say is that James . . . uh, well, James . . ." She cleared her throat and took a deep breath. "James raped my daughter, Lenore."

"What?" Jimmy just about leaped from his chair. "What are you saying?" He turned and looked at Hattie with wide eyes. "Is this true, Aunt Hattie?"

She nodded sadly. "I'm sorry to say that it is. I've known about this for years. I tried to tell Esther at James's funeral, but she just—"

"That's what that was about?" Jimmy's eyes were bright, and his face was flushed with emotion.

Esther felt a wave of pity for her stepson. "I'm sorry, Jimmy. Believe me, we've all been hurt by this."

"Not nearly as much as poor Lenore," Hattie said.

"How do you know this is true?" Felicity demanded in an ice-cold voice. "I mean, how dare you go about making these kinds of serious accusations against a man who's not even here to defend himself?" She pointed at Hattie. "You, his own sister?" And then she pointed at Esther. "And his widow?" She shook her head. "How dare you?" She stood up and started to cry. "And right before Christmas too. I think you just want to ruin Christmas, and my—my party. I think you are both—both—evil!" She ran from the room sobbing.

"Do you want to go to her?" Esther asked Jimmy in a weary voice.

He just shook his head and slowly exhaled. "She'll get over it."

"Now, I feel absolutely terrible to have brought this sad news with me," Hattie said. "It wasn't my intention at all, but when I learned about Christine being Lenore's daughter, well, I just thought it was the right thing to do." She frowned. "Unfortunately, I hadn't really thought about it being Christmas and all. It does seem like bad timing on my part. I hope Felicity can forgive me."

"You were right to tell us this, Hattie," Esther said. "Christmas or not, this wasn't a secret to keep hidden."

Jimmy was still shaking his head, but now tears were streaming down his cheeks. "I just can't—can't believe that my dad would do something—something so—so horrible like that."

Esther nodded and then reached for his hand. "I know how you feel, Jimmy. This afternoon I was a complete crazy woman. Why, you should've seen me. I was breaking things and throwing things and—"

"Really?" Jimmy studied his stepmother more closely.

"It's true," Hattie said. "I only just finished cleaning it up, but the wreckage she left behind was something to behold."

"I feel like I'd like to break something too," Jimmy said in a flat voice.

"Be my guest," Esther said calmly. "Anything in here you'd like to take your hand to? Or maybe there's something left in the den that wasn't broken."

He sighed and looked down at his plate, one of the blue willow plates from her side of the family. Esther braced herself, afraid he was going to pick it up and throw it. And from where he was sitting and with his kind of arm, he could probably take out one of the French doors across from them. She prepared herself for a loud crash.

But he didn't throw it. "I know I have to forgive him," he finally said. "But at the moment, I just don't feel much like it. If he were here right now, I'd probably really let him have it. I feel like everything I ever believed about him has suddenly become a big, fat, ugly lie."

"If it helps," Hattie said in a gentle voice, "James was extremely sorry for what happened. Esther has all the letters he wrote to me during that time, shortly before he died . . . He confessed to everything in those letters, and he was very remorseful. Maybe you should read them too, Jimmy. It might help you understand better. Do you mind, Esther?"

"Not at all. I think it's a good idea. They're probably still on his desk."

Hattie left to go get them, and Jimmy leaned back in his chair. "I feel like somebody just knocked the wind out of me, Mom. Like I can't quite catch my breath."

"I know. Believe me, I know."

"Does Christine know about this yet?"

"Hattie told her."

"How did she take it?"

"She was understandably upset."

"Maybe that's why she left the house early today. Felicity was complaining about that tonight. She thought Christine was just being flaky."

"*Flaky* is not a word I would use to describe your half sister."

Jimmy's eyes opened wide. "You're absolutely right, Mom. Wow, I hadn't even thought of it like that. This *would* make her my half sister." He almost smiled. "Well, that's pretty cool."

Esther felt a small wave of relief.

"What's pretty cool?" Felicity snapped as she stepped back into the room, her eyes still red and swollen from crying.

"Christine is my half sister," Jimmy said with genuine enthusiasm. "I knew there was something familiar about that girl. She felt like family to me." Now he was grinning. "That means she's Jamie and Casey's aunt. Man, that's so cool."

"Oh, Jimmy!" Felicity sank back into her chair, folded her arms across her chest, and scowled at him. "How do we even know this is true? I mean, Christine waltzes in here out of nowhere, and then she starts making all these claims and painting your dad out to be some sort of pervert who raped—"

"Felicity!" Esther felt her nostrils flare in anger, an unattractive habit she normally tried to avoid. "That is enough!" she said in her sternest voice. "You obviously don't have your facts straight about any of this."

"That's right, Felice," Jimmy said more gently. "Aunt Hattie has letters from Dad, confessing the whole thing to her."

"And here they are." Aunt Hattie set the bundle in front of Jimmy.

"Are you sure they're authentic?" Felicity asked in a small voice.

"Of course," Hattie said, slightly affronted. "Do you think I'd make something like this up about my own beloved brother? It was hard enough for me to know about this personally. Can you imagine how I struggled before I decided to tell the rest of you?"

"But the good news is that this makes Christine my half sister," Jimmy said. "And she's your niece, Aunt Hattie."

Hattie smiled. "Yes, I know. I'm so pleased."

"And my granddaughter," Esther said. "That is, if she hasn't given up on the bunch of us for jerking her around like this. Poor girl. She probably thinks she's suddenly landed in the loony family."

"Well, hopefully, we can make it up to her tomorrow," Hattie said.

"This will be her first Christmas with us," Jimmy said. "Our family is growing."

"So are we still on for the party?" Felicity asked in a tired voice. "Not that I really care so much anymore. Fact is, I wish I'd never agreed to this party in the first place. At the rate we're going, the whole thing will probably be a total disaster anyway."

"It's going to be okay, Felice," Jimmy reassured her.

"Yeah, right." She looked unconvinced. "Well, maybe we can stand around the Christmas tree and announce that the late great James Daniels was really a fraud who raped his stepdaughter."

"Felicity!" Jimmy's eyes narrowed, and Esther suspected that his wife had pushed it too far even for him this time. "That's totally uncalled for."

"Well, you people are so into making the truth known. Maybe everyone in town should know about this nasty little business. Maybe we should take out an ad—"

"Knock it off!" Jimmy stood. "I think we should go now. I'm sorry, Mom, Aunt Hattie. Felicity spoke way out of line just now."

"Don't apologize for me." Felicity stood up and reached for her coat slung over the back of her chair. "I'm not a child, you know."

"Then stop acting like one."

She looked at Jimmy as if he'd slapped her, and then she hurried from the room.

"Thanks for dinner," Jimmy said briskly. He jerked his arms into his jacket and shook his head. "Hopefully, Felicity and I can get this smoothed over before we ruin the holidays completely."

"Hopefully," Esther said without getting up.

"Good-night," Hattie said, ever cheerful. "Drive safely on the snow."

Esther exhaled loudly after the front door closed. "Well."

"Now, that didn't go too badly," Hattie said with a funny little grin.

Esther looked at her sister-in-law in wonder, and then they both laughed.

"I just hope Christine is all right," Esther said as she refolded her napkin and set it beside the plate.

"Well, I know I'll be saying a special prayer for that sweet little girl tonight."

Esther felt her brows lift slightly. "Really, Hattie? You've actually become a praying woman?"

She smiled. "Indeed, I have."

"Does this mean you believe in God and go to church and do all those churchy things that churchy people do?"

"I do believe in God, Esther, and I do go to church when I have a notion to. And I do pray and even read my Bible on occasion. But I wouldn't necessarily classify myself as a churchy person. I suppose it truly is hard to teach an old dog new tricks."

"So what on earth brought all this on?" Esther knew her voice sounded skeptical, perhaps even harsh, but she couldn't help herself. "I remember when you and Hal used to carouse and drink and gamble in Vegas with the best of them."

Hattie winked at her. "I figured at my age it was best to cover all my bets regarding the hereafter. I decided if God really was up there, and if he really did care about old Hattie, well, I thought it might be wise for old Hattie to give him a fair shot. And you know what, I think he does."

Esther considered this. "Very interesting, Hattie."

"You should give it some thought yourself, Esther. No offense, but you aren't getting any younger either."

"Thanks a lot."

Hattie's lips pressed together, and she grew quiet as if she were contemplating something. "There's another thing, Esther."

"Oh, no . . ." Esther held up her hands. "If it's more bad news about James, well, you better just sit on it for the time being. I'm not sure if I can handle anything else—"

"No, no, nothing like that. It's not anything bad. But you're right, it is about James. It's something he said to me on the phone about a week or so before he passed away."

Esther took in a quick breath, braced herself, and waited for Hattie to continue.

"At the time I wasn't too sure what to think. To be honest, I was still quite irked with him. Oh, I'd forgiven him all right, how could I not? But I secretly resented that he'd dumped this whole nasty business into my lap. It reminded me of when we were kids and he'd do something wrong and old Hattie would take the blame. But that evening when he called me, he told me that he'd made his peace with God. Now, I wasn't too sure what he meant by that. At that time in my life, I hadn't given God a second thought. But all these years later, I like to believe he meant that he'd received God's forgiveness. Although this is partial speculation on my part. But those were his words. He said, 'Don't worry about me, Hattie. I've made my peace with God.' And not long after that he died."

"Oh." Esther looked at the messy table before them and sighed. "Let's just leave this until tomorrow. I'm completely exhausted. I feel like I could sleep for a week."

"You and me both, Esther."

Esther imagined how the two of them must look as they slowly made their way through the semidarkened house. She, old and angular and clumsier than usual as she fumbled along on her crutches, and Hattie, short and round, taking her quick little steps alongside her. What a pair they made.

When Esther finally got herself into bed, she felt completely drained, but as she closed her eyes she thought of Christine and suddenly remembered what Hattie had said about praying for her tonight. Maybe it wouldn't hurt to give it a shot herself. At least she could do it for her granddaughter's sake, since she seemed to take this God thing pretty seriously.

"Well, God . . . ," she began slowly, "I know we're not really on much of a first name basis quite yet . . . I'm not even sure we'll ever be. But if you're up there listening, will you please watch out for my dear granddaughter tonight? Take care of her and bring her back to us safe and sound for Christmas. I'd really appreciate that. Amen."

19

Without bothering to remove her snow-dusted parka, Christine went straight for the phone in her dorm room. Her hands felt shaky as she attempted to dial the correct digits for the long-distance number to the mission station. Thankfully, she got it right the first time. She sighed in relief when a woman with an accent confirmed this on the other end. But when she asked for her father, she felt her heart drop to her snow-encrusted boots.

"I'm sorry," the woman said, "but Mr. Bradley has gone to spend the holidays with the Richards family. Their station is in the jungle, but we can reach your father by radio if it's an emergency."

"No, no . . ." Christine sighed. "It's not an emergency."

"Did you call to wish him a Merry Christmas?"

"Yes," Christine said sadly. "I'm sure he's having a wonderful time."

"Oh yes," the woman said. "Your father is a sweet man. He was taking a lot of goodies out to share with the villagers. He's like a regular Saint Nick."

Despite herself, Christine smiled. "Yes, he is."

"God bless you," the woman said.

Christine hung up the phone and tried to imagine what it would be like to be down in Brazil, where summer was in full bloom right now. As much as she'd looked forward to a white Christmas, she would trade it in a heartbeat just to be down there in the heat and humidity with her dad.

"A regular Saint Nick," she said to herself. And even though it was the middle of the afternoon, she flopped down on her bed in total defeat. "So what would *you* do, Dad, if you were in my shoes right now?" The tears she'd been holding back began to fall freely. Not only for herself, although, to be honest, she was desperately homesick and lonely, more than she had ever been in her life. But mostly she felt sad for her mother—rather, her birth mother—Lenore. To think what that poor girl, a year younger than Christine, had endured during the last year of her life. So unfair and unjust. Christine could hardly even imagine it. It was so wrong!

"How could you let that happen to her, God?" she demanded. "And then to just let her die after all she'd been through? What was the purpose in all that?"

But no answers came, and before long the loneliness and emptiness of the vacated dormitory began to press against her, almost like a physical thing, breathing down her neck in short, chilly breaths. To remain in the isolation of that room for one more moment felt unendurable. So she pulled on her parka and gloves and headed over to her church. She hoped she might catch Pastor Reinhart and ask him some of these perplexing questions. He might not have all the answers, but at least he'd listen.

But when she arrived at the old brick church on Oak Street, she suddenly remembered that they'd opened their doors to offer shelter to the homeless during the holidays. Apparently, they did this every year at Christmastime. There was a homeless shelter downtown and a mission, but those ministries catered mostly to single adults. But the church went out of their way to create a special place where homeless families could gather and feel comfortable for a few days. Of course, Christine had been so distracted with her grandmother's family and all her related problems that she'd completely wiped it from her mind.

"Christine," Beth Maxwell called when Christine had barely reached the office. "What are you doing here?"

"Looking for Pastor Reinhart."

"He's in the kitchen at the moment."

"Thanks."

"Hey," Beth said hopefully, "before you skitter away, what are you doing the rest of the day?"

Christine shrugged. "Not much."

"Well, we're a little shorthanded," Beth said. Then she explained how she had broken the shelter kids into three age groups. "The teens are being treated to a free Christmas shopping spree at the local discount store, followed by a movie. And the middle graders are on their way to the skating rink, but the little kids were supposed to hang out here at the church for craft projects, snacks, and a special Christmas video."

"Sounds good."

"The problem is that Candace Everly was supposed to be in charge of the little kids today, but her own kids just came down with the chicken pox, so she had to stay home. So we could really use your help, if you're willing."

"Sure," Christine said. Actually, she was happy to oblige. The last thing she wanted right now was to return to her ghost-town dorm and then sit around feeling sorry for herself. Instead she spent an amazingly stress-free afternoon with the youngest of the kids. Her biggest worry was whether or not they would run out of sequins and glitter as she helped their sticky little fingers cut and glue pieces of colored felt until they finally resembled Christmas stockings. She was surprised at how the time seemed to fly, and even after her responsibilities with the children were finished, Christine offered to stay on and help with dinner too.

"This is awfully nice of you, Christine," Pastor Reinhart said as she helped clean up afterward.

"Actually, it's kind of selfish," she admitted. "It helps keep my mind off of my own family troubles."

"You want to talk about it?" he asked.

But her problems suddenly seemed small in comparison with the problems of the families her church was trying to serve. She couldn't help but notice how poor they seemed, or how many of the parents' faces looked so apathetic or hopeless. She couldn't imagine how it would feel to be broke and homeless, especially during Christmas. And then to have children depending on them as well. It was so incredibly sad. But at least they had each other. That was something.

She felt reluctant to leave when Beth offered her a lift home. Of course, she knew it would be silly for her to take up one of the precious beds in the church's makeshift shelter, but it seemed almost preferable to returning to her empty dorm. In some ways she wasn't much more than homeless herself. Just the same, she accepted the ride and was thankful not to have to walk through what now appeared to be almost six inches of accumulated snow.

"Are you sure you want to stay by yourself at the dorm during Christmas?" Beth asked for the third time. She'd been incredulous that Christine had chosen to spend her holidays by herself at the dorm. "Really," she assured her. "You know you'd be welcome at my house."

"Thanks," Christine said. "But I'm fine, really. And I plan to come help out at the shelter again tomorrow, and then there's the candlelight service later on. Before I know it, Christmas will be over and done with and winter classes will be starting up again."

"Okay," Beth said. "Guess I'll see you tomorrow, then."

Christine trudged up the steps to her dorm, her tracks the only ones breaking into the most recent layer of snow. Of course, it made no sense to shovel the steps when the dorm was mostly empty. Plus, it was the holidays and the maintenance people were probably enjoying some time off. It also made little sense to run the big furnace at full blast, and a notice had been posted before winter break so that students would be prepared for the cooler temperatures. But it seemed to be getting colder and colder with each passing night.

Christine tried to imagine her dad in a steamy jungle setting, dressed as a jolly old elf and handing out gifts to the surprised indigenous locals and missionary kids. But suddenly all she could think of was poisonous spiders, gigantic snakes, and prowling panthers . . . and to her it seemed more perilous than ever for her sweet and unsuspecting father to be so far from home. She fervently prayed for his safety until she finally fell asleep.

20

Esther peered out the front window again. Long, blue shadows were falling across the snow, and the little white lights had come on and were starting to twinkle with false cheer. "Has anyone heard anything from Christine?" she asked.

"I've left two messages at her dorm," Jimmy said as he set a load of birch logs in the basket next to the fireplace. "Mind if I start this fire up now?"

"Go ahead," Felicity called from the dining room, where Esther had observed her arranging enough food to feed a small army. "We want it going nicely when the guests start to arrive."

"It's warm enough in here already," Esther snapped as she headed back toward her dining room to survey Felicity's latest damages. Felicity might be all gladness and joy today, and she'd even apologized for her thoughtless remarks last night, but Esther still felt certain that young woman was out to sabotage them all.

"Open a window if you're too warm," Felicity called in a voice as sweet as her heavily frosted Santa cookies.

It had grated on Esther's nerves all day—the way her daughter-in-law had waltzed in here as if everything was just fine. Oh, she'd done her little apology, with Jimmy at her elbow as if he'd personally coached her on the drive over. But Esther wasn't convinced. Now she hovered around Felicity, feeling a bit like a vulture on crutches. Scowling from her position in the doorway, she watched as Felicity flitted around the ornately decorated dining room table in her pretty red velvet party dress. *Queen for a day*, Esther thought as she turned in disgust, heading for the solitude of the den, what used to be James's den but was now her only haven in this normally quiet house that had suddenly turned into a three-ring circus. *Well, let them party if they must*, she thought as she closed the door behind her. Let stupid Felicity have her fun!

Oh, she knew she shouldn't take out her anger on poor Felicity. Why, that was like kicking the puppy who'd just chewed up your three-hundred-dollar shoes. What was the point? But Hattie had confessed to Esther during breakfast that morning that she felt fairly certain that Christine had overheard some of Felicity's thoughtless remarks the previous day. And now Esther felt certain that if Felicity had only possessed a little more sense and had treated Christine just a little better, well, maybe Christine would still be here with them today. And she'd told Jimmy as much that morning when he'd delivered the "special" load of firewood—special because it was birch and supposed to be "white and pretty." *Pretty, my foot*, she'd thought. *It's only firewood, for Pete's sake!*

"Christine is a sensible girl," Jimmy had reassured her. "I don't think she'd let something Felicity said upset her. Everyone knows that Felicity sometimes speaks without thinking."

"Sometimes?" Esther felt her left brow arch.

"Oh, Mom, Felicity may have her faults, but she's really not trying to hurt anyone intentionally. And, if it makes you feel any better, she was really very sorry by the time we got home last night. She almost called you, but it was getting pretty late by the time we got the kids to bed."

Be that as it may, Felicity had still done little besides the stilted apology to convince Esther of her contrition. And Esther felt seriously fed up with her daughter-in-law as she sank down into the big leather chair behind James's old desk. She leaned back and looked around her. Hattie had done a good job of cleaning up. And the den actually looked much better with all of James's ridiculous paraphernalia removed. Much more calming and peaceful. She should've done it years ago.

Esther looked at the black desk phone and even picked up the receiver. But then she'd already called that number several times and left at least two, maybe three, messages. Still, she supposed it wouldn't hurt to try again. But she was answered by the same old thing; after four rings the blasted machine came on again.

"You've reached the number of Christine Bradley and Brianna Taylor. Please—" Esther put the receiver back in the cradle with a thud. *Where could that girl be?* As far as Esther knew she didn't have any relatives nearby and all her friends had gone home for the holidays. Perhaps she'd called one of them up, desperate to escape the insanity of the Daniels family, and begged to be included in some festivity. Maybe she was off at some ski lodge, having a good time with friends and drinking hot toddies right now. That's what Esther would've been doing at the same age. Goodness, how many times had she opted for some expensive and scintillating outing with friends over going home to spend time with family? And did she regret it now? Well, of course she did. But not completely.

"Oh, who can figure such things out?" she said to herself. She felt exasperated and agitated and suddenly longed for a cigarette like she hadn't done in years. Oh, she knew it was perfectly ridiculous and would probably make her sick, but she simply felt the need for something to calm her nerves. She began jerking open the drawers to James's desk. Surely, he must've left something behind, since he'd smoked right up to the day he died. Naturally, the drawers were full of all sorts of odd things, and she wished she'd taken the time to dump their contents onto the floor yesterday. Perhaps Hattie would've gotten rid of all that junk too. Not that she wished to turn Hattie into her personal maid. Actually, she was becoming rather fond of her previously estranged sister-in-law. But right now Hattie was having a little nap, refreshing herself before the guests started to arrive, and all Esther wanted was a stupid cigarette!

Of course, Esther knew she might've been wise to have followed Hattie's lead and taken a nap. After all, she had every reason to excuse herself from all of Felicity's hubbub. She could've said, "I'm so sorry, but I'm recovering from a bad sprain and really need my rest." She'd be sorry once the party really got going. The extra people in her home had begun to wear her already frazzled nerves thin.

Good-night, why couldn't she find any darn cigarettes?

"Voila!" she said triumphantly when she finally unearthed a sleek silver case with the initials JD on it. She'd gotten him this for their fifteenth anniversary, shortly before he became ill and was told to give up smoking, which he did not.

The case felt light, and she expected it to be empty as she popped it open, but there, as if appointed by fate, lay one lonely cigarette.

"Ahhh." She picked it up and smelled the pungent, earthy smell of stale tobacco. Then she put it to her lips before she looked around and realized she needed a light. After more digging and hunting, she finally discovered a dusty old book of matches. She blew off the dust and examined the faded photo on the front. Something about that large pink building and palm trees seemed vaguely familiar. Without her reading glasses, she was forced to hold it at arm's length, squinting to read the fine print. *The Hotel Marquise.* Ah, yes, it was where she and James had stayed during their honeymoon in the Bahamas—about twenty-three years ago now. She set the cigarette and matchbook on the surface of the desk, then pulled back her hand as if these items were hot coals. Then, as if mesmerized, she just stared at them.

Is this what life eventually boils down to? A stale cigarette and a dusty book of matches? Two seemingly innocent items that burn you clear to your soul? She pushed herself up from the chair and limped painfully over to the leather sofa. She fell down onto it in a broken heap, clutched a tapestry-covered cushion, and began to sob. "I am nothing but a useless old woman," she moaned. "I have led a foolish and shallow life with nothing to show for it but ashes and dust . . . ashes and dust. Nothing left . . . but ashes and dust."

21

Christine had managed to maintain a brave front for the whole day as she poured all her energy into the homeless shelter. But by that evening, she felt worn and weary, and just slightly beaten. It wasn't the work so much, although she couldn't remember having labored so long or so hard in her life. Being young and healthy, she'd stepped up and volunteered for the hardest task of all, kitchen crew. And not just for a one-meal shift or cleanup or setup; no, she'd stuck her foot in her mouth and volunteered to help out with everything for the entire day. And, naturally, they were happy to have her.

Still, it wasn't the work that had eventually worn her down, but rather her surrounding circumstances. Seeing and interacting with all those homeless families, those children who seemed hungry for not only food but also the slightest speck of attention, those young single mothers with worn-out shoes and empty eyes.

Well, it had finally managed to wear her down, and now that the day was over, her cheeks were tired from smiling and she felt seriously depressed. But perhaps the most shameful part of all this was that she wasn't just depressed over their sad lots in life and how they had nothing, no homes, no money, no means. No, that might actually seem noble or admirable, expected even.

If the truth were told, and she hoped it never would be, Christine was feeling sorry for herself because at least those poor homeless people had fragments of their families around them during Christmas, whereas she felt entirely cut off and alone. And to realize that she was actually feeling jealous of homeless families—now, really, how pathetic was that?

If she hadn't been so tired, so thoroughly down and out, she might've found her situation to be somewhat humorous. She might've imagined herself talking to her dad on the phone after the New Year and telling him the whole embarrassing story, and then they would both laugh and he would promise that they would have a grand Christmas after he came home in two years, or better yet, maybe they could figure out a way to fly her down there for Christmas next year.

But as she slipped into the back pew of the packed church, she felt no joy, no mirth, no Christmas cheer. In fact, she wondered why she'd even bothered to come to the candlelight service at all. Chances were it would only depress her more as she saw families clustered together, sharing candles and smiles and warm embraces. The old man beside her smiled and nodded, then turned his attention back to the pulpit. She didn't recognize him, but she'd been attending this church only a few months and hadn't had a chance to meet everyone.

She tried to pay attention as Pastor Reinhart spoke of the first Christmas, but she found herself drifting in and out. Of course, she'd heard the Christmas message so many times that she knew it by heart. Maybe she was just tired. Maybe she should just go home before she nodded off to sleep and really embarrassed herself.

She stood up and slipped unnoticed out the back of the church and then out the door to the street. But before she turned to walk back to her dorm, she paused to look at the nativity scene that was set up in front of the church. Oh, she'd seen it before and had even admired the painted life-size plywood figures of Mary and Joseph, the shepherds and angels and animals, all propped up beneath the straw-covered roof of a "stable." And they almost looked real in the soft spotlights tonight. Christine studied Mary and the way her sad eyes seemed to gaze fondly at the baby in the manger. Mary had been even younger than Christine when she'd been chosen to bear God's child. A teen mother. *Not so unlike Lenore*, Christine thought. It couldn't have been easy for either of them. Surely, Mary must've had times when she wondered what God was up to. It would've been a challenge to be the mother of God's son, and although she was called "blessed," she certainly must've suffered some too.

Christine knew that Lenore had suffered dearly for the baby she carried as well. To be only eighteen and to stand against her parents, fighting to protect her baby's life—Christine's life. She shuddered. Not so different from Mary in some ways.

Christine pulled on her gloves and began walking toward her dorm. But as she walked she considered her birth mother's life and how it was similar to Mary's. Surely, God's hand had been on Lenore during those hard times. How else would she have been befriended by Christine's loving parents? Oh, Christine knew that God hadn't willed for Lenore to be raped. No, that was just one of those unfortunate circumstances where sin got in the way. But, ultimately, according to Christine's father, Lenore had been happy to give birth, and she'd been pleased and proud of her baby daughter. And although it wasn't easy to give her up, Lenore had entrusted Christine to this kind and generous couple. And Christine's parents had been overjoyed at Lenore's incredible gift of love.

Christine stopped on a corner and looked up at the dark sky. "Thank you, God," she whispered, finally believing that perhaps her life wasn't a mistake after all, that perhaps God was still in control, that he still loved her and wanted the best for her.

She continued to walk, still thinking about young Lenore and her brave decision to keep her baby despite the circumstances. Christine wasn't sure she would be as brave under similar conditions. Suddenly she was flooded with gratitude and respect for her birth mother. Suddenly she wished there was a way she could tell her. She stopped again. "Please, God," she whispered to the night. "Please, tell my mother Lenore I want to say thank you to her too." Christine realized it was probably a foolish prayer, but she meant it with her whole heart. She stood there for a long moment, just silently staring into the almost-black sky, when suddenly she noticed a star breaking through the clouds, as if it was peering down at her, as if it was winking. Oh, she knew it was silly and probably her imagination, but it seemed like a sign. As if Lenore was trying to reassure her that all was well in heaven. "Thank you," Christine breathed.

And then she saw another star, just as bright as the first, popping out right next to the other one. The only two stars she could see in the entire night sky. Suddenly Christine laughed as she imagined her two mothers holding hands in heaven. "And tell my mother Marie I said thank you too," she whispered. She stood there just staring at the pair of twinkling stars, and then suddenly she saw a third star, directly across from the other two, making a perfect triangle. "And, while you're at it, please tell Jesus's mother Mary I said thank you too."

Then, with a lighter heart than she'd had in weeks, Christine walked back to the dorm. She knew that not everything was resolved, and she knew she still had to figure out what her role would be with the Daniels family. But she also knew that things had changed between her and Lenore. She knew that she'd be forever grateful for her birth mother, forever thankful that she'd saved Christine's life. And she owed it to Lenore to do whatever she could for her surviving family.

Christine had barely closed the door to her room before she saw the message light flashing on her answering machine. Hoping it was her dad, she turned it on. "You have seven messages," the electronic voice said. Surprised at the number, she played them all to discover that none were from her dad. But she was relieved, since the only reason she'd hear from him right now would probably be due to an emergency. Besides, three of the messages were from her grandmother, all urging her to come over to the house, to bring her things, and to stay until New Year's. And one message was from Aunt Hattie, saying how much she missed her little niece and to please come back by the house before she had to return home. And two were from Jimmy, saying that he was so happy to learn that she was his half sister and would she please give them a call as soon as she got in. And one was actually from Felicity, an apology of sorts, saying that she hoped Christine hadn't misunderstood her, but that that sometimes happened, and how much the children would love to see her for Christmas.

"Well." Christine picked up the phone and quickly dialed. She waited through several rings until she heard Jimmy's voice over what sounded like a houseful of others.

"Christine!" he boomed. "Merry Christmas! Are you coming over?"

"I could," she began. "If it's not too late."

"Never too late for you. Are you at your dorm right now? How about I pop over and pick you up? I don't like the idea of my little sister walking by herself at night."

So it was settled. Christine hurried to change her clothes. No sense showing up in her soiled kitchen clothes that smelled like green beans and turkey gravy. Then she grabbed the photo album she'd assembled for Grandmother. She wished she'd taken time to do something for the others. Oh well, maybe next year.

Jimmy cheerfully filled her in on all the happenings of the day and the party as they drove. "A lot of Felicity's family and friends are there. And as you can imagine, Mom's been lying low for most of the evening. I think she's been worried about you." He parked the car in the spot still left in the driveway. But the side streets were filled with cars.

"I'm sorry," Christine said. "I've been helping at my church, but I should've called."

"Hey, I don't blame you," he said as they reached the front door. Then suddenly he hugged her. "And just so you know, I'm really glad that you're my sister, Christine. Welcome to the family. Really." Then they walked inside, and he took her coat and nudged her down the hallway. "Your grandmother is in the den," he whispered.

Before anyone noticed her arrival, Christine slipped off to find her. She tapped lightly on the den door, but due to the noise from the party—a boisterous group was attempting to sing "The Twelve Days of Christmas" around the piano—she decided to simply let herself in. And there, sitting behind the big mahogany desk, was her grandmother, head bent down as she held a match in a somewhat shaky hand to light a rather bent cigarette.

"Grandmother?"

She looked up at Christine, her face an odd mixture of simultaneous embarrassment and pleasure. "Oh! You're here," she sputtered through the smoke.

"Yeah." Christine smiled. "Merry Christmas, Grandmother."

She sheepishly held out the cigarette. "I thought I needed this, but . . ."

"Don't let me stop you," Christine said as she sat down in the chair across from the desk, placing the photo album in her lap.

"Do you think smoking is a sin?" her grandmother asked, still holding the cigarette at a distance as if she wasn't quite sure what to do with it.

"I think God's the only one who can determine that," Christine said with a smile.

"Really?" Esther looked at her cigarette with curiosity, then took a tentative puff followed by a short fit of coughing. "Hand me that ashtray, will you?"

Christine reached for the brass dish on the coffee table and set it on the desk, watching as her grandmother snuffed the cigarette out and sighed.

"It was just for old times' sake," Grandmother said, still sputtering. "But I guess my lungs weren't ready for it."

"I have something for you," Christine said. "For old times' sake."

"Really?" Grandmother leaned forward with interest, and Christine slid the photo album across the smooth surface of the desk.

"Sorry, I didn't have time to wrap it."

Esther slowly opened the album, then just stared at the array of photos before her. It was only the first page, and only shots of Christine as a newborn, a rather red and wrinkly looking baby. After what seemed several minutes her grandmother turned to the next page, staring again with equal fascination.

Christine leaned over the desk to see the album more clearly. She wondered if there was something more fascinating than she'd realized. "That was my first birthday," Christine said, pointing to the redheaded infant dressed like an elf in green velvet.

Esther nodded without speaking, and Christine wondered if perhaps this wasn't such a good idea after all. But she sat, waiting patiently while her grandmother slowly worked her way through the book. The last pictures had been taken at Christine's high school graduation, and then there was one of her and her father shortly before he left for Brazil.

"Thank you," Esther said in a low voice.

"I hope it's okay."

Her grandmother looked at her. "Are you kidding? Okay? Why, it's one of the most beautiful gifts I've ever received. Thank you." She flipped back through it again, staring in wonder at the photos, then suddenly looked up. "So you must have a December birthday too."

Christine nodded.

"What day is it?"

Christine never liked to answer this question, but she finally said, "The twenty-fifth."

"Christmas day?"

She nodded. "Yeah. My parents called me their Christmas present."

Her grandmother smiled. "I can understand that." She looked back down at the book. "Now, can you tell me more about what's going on in these pictures?" she asked. "Like where were you when this was taken?"

So for the next hour or so, Christine attempted to commentate on the pictorial tour of her life.

"Hello in there," Jimmy called as he poked his head in the door. "Everything okay?"

"Yes, of course," Esther said. "How's the party going?"

"Nearly everyone has gone home now, except for immediate family."

"Is it that late?" Esther looked at her watch. "Good heavens, it's half past eleven."

"You two care to join us for a cup of peppermint cocoa?"

"Yes," Esther said. "In fact, I have a little announcement to make."

22

After everyone had gathered comfortably in the living room, where a cheerful fire was still snapping in the fireplace, Jimmy brought out a tray of cocoa cups, each one topped with a dollop of whipping cream and garnished with a candy cane.

"Remember who started this tradition?" Jimmy asked as he handed Grandmother a steaming cup.

"Haven't we always done this?" Felicity said as she picked up a cup for herself.

"Well, I never did it myself," Jimmy said as he handed Christine a cup. "Not until Dad married Mom, that is." He handed Aunt Hattie a cup. "But I believe it was Lenore's tradition to have cocoa before bed on Christmas Eve."

"To give you sweet dreams," Grandmother said in a voice full of reflection.

Jimmy sat down next to his wife. "Works for me."

"Too late for them," Aunt Hattie said as she nodded to Jamie and Casey, who were curled up in sleeping bags beneath the Christmas tree.

"It was Jamie's idea to bring the sleeping bags," Jimmy said. "But don't worry, Mom, they don't need to spend the night here."

She waved her hand. "Oh, that's all right, they're welcome to stay if they like."

Jimmy blinked, then Felicity spoke quickly. "No, we have to go over to my mom's in the morning. She's making waffles."

"Good for you," Grandmother said. "Good for Janet." She looked around the room, pausing to look at each face before she continued to speak. "As I told you, I have a little announcement to make tonight. But I didn't want to make it until everyone was here." She looked directly at Christine. "My family isn't very big, but you're all important to me. As you know, I've been in contact with my lawyer regarding my will. He made a draft today, and I will sign it after the holidays." She chuckled. "And be assured, if I should kick the bucket between now and then, the changes I made today will be in effect."

Christine glanced over at Jimmy and Felicity. She could tell by Felicity's creased brow that she was worried. And Christine knew that all this talk about changing the will had been upsetting to her. Suddenly Christine wished that she could just disappear. She had no idea what her grandmother was up to, but she was worried that her own presence had been the catalyst behind it.

"Rather than wait for my timely or untimely demise, I've decided to make my wishes known while I'm still around to make sure no bickering occurs after I'm gone." She turned and looked directly at Felicity. "Because despite what I've said about money all these years, I know as well as anyone that it will never buy you happiness. Just the same, I know that's a whole lot easier to say when money's not an issue." She cleared her throat, then glanced over at Aunt Hattie. "Sorry you have to hear all this again, Hattie."

"That's perfectly all right, dear. You go right ahead."

"So what I have decided to do is to disburse some of your inheritance now," Grandmother said. "Not all of it, mind you. Some things are better left until the end. But I have decided that it makes no sense for an old woman like me to sit on a pile of money while some folks are struggling to make ends meet."

"Oh, Mom," Jimmy began. "You don't need to—"

"You just hush now, Jimmy. You're a good boy, and I love you like my own, but when it comes to money sense you don't always get it." She shook her finger at him, then smiled. "Anyway, as I was saying . . . I want everything to be perfectly clear. I know how easy it is to get confused when families and wealth merge in marriages. I want all my cards laid out on the table. You see, when Christine's mother left home more than twenty years ago, she had a good-size savings account that her father had started for her for college when she was just an infant. This was an account that I continued to add to over the years, hoping that someday she would come home and I would—" She choked slightly, and Aunt Hattie patted her hand.

"Anyway, at first I just wanted to change my will to reflect that this savings is to go to Christine. Because that seems only fair. But that's when I decided that it's usually the very times when kids need money that they don't have it. And that's when I decided to do a little disbursing this Christmas." She held out two envelopes. One she pointed in Christine's direction, the other in Jimmy's. "Well, come on, here you go. Merry Christmas."

Jimmy got up and got his envelope, but Christine felt like she couldn't move. Then Jimmy got hers and handed it to her. "Come on, Christine, don't be upsetting your grandma on Christmas Eve."

"That's right," said Grandmother. "And like I said, that's your inheritance for now. I plan to keep my house and enough to live comfortably on for . . . well, at least until I see those grandchildren grow up." She looked at Christine. "And perhaps see some great-grandchildren from you. In due time, that is. No hurry."

Christine felt her cheeks blushing. Then without looking inside the envelope, she got up and went over to hug her grandmother. "Thanks," she whispered.

"Thank *you*," Grandmother said.

When Christine stepped back she could see her grandmother's blue eyes glistening with tears, but for a change they seemed like tears of joy.

Just then the bell on the mantle clock began to ring.

"Look, everyone, it's midnight now," Jimmy said. "Merry Christmas, everyone!"

"Happy birthday, Christine," Grandmother said.

"No way," said Jimmy. "You're a Christmas baby?"

She nodded with embarrassment.

"Happy birthday, dear," Aunt Hattie said with a smile.

"Happy birthday," Felicity said. "Just wait'll Jamie hears about this. He thought it was bad being born the week before Christmas."

Christine nodded. "Yeah, it always made having parties a little awkward. But it was kind of fun too."

"Her parents called her their Christmas present," Grandmother said with a bright smile.

"That makes me think of something," Aunt Hattie said as she held up her cocoa cup. "I'd like to propose a Christmas toast."

Everyone else held up their cups and waited.

"Here's to Christmas Past," began Aunt Hattie. "The gift we keep with us forever. And here's to Christmas Future." She glanced at the children peacefully snoozing beneath the Christmas tree. "The gift that is yet to come. And here's to Christmas Present." Aunt Hattie nodded to Christine and smiled. "The gift we open today!"

ANGELS
In the
SNOW

1

The isolation felt complete now. Snowflakes tumbled nonstop from a pewter sky, silently encompassing her like a living, moving fortress. Claire experienced a strange sense of comfort in being cut off from the rest of the world with such cold totality. She glanced over at her cell phone still securely plugged into the electrical outlet to recharge its battery, her only link to civilization if she were to be snowed in.

"It could happen," Jeannie, her art rep, had warned with her usual sage type of wisdom. "You've got to be ready for anything up there in the mountains. We always keep the cabin stocked with nonperishables, candles, matches, and whatever you might need until you can be dug out, or the snow melts, whichever comes first. And either one might not be for weeks. So don't let that November sunshine fool you, honey; you could get a blizzard at the drop of a hat."

Claire dropped her black felt walking hat onto the old maple table by the window and sighed deeply. Hopefully this change in weather wouldn't put a damper on her daily walks. Her hike through the woods seemed the only part of her day that she actually looked forward to, and she wasn't about to give it up to bad weather.

She looked again at her cell phone, this time even picking it up and fingering the small buttons. It wasn't too late to change her mind about all this. Maybe it was too extreme, or just plumb crazy, as her father had said from his home down in sunny Palm Springs. She quickly dialed Jeannie's number then waited impatiently for the assistant to put her on the line.

"Oh, Jeannie, I'm glad I caught you," she said finally, trying to disguise the tight feeling of unease that had crept inside her chest.

"Claire!" exclaimed Jeannie. "How's it going? Produced any masterpieces yet? I saw Henri just yesterday and promised him you'd have something very special for him in time for his holiday exhibition."

Claire groaned. "Don't make promises you can't keep."

"Oh, come on, kiddo. You've got to break free from this little slump of yours."

"*Little* slump?" Claire sighed deeply. "And, please, don't start another pep talk—"

"It's not a pep talk. It's just the facts. You know that I, of all people, hate to appear insensitive to the delicate nature of a talented *arteest*, but it's been over a year. You've got to move on, honey. Remember, *you* weren't the one who died in that accident. You've got to keep living, kiddo. What would Scott think if he knew you'd quit your art like this. Or Jeremy for that matter—"

"Oh, stop, Jeannie!" The tightness in her chest exploded into hot, red sparks, and her pulse began to pound against her temples. "I don't even know why I listen to you!"

"Okay, okay." The voice on the other end instantly became calm and soothing. "I'm sorry, Claire, I really don't want to push you too hard. It's a good sign that you're actually getting angry with me—a healthy emotion, as my shrink would say. Now, listen to me. I want you to walk over to your easel right now—it is set up, isn't it?"

"Sure," lied Claire as she stared at her still unpacked art supplies lying heaped against the wall by the door, right where she had dropped them several days before.

"Okay, now go over and pick up a tube of paint—*any* color." Jeannie paused as if allowing time for Claire to follow her simple directions, although Claire did not. "Okay, now," continued Jeannie as if speaking to a small child, "just squirt a little paint onto your palette. . . . Now then, pick up a brush—*any* brush—and just start wiping that paint around on the canvas. Don't even bother trying to make it look like anything, Claire. Just start brushing it on—just swish-swish, free as the breeze. . . . You can even pretend that you're painting the side of a barn if you like, as long as you

294

keep moving that brush. Like the Nike ad says, *just do it!* Okay, honey?"

Completely ignoring Jeannie's directions, Claire stared blankly out the front window, watching as white flakes floated down, filtering through pine trees, barely distinguishable against the sky. "It's snowing here," she said without emotion.

"Great. Perfect reflective light for painting. Now, you've got plenty of firewood and lots of provisions. Even if the electricity should go out you'll be absolutely fine; just remember to bundle up and keep that woodstove stoked up during the night."

Claire tried to remember why she'd called Jeannie in the first place. Certainly not for this. "Thanks, Jeannie," she said flatly. "I'll get right to work."

"Good girl." Jeannie paused. "And someday you'll thank me for this."

Claire sighed. "I sure hope so." She hung up and walked over to her art supplies, trying to remember exactly what it was that Jeannie had told her to do. It wasn't that Claire wanted to be difficult—and she knew that Jeannie *believed* she had her best interest at heart—it was just that Claire couldn't help it. But she would give it a try.

Mechanically, she released the bands from her easel, unfolded its spindly legs, then set it at an angle by the south window. Then she set up a small card table and slowly unpacked her art supplies, handling each single item as if she'd never seen such a thing before. She carefully arranged all her materials, lining up the brushes by width and size, fanning the tubes of acrylic paint into a perfect color wheel. She hadn't brought her oils with her. Perhaps it was laziness, or maybe she just wasn't ready to face that smell again. She stacked the clean palettes and folded her rags and set her water containers in a neat row, until the card table looked like an ad for an art supply store. With everything meticulously arranged, she stepped back and surveyed her work, nodding her head in grim satisfaction.

"Very nice, Claire," she said in a sarcastic tone. Never had she been so meticulous about her supplies. Usually caught up in the flurry of the creative process, she had been one to work like a chaotic whirlwind, surrounded by an incredible mess of squinched-up paint tubes, smelly rags, and dirty brushes soaking in grimy jars of mud-colored linseed oil. She remembered how Scott would step cautiously into her studio with a look of mock horror on his face.

"Oh, no, it looks like Hurricane Claire has struck again," he would tease. But then he would peer over her shoulder and praise—no, almost worship—her work. Never a critic, Scott had always believed her infallible as an artist and as a human. As a housekeeper, well now, that was another story.

Determined to obey her rep's directives, Claire opened a fresh tube of paint. Cobalt blue. She squeezed a generous amount onto her clean white palette. It was a harsh, cold, sterile shade of blue, and she knew nothing in nature that was exactly that color—other than her heart perhaps. Then randomly she selected a brush, "any brush," as Jeannie had instructed. And like a machine, she began to work the fresh paint back and forth across the clean palette. Swish-swish, swish-swish. Perfect consistency. Then she lifted the filled and ready brush, holding it just inches from the clean white canvas. And there her hand stopped as if her elbow joint had been flash frozen. She took a deep steadying breath and even closed her eyes, willing herself to move her hand forward, to make just one brush stroke.

"Do like Jeannie said," she told herself through clenched teeth. "Just pretend you're painting the side of a barn!" But her fingers locked themselves like a vise around the wooden brush handle, and the frozen arm refused to move. How long she stood there with her arm poised in midair she did not know, but finally she realized that the little cabin had grown dark and cold inside, and long, dusky shadows now stretched over the thin blanket of snow that had covered the ground outside. After cleaning the brush, she went to rescue the few small embers still glowing in the woodstove, throwing on some thin sticks of kindling and blowing fiercely until a tiny flame began to flicker at last. She warmed her hands over the tiny fire, then quickly added more logs, filling the stove and closing the door with a loud empty clang.

Without eating, she went to bed, pulling the thick eiderdown comforter up to her nose. And once again she dreamed of them. They were walking just ahead of her, close enough that she could recognize their straight backs and nicely squared shoulders; both had curly brown hair, the color of burnt sienna. And, although the boy's head didn't even reach the man's shoulder, they both walked with that same loose-jointed gait that told you they were related. Father and son. But as close as they seemed to her, they were always just out of reach—out of earshot. And no matter how hard she ran after them, screaming and yelling their names, they never turned to see her, they did not heed her voice. Only this dream was slightly altered from her usual one; in this dream they weren't walking on the beach, they were walking through the freshly fallen snow.

2

Claire awoke while it was still dark and wondered where she was, then realized by the chill in the air that this was the cabin. Too quiet and still and dark to be her loft apartment in the city. And far too cold. Across the room, she saw the small red embers, burned down low again, staring back at her like animal eyes. Hungry eyes. The fire craved more wood. She crawled out of bed, her bare feet cringing at the touch of the cold wood floor. Dragging the comforter along with her like a robe, she stuffed more wood into the woodstove, closing the door with a clank. Then she pulled the one easy chair over to the east window and, wrapping the comforter all around her, pulled her knees up to her chin and waited for morning to come.

At last she saw a sliver of golden light cutting through the dark silhouettes of evergreen trees. More snow had fallen during the night. It now looked to be several inches deep but not enough to prevent her from taking her daily trek to the little footbridge and back again. It was the one actual pleasure in her day. But she held it out for herself like a reward, her proverbial carrot for getting through what needed to be done.

It was upon arriving at the cabin that she'd made her detailed list of daily chores (things that Jeannie had told her must be done in order to survive). And then Claire had created a rigid schedule that, after only a week, she'd managed to stick to almost religiously. First she showered (whether she wanted to or not), then brewed a pot of strong coffee while she started herself some breakfast, usually oatmeal, canned fruit, and a piece of toast. These she forced down, mostly, reminding herself how the doctor had warned that to lose any more weight would seriously threaten her health. Afterwards, she would meticulously wash the dishes in the old soapstone sink, then carefully clean the small one-room cabin, plus bathroom, taking more time than she'd ever spent in her large rambling home before the accident, before she'd moved to her loft apartment.

When everything was spotless, she would go outside and restock the firewood box beside the front door as well as refill the copper washtub next to the woodstove. After this she split a small pile of kindling that went into the big wicker basket right next to the copper washtub—nice and neat. Finally she would carefully check her supplies to see if she needed to make the twenty-minute drive to the closest store for bread or eggs or fresh produce. And since she had made that trip just yesterday, the cupboards were nicely stocked. But today, thanks to the snow, she had two more tasks to add to her list. She picked up the old broom and neatly swept the powdery snow that had blown across the wide front porch. Then she found a snow shovel and shoveled through what couldn't have been more than four inches of light snow to create a little path that connected the small cabin to the nearby garage and attached woodshed.

Going back inside, she shook out the heavy suede working gloves that she'd located in the shed, placing them close to the fire to warm and to dry. She glanced at her watch and sighed. Just barely noon—she was getting too good at this. And so far she had not allowed herself to take her walk before two o'clock, on a pretense that she was "working" until then. Although she wasn't a bit hungry, she fixed herself a lunch of sliced apple and cheese and crackers, arranging them prettily on an old-fashioned plate of blue and white. This she set on the small maple table and slowly consumed, eating each bite slowly, yet barely tasting it. After brewing a small pot of green tea, she settled into the easy chair and opened a book on "igniting the creative spirit." She would attempt to read the first chapter, again, until two o'clock.

All morning long she had managed to ignore the card table with her neatly arrayed art supplies as well as the waiting canvas still standing at attention by the window. And she sat with her back to these instruments now, distracting herself with the black-and-white pages before her. Yet the words and letters danced off the smooth paper, never reaching the interior of her mind as she absently turned the pages. The familiar tightness in her chest was returning, and she glanced once again at her watch. Only one-thirty.

Gritting her teeth, Claire closed the book and stared out the window at the tall pine trees, their long needles clinging like slender fingers to fresh clumps of snow just starting to soften and melt in the sun. She *must* adhere to her schedule, she warned herself. Otherwise her little world would quickly fall apart and go spinning out of control. She closed her eyes and tried to pray, but as usual the words would not form themselves, would not come to her, not even in thoughts. Her heart recoiled within her, blank and empty—numb, except for that usual burning ache that never seemed to lessen, never seemed to leave her at all. And if, in fact, the pain were to leave, what would she be left with?

At exactly one-fifty-six she slowly rose from her chair and began to prepare for her walk. She laced up her sturdy leather hiking boots, wound a soft charcoal-colored scarf around her neck, buttoned up her heavy woolen coat, and placed her black felt hat on her head. Standing before a foggy antique mirror by the door, she stuffed her shoulder-length blond hair up inside the hat, then pulled the narrow brim down lower, clear to her eyebrows.

In the mirror her small pointed face looked ghostly pale surrounded by the severity of the black hat, and her eyes peered out from beneath the brim like two gray pools of sadness. But her ghostlike appearance hardly mattered since she never met anyone on her solitary walks. And, although she knew there were other cabins somewhere in this vicinity, she had yet to see a single person since her arrival, other than someone driving a dark red Suburban down the road too fast a couple of times, and of course, the old woman who ran the store at Saddle Springs. Claire slowly pulled on her knit gloves and looked at the clock over the kitchen stove. Ah, exactly two. Finally, she could set out on her walk.

She followed the same path every day, the only path she knew. It had been easy to recognize the trail before the first snow had fallen, since the packed-down dirt clearly marked the way through the woods. But now all was white. Fortunately, she'd memorized the way by now. She knew exactly how the narrow trail meandered through the pine forest, curving to the left then taking a sharp right turn at the big dead tree. The first time she had seen this huge, fallen juniper tree, she had actually wept. Seeing it laying there so helplessly, like old bleached bones with each branch still intact, had touched some hidden nerve within her. Obviously it had been cut down, for the old gray stump was sawn smoothly through, revealing faded rings from forgone years. But why had it been so mercilessly toppled like that? It had once been tall and majestic, one of the largest junipers in the forest. Why had it been left behind—not even used for timber? The sad waste of it all had overwhelmed her that first day, and she had stood there and mourned for the better part of an hour.

But with each subsequent day and walk, she'd grown accustomed to the fallen tree and now actually looked forward to seeing it, like an old friend. Its narrow top pointed like a twisty old finger directing her down the path where the woods would thin a bit and the trail would grow straighter. This thinning, she decided, was the result of an earlier forest fire, for she had spotted some large blackened stumps in the clearing, hunkered close to the ground like dark gnomes keeping their secrets close to their chests. And all around these hunchbacked darkened creatures grew smaller trees, healthy and supple and green, planted by nature to replace what had been so cruelly lost.

But today, as she walked along the path, everything looked altered and changed, draped in its fresh blanket of snow. Clean and white, pristine. Almost invigorating. But invigorating was an emotion she could only imagine and barely remember. Still, while walking along the forested area, she couldn't help but look around her in wonder.

Snow remained a novelty to one who had grown up in Southern California and only skied a few times in her life. Against the fresh blue sky, tall ponderosa pines stood like sentries, holding their rounded snowballs like artillery in their long, sparkling green needles. And fallen logs, previously dark and moldering, were now respectfully shrouded in clean white sheets, as if to rest in peace. She noticed sets of squirrel and rabbit tracks and some bigger tracks, maybe raccoon, crisscrossing each other here and there, and also the sharp two-toed spike tracks of dear. The pine forest wearing its first cloak of snow had become a new place. Strange and coldly beautiful.

She came to the old dead tree, just before the burn area, and actually gasped at its transformed beauty. Each twisted bare branch and gnarled twig, now dusted in a thin veneer of white powder and illuminated by the afternoon sun, glistened like polished silver and were a soft contrast against the brilliant blue backdrop of sky. The phrase "breathtakingly beautiful" had always sounded phony to her, but that is exactly how she would describe this scene. Before the accident she would have raced back to the cabin for her camera and then used a whole roll of film trying to catch every single angle and shadow and light just right. Then she'd have waited impatiently for the photos to be developed, imagining the final image in oils on a wide canvas. But now she simply stood and stared, almost afraid to breathe. Such beauty was terrifying to her now. She took a deep breath and continued to walk, leaving the fallen tree behind her, its image still burning itself into her brain, making it nearly impossible to see the trail ahead. Finally, after several minutes of walking, she regained her focus and began to look around again.

The clearing, void of tall tree shadows, grew so bright that she longed for her dark glasses, and for the first time she understood how it was that a person could actually become snow-blind. Even though her eyes were adjusting to the stunning brightness, she was still forced to keep them focused downward, mostly to the trail before her. And that's when she began to notice another type of tracks—in fact, two sets. *Human tracks.*

Claire frowned. Up until now she had imagined that this entire section of woods belonged to her, and to her alone. She thought of this as *her woods.* And she didn't want to share *her woods* with anyone who was walking on two legs. The tracks headed in the same direction she normally walked, the way she was walking right now. She knew she could choose to turn around and head straight back to her cabin. But as a result her walk would be cut short. Her only other option was to continue along her regular path and risk the chance of running into these two interlopers. Because surely they, like her, would eventually turn back and return to wherever it was they had come from—these people who were trespassing in *her* woods.

Oh, she knew this was all ridiculous. After all, the trail was part of the National Forest, put there for anyone and everyone to use and to enjoy. And she also knew that other cabins, spotted here and there, likely had inhabitants who relished the pleasures of a hike in the woods just as much as she, but up until now—with the help of the snow—she'd never seen any signs and had simply preferred to imagine that her little borrowed cabin was the only one within miles. It was that sort of isolation that had compelled her to come here; she had longed for that deep sort of loneliness—both within and without. Of course, Jeannie had mentioned there were others around, but she'd also said the majority of cabins sat vacant during most of the winter months. Too hard to get in and out of, too difficult to cross over the mountain pass once the snows came.

Claire kept walking, ignoring the human tracks and hoping she wouldn't come face-to-face with their owners and spoil her sense of isolation altogether. Hopefully this was a one-time thing, tourists who had stopped their car along the road to take a walk and enjoy the snow before continuing on their merry way. To her relief she walked all the way to the footbridge (her turn-back point) without seeing a living creature other than three brown does and a good-sized buck with a nice set of antlers. She turned back in triumph, pleased that she had *not* run into the owners of the human tracks as she walked back to the cabin. All in all, her leisurely paced walk usually took just less than two hours. Of course, if she walked faster she could probably cut that time in half, but then, why would she want to do that?

Back at the cabin she managed to distract herself from seeing her easel again, although she could feel its stiff presence, still standing guard at the window and perhaps even mocking her now. She was able to avoid it completely until it was nearly dark outside. And that didn't take long, for the darkness of imposing winter came more quickly with each passing day. Ignoring the electric lights, she lit a kerosene lamp and watched as its golden glow filled the room with a soft-edged, murky sort of light. She liked how the lamp created deep shadows, illuminating the wood surfaces with richness and warmth. And that's when her easel and art supplies faded into the shadows, into oblivion, finally allowing her to pretend they didn't exist at all.

She then began her evening routine. Not all that much different than the morning one. But after the last dinner dish was washed and dried and set into the old pine cupboard next to the sink, that familiar tightness began to build in her chest again. With each day (and it was always worse at night) it felt as if the burning, aching sensation was growing larger and larger, taking up even more space inside her. Instead of diminishing over time, it only seemed to increase. She had hoped that a drastic change like living alone in the woods might somehow change something—break something. But, if anything, it only seemed to amplify and magnify her pain and loneliness. And she knew she wasn't big enough to contain it all. In fact, she felt certain that in time she would simply burst open from it. And so, once again, she tried to pray.

Pressing her lips tightly together she closed her eyes and willed a prayer to form itself within her. *Please, God!* Only two little words, but it was a start and all she could muster. And as small and insignificant as it seemed, she felt surely it must be progress. As a result she relaxed a little, trying to remember the time in her life when she had known how to pray—a time when it had been as simple as breathing. Sometimes she had spoken the words out loud, but usually she just whispered them in the privacy of her own heart. Either way, she'd always been certain that God had listened. Up until the accident, that is. That's when the painful silence had begun. *Please, God!* her heart cried out again. *Please, please, help me.*

The next day, after a slightly better night's rest than usual, Claire finished her morning routine earlier than normal and decided to break her own rules by starting her walk *before* two o'clock. Another couple inches of snow had fallen during the night, almost but not completely erasing her steps from yesterday's walk. The fresh snow made it slightly more difficult to walk, but the effort was well worthwhile. The forest was stunningly beautiful, somewhat heartening, and nearly invigorating. *Nearly.* But once again, shortly after she reached the dead tree that pointed toward the clearing, she noticed the two sets of human tracks. Fresh tracks that had been made that day.

She stood for a long moment before deciding to simply ignore them and continue. But after only a few steps, she paused and examined the tracks more closely. She placed her foot next to the one imprint and noticed that it was quite a bit larger than her own boot—probably that of a man. Then she placed her foot beside the other imprint to find that these prints were smaller than hers. Obviously, a child's. So a man and a child had walked along this path today—and perhaps yesterday too. She sighed and continued on her way. She must simply forget that someone else had recently walked here—convince herself she was really alone in *her woods.* She would not consider the man and child hiking along somewhere ahead of her. But she couldn't help herself. Unwillingly, she began to envision the two walkers on the path before her. And it was an unwelcome image—that of father and son, laughing and talking as they walked along together. Alive and well, and enjoying life! It was like a sharp slap in the face, and it felt totally unfair—unjust even.

Reaching the clearing, she noticed how the two sets of tracks had left the main trail, diverting to the right. She followed the tracks with her eyes, curious as to where they might be going. And that's when she saw them. Like bas-relief images in white plaster, pressed into the snow were two distinct snow angels, their wings now glistening in the afternoon sun. She stood still, staring in wonder at the simple beauty of the snow art. It was the warm trickle of tears falling down her cold cheeks that reminded her it was time to move on, to force her eyes from this sight and forge ahead. She tried not to notice where the two sets of tracks came back onto the main trail again and continued before her.

But, as she walked along, her eyes focusing on the stumps and small trees, her original image of the strangers hiking on the trail up ahead of her altered—be it ever so slightly. Suddenly she envisioned the pair—father and son—striding along with a similar loose, long-legged gait. She imagined their curly, dark-brown heads the color of burnt sienna bobbing along, their straight backs and squared shoulders moving steadily forward. The painful familiarity made her swallow hard in disbelief. Then she blinked back fresh tears as her heart began to pound furiously. And suddenly she began to walk faster—much faster—until she was running breathlessly toward the bridge.

3

When Claire finally reached the footbridge, the tracks just kept going. She could see them curving off to the right, heading into the trees up ahead. Going where? She clung to the snow-covered wooden railing and gasped to catch her breath.

"Claire, you're crazy," she said out loud. She stared at the footprints continuing beyond the footbridge and seriously considered following them. But to where? And that's when she noticed that a thick band of clouds had rolled in, beginning to blot out the sunlight. These clouds were quickly filling the sky and were probably full of snow. But how could she not keep following the mysterious footprints? What if? She walked a short distance before she noticed that snowflakes were already tumbling from the sky. Not timid flakes, but large, heavy ones.

Shielding her eyes from the spinning flakes, she looked ahead but saw no sign of any living thing. She could barely discern the trail now washed in a swirling blur of white. These recently made tracks would soon be obscured by the rapidly falling snow—and yet . . . glancing over her shoulder, she looked at the trail behind her, only to see that it too was fading fast. Her heart pounded in her temples, echoing loudly in her ears. Whether it was exertion or fear, she wasn't sure. Perhaps both. She took a few more steps forward, knowing full well that she was making a foolhardy decision—or perhaps she was just slightly crazed—then she froze in her steps. Just whom was she following, *really?* She looked up to the moving mass of white above her and tried, once again, to pray. Raising both gloved fists into the air, she raged at God for her losses. Then, several minutes later, humbled by her own audacity, she meekly pleaded for his help. But this time her prayer was more than just a few words. Partially unintelligible perhaps, but it was an honest cry from the heart.

Finally she turned around and trudged back across the bridge and down what she hoped was the trail. The falling flakes abated slightly, and she was barely able to retrace the three sets of footprints, but by the time she reached the place in the clearing where the snow angels had been, she was disappointed to see that they had been nearly obliterated by the new snow. Taking advantage of this brief lull in the storm, and before she lost her trail completely, she jogged all the way back to the cabin.

Warm from her exertion, Claire paused on the cabin's covered porch to catch her breath as she peered out on the falling snow. It was coming down fast again, and the wind had picked up and was now swirling the flakes into moving walls that obscured all vision beyond twenty feet. As she shook off her snow-coated jacket and hat and gloves, she realized with chilling clarity how close she'd actually come to being out there in what appeared to be turning into something of a blizzard. "Thank you, God." She spoke the words aloud, almost startled at the sound of her own voice against the backdrop of the snow-muffled wind.

She stoked the fire and glanced up at the clock. It wasn't even two yet. She still had several hours to fill before the day would mercifully come to an end. Walking over to the window, Claire stared out onto the drape of whiteness that enclosed her. She could feel the canvas right next to her, still situated on its easel. It felt as if it were pulling her, tugging her toward it like a magnet. Could she?

Claire went over to the card table and looked at yesterday's pallet still stained with the stark unforgiving shade of cobalt blue. After setting it aside, she picked up a fresh white pallet, then looked blankly at the rainbow circle of paint tubes arranged so neatly on the card table. But it was as if the colors frightened or maybe just intimidated her, and finally, as if in surrender, she picked up a tube of titanium white. She held the tube in her hand, gently squeezing it, feeling it give beneath her fingers. Then she opened the cap and bravely pushed a small mound of paint onto the pallet. She stared at the stark white paint—barely distinguishable from the white pallet— then glanced up.

Peering out the window again, Claire studied the swirling, whirling whiteness before her. But it wasn't really pure white, she observed. She squinted her eyes as if to separate the tiniest traces of color hidden within its whiteness. No, it had a faint bit of green in it. Or maybe it was blue. And just a smidgen of black, to gray it ever so slightly in places. Taking up her pallet knife, she began to spread the white paint, adding just the faintest touches of green, blue, black . . . as needed. And like a woman possessed, she began to smear paint across the canvas, working faster and faster until the entire surface was covered. Washed in a sea of white.

Feeling weak and almost breathless from the effort, she finally stepped back and studied her artistic accomplishment. She stared at the whitened canvas for a long time and finally began to laugh, but it wasn't a mirthful laugh. Instead it was filled with self-doubt and deprecation. "Claire, you have totally lost it now." She threw down her pallet knife and wiped her hands on a damp rag, then collapsed on her bed in hopeless tears.

Several hours later, she awoke to a darkened cabin and the sound of the howling wind. But as she rose to check on the nearly dead fire, she thought she heard another sound as well. A quiet moaning sound—or perhaps it was simply the wind crying out of pure loneliness. Or maybe . . . maybe she was simply losing her mind altogether. She stood silently before the door, straining her ears to listen. And once again, she felt certain she was hearing another sound, something other than the wind.

She opened the door to a blast of cold and snow, and there huddled on her porch, just a few feet from the door, was some sort of animal. She started to back up and close the door as she remembered how Lucy McCullough, the owner of the small store, had recently told her about a rabid raccoon that had turned vicious on a family that had been "foolish enough to feed the durned thing." But this looked bigger than a raccoon. The animal slowly lifted its head, and despite its coating of snow, Claire could tell it was of a canine nature. But even so, she wasn't sure if it was wolf or dog—although she felt fairly certain there were no wolves in these parts. The animal moaned again, appearing to be in pain.

"Are you hurt?" she asked softly.

The animal struggled to its feet; she was certain it was a dog— some sort of shepherd mix. Still, she wasn't sure what to do. What if it was vicious or rabid? It walked slowly toward her, and when it got closer to the light coming from inside the cabin, she could tell by its eyes that it wasn't going to hurt her. She wasn't even sure how she knew this, but somehow she just did.

"Do you want to come in?" She held the door open wide, but the nearly frozen dog just stood there in front of the door, as if it were afraid to actually step inside.

"I won't hurt you," she promised, kneeling by the shivering dog. She carefully reached out her hand, keeping her fingers tucked into her palm the way Scott had once shown her long, long ago. The dog looked at her with soulful brown eyes, and she gently stroked his head. "Come on in, fella," she urged. "Come warm yourself by my fire."

She coaxed him into the cabin and shut the door against the storm. "You wait here while I get a towel to dry you with." She quickly wiped the snow off her bare feet and went to retrieve a couple of towels. Then, speaking in a calm voice, she led the dog over to the fire where she gently toweled him dry with one towel and, making a bed of the other, helped him to lie down. He looked up with ap-preciative eyes.

"What in the world are you doing out on your own on a night like this?" she asked as she looked through her cupboards for what might possibly be an appropriate meal for a half frozen dog. Finally deciding on a can of stew that she figured they both could share since she hadn't eaten dinner, she searched out a couple of earthenware bowls to use for the dog's water and food. She warmed the stew just slightly before generously filling his bowl.

The dog's tail began to thump against the floor as she situated the filled bowls before him. Then he stood somewhat unsteadily and began to lap, first from the water and then from the stew, which he quickly eliminated, licking the bowl clean as if to say thank you. Picking up the empty bowl, she noticed how he gingerly held his front left leg just slightly off the floor, as if it was hurting him. When he lay down again, she knelt to check it. She couldn't find any open cuts or wounds but noticed that he seemed to flinch when she touched what appeared to be a swollen joint.

"Did you hurt your leg, boy?"

His tail thumped against the floor, and he looked up with trusting eyes.

"Well, you'll just have to take it easy for now. Enjoy a warm night by the fire, and tomorrow I'll phone the store and see if anyone is missing you." She'd already noticed the dog wore no collar, but it was possible he'd slipped out of it. And surely old Lucy at the store would know if a dog had gone missing lately.

Claire set her bowl of stew on the table and sat down to eat, unable to take her eyes off this unexpected visitor. She'd never had a dog of her own. Her mother had always claimed they were too messy, and Scott, although he loved animals, suffered from allergies. And it wasn't that she'd ever really wanted a dog before, other than that short spell during childhood, somewhere between nine and ten.

She stoked the fire against the night and then refilled the dog's bowl with fresh water before she turned off the lights and made her way to bed. As she lay in bed, she remembered how utterly stricken she'd been earlier this same evening, and suddenly she realized how she no longer felt so completely helpless and hopeless. As odd as it was, this stray dog had provided a good distraction for her. Even now, seeing his silhouette by the firelight and hearing his even breathing brought a strange sense of comfort. But he's only a dog, she told herself, and someone is probably missing him right now.

Once again, she prayed. Only this time it came more naturally. Oh, it wasn't easy by any means, but she was at least able to form actual words and partial sentences in her mind, and somehow they made sense to her. She just hoped they made sense to God.

4

Claire awoke to something nudging her elbow. Startled from her deep and thankfully dreamless sleep, she looked over to see a pair of brown soulful eyes staring back at her. It took her a few seconds to remember last night's visitor, but it was obvious that the dog was still there, now peering at her in what seemed a fairly urgent manner.

"Poor thing," she muttered as she climbed from her bed. "I forgot all about you." Pulling on her robe, she glanced at the clock. "My goodness, it's after eight o'clock. I can't believe I slept that long." She reached down and patted the dog's head. "I'll bet you need to go out now, don't you?" She went to open the door, noticing once again how the dog painfully limped just to cross the room.

"There you go, boy." She waited as he slowly made his way through the threshold. "Now take it easy on that leg." She grabbed a few pieces of firewood then watched uneasily from the porch as the dog picked his way through what was now close to a foot of snow. Finally he relieved himself on a nearby tree. The weather seemed to be clearing up some with the promise of sunshine on the western horizon. The dog paused, sniffing the air, and Claire wondered if he might be thinking this break in the storm was a good time to return to his home. But it worried her to imagine him trying to make his way very far through the snow on that lame front leg. She knew he needed to give it a good rest.

But as if to show his good sense, the dog turned around and slowly limped back onto the porch. His tail wagged when he approached her, but once again he stopped at the door, as if waiting for another invitation to come inside.

"Come on in, boy. It's freezing out here, and I'll bet you'd like some breakfast." His tail wagged faster, and he followed her back inside the house, watching with patient eyes as she laid more sticks on the embers and blew to encourage the flames. "How about a real breakfast this morning?" she said, opening the refrigerator and pulling out an untouched carton of eggs. She scrambled up several and even grated some Swiss cheese on top while the bread toasted and the coffee perked. Then she dished up a good portion of eggs along with some torn-up pieces of toast into the same earthenware bowl she had used last night, even taking a moment to blow on the eggs to help them cool.

"There you go, boy." She set down the bowl. "Hope you don't mind eating people food." She dished up her own breakfast, but by the time she sat down at the table, the dog had already licked his bowl clean. "Guess you like my cooking."

Satisfied, the dog returned to his spot by the fire and carefully settled himself onto the makeshift towel bed, groaning just slightly as he licked the swollen joint that seemed to be troubling him.

After breakfast, Claire washed up the dishes to pass the time until nine when she could call Lucy at the store.

"Missing dog?" said the old woman. "You say you're missing a dog?"

"No," Claire corrected her. "I mean I have what must be a missing dog. He's at my house right now, but he's not mine."

"Oh. A stray, you mean?"

"He's a well-mannered dog. I'm guessing he ran away or got lost."

"Any ID?"

"No, he doesn't even have a collar."

"Well, he's probably a stray then."

"But he's an awfully nice dog, and he doesn't look malnourished, although he's got an injured leg. Have you heard of anyone who's missing a dog?"

"Well, let's see. Arlen Crandall lost his tabby cat 'bout a month back. But then that cat was as old as Methuselah, probably older than old Arlen himself."

"Any dogs missing?"

"Not that I've heard of. When'd you find him?"

"Just last night. He showed up at my door during the snowstorm."

"Lucky for him you took him in. It was pretty nasty last night—winds were up to forty miles an hour."

"Yeah, I'm glad I heard him over the wind."

"You say he's got a hurt leg?"

"Yes. He's limping, but I don't see an open wound or any sign of infection. Still, the joint is pretty swollen. I wonder if I should try to get him to a vet."

"Land sakes, no," said Lucy. Claire could hear her munching on something as she talked. "Don't waste good money on a vet for somebody else's dog. Besides, it's probably just a sprain, and ain't nothing no vet can do for a sprain anyway."

"I suppose. . . . Well, if anyone mentions a missing dog—he's some kind of shepherd or collie mix, I think—will you have them call me?" Claire repeated her cell phone number twice to make sure Lucy got it right, then hung up.

"Looks like you'll be hanging out with me for the time being," she informed the dog as she began working her morning schedule. But he seemed content to watch her from his post by the fire.

Once again, she completed her tasks more quickly than usual, and it was only eleven when she decided she'd break her daily routine for the second time. "No reason not to take a walk early today," she said as she glanced outside to see the sunlight breaking through. "Who knows, it could be snowing by two." She reached for her coat, then remembering, she glanced over at her disabled canine houseguest. "Oh." She frowned. "I'll bet you're not up for a walk, now, are you?" His tail thumped, but he didn't move from the warmth of his spot by the fire.

"No, of course not." She rehung her coat. "I forgot about your bad leg." She sighed and looked around the small cabin until her eyes came to rest on the canvas from yesterday. She stood and stared at the back of it for several minutes. She'd purposely avoided it all morning, but now she hesitantly approached it. Perhaps she was ready to examine her work more closely now. Maybe she would understand what it was she'd been trying to accomplish yesterday. She stood in front of the painting, her arms folded across her chest, and just looked. For a long time, she stared into it, hoping to see something—anything at all. But all she saw was white—shades upon shades of white.

Finally, to give her eyes relief, she redirected her gaze out the window, studying the snow-covered pines glistening in the sunlight. A pleasant scene, like something you might see on a Christmas card, but nothing spectacular. Nothing worthy of actually painting into a landscape. But then again, what would it hurt to try? It wasn't like she was doing much of anything else anyway. And so, once again, she arranged her paints on the pallet, some white and a bit of green and black. And then, with the scene out the window to guide her, she began to paint, carefully layering snow-covered trees to her blanket of white. She worked for several hours, but when she finally stopped, she felt disappointed. It was as if she'd become snow-blinded by her own creation, and for all she could tell it was simply layer after layer of unfeeling white. She turned from her work in frustration. "I *cannot* do this!" she exclaimed, throwing down her pallet knife in disgust.

She'd almost forgotten about her visitor and was startled to hear his tail now thump-thump-thumping against the floor. "Oh!" She looked over to see him sitting by the door. "I'm sorry. I'll bet you need to go out again." She reached for her coat and let him out, then went to the shed to fetch another load of firewood as she waited for him. But as she carried the wood back to the house, she noticed the dog had wandered over and sat down right next to the garage door.

"What is it, boy?" she called, stacking the firewood by her front door. "Don't you want to come back inside now?"

The dog remained there as if waiting for something. She walked over to the garage and patted his head. "What's up, boy? You think there's something interesting in there? Something you need to see?" She lifted open the garage door and held out her hand. "See, boy, it's just my Jeep." The dog limped over to the Jeep and stood right by the door, wagging his tail like he wanted to get in and go somewhere. "You want to get in the Jeep?" she asked incredulously. He sat down right next to the door and waited.

She scratched her head. "Looks like you want to take a ride, boy. Maybe you think we'll find your owners. Well, hang on while I go get my keys. I guess it wouldn't hurt to go down to the store and see if anyone's been looking for you."

Still, as she hurried back to the house to get her keys, she wasn't entirely happy about the prospects of discovering this sweet dog's owners. But suppressing these troubling thoughts, she helped load the injured dog into the passenger's seat and started the engine. She slowly plowed her way through the long driveway until she finally reached the unplowed road. "I thought Jeannie said they maintained this road year 'round," she muttered, maneuvering the Jeep through the snow. "Good thing I've got four-wheel drive." She smiled to herself as she remembered a few years back when Scott had picked out their new Jeep Cherokee. She had teased him over the unlikelihood that they'd ever actually need an off-road vehicle for their urban lifestyle in the Bay Area. "You just never know," he'd said with a twinkle in his eye.

"You just never know," she repeated as she glanced over at her well-mannered canine passenger. "Well, it sure looks like you've been in a car before." She half expected him to start barking when they reached a particular crossroad, like perhaps he was going to direct her to his home. But he just sat quietly, happily gazing out the window as if he rode around with strangers all the time.

After about thirty minutes of slow going, they reached the store and Claire carefully unloaded the dog. He stayed right at her heels, following her up to the front door. It hadn't even occurred to her until then that she didn't have a leash for him. But then she wasn't used to dogs or what to expect, and besides, this one almost seemed like he was leading her instead of the other way around. "Okay, you wait here, boy," she instructed him. "I don't know if Lucy likes dogs in her store or not." Obediently, as though he understood, the dog sat down on the porch.

The little brass bell on the door jingled as Claire entered, and old Lucy looked up from behind the cash register where she was reading a newspaper. "Hello there," she called.

316

"Hi, Lucy. I thought I'd stop by to—"

"No one's been in here today to complain 'bout a lost dog," she said with a frown as she folded her paper. "Fact is, ain't no one been in here today doing much of anything."

"Oh." Claire looked around the small but well-stocked store. "Well, I guess I might as well pick up a few things while I'm here then."

Lucy looked up with what seemed somewhat skeptical interest. "You still thinking you're gonna winter here?"

Claire nodded. "I—uh—I think so. Well, at least until Christmas."

"And you sure you're stocked up?"

"I think so."

"*Think* so? Or *know* so?" Suddenly Lucy was rattling off a list of all kinds of things—everything from toilet paper to coffee to canned meat to candles. "Just in case the electricity goes out, you know. We lost power for near a week a few years back when a tree blew down and took out the power lines with it. Not only that but a body can run out of all sorts of things during a long stint of being snowed in up here. You newcomers just don't understand what it takes to survive in the mountains when three feet of snow can fall within twenty-four hours."

"But my friend told me that the roads get plowed here . . . eventually."

Lucy rolled her eyes and laughed. "The key word being *eventually*. And unless you have a snowmobile or are ready to trek all day and night on snowshoes, you could be stuck but good. And you might as well know right up front that I don't make deliveries."

"Well, maybe I should pick up some extra things then," said Claire. "As well as some dog food and dog things."

By the time Claire got out of the store, she'd spent more than a hundred dollars and wasn't sure if she was being wise or had just been duped by a sharp old businesswoman. Whatever the case, she figured she or someone else would use the supplies . . . eventually. The dog was still waiting on the porch.

"Hey, boy," she said as she opened a box of chew bones and gave him one. "You're a good dog." He quickly munched down the treat then followed her to the Jeep, watching while she loaded her supplies into the back. She paused to pull the new red collar from the top of the last box and bent down to slip it around the dog's neck. "Just until we find your owners, and in case I need to leash you up—not that I expect to—you seem to stay pretty close as it is. And it doesn't look like you'll be ready for a walk any time soon." Then she hoisted him back into the passenger seat. "Don't you look handsome." She stroked his smooth head and rearranged his collar so his tufts of ebony and honey colored fur hung neatly over it, then went around to the driver's seat.

"No one's called about you yet," she told him as she drove away from the store. Then she smiled—actually smiled. "But that's okay with me."

It was just getting dusky when they reached the cabin, and she wondered where on earth the day had gone. More snow was beginning to fall as she carried her supplies inside. Then, remembering Lucy's strong words of warning, she decided to get a few more loads of firewood stacked on the porch before dark and even took time to chop some more kindling. As she worked—quickly, before the light faded—the dog stayed with her, limping back and forth between the house and the woodshed.

"You're such a good companion," she said as she finally stacked the last piece of wood by the door and brushed off her hands. "And I'll bet you're hungry now." Claire paused to stomp the snow off her boots. "I know I am." The realization of her statement hit her as she shook off her hat. "It's true, I'm actually hungry!"

5

Snow fell silently and steadily throughout the night. By the time Claire got up the next morning, there appeared to be about eighteen inches of accumulation. She took the broom along with her when she let the dog out, sweeping away the feather light powder that had drifted onto the porch. Taking in a deep breath of cold mountain air, she held it for a long moment, experiencing the chill in her lungs, then slowly exhaled. Lovely. It really was lovely. She hadn't noticed how clean and fresh it had felt before. The morning sun was peeking beneath a layer of clouds now, shining like a golden beacon through the trees, illuminating everything in its path with a wide stream of heavenly light.

If only she could take a walk today. She glanced over to the dog limping back toward her, his tail wagging. His leg did seem slightly better, but not well enough for a walk. And how could she leave her poor faithful companion all alone? What if he didn't understand? Or thought she had abandoned him? No, her daily walks would have to be kept on hold for a while longer.

"I wish you had a name, boy." She patted him on the head. "Well, I suppose you do have a name. I just don't know it." She thought for a minute. "Maybe I should just give you one." But what if she gave him a name and then his owners suddenly showed up to collect him. Perhaps it was better not to get too attached. Or to wait and see what happened first. She finished up with her outdoor chores, shoveling the paths, stacking more wood, and chopping more kindling.

"Maybe old Lucy was right," she said to the dog as she stomped the snow off her boots. "I suppose we could get snowed in here." She squinted up at the morning sun still filtering through the trees. "Although that doesn't seem very likely right now."

Back in the cabin, she wondered what she could do to pass the time. She stood and studied her snowy painting from the previous two days and finally just shook her head. "An exercise in futility," she muttered. Then she removed the canvas, leaned it against the wall, and replaced it with a blank one. Once again she stood for a long while, just staring out the window, gazing on the patterns of light and shadows that played through the trees. Could she possibly capture it? And what would it hurt to try?

She worked so long and hard that she completely forgot about lunch, and only when the outside shadows grew long and somber did she pause to turn away from her work and finally look up at the clock. "Good grief!" She noticed the dog now standing at her feet, looking up expectantly, as if he needed to go out again. "Whatever happened to the day?"

She set aside her brush and let him out, taking a moment to stretch her stiff arms and shoulders and shaking the cobwebs out of her head as she breathed in the fresh icy air. "Hey, it looks like you're walking better now, boy." She bent down and gave him a good scratch behind the ears. "Tell me, do you have a master somewhere? Someone who's looking for you and missing you just desperately?" She shook her head. "Well, if you were my dog, I'd have been combing the neighborhood for you. And the first place I'd have checked was Lucy's store." She stood up. "And if no one calls for you by tomorrow, well, we're giving you a name—and that's that."

After stoking up the faltering fire, she fixed dinner for them both, then busied herself with cleaning and straightening—afraid to allow herself to go back and review her day's work. She knew she would only be disappointed with a painting that held nothing more than snow and trees and, oh yes, light. And although the snow scene was better than a blank canvas, it certainly wasn't a landscape that Jeannie could interest Henri, or anyone else for that matter, in showing. But at least she was painting. That was something. For three days now she had actually worked—a real breakthrough. And it seemed no coincidence that this change had come only after she'd really broken down and prayed to God to help her. She hung a polished copper pot back on the rack and thought. Hadn't that been about the same time that the dog had come into her life too?

So that night when Claire went to bed, she remembered to thank God for sending help. Maybe it did come in the form of a dog, but it was help just the same, and she knew it. Now if only she could keep this dog.

The next morning she awoke to the sound of her cell phone ringing. Certain it must be Jeannie checking up on her, she eagerly jumped out of bed, ready to tell her (and honestly this time) that she'd actually made a little progress—that she'd been painting! But it was a man's voice on the phone, and one she didn't recognize.

"This is Rick Marks," said a gruff voice. "I hear you've got my dog."

She felt her heart plunge like a rock as she looked at the dog now wagging his tail at her feet. She could tell he was ready to be let out. "Did you lose a pet?" she asked weakly as she walked across the room to open the door for the dog.

"Yeah, he ran off."

"Really?" She thought about this. "Are you sure this is your dog? I mean, he doesn't really seem like the type to run off—"

He laughed, but not in a nice way. "Aw, that mutt's always running off."

She didn't like this man calling the dog a mutt. "Well, maybe you should describe him to me. Maybe we're not talking about the same dog."

But when Rick described the shepherd-collie mix right down to the patch of white beneath his chin, she knew they were talking about the same dog. "What's his name?" she asked in a quiet voice.

"Mike."

"Oh." She looked out the window to see the dog, rather, Mike, now making his way back onto her porch, his limp barely noticeable. "What happened to his leg?" she asked, not even sure why, perhaps only as a stall tactic.

"His leg?"

"Yes, he had a bad leg when he first showed up."

"Well, he was perfectly fine last time I saw him."

She sensed hesitation in his voice and felt a flicker of hope. "Does that mean you might not want him back?"

"Aw, he's my dog, lady. Of course, I still want him back."

"Right." She mechanically gave him directions to her house. "But that snow's pretty deep," she added. "And the roads haven't been plowed over here. Are you sure you can make it here okay?"

"It'd take a heck of lot more snow than this to keep me off the road."

Claire dressed quickly, then made sure that Mike got a good meal before his master arrived to take him away. After the dog finished licking the bowl clean, Claire knelt down on the floor and wrapped her arms around the soft fur of his neck. "You are such a good dog," she said. "I can't believe you're going to leave me now." She ran her hands down the silky coat on his back. "Thank you for coming to—to—" Her voice broke, and she buried her face in his neck and sobbed for several minutes. Finally she stopped, feeling his warm wet tongue now licking her face, as if to comfort her.

At the same time she heard the rumble of an engine pulling up her driveway. The dog's muscles tightened when the sound grew louder, and his ears peaked to attention. Then he gave a low growl and a couple of sharp barks. It was the first time she'd heard him bark. She peered out the window to see one of those ridiculously tall pickups with the huge oversized tires plowing up her driveway. It was painted a garish metallic blue and was trimmed with a row of lights that made it look like something from another planet. A heavyset man in a plaid flannel shirt climbed out and ambled up to her door, knocking loudly and causing the dog to bark again.

She stood by the door for a moment, unsure whether she actually wanted this man to come inside her house, much less to know that she was living out here all alone. Finally she decided to simply step outside with the dog.

"Hello," she said stiffly as she closed the door behind her.

He tipped his head slightly then grinned as he carefully took in her appearance. "Howdy, ma'am. I don't recall catching your name."

She forced a smile. No sense in being hostile. "My name's Claire."

"You're new 'round here."

She nodded. "Yes. Just visiting. It's my friend's cabin."

"Well, I still don't know how Mike found his way clear over here," said Rick, scratching his head as he looked at the dog. "It's time to go home, buddy. Go get in the truck now."

But the dog just sat there, as if rooted to the porch next to Claire's feet. She restrained herself from reaching down to pat his head and say, "good dog."

"I *said*, go get in the truck, Mike!" Rick spoke in a sharp tone and pointed to the pickup. The dog began to slowly walk toward the truck, his tail pointed straight down like a rod.

"He's better, but his leg's still hurting him some," said Claire, following the dog with her eyes. "He might need some help getting up there."

Rick made a snorting laugh. "Well, I guess I could give him a hand, just this once. There's no sense in pampering your animals too much." He easily hoisted the dog into the pickup bed that was partially filled with snow, then stepped back. Claire noticed there was no tailgate on the truck.

"Won't he slip out and hurt himself?"

Rick laughed again. "He's ridden like this his whole life." Then he noticed the collar and quickly slipped it off. "And he don't need no fancy collars neither." He handed it to her. "Sorry that he troubled you."

"He was no trouble." Just then Claire considered offering him money for the dog, wondering if that would be an insult or not. "Uh—you wouldn't be interested in selling Mike, would you?"

He laughed again. "Nah, my other dogs have been acting up since he's been gone. He may not be much, but he's a good ol' dog."

She nodded, fighting to hold back tears and telling herself she was a fool for caring so much in the first place. "Yeah, he is." Then she turned back to the house, unable to look at the dog again, afraid she would completely break down in front of this less than sensitive man.

She listened as the truck's loud engine started up again and waited until the sound became a dull rumble then faded away to nothing before she collapsed on her bed and sobbed uncontrollably. "Why, God?" she cried. "Why would you send this sweet dog to comfort me and then just snatch him away? Why?"

6

Claire was unable to paint a single stroke for the remainder of the day. Instead, she paced about the cabin like a caged animal, cleaning and straightening what already looked perfectly neat. Finally at two o'clock sharp she allowed herself to leave the confines of the cabin. The snow was well over a foot deep now—the deepest she'd walked in so far—and it made for hard work, not to mention slower. But she didn't care. Perhaps the effort would be so taxing that she might forget all about the dog, at least temporarily. She should've known better than to let her heart become so attached—and to a silly animal! She trudged steadily along, hardly lifting her eyes from the ground, just following the trail—step after step—until she finally reached the dead tree. There she stopped to catch her breath and look around. But instead of seeing the beauty she'd been so fascinated by before, everything looked dull and flat and starkly white to her. Uninteresting even. And now a lifeless layer of heavy cloud hung low overhead. It was the color of an old nickel and probably filled with more snow. But she didn't really care. Let it snow.

She turned to the right, as usual, and began moving toward the old footbridge, when she noticed those same two pairs of footprints as she'd seen before. Due to her recent distractions, first with the dog and then her painting, she'd almost forgotten about those sets of disturbing footprints. But now, here they were once again, and with fresh clarity, as if they'd just been made today. And while they weren't quite as distinct as before because, like her, the walkers had been forced to trudge along slowly cutting their way through the thick snow, they were clearly the same sets of footprints—one large, one small. She walked along, following them, unwilling to step right in their tracks; yet, it was much easier to walk where they had already stepped. Once again, she wondered, to whom did they belong? Who had been out here walking in all this snow today? Perhaps they'd passed by just moments ago, for the imprints appeared fresh.

Maybe it was because she was tired, or simply just sad, but it didn't take long before she began to imagine the two of them again. Father and son, strolling along—maybe they were hand in hand this time, the dad helping the boy through the deep snow, but still they'd be walking with that slow, distinctive gait. She tried to go faster now, hoping to spy them as she came around the bend in the trail up ahead, but when she turned the corner all she saw was snow and trees. And more snow and trees . . . nothing but snow and trees.

By the time she reached the bridge, the clouds had grown thicker and darker, and she knew she should turn back, but somehow she just couldn't. And as tired as she was, she continued, panting breathlessly as she trudged through the thick layer of snow, following doggedly without looking up. Finally, maybe thirty minutes later, she noticed fat snowflakes were falling quickly now, and, despite her desperation to find the mysterious walkers, she knew she must turn back. For the second time, she had embarked on a fool's errand, and one that could easily turn lethal if she didn't return to her senses.

She couldn't even be sure how she finally made it back to the cabin that late afternoon. But somehow she did. By the time she reached her driveway, her vision was almost completely obscured by the swirling snow and a bluish light that was fading fast. She went inside, stripped off her snow-coated, sweat-soaked clothing, and collapsed into bed without even eating dinner.

That night she dreamed she was caught out in the woods—in the midst of a howling blizzard and waist high snow. She was freezing cold, and as hard as she tried, she couldn't push her way through the deep snow. She felt trapped in quicksand and could feel herself being pulled down, down, down. And after a while she lost all strength to resist. She no longer cared. She entirely lost her will to fight. Better to give in, to just allow its cold forces to swallow her up. And then she would be no more. Feel no more. Escape.

But just as she yielded, resting her face in the cold, white snow, two angels appeared—one on either side. They were brilliantly white, even whiter than the snow! She couldn't see the features on their faces because they glowed so brightly—like burning kerosene lamps. Still she could feel them near her, and each one held securely to an arm as they guided her through the snowstorm. They even lifted her up as if she were lighter than a rag doll, her feet trailing helplessly through the snow. And then they carried her up higher, as if she were lighter than a feather, and the three of them flew like birds above the evergreen treetops, up over the falling snow and the layer of clouds. She wanted to ask the angels their names but was so awed by them she was unable to find her voice to speak. It was a delightful dream, really, and she was sorry to wake up. But flying through the snowstorm with the angels had made her cold, and when she awoke, she was shivering in the darkness.

She looked across the coal-black room to see the fire had gone completely out. And why not, when she hadn't even bothered to stoke it up after her wild and reckless walk? Now she paid for her mistake as her feet touched the icy floor and she struggled with freezing fingers to wad up old newspaper and stack the kindling. Her hands shook from the cold as she lit a match and held it to her little mound, blowing gently to help the fragile flame grow stronger.

Wrapped in a quilt, she huddled before the fire for more than an hour before she finally began to feel free of the icy grip that had laid hold of her. And by then, despite the hour, she was wide awake and unable to sleep, still fascinated by her captivating dream. Finally, she made a pot of strong coffee and went over to look at her two recently painted canvases, hopeful she might see something worthwhile in their content. She stared for a while then frowned. Nothing more than boring snowscapes—layers of white upon white upon white. Lifeless and blah. Not even good enough to be reproduced into Christmas wrapping paper!

How long she stood there, she couldn't remember, but suddenly like a flash of light in the midst of hopeless darkness, it hit her. She moved a couple of lamps nearer her easel, then picked up a fresh pallet and opened a tube of paint. Those paintings simply weren't finished yet.

She worked with a frenzy—a creative compulsion unlike any she'd ever known before—only pausing on occasion to stretch out her stiff arm and briefly sip on her long since cold coffee. Still working, she hardly noticed when the sun came up, although she appreciated the improved light, but she continued relentlessly on until it was nearly noon. Finally, her back and shoulders burned like fire and she was forced to stop, to step back and simply close her eyes.

Without even allowing herself the opportunity to pause and evaluate her work (for fear she would be sadly disheartened) she turned toward the kitchen area and opened a can of tomato soup, quickly heated it, then sat down at the table to eat in silence. She imagined how she must look, unwashed and unkempt, huddled there still wrapped in the worn quilt, eating her lukewarm soup with only the sound of the clock ticking and the clink of the spoon against the ceramic bowl.

"I'm a madwoman," she said aloud as she set the empty bowl into the sink with a loud thunk. Suddenly, she imagined her favorite artist—Vincent Van Gogh—and the way he had cut off his ear and done other strange things, and for the first time she thought perhaps she almost understood. Sighing loudly, she paced the floor, careful to keep from accidentally seeing her recent painting, still unwilling to look at her work. "And now I'm even starting to talk to myself," she mused.

Then in sheer exhaustion, she stoked her dwindling fire and allowed herself a short nap before she returned once again to her unsettling creation. She worked until dusk this time and, lamenting the loss of good light, turned the easel toward the wall (still afraid to really look) and fixed herself a bowl of undercooked oatmeal for dinner. She knew her eyes were too tired to keep painting anymore tonight, especially if she didn't want to sacrifice the quality of her work— assuming there was any quality. And so she simply sat in the easy chair and closed her burning eyes, wondering how in the world she would ever be able to survive this soul-wrenching loneliness. It was odd though, while she had definitely felt the pain of loss, she hadn't really noticed the loneliness so much before. In fact, her solitude had been somewhat welcome when she'd first come to the cabin. But somewhere along the line, something in these circumstances had changed. Maybe it was her.

Just then, she heard a scratching sound followed by a sharp bark.

"Mike!" she cried, leaping from her chair and dropping the quilt to the floor. Sure enough, when she flung open the door, there was the dog all covered with snow. She told him to come, and, as he gave himself a shake, she ran for the towel, happily drying him off by the fire.

"Oh, what on earth are you doing out in this horrible weather, you silly old dog?" Then she hugged him, and he wagged his tail. "I'll bet you're hungry." She quickly found his dishes and filled them with food and water. She set them before him, watching with pleasure as he hungrily devoured every bite. She knew she should contact Rick. But she didn't have his phone number. And besides, it was dark out, and she wasn't eager to see him standing on her doorstep tonight. It would have to wait until morning. In the meantime, she would simply enjoy this unexpected visit from her dear old friend.

Having Mike (or Michael as she had decided to call him) made it easier to go to bed that night. It was such a comfort to hear the dog's even breathing as he slept by the warmth of the fire. But before she drifted to sleep she prayed. First she thanked God for returning Michael to her, and then she asked that she might somehow keep him for good this time. She knew it was a long shot but figured she had nothing to lose.

The next morning she awoke early, refreshed by a good night's sleep. She couldn't actually remember if she'd dreamt of angels again or not, but she was heartened to see her friend Michael still sleeping peacefully by the fire. But his head popped up as soon as he heard her footsteps. Soon his tail was thumping against the planks of the wood floor, and she knew he was waiting to be let out. She watched him make his way down the porch and into the snow, his limp barely noticeable now. She knew she had to make some kind of an attempt to reach Rick today, but she was in no hurry. And once again she prayed that God would somehow allow her to keep Michael.

After breakfast, she went over to yesterday's canvas and hesitantly turned the easel around, allowing the morning light to wash across it. She felt her hand go to her mouth as she gasped in wonder. Had she really painted *that*? She moved closer and, narrowing her eyes, studied it carefully. Incredible! There amidst the trees and snowy background she'd painted a few days back were several—what would she call them—celestial beings? No, they were simply angels. And they were artfully tucked here and there, almost so that you wouldn't notice. Some angels were partially hidden behind trees, some translucently visible in the foreground. But each angel was painted in varying shades of white—in fact the entire picture was little more than shades of white upon white. If you squinted, it looked like little more than a snowstorm. But if you looked closely, the angels were clearly there. It was amazing, really. She closed her eyes and shook her head sharply, then looked again—almost thinking she'd imagined this whole thing or was dreaming again.

"Did I really paint that?" she said aloud, drawing the attention of Michael who walked over and looked up with canine curiosity. She turned to him. "What do you think, boy?"

His tail wagged as if to give approval, although Claire knew he was simply responding to her voice. And then she began to laugh. "Oh, man, Jeannie's going to think I've gone totally off the deep end." She went to put on the coffee. "First of all, I'm talking not just to myself but to a dog as well. And next off, I've started to not only believe in angels but to paint pictures of them too."

She took her coffee mug back over to the painting, ready to look again, to see if it was really as good as she'd first thought. Perhaps she wasn't really seeing things as they were—another symptom of insanity. But this time she liked the painting even more. Of course, this alone should have disturbed her since she didn't usually like her finished work at all. And despite the opinions and approval of others, she was always her worst critic. "Maybe I am losing it, Michael," she said, taking a sip of hot coffee. "But I really think God's sending me angels to help me through this—this thing." She reached down and patted his head. "And if I'm smart I'll keep this little bit of information to myself. But I honestly think you might be an angel too."

Still, and as much as she hated to, she knew she needed to make an attempt to reach Rick. Finally, she decided to just get it over with and dialed information, but was informed that his number was unlisted. She decided to call Lucy at the store and see if she might know something more.

"Yeah, Rick got your number from me the other day, but he didn't bother to leave me his number for you." Lucy cleared her throat. "He's not the friendliest guy around, if you didn't notice."

"Well, he picked up his dog the other day, but late last night he came back."

"Rick?" Old Lucy let out a hoot. "Why, he's a married man—still, I wouldn't put it past—"

"No, no. Not Rick. The *dog* came back."

"Oh, well, that's not so bad. But still, that's a nuisance now, isn't it? Rick ought to be fined for letting his animals run wild like that."

"I don't really mind. I mean I like the dog, a lot. I honestly wish Rick would let me buy the dog from him."

"Well, why don't you then?"

"I offered, but he didn't seem too interested."

Lucy made a noise that sounded like *harrumph*. "Well, from what I've heard, that man has more dogs than a body needs, and his own family hardly has food on the table. Fact is, he's run up his bill at the store again."

Claire sighed. "Well, if you see him, would you tell him I'm willing to pay good money for this dog?"

"*Good* money?" Lucy laughed. "You sure you want me saying it just like that? Don't you know he's bound to take advantage of you?"

"Well, say it however you think best. You're the businesswoman, Lucy."

"That's absolutely right, honey. You leave it all up to me and I'll have that man paying you to keep his dog."

"Oh, I don't want that—"

"Well, one way or another, you just trust me, and I think we can work this thing out just fine."

"Thanks, Lucy."

"By the way, how's your painting coming along these days?"

"Actually, I think I've made a real breakthrough."

"Well, good for you, honey. You keep it up now."

Claire hung up the phone feeling slightly more optimistic. She knew Lucy would be a better match against someone like Rick than herself, but she still wasn't too sure he'd be willing to part with his "good ol' dog" as he'd put it. Although, now that she thought about it, she'd given up awfully easily. She knew Lucy wouldn't give in like that.

Claire got out the other snowscape now, the second one she'd painted, the one with beams of sunlight filtering through the trees. With trembling hands, she set it on the easel and stepped back. But before she picked up a brush, she closed her eyes and breathed deeply, attempting to remember the vivid angel dream from the previous night. And then she prayed that God would guide her hands, and her heart, and she began.

It was after two o'clock by the time she paused. She felt Michael's nose pressing against the back of her calf, as if to gently get her attention. She sighed and stepped back, glancing down at the dog. "I'll bet you need to go out again." He wagged his tail. Noticing hunger pains, she grabbed an apple and a chunk of cheese; the latter she shared with Michael, then she got her coat and hat and headed out the door.

"I think you could use a little exercise today," she said, heading toward the road. "Not too much, mind you, but just enough to keep that leg getting stronger." They walked slowly down the trail; it was still slightly packed from yesterday's trek, although a fresh layer of snow softened her previous tracks. The sun was trying to break through a thin veneer of fog that hung suspended through the trees like a transparent fluffy quilt, resulting in a soft, gentle sort of light—almost heavenly. It would be the perfect backdrop for her next painting! She paused now and again, allowing Michael a chance to rest his leg as she tried to memorize the scene before her. Would she be able to capture that kind of mysterious light, that downy softness? She played with various ideas for technique while she walked, praying once again that God would continue to lead her along this intriguing artist's journey she seemed to be on.

She went as far as the dead tree, curious whether or not she'd see those two sets of tracks today. But spying no fresh tracks, she decided to turn back. "I think this is far enough for you, Michael." She felt a keen sense of disappointment as they walked back. She had so wanted to see those tracks again, for as much as they disturbed and frightened her, they also gave her a strange sense of hope. Oh, she knew they couldn't *really* be angels—at least not likely—because angels surely wouldn't go tramping through the woods in snow boots. And she knew it wasn't *really* Scott and Jeremy—despite her wild imaginings. For that was impossible and ridiculous, a little insane even. But something inside her, something she dared not consciously consider let alone acknowledge, still longed for a miracle.

7

〠

Claire dreamed of Scott and Jeremy again. This time it was the old familiar beach scene with them just up ahead and her unable to catch up or make them aware of her presence. And once again she awoke with pounding heart and clenched fists—frustrated that she couldn't even catch a glimpse of their faces. She got out of bed and though it was still quite early and very dark, she turned on lights and threw fresh wood on the fire. Michael watched her curiously but didn't budge from his cozy bed by the hearth.

"It's okay, Michael," she said soothingly as she quietly closed the woodstove door. "You can't help that you've linked yourself up with a madwoman. Don't mind me. I think I'll just work on my painting a little." And so she returned to her easel and the third canvas she'd started during the last week. She was trying to capture the misty light from their walk the previous day. She knew it would be a perfect backdrop for more angels—if they would only come to her again. She'd hoped to have that dream, the one where they lifted her up to fly. But instead she'd been frustrated by the old one, and it was still haunting her now. Perhaps she could lose herself and forget about it in the process of painting.

It took Michael's nudge of reality to bring her back into the present. She paused long enough to let him out and fix them both a bit of breakfast. But then she went straight back to her work. This picture felt special somehow—as if it might actually capture the images of Scott and Jeremy. Of course, she knew the departed weren't actually real angels—she'd gone to Sunday school and church long enough to know that. Angels were heavenly beings, created by God, who went as messengers and helpers and whatnot . . . while humans, once in heaven, were supposedly given heavenly bodies (although how could one really know for sure until that day came?) and were supposed to be somehow *different* from angels. Now what exactly that difference was, or how it looked, was a complete mystery to her. And so, if she wanted to imagine her deceased husband and son as angels, well, who on earth was going to argue with her about it?

It wasn't until the late afternoon shadows came that she realized she had painted too long for them to take their daily walk. "I'm so sorry, Michael," she said, glancing at the clock and setting her brush down. "We could still go out for a bit and stretch our legs."

The snow was a dusky blue now, and when Claire looked to the eastern sky, she could see a nearly full moon shining through the trees, casting its pearly shadow through their black silhouettes. She stood in awed amazement, wondering once again if she could feasibly capture this beautiful work of creation. Would it be possible to reflect this kind of magical twilight in the medium of mere paints and canvas? And even if she could, would the angels work with it? And was she absolutely crazy to go on painting these snowscapes with angels anyway? Who would ever be interested in such things? It was highly possible that she had become compulsively obsessed with something that everyone else would just laugh at or dismiss as too sweet and overly sentimental.

She picked up the stick that Michael had just dropped at her feet and tossed it across the snow again. Not that her angels were childish or cherublike by any means. No, with her impressionist style they came across as more mysterious and strong and active—in motion somehow. At least that's how it seemed to her. But, she wondered as she impatiently waited for Michael to return with the stick again, what about what she'd painted today? Was it really what she thought it was? Was it all she hoped it would be? Who was she fooling anyway?

"Come on, boy!" she urged, heading back to the porch, stomping her boots as she opened the door.

She didn't allow herself to view the painting until she fixed them both a good dinner and cleaned up afterwards. After making herself a cup of strong tea, she set a floor lamp next to her easel and turned the easel so it faced the easy chair. Then she situated herself comfortably in the chair and looked up, unsure of what she expected to see. The painting looked different in the cabin's mellow golden lamplight—more alive and real somehow, as if the faces contained expressions she hadn't even painted there. She stared in silent wonder for a long while—until the tea in her cup grew as cold as the tears on her face. Then she slowly rose from the chair, turned off the light, and prepared for bed.

The next morning she didn't look at the previous day's painting. Promising herself to begin her twilight painting as soon as she finished her chores and took Michael for a short walk she set the haunting painting aside—in a dark corner where she could barely see it. Her reason for wanting to take an earlier walk was twofold (if the truth were to be known). Partly so she could be back in time to paint until evening when she might once again catch a glimpse of the moonlit scene, and partly in case she and Michael decided to walk further—to see where those footprints in the snow really went. She felt she owed it to herself—not to mention her sanity—to do so. But just as she was washing the last breakfast dish, the phone rang.

"I hear you got my dog over there again."

"Hello, Rick." She tried to make her voice sound cheerful and pleasant.

"Lucy's been telling me you want to buy him."

"That's right." Remembering Lucy's warning, she tried not to sound overly eager.

"Well, I told Lucy that I ain't too interested in selling him, but then she reminded me how my bill's just a little overdue—" He made a shushing sound. "I know, Lucy. Just give me a minute, would you?"

"Are you at the store right now?"

"Yeah, and Lucy's here acting like she's some kind of dog broker or something, like she's supposed to be handling all this for you."

"Well, I told her to go ahead and make you an offer."

"Like I said, I'm not real eager to sell Mike. He's a good—"

"Gimme that phone, Rick." It was Lucy's voice now. "Okay, Claire, if you want, I'll just handle this for you. You just give me the word, and I'll strike a deal that everyone can be happy with."

"Sure, Lucy. Do what you think is best. I just want to be certain I get to keep the dog, but I sure don't want him to cost a fortune either. Not that he's not worth it. Let's see, I'm willing to go a hundred dollars to start with."

"Nah, you're right, he's not worth much. I think thirty bucks is a right generous offer too."

"Thirty?" Claire frowned. "I just said—"

"Now, I myself wouldn't have given Rick a dollar for that old mutt."

"But, Lucy—"

"Well, Rick's standing here holding up five fingers in front of my nose and saying 'fifty.'"

"Fifty is fine!" Claire said with excitement. "I'll gladly pay—"

"Claire says she won't go over forty, Rick. How old's that dog anyhow?"

"Lucy!" yelled Claire. "I'll pay fifty!"

"Four years old, you say." Lucy made a tsk-tsk sound. "Why, ain't that about half a lifetime for a mutt?"

"Please, Lucy!" Claire looked down at Michael hopefully.

"Okay, Rick, Claire has agreed to forty-five. But that's her final offer."

"Lucy!"

"All right, honey. It's all settled. Forty-five it is. That'll just cover Rick's bill and that pack of cigarettes he's pocketing right now. The dog is yours—you can settle up with me later."

"Thanks, Lucy." Claire felt slightly weak. "But I'd be happy to give him fifty."

"You drive a hard bargain, honey, but Rick is holding at forty-five."

Claire's hand was shaking as she set down her cell phone. "That woman!" Then she turned to the dog. "Michael, you really belong to me now!"

The sun shone down brightly as they set out for their walk that morning. Its warmth made the snow soften and melt, sinking down into itself. This also made for easier walking and distinct footprints. But when they reached the tree, she found no new sets of footprints—only faded mushy ones from days before.

"Oh, well," she said as she turned around. "I have enough to be thankful for today." She patted Michael's head. "You belong to me now."

She spent the afternoon trying to recapture the mood and colors of the twilight evening and moon from the night before. It felt odd to be using such dark colors on the canvas this time—lots of blue and black. And she didn't really like it. Finally, late in the afternoon, she stopped, realizing that this was her chance to go see it again. She bundled up and then carried a kitchen chair out onto the porch, settling herself in to witness the spectacle unfold. As she watched the shadows grow longer, the dusky blue of the snow, and finally the now full moon appear, it occurred to her that the colors here were quite similar to Van Gogh's *Starry Night*. She waited a while longer until a few stars appeared and thought perhaps that was what the scene was missing. Then, chilled from the cold, she and Michael went back inside where she fixed their dinner with golden stars still dancing in her head.

And then she painted. Late into the night, she worked, thinking (or just hoping) that she was finally getting it. Whatever *it* was. But it was three in the morning by the time she quit, falling exhausted into her bed with her clothes still on.

The phone awakened her, and groggily she answered, afraid it might be Rick having changed his mind and now demanding that she return his dog to him. But instead it was Jeannie.

"Hi, kiddo; I thought it was about time for a check-up call. How's it going?"

"Okay." Claire yawned and pulled the quilt around her as she threw some sticks onto the embers.

"So, how's the painting coming along?"

"Pretty good, actually." Claire brightened, still not fully awake, but ready to tell Jeannie about her breakthrough. "You see, I got this dog named Michael—he's kind of like my angel, you know. Hey, isn't Michael an angel name? Like the one who protects or something?

Or maybe that's Gabriel. Anyway, this guy's name is Michael." She walked over and opened the door to let the dog out.

"Well, good," Jeannie paused. "That sounds real good. But what about the painting?"

"That's what I'm trying to tell you, Jeannie. I've been able to paint again. I mean, ever since Michael came, I've been painting. First I thought I was just painting snow—everything was just white-white-white. Then I saw these angels—well, not actually saw them, I guess. But I dreamt them, and it felt real. And I thought, hey, those snow-scapes just need some angels thrown in."

"Snowscapes? Angels?" Jeannie sounded skeptical.

"Oh, don't worry, they're not like cherubs or something you'd hang on your Christmas tree. And if you squint your eyes you almost can't see them—"

"Uh, what else have you done, Claire?"

"You mean besides angels?"

"Yeah. What else you got cooking?"

"Nothing really. Just angels. It's like I can't paint anything but angels and snow right now. I know it sounds weird, but I think it's a real breakthrough."

"Uh-huh."

"I can hear that sound in your voice, Jeannie." Claire took in a quick breath. "It's like you think I'm going wacko or something. And I have to admit I've had these same concerns myself—I mean especially when I started relating to how Vincent cut off his ear and everything—"

"Claire!"

"I'm sorry, Jeannie. I don't mean to sound crazy. And really, I'm just fine, really I am. I think this angel thing all started when I first saw those footprints in the snow. I mean they look exactly like Scott and Jeremy's, and I keep thinking maybe they're out here—just walking around in the—"

"That does it, Claire. I'm coming out."

"But you don't need—"

"Yes, I do. I need to do an ear count on you. And I don't even care what day it is."

339

"What day is it?"

"Oh, you poor thing. You don't even know what day it is? Why, it's Thanksgiving, of course."

"Thanksgiving?" Claire considered this.

"Yes. And I'm coming out. I'll even bring a turkey. And maybe some friends too. You ready for company?"

"Uh, well . . ." Claire looked around the small cabin, at herself still dressed in her rumpled clothes from the day before. "Yeah, sure. If you really want to—"

"I'll see you around two then. Don't do anything foolish before I get there."

Claire hung up the phone feeling slightly stunned. And she'd forgotten to warn Jeannie about the snow on the roads. She went to let Michael back inside and looked around. Fortunately, yesterday's sun had melted it down some, and it looked to be doing the same today. But was it really Thanksgiving? She scratched her head. How had she missed that? Maybe she really was going crazy. Oh, well, they always say you're the last one to find out.

8

Claire carefully stacked her paintings against the wall, then draped them with a sheet. It wasn't that she wanted to hide them exactly. And yet she wasn't eager to have them viewed either. Not by strangers certainly. Not even by Jeannie. Then she went to work preparing what she hoped would be some adequate side dishes to accompany Jeannie's turkey. Midway through the day she decided to call her dad. She knew he wasn't much into holidays, hadn't been since her mother died more than ten years ago.

"Hi, Daddy. Happy Thanksgiving."

"Hey, sweetie, how're you doing out there in the middle of nowhere's-ville?"

"I'm doing okay. I've been painting."

"Really? Good for you. Maybe you were right about needing all that isolation after all. Although I know I couldn't handle it myself. I needed you and all my friends around after I lost your mother."

"Well, I wouldn't want to live out here indefinitely. But for the time being, I think it's doing the trick."

"I'm glad to hear it. I've really been praying for you, Claire."

"Thanks, Daddy. I can tell that somebody has. So, you doing anything special for Thanksgiving?"

"Hank and I played eighteen holes this morning, and he's here right now trying to talk me into coming over to his place this afternoon, but I don't know."

"Oh, you should go, Daddy. Remember what you just said about needing your friends."

"Yeah, I suppose you're right. But what about you? You got any neighbors out there in the sticks wanting to eat turkey with you?"

"Actually, Jeannie's coming up. Maybe bringing some friends too."

"Well, good for Jeannie. She's a good ol' gal."

"Yeah." Claire glanced over at the shrouded canvases. "But I'm not sure that I want her to see my paintings just yet."

"Why's that?"

"Oh, I don't know. I guess I'm afraid she'll think they're weird. Or worse yet, she might think they're terrible and then be afraid to tell me for fear that I might completely fall apart and never paint again."

He laughed. "I've never known Jeannie to be anything but honest. And why would she think they're weird?"

"They have angels in them, Daddy."

"Angels?"

Claire bit her lip and waited.

"Well, what's wrong with angels anyway? Lots of Renaissance painters painted angels, didn't they?"

"Yeah. But my style isn't exactly Renaissance, you know, it's more impressionistic. And I can't think of too many impressionists who were into angels."

He chuckled. "Maybe it's time for a first. I think it sounds great, Claire. If you want to paint angels, you just go ahead and paint angels. And if Jeannie can't sell them, well then, I'll buy one, and I'll bet Hank will too. Right, Hank?"

"Oh, I forgot you have Hank there, Daddy. I better get back to my kitchen work anyway. Give him my love, and Marie too."

"You bet. Now you have a good day, sweetheart. And don't worry about those angels; if you don't want to show them to anyone yet, then don't."

She set down the phone and went back to her cooking. It was a challenge to make anything too festive with her spartan ingredients, but then she wasn't an artist for nothing. By two o'clock she had concocted an apple pie with a festively decorated crust complete with sculpted pastry leaves (hopefully it would taste as good as it looked). And she put together a pretty looking cheese and cracker plate, even if it only contained three ordinary types of cheeses cut into interesting shapes. What she lacked in food variety she hoped to make up for with ingenuity. She even managed to put together a centerpiece using pinecones, juniper berries, moss, and some emergency candles. And it wasn't half bad, although she knew the candles wouldn't last long once lit.

As it turned out, Jeannie only managed to entice one friend to drive up the mountain pass with her, her old friend Leo Goldberg. Claire only knew Leo casually, as someone loosely connected with the art world in the Bay Area and someone Jeannie had dated off and on over the past few years but had never seemed terribly serious about.

"Claire, you look lovely," said Leo as they walked in the door. Then after setting a large cardboard box on the table, he took both her hands in his. "The mountain air must agree with you."

"Yes," agreed Jeannie as she removed her big wool cape and gave Claire a kiss. "You've even got roses in your cheeks."

Claire smiled. "Oh, I'm so glad you came up, Jeannie."

"Well, to be honest, I was worried you might be up here gnawing on a table leg and mumbling to yourself."

"Yes, she was beside herself thinking you might've lopped off an ear." Leo looked at her carefully. "But they both appear to be intact."

Claire forced an awkward smile. "Actually, that might not be too far from the truth." She patted the dog's head. "But this guy has been good company for me."

"Okay, let's get this turkey into the oven to heat," said Jeannie. "And then I want to see those paintings."

"Did you actually cook this?" Claire opened the oven door and slid the golden brown turkey inside.

Jeannie laughed. "Are you kidding? I'm a city girl, and I know how to survive in the city—it's called take-out."

Leo began unpacking other food items, and he and Jeannie continued to laugh and joke about her lack of culinary skills. But suddenly the cabin began to feel overly full and slightly stuffy to Claire. She found herself stepping away from them. And she felt relieved that Jeannie had brought only one friend.

"Do you guys want to take a walk before dinner?" she asked, longing for fresh air and hoping to distract them from wanting to see her art just yet.

"Hmmm?" Jeannie looked outside the window and tapped the toe of her soft leather high-heeled boots. "I didn't exactly wear hiking boots, if you know what I mean."

"Right." Claire pointed to the chairs at the maple table. "Why don't you both sit down? Would you like some coffee or tea? I have hot water all ready."

"Tea sounds lovely." Jeannie sat down at the table, but Claire saw her eyeing the draped canvases off to her right.

Claire poured the hot water into the teapot, breathing deeply as she gazed out the window above the sink, willing herself to relax.

"Those your paintings?" asked Jeannie, as stubborn as ever.

Claire waited while the tea steeped in the pot before she returned to the table. "Yeah. But I'm not sure they're ready to be—"

"Jeannie says you've been painting angels." Leo leaned back in his chair and crossed his leg, an unreadable expression across his face. "I suppose you haven't heard that the angel trend is over now."

"Oh, Leo." Jeannie frowned and waved her hand. "Angels have been around forever."

Claire sat down with them and poured tea. "So, do you mean to say that you believe in them too, Jeannie?"

Jeannie laughed. "I *mean* that they've been represented in various art forms for thousands of years. Good grief, you can probably find them carved into some cave walls from prehistoric times. So they're certainly not only a modern-day fad, although Leo's right," she cleared her throat, "our latest angel trend is probably over by now. But that shouldn't matter—not really." Still there was something unconvincing in Jeannie's voice, like she was only trying to humor Claire.

"Cheese and crackers?" Claire hopped up to get the platter she'd so carefully prepared earlier.

"Very pretty," said Leo as he took one.

"Well, I didn't really shop for Thanksgiving," she admitted. "My pantry was a little, shall we say, boring, so I thought I better at least try to make it look good."

"But back to the paintings." Jeannie nodded toward the canvases again. "You don't really want to keep me in suspense like this, do you?"

Claire smiled. "Actually, I do."

Jeannie leaned her head back and groaned. "Whatever for?"

"Well, I'd like to enjoy your company and the dinner before . . ."

"Before what?" asked Leo.

"She's afraid we're going to hate them." Jeannie shrugged. "Well, even if they're not very good, Claire, at least you are painting. That's the main thing. And you've only been up here—what? A few weeks now. There's time to do more. I know how fast you work once you get going." She winked at Leo. "That's one thing I love about my impressionists, they usually work in a whirlwind of inspiration—producing a volume of paintings in a short amount of time."

Claire glanced at Leo. "Forgive me, Leo, but I've forgotten exactly what your connection to the art world is."

He grinned. "You may be sorry you asked."

Jeannie rolled her eyes. "Claire, honestly!"

He waved his hand. "Oh, it's all right, Jeannie—"

"No, Claire should know better than this. For heaven's sake, Leo is an art critic with the *Times*."

Claire slapped her forehead. "Oh, that's right. I'm sorry. But Jeannie can vouch for the fact that I go out of my way to remain oblivious in that area. I'm that proverbial ostrich with my head—well, who knows where? I just don't pay much attention to the reviews. I figure if someone praised my work I might turn into a prima donna and sit around on my laurels all day. And, on the other hand, if someone criticizes my work, I'm sure to take it personally and never want to paint again. And I've already been creatively paralyzed for over a year now. So, for me, it's better not to know. Besides I trust that Jeannie's keeping up with all that, and she sort of lets me know, gently, how I'm being received out there."

Leo ran his fingers down his goatee beard. "Then you probably want me to keep my mouth shut if I take a peek at your work today?"

Claire sighed. "I don't know. I probably don't really want anyone to look at it just yet."

"Come on," said Jeannie. "You can't possibly think I'd drive all the way up here and then leave without even looking."

"I thought you said this was a mental health visit," teased Claire.

Leo laughed. "Yes, and I also heard you've been chasing angels in the woods."

Claire looked down at the table.

"I'm sorry," said Leo. "I didn't mean to—"

"Oh, come on," urged Jeannie. "Claire isn't as thin-skinned as that. Are you, Claire?"

Claire looked up. "No. But you're right, Leo. I have been chasing angels in the woods."

"Well, good for you." He clapped his hands. "I like an artist with spirit and passion. It's always sure to show through in their work."

"So, you don't think I'm crazy? I mean, did Jeannie tell you that I found footprints and that I thought they belonged to my deceased husband and son—or maybe angels?"

He smiled. "Yes. I think it's a charming story. And who are we to say what's real and what's not? If it seems real to you—"

"Enough!" Jeannie stood up. "Please, don't encourage her along these lines, Leo. Claire's been through a lot this past year. She needs to move on now."

"But perhaps this is part of the moving on process for her," he argued. "Maybe she needs to chase angels in the woods to escape something. Maybe it's how she'll become free of her grief. Who are we to say?"

Jeannie sat down again. "Oh, I don't know. I just want to see her get better. And all this talk of angels-angels-angels . . . frankly it worries me."

Claire reached over and patted Jeannie's hand. "I appreciate your concern. To be honest, it worries me a little too. Sometimes, in the middle of the day when I'm doing something ordinary like heating soup or feeding the dog, I think all my obsession with angels is pure nonsense. But then, at other times, like in the silence of the snowy woods, or in the middle of the night . . . well, I'm not so sure."

"A lot of people believe in angels," said Leo quietly. "There are all kinds of books written about them."

"You two." Jeannie pressed her lips together and shook her head.

"Have you read any books on angels, Leo?" Claire leaned forward, eager to hear anything he had to say on the subject.

"No, but my mother has. She happens to be a devout believer in angels."

Claire sighed. "It's encouraging to know I'm not alone."

"Come now," said Jeannie. "It worries me to think of you out there in the snow trying to track down your dead husband and son—forgive me for being so blunt, Claire. But it sounds pretty outrageous to me."

"Oh, I don't really think it's them. . . ." She gazed out the window with a longing to be out there, walking in the cool snow.

"But you *want* it to be," said Jeannie. "That's almost as bad."

"Of course, she wants it to be them," defended Leo. "Who wouldn't want to see their departed loved ones again, if they could?"

Claire nodded. "But at the same time, I know I need to let them go. I know I need to accept that those footprints out there probably don't really belong to them."

"*Probably?*" Jeannie lifted an eyebrow.

"Okay, they *don't* belong to them."

"That's better." Jeannie glanced up at the clock. "I'll bet that turkey's almost heated by now. We should warm up those potatoes and gravy and rolls too."

The three of them enjoyed a homey and delicious dinner, and Michael enjoyed the treats tossed his way from the table. Then Jeannie helped clean up while Claire made coffee to go with their pie. Finally, they were all sitting at the table, leaning back in their chairs and feeling stuffed and content.

"It's times like this when I wish I still smoked my pipe," said Leo as he patted his full midsection.

Jeannie stood and walked slowly over to the paintings. "The time has come, Claire. Are you ready?"

Claire took in a deep breath. "Are you two ready?"

Leo rubbed his hands together. "Well, if anticipation has anything to do with it, you've sure got me going, Claire."

Claire walked over to the paintings, wondering about the best way to do this. "All right," she finally said, "if we're going to have an art show, you need to give me a couple of minutes to set up, okay?"

"Maybe we should step outside for a breath of fresh air," suggested Leo.

"Good idea," said Claire. "I'm sure Michael would enjoy stretching his legs a bit too."

With the cabin to herself, Claire rearranged the table and chairs and lights to best accommodate and display her work. She set four of the paintings on the chairs and finally placed the picture of Scott and Jeremy on the easel, draping it with the sheet, still unwilling to show it to anyone. Then she went outside to invite them back in.

Her voice actually trembled as she spoke. "Okay, the gallery is officially open."

"I'm so excited," said Leo. And that alone filled Claire with dread. An art critic! What had Jeannie been thinking?

Claire lurked behind them as they entered the cabin. She stood silently as they viewed the works, watching their every move, waiting for their reactions. But Jeannie and Leo said nothing—absolutely nothing. They simply moved about the crowded space, situating themselves to best view her various works.

"Perhaps if they were framed," she finally said weakly, almost inaudibly.

The floor squeaked beneath Leo as he moved to get a better look at the night painting. His hands hung loosely at his sides. But still he said nothing.

"Oh, I should've known," muttered Claire. "I never should've. . . ." She walked over to the sink and stared blankly out the window, wishing desperately that her company would just quietly turn and leave. Or perhaps she could leave, maybe just vanish into the air, like an angel.

Finally, Jeannie spoke, but her voice was different somehow; perhaps it was strained by all this. "What's under this, Claire?" She was standing before the easel now.

Claire stepped up to the easel. Well, why not get it over with. She might as well let them see it all. Like a felon about to be sentenced, she pulled the sheet from the painting, then stepped back, unable to actually look at it herself. Oh, if only this cabin had another room, besides the bathroom, where she might run and hide. She felt her teeth clenching and wished that this day could be over—that Jeannie and Leo could politely excuse themselves and get in Jeannie's BMW and just leave. But still they stood there, just looking in silence. As if they were too embarrassed to speak. And Claire felt as if she were standing before the two of them naked and ashamed, with nowhere to hide.

At last Jeannie turned around and faced her. But her expression was confusing. Was she upset? Angry? Frustrated by Claire's lame excuse for art? Then Claire noticed there were real tears in Jeannie's eyes.

Jeannie pulled out a handkerchief and daubed at her eyes. "These are beautiful, Claire."

"Really?" Claire grabbed Jeannie by the arms. "Tell me the truth, Jeannie. Are you just saying that? Are you afraid I've totally lost it, gone off the deep end, and you don't want to tell me for fear I'll completely crack up, and you'll have to get the men in the white coats and—"

"No!" Jeannie leaned forward and looked directly into Claire's eyes. "I *mean* it. I'm perfectly serious. These are the best things you've ever done."

Now Claire felt tears filling her own eyes. "What about you, Leo?" she asked in a shaky voice. "What do you think?"

He turned around to face her. His expression was still impossible to read, but if anything he looked slightly frightened.

"Are you okay?" she asked, stepping closer.

He nodded and took a deep breath. "You really want my opinion, Claire? Despite what you said earlier about critics?"

She considered this, then nodded. "Yes. Tell me the truth."

"These are brilliant." He rubbed his goatee thoughtfully. "I can't even think of the right words to describe them—and I'm a writer—inspired, holy, powerful, inspirational, amazing . . . that's just for starters."

She felt her knees growing weak and eased herself down into the easy chair, placing her head in her hands as she sobbed in pure relief. She felt both of them near her, their hands resting on her shoulders as they waited for this moment to pass. Finally, she looked up at them and asked, "Are you guys telling me the truth? *For real?*"

They both nodded.

"I have to take these with me, Claire. Henri must see them at once. If it's at all possible, we have to get a show scheduled before Christmas, even if that means moving some things around. Do you think you'll have any more done by then?"

"I—I don't know. It's like they come to me—like Leo said—in inspiration. Like God is actually guiding my hand."

"I believe that," said Leo.

Jeannie nodded. "Well, whatever it takes, if you can do more, it'll help the show."

"Are you sure, Jeannie? I mean, like Leo said, angels aren't really in vogue right now. And what if Henri doesn't—"

"You let me figure this out."

"But you really think anyone would want to buy them?"

Jeannie pressed her lips together. "Well, you can just never tell about these things. I've seen work that I thought was amazing and brilliant before, but the public just didn't seem to get it. I suppose that could happen."

Leo nodded thoughtfully. "Yes, I've seen it too. I've given artists the best reviews and then watched them sink into oblivion."

Claire looked down at her lap. "Yeah, I know what you mean."

"But we've got to give it a try," said Jeannie. She glanced at her watch. "And we should probably be on our way now, Claire."

Claire stood and took Jeannie's hand. "Thanks so much for everything."

"I'll load up the pictures," said Leo. "Do you have any spare blankets to wrap them in?"

"There are some in that closet by the bathroom," instructed Jeannie.

"The one on the easel . . ." Claire began with hesitation.

"Yes?" Jeannie nodded.

"I don't really want to sell that one."

"I didn't think you would." Jeannie put her hand on Claire's shoulder. "But can you let it be in the show?"

Claire glanced over at the painting, knowing she would miss it but also knowing it might be better to have it away from her, for now. "Yes. You can take it."

"Good."

After the paintings were loaded, Jeannie turned to Claire. "About those footprints in the woods?"

"Yes?"

"Well, maybe they are something more. I mean, you never know."

Claire smiled. "Or maybe you're just saying that because you like the inspiration they provided."

Jeannie grinned. "Maybe."

"So you like representing a mad artist, now, do you?"

Jeannie shook her head. "No. I like representing *you*. I definitely do *not* want you to go mad. And if necessary, I recommend you search out those footprints if only to prove to yourself they belong to a couple of perfectly normal human beings just out enjoying nature the same as you."

"Yes, I may do that."

"I just want you to stay healthy, kiddo." Then Jeannie leaned over and gave her a kiss on the cheek. "You take care of yourself now. And don't you quit believing in angels!"

"That's right," called Leo. "I can't wait to tell my mom about you!"

9

For the next two weeks, Claire divided her time between painting and walking and daily chores, all this with Michael by her side. Painting came more easily to her now; it almost seemed that something new had been unleashed or maybe broken when Claire heard the approval of two art professionals. And it wasn't that her art was dependent on the opinions of others, but under the circumstances, she appreciated it.

She had suspected she wouldn't be able to keep up the frenzied, somewhat crazed pace of her original angel pieces. But she'd known even then that it was slightly fanatical, almost over the edge. Now she was thankful to simply continue. Plus she noticed that a quiet peace seemed to accompany her as she worked. And to Jeannie's great pleasure, Claire managed to create four more paintings for the show. She could hardly contain herself as she told Jeannie the good news on the phone.

"I can't wait to see them," exclaimed Jeannie. "I'll send a courier to pick them up. If I get right on it, he could be there by late this afternoon."

"They're a lot like the earliest ones," explained Claire as she studied her latest painting. "Mostly shades of white on white and snow-covered trees with angels here and there. Sometimes I worry that the angels are too subtle; I'm afraid the viewer could almost miss them."

"Yeah, but once they see them, they'd wonder how they ever missed them in the first place."

"I hope you're right." Claire said, washing out a dirty brush.

"Of course, I'm right. Everything's all set too. The show will begin this weekend. Did I tell you that Henri actually postponed an *Andrew Banks* show until *after* the New Year—can you believe it? Just so he could squeeze your show in *before* Christmas. He's such a doll. And he plans to run it for three weeks—it's his best-selling season of the year, you know. Can you believe our luck with this timing?"

Claire bit into her lip. "I just hope he's not disappointed."

"What do you mean?"

"I mean it could be a total flop."

"Well, you let us worry about that, kiddo. You just keep on chasing those amazing angels."

Claire sighed. "That's got me worried."

"What's wrong, sweetie?"

"Well, I've been having those old dreams again. And I can't quit thinking about those—those footprints in the snow. I know it sounds crazy, Jeannie, and I don't really believe it right now, but sometimes in the middle of the night, I feel just certain that they belong to Scott and Jeremy."

"Claire, you know it can't really be—"

"Oh, I know, I know—at least my head knows, most of the time anyway. But it's this whole angel thing that's got me going. And strange things have happened to other people. Lucy at the store was telling me just yesterday that a friend of hers is certain he saw Big Foot a few years ago. So how can I be so certain that it isn't them? What if it is?"

Jeannie exhaled loudly. "Well, as your rep, I shouldn't even say this—it's like shooting myself in the foot—or telling you to kill off your muse . . . but as your friend I know I have to speak up." She cleared her throat. "Claire, it's like I said before, I think it's time you followed those footprints—to their final conclusion, I mean. Then, and only then, you will see that they belong to a pair of perfectly ordinary human beings—flesh and blood . . . not feathers and angel dust. Come to think of it, it could be the old couple that has a place down the road a ways. They used to walk pretty regularly as I recall. I think their name was Henson or Henderson. And she was a real tiny lady; I'll bet she could have child-sized feet."

"Yeah, you're probably right." Claire considered an older couple walking through the snowy woods. Yes, it could happen. "I've tried to follow the footprints before, but for one reason or another, I always turned back. Lately I've been thinking about following them again, but. . . ." She paused, uncertain.

"The illusion would be over."

Claire swallowed. "Yeah. That's what I'm thinking."

"Well, maybe it's time to end this thing—to really move on, you know? I realize that life dealt you a really low blow in losing Scott and Jeremy. But you've got a bright future, kiddo. And there are all kinds of good things in store for you, but you need to be ready for them. And even if this means it's the end of your—uh—angel era, I'm sure you'll still be inspired to paint something else equally wonderful, in time. Talent like yours doesn't come along every day."

Claire was ready for this conversation to end. "I hope you're right, Jeannie; I want to believe you."

"Trust me, sweetie, it's not healthy for you to live in a fantasy world." She paused, then laughed. "And as greedy as I am to have you producing more of those lovely angel paintings, I'm not willing to see you sacrifice your emotional well-being for them."

"Thanks. I appreciate your honesty."

"And, don't forget, I want you here for the opening of the show."

"What day is that again?"

"This Friday night. Come at seven for the preview showing. I have some people I want you to meet. Shall I send someone for you?"

"No. I can drive. I'm just not sure what to do about Michael."

"Michael?"

"My dog."

"Oh, yeah. Why not bring him along?"

"I would, except the landlord doesn't allow pets in my apartment."

"Oh." She could hear Jeannie tapping her pencil on the phone

354

now, her sign that it was time to hang up. "Well, you know I'm not crazy about dogs, but I suppose he could stay at my place."

"Thanks, Jeannie. I might have to take you up on that."

"See you on Friday then.

After another restless night, haunted by the same old dream, Claire decided that Jeannie was right. It was time to follow those footprints and just get it over with. And, after all, why shouldn't she become acquainted with her neighbors, the Hendersons, or whoever they were. If they were real neighbors, that is.

"Ready for a nice long walk?" she asked Michael after putting away the last of the breakfast dishes.

He wagged his tail in response and waited by the door as she slowly bundled up. Several inches of fresh snow had fallen the night before, and the temperature had dropped since yesterday. She took a few minutes to stack more firewood on the porch, then the two of them set out. As she walked, she wondered if she shouldn't just pack things up this week. Hadn't she accomplished what she'd set out to do? To break the bond that had kept her from painting? What other reason was there to stay? She looked at Michael happily running ahead of her. That "no dog" policy at her loft apartment did present a bit of a problem, but perhaps she could sublet it and find a new place. But where?

She shook her head, as if to dispose of these troubling thoughts. Why not just enjoy the day, the walk, the snow? After all, if she decided to stay in San Francisco after the opening, it could be her last chance to be here and to do this. She took in a deep breath and looked up at the sky. She hadn't noticed earlier that it had that heavy look again—that dull gray density that could possibly mean more snow. Hopefully it would hold off until later that afternoon. By then she'd have met the old couple and be safely back at her cabin, probably packing up to leave. She'd have to remember to take some time to stop by and say good-bye to old Lucy. Lucy had been a real godsend, especially when it came to securing the deal with Michael. Claire smiled to herself as she recalled Lucy's surprised face when she'd gone in to settle up Rick's bill for the dog.

Claire had painted a small angel picture for her on an old piece of board she'd found in the shed. Nothing really special, but Lucy had been deeply touched.

"I'll hang it right here by the cash register," she'd promised. "Why, it's my first piece of honest to goodness art—and from a real live artist too!"

Claire and Michael trekked through the woods until they reached the dead tree. And there, to her surprise, were two sets of fresh tracks, clearly visible, as if they'd just been made. This was more than she'd hoped for! She'd expected to at least discover some old tracks that were still discernable, but nothing as plain as these. She looked up the trail, half expecting to see an old couple slowly walking along. But there was no one. Still, she should have no problem following these footprints to their "final conclusion," as Jeannie had put it. And if she hurried she might actually catch up with them.

She walked fast. Pausing at the footbridge to catch her breath, she glanced up at the sky with slight apprehension. The clouds seemed a little lower now, but no flakes were falling as yet. Still she could never be sure. "Okay, boy, ready to go?"

Michael turned around as if to head back toward home as usual. "No, we're going this way today, Michael," Claire said.

He looked at her curiously, then joined her, tail wagging eagerly.

"Yes, we're going to meet our neighbors," she announced as they continued on, her heart beating a little faster in anticipation.

After about ten minutes of fast walking, Claire noticed it had begun to snow. Nothing threatening, just a few random flakes. But the farther she got from the turning point of the footbridge, the more her heart began to pound. What in the world was she doing? And why? Tracking footprints that belonged to a couple of old-timers? What did she really hope to prove by this anyway? And what if the footprints simply went on and on—traveling off into nowhere? What if she and Michael were to become lost out here, all alone in the wilderness with no one for miles around? Who would ever think to check on them or go out to look? She stopped and glanced nervously at the trail behind her. Should she turn back? It wasn't too late to stop and retrace her steps. And yet something beyond herself, something deep within, seemed to drive and compel her forward. And so she continued, praying silently as she went.

The footprints continued up over a slight hill, then curved off to the right. The snow was falling harder as she and Michael descended the hill, and she could feel it blowing around her in little flurries. And visibility began to decrease.

"It can't be too far ahead," she said aloud, to assure herself as much as Michael. She noticed that the footprints were becoming less distinct; they were slowly being devoured by the quickly falling snow. "We've got to hurry, Michael!"

Claire began to jog, keeping her eyes focused on the ground ahead of her, afraid if she made one wrong turn, she and Michael might be lost out here forever. She paused once to look behind her. At least her freshly made footprints were still fairly clear; she ought to be able to follow them home if weather forced them to turn back. She tried to envision the older couple out walking in the snow. But somehow it just didn't fit. And then she remembered the pair of snow angels—one big, one small. Surely an elderly couple wouldn't lie down on the snow and make snow angels—would they? And if the rapidly fading footprints in front of her didn't belong to that elderly couple, whom did they belong to? Could it be?

She continued jogging, a tight feeling wrapping itself around her chest with each step. The snow was falling even faster now, and the trail was a blur. She couldn't even be sure she was still following the footprints. Perhaps she had stumbled onto a deer trail. She knew how they crisscrossed the National Forest. A person could become lost for weeks following such a trail.

"Oh, dear God," she cried out breathlessly as she continued pressing on. "Help me!"

Finally, she stopped running and bent over, her chest heaving up and down from the exertion. She wasn't even sure how long she'd been traveling, but a knifelike pain stabbed into her right side, and her lungs burned like fire. She knew she could run no farther. Her legs felt like lead, and her heart was consumed with fear. She knew she was lost. And all around her was white and swirling snow, thick and opaque, like a living blanket that wanted to suffocate her. She looked all around, unable to see her dog.

"Michael!" she screamed. But her voice sounded dull, hushed by the deadening acoustics of the snow and the wind. "Michael!" she cried again, turning around in a circle. "Please, come here, boy!"

10

Claire never knew for sure how she got there. Perhaps it was like in her angel dream, with a pair of invisible celestial beings lifting her up and carrying her along, high above the storm. Or maybe it was Michael, her angel dog, who had led her to safety. She could only imagine. But somehow, both she and her faithful companion emerged half frozen from the snowy woods. And seeing a faint golden light up ahead, she stumbled stubbornly toward it, forcing one icy foot in front of the other until she collapsed on the porch of a cabin not much larger than her own.

And even then she couldn't remember anyone coming to the door, or opening it up and saying, "Hello, and what have we here?" In fact, she later learned she had never even made it to the door. It was Michael's persistent scratching and loud barks that had finally aroused the attention of the tenants. The first thing Claire remembered was sitting in front of the big river rock fireplace, her bare feet wrapped in a soft woolen throw, and a young girl, about age ten, Claire guessed, holding a thick mug of hot tea before her.

"Can you drink this?" asked the girl in a quiet voice.

"Thank you." Claire believed she said those words, although she couldn't be sure. But she did recall taking the warm mug into her hands and eagerly wrapping her cold fingers around its exterior, then slowly drinking the hot contents.

"My dad's calling for help," said the girl.

Claire felt her eyes open more widely. "Help?"

"For you. He thinks you have hyperthermia."

Claire thought she may have smiled at that. "You mean hypo-thermia?"

The girl solemnly nodded. "You looked frozen."

"My dog?" Suddenly Claire remembered being unable to see Michael in the snow. The girl pointed to her left and, curled right next to Claire's bundled feet, Michael rested by the warmth of the fire.

"He's okay." The girl ran her hand along Michael's still damp coat. "He's a good dog, isn't he?"

Claire nodded. "Thank you for helping us. My name is Claire. I live in a cabin—"

"Has she come to?" This came from a male voice, and he sounded worried. Claire turned to see a man now entering the room. His blond hair looked disheveled and his beard in need of a trim. "Are you okay?" He came over and knelt in front of Claire, peering into her eyes as if to discern her mental stability as much as her physical well-being.

"I think I'm fine," she answered, feeling like the village idiot. "I—uh—got lost in the snow."

"I can understand that," he said, standing to peer out the window. "It's turned into a real blizzard out there."

"I'm sorry to trouble you—"

"Good grief, you're no trouble. You and your dog looked like you were about to freeze out there."

"I'm so glad we stumbled onto your house."

"I'll say. You must've had a guardian angel watching over you."

She looked at him closely. "An angel?"

He laughed. "Well, who knows? But how are you feeling now? It doesn't look like you're suffering from frostbite. Fortunately you were well bundled up. But I suspect you worked up a sweat trying to find your way through the snow, and you were getting pretty chilled."

She nodded, noticing now that her heavy wool jacket had been replaced by a thick polar-fleece blanket. "Yes, we were running—I got scared—"

"I was afraid you might have hypothermia. You were shivering pretty badly. I called 911, and they told me just to get you warm and that it would take them at least two hours to get anyone out here, due to the weather."

"Oh, I don't need anyone—"

"Right, I'll let them know."

"I'm actually starting to feel warmer now." She looked up into his eyes, noticing that they were a mixture of blue and gray and perhaps a mossy green. Interesting really. "I should probably get going."

He laughed. "Not in this weather, you don't."

She looked out at the snow still swirling in menacing circles. "I suppose you're right."

"We'll give you a ride home as soon as you've had a chance to get thoroughly warm and when the weather abates some."

"Thanks." She looked over at the girl who was still peering at her curiously. "Thanks for everything."

"It was your dog that got Anna's attention." He nodded to the girl. "He was scratching and barking. Pretty smart dog, that one."

Michael opened his eyes and looked up now, his tail thumping on the floor.

She reached down to pat his head. "Good boy, Michael."

"Michael?" said the girl. "Is that his name?"

"Yes," Claire answered her then looked back at the man. "And as I was just telling your—uh, your daughter?"

He nodded. "That's right."

"That my name is Claire Andrews, and I live in a cabin over on Ridge Road."

"I'm Garret Henderson—"

"Oh, are your parents the Hendersons—" she interrupted, then laughed. "I mean do they own this place? My friend mentioned an older couple named—"

"Yes, Marge and Carl. They stay here during the warmer months. But usually this place is abandoned in winter."

Anna nodded. "You're lucky we were here."

"I'll say."

"What I can't figure out is what you were doing this far from home." Garret scratched his already messy hair. "And in weather like this."

"I know. I must seem like a crazy woman to be out in this." She frowned. "Actually, it's kind of a long story."

"And you should probably rest." Garret stepped back. "And I need to call those 911 folks back and let them know we don't need an ambulance or anything."

"Right." Claire leaned her head back into the comfortable chair and closed her eyes. She felt so silly about her quest now—trekking off in the middle of a snowstorm to find her lost angels. Good grief, had she been mad? And, of course, Jeannie had been right. Two perfectly normal human beings. No feathers or angel dust anywhere.

"More tea?" offered Anna.

Claire opened her eyes to see Anna with her hand out, ready to take the nearly empty mug. The girl had a lovely oval-shaped face with clear blue eyes. Her hair, slightly darker than her father's, was about the color of polished oak. "Thank you," said Claire, "more tea would be nice."

When Anna returned, Claire asked her how old she was.

"I'll be eleven next month," she said proudly.

Claire nodded. "That was about my guess."

"I'm really supposed to be in school right now, but I got special permission to be with my dad while he works on his book."

"His book?"

"Yeah." Anna smiled brightly. "My dad is an author."

"Cool." Claire took a sip of tea. She wanted to ask about Anna's mother but couldn't quite put this question into words, at least not into words that didn't sound rude or intrusive.

"We've been here since school started in September. I'm doing home school until we go back and I can be in my class again." She frowned.

"And you're not looking forward to that?"

"Not really. I like it out here. And I think I learn more doing home school than I do at real school. My dad's a good teacher."

"What kind of books does your dad write?"

"Novels." Anna's eyes grew wide. "That means they're fiction, which is the same as not being true. Oh, it's not that my dad tells lies, but he makes his stories up, you know?"

Claire smiled. "Yes, I know."

"Actually, he writes historical novels."

A light went on. "Does your dad go by the name of G. A. Henderson?"

"Yeah. Garret Allen Henderson." She nodded proudly. "That's him."

"I've read some of his books. He's good."

Anna's face grew brighter than ever, and suddenly Claire wished she could paint her. She would be a perfect model for an angel. Not that Claire had needed models before, but the idea appealed to her now.

"Well, I think I finally convinced them that you were okay," said Garret, coming back into the room. "But they were pretty determined to send out an ambulance."

"I'm sorry to cause so much trouble."

"Oh, it's okay. I think I needed a break anyway."

"Yeah, he has barely stopped working today," complained Anna.

"She told me that you're an author," said Claire. "I've actually read a few of your books—and liked them."

He smiled—kind of a crooked smile but sincere, and nice. "Thanks. I guess you'd have to say that though, wouldn't you. You wouldn't want to risk me throwing you back out in the freezing snow again."

She laughed. "No, really. I did like them. You're very good."

He shook his head. "Well, I'm not so sure about that anymore. It's taken me nearly two years to finish this last one, and even now, I'm . . ." He sighed deeply. "Well, just not too sure."

"I'll bet it's the best thing you've ever done."

He looked at her curiously. "Don't know what makes you think so. But let's hope you're right."

"Well, I think we sometimes become the most critical of our work when it's really the best."

"Are you a writer?"

She smiled. "No. Actually I'm an artist."

"An artist?" Anna's eyes grew wide. "A real artist?"

"Oh, no." Garret held his hands in mock alarm. "Now, you've gone and done it. You didn't realize that Anna is absolutely enamored by artists. She'll probably never let you go home now."

Claire laughed. "A girl after my own heart. Well, don't worry, Anna, I used to be just like that too. That is, until I got to meet way too many artists. Although I must admit I still get giddy sometimes when I meet someone I really admire."

"Yeah," said Garret. "I'm like that too—with authors."

"What kind of art do you do?" Anna asked eagerly.

"Maybe I should leave you girls on your own for a while," said Garret. "Perhaps I can finish this chapter up before I take you home. I was just getting into the groove, you know, before you got here."

"Of course," Claire waved her hand. "I absolutely understand. I'm the same way with my art."

For the next hour, Claire and Anna talked about art. And Anna shyly showed her own sketches and watercolors, which Claire actually thought were quite well done for a girl that age—and told her so. Then Claire helped Anna prepare a light lunch of soup and grilled cheese sandwiches.

"I can cook almost anything," said Anna as she set the plate of sandwiches on the table.

"I believe it." Claire nodded. "You look like you know your way around the kitchen."

"Do I smell something?" Garret poked his head out from what Claire suspected was both an office and bedroom, since the cabin hadn't appeared large enough to have more than two bedrooms, plus the loft above.

"Just in time," said Anna. "We might've eaten them all up without you." She grinned at him. "Since I know you didn't want to be disturbed."

They all sat down at the table, then Garret and Anna bowed their heads to pray. Claire followed suit, both pleased and surprised by the gesture. After Garret said a quick but earnest sounding prayer, they all began to eat.

"Claire told me that she's been painting pictures of angels lately," Anna informed her father.

"I'd invite Anna to see them," explained Claire, "but they were just picked up yesterday for an art show this coming weekend."

"Where's the show?" asked Garret as he dipped his spoon into his soup.

"A gallery called The Blue Moon. It's in San Francisco."

"Hey, I know where that is," said Garret. "That's a pretty swanky joint."

"Henri LaFollete is the owner—and a friend of mine."

"Lucky you."

Claire considered his words without responding. "I told Anna I wished that I could paint her."

"Could she, Daddy?"

He frowned slightly. "I guess so; I mean, if she really wants to."

"Yes, I'd love to." Suddenly Claire remembered how her time in the mountains seemed to be coming to an end this week, how she'd been considering returning to the city for good on Thursday. "I guess I should say if I come back, that is."

"*If* you come back?" Anna frowned. "You mean you're leaving? I just barely get to meet my first real live artist and now you're leaving me? Already?"

"Hey, Anna, you don't want to make our guest feel—"

"Oh, it's okay. I can understand how she feels." Claire turned to Anna. "I'm not completely sure about leaving. I've still got some things to work out. For one thing, I'm not allowed to keep a dog in my apartment in the city. And I can't bear to part with Michael—"

"We could take care of him for you," said Anna eagerly. "I'd love to have a dog for a while. I'd take him for walks and brush him and everything."

Claire glanced uncomfortably at Garret who seemed to be remaining fairly silent just now. "Oh, I couldn't impose," she said. "First of all, I land on your doorstep in the midst of a blizzard, and then to leave my dog while I'm gone—"

"Oh, please," begged Anna the way only a ten-year-old can. "Can we take care of Michael? Please, Daddy?"

Garret cleared his throat and daubed his mouth with a napkin. "You'll have to let me think about this, Anna."

"But, Daddy—"

He stood. "Please, Anna. We'll discuss it later."

11

|||||||||||||||||||||||

Later that evening, Claire wondered if she hadn't simply imagined the events of the day. And that strange but unforgettable encounter with Garret and Anna—perhaps she'd simply dreamed it. She busied herself with packing up her art supplies. Then, just as she closed the big wooden case, she wondered if she was really ready to leave yet. She looked over to where Michael was sleeping soundly by the fire—surely exhausted from his freezing trek through the woods today—proof that perhaps it was real after all. She knew she could take him to San Francisco with her, leave him with Jeannie, and begin searching for a new place that allowed dogs. But she couldn't erase the sound of Anna's voice, pleading to keep the dog for her. Surely the girl was a bit lonely, staying out here with only her father for company. And while Garret seemed a nice man, on first acquaintance anyway, he did appear slightly moody. What had started out for her as a magical visit had eventually deteriorated into what felt like a hastily ended intrusion (of course, she'd been the intruder).

She'd almost considered inviting them into her cabin, to give Anna a close-up look at the life of a "real artist." Not that it was anything terribly interesting, but the girl had seemed so completely fascinated by it all. But after the way Garret had suddenly turned quite chilly toward her, all she could think of was escaping him and his unreadable scrutiny. If that's what it really was. And she couldn't even be sure of that. It was quite possible that she was just overreacting to everything, due to life in general plus her isolation of late. Perhaps she'd simply misplaced or forgotten all her previous social skills.

She realized now that she'd been pacing back and forth, completely unsettled by all this. And perhaps, if she were to be truly honest with herself, she could face the real reason for her unrest. Maybe the most disturbing part of her day was that she never did find Scott and Jeremy at the end of the trail. And she never stumbled across angels either. Well, at least not that she could remember. But then, who knew what may have accompanied her through the snowy woods, guiding her to safety. Still, it didn't matter. For, somehow, she knew that the events of the day were meant to force her to let go—to accept that Scott and Jeremy were gone now. And she would not see them again until it was time for her to leave this earth permanently too. She considered how close she may have been to actually joining them today and shuddered. Surprisingly, she was relieved to be alive. She wrapped her arms around herself and prayed a silent thank-you prayer. For the first time in nearly eighteen months, she realized she really did want to live after all.

That night she slept dreamlessly. Or if she had dreamed, she hadn't been disturbed by the content. She awoke feeling refreshed and renewed. But still she needed to decide what to do. Pack everything up and leave for good or plan on returning after the show? On one hand, it felt as if her work here was done. She'd made her painting breakthrough—as well as her emotional and even spiritual one too. Really, she was ready to go. Then why didn't she feel ready? With Christmas just around the corner, she knew the smart thing would be to go home. Why would she want to spend the holidays here, all alone—in such complete isolation?

She wondered what Anna and Garret would do during Christmas. Was there a wife and mother somewhere? If so, where? But why was she troubling herself with all these questions that had absolutely nothing to do with her?

"What do you think, Michael?" she asked as they walked outside. "You want to go for a really long ride today?"

His tail began to wag, and as crazy as it seemed, she let that be her sign—at the same time chiding herself for allowing the least necessary piece of canine anatomy to be the deciding factor of her fate. But it was better than flipping a coin. Still, by the time she got the cabin completely cleared out and the back of her Jeep packed, she felt unsure. And it bothered her that Anna would be expecting to hear from her again about caring for the dog.

Finally she decided to go back inside and write Anna a quick note that she could leave with Lucy (who also handled what little mail came to the local post office boxes). Apologizing for her change in plans, Claire wrote that she'd decided it was time for her to leave for good, and she had no choice but to take Michael along with her. She also encouraged Anna to continue pursuing her art dreams and thanked her and her father once again for rescuing her. Then she signed her name and sealed the envelope. She didn't bother to put a return address on it since it wasn't being mailed from the city, and there was little chance that Lucy wouldn't get it into the right box. Then she took one last look around the cabin, making sure everything was in its place, and much cleaner and nicer than when she'd first arrived. She locked the door and slipped the key back into the secret hiding place and, telling herself that she was doing the right thing, left.

But she felt a lump growing in her throat as she navigated the Jeep through the accumulation of snow—the roads had only been plowed once and that had been a couple weeks earlier. By the time she reached the store, she had recovered.

"Can you put this in the Henderson post office box?" she asked.

"Sure." Lucy examined the name on the front. "Oh, so you've met young Anna, have you? Isn't she the sweetest little thing?"

Claire nodded. "Yes. And she aspires to be an artist too."

"Well, isn't that perfect. Maybe you can give her some lessons—"

"Actually, I'm leaving now, Lucy."

"Leaving?" Lucy frowned. "You mean for good?"

"Yes. I think I've accomplished what I set out to do here."

Lucy leaned forward as if examining Claire. "And what was that, exactly?"

Claire smiled. "I needed to get back to my art. I'd been sort of blocked, if you know what I mean."

"Blocked? A good artist like you?" Lucy shook her head. "What in tarnation could block someone with your kind of talent?"

Claire had never divulged any of her history to this old woman before, but considering how Lucy had been such a good friend, not to mention working out the deal with her dog, she didn't mind telling her a bit more now. "Actually, I lost my husband and son about a year and a half ago and—"

"Oh, dear!" Lucy reached over and grabbed her hand in hers. "You don't have to explain another thing, honey. I know exactly what you mean. Why, when I lost my Walter, about ten years back, I was a perfect mess. Good grief, it took me several years to pull myself together. I let the store just go to wrack and ruin—Walter would've been furious with me." She laughed. "Maybe he was."

"But it looks like you're doing fine now."

"And so are you, honey. You're doing just fine. I can tell."

"Thanks for being a friend." Claire smiled. "I appreciate it."

"Well, you come back and visit now, ya hear?"

Claire waved as she opened the door. "I'll try to, Lucy. Maybe when the weather gets warm again."

The driving was much better on the main highway, with the pavement fairly clean and dry. They made a quick lunch stop and a couple of stops in between, but the closer Claire got to the city, the more excited she became.

"I've got a big show this weekend," she told Michael as she drove. "And you'll have to spend some time on your own for a while, over at Jeannie's, but you'll be okay, won't you?" She reached over and patted his head. "And I'll see about getting us into a bigger place, something with a yard for you to play in." She frowned. A yard? In the city? Who was she kidding? "Well, who knows, maybe we'll move out of the city." She smiled at the thought. "Actually, we can move wherever we want, Michael." She took in a deep breath, exhaling in a happy sigh. "Because I'm doing better. And I'm ready to move on." She almost regretted selling her big house now. But it had seemed too large and empty after losing Scott and Jeremy. And even with a dog she wouldn't need that much space now. No, it had been the right thing to do. She knew she'd find the perfect place eventually. She believed that God was directing her path from here on out.

On a hopeful hunch, she decided to give her landlord a call before she got to the city, just to see if there might be the slightest chance to get her lease changed to include a pet, even if it cost more. She explained the situation about adopting Michael in what she hoped was heartwarming detail, telling how he was an amazingly well-trained animal and how she would take all financial responsibility for everything and anything. And after a long pause he finally agreed to let her keep the dog, but only until Christmas.

"I'm sorry," he said, "but that's the best I can offer. And it's only because you've been a really good tenant. Unfortunately, I've had trouble with people and pets before. So I just can't allow more than a couple of weeks. However, if you're wanting to sublet your place, I do know of a woman who's looking for something just like it."

"Great, can you let her know I'm interested?"

"Sure."

She turned off her phone. "Well, Michael, we've got until Christmas to figure this out."

It was nearly midnight by the time she'd unloaded and put away everything from the Jeep. Michael had faithfully followed her up and down the three flights of stairs, and she hoped that maybe this would help to familiarize him with his new surroundings. She felt bad about uprooting this country dog to such an urban setting. But amazingly, he seemed to be fairly happy. Still, he didn't let her out of his sight.

"We'll lay low tomorrow," she promised him as she arranged an old army blanket for his bed right next to her own. She was glad that she'd returned a day before the opening; it would give them both more time to adjust. Being back in her old bed was a little unsettling. She recalled all the sleepless nights she'd spent tossing and turning there before. But perhaps it would be different now. Maybe this was the true litmus test as to whether she was really moving on or not.

To her surprise she slept fairly soundly again. Other than waking up a couple of times when she heard street noises below—a startling change after the silence of the cabin—she really did sleep well.

By midmorning, she was bored with puttering about her low-maintenance loft apartment, and she'd already taken Michael for a short romp in the nearby city park—a mere slip of land wedged between the packed-in housing. Finally she decided to set up her easel, ready to attempt an idea that had sprung up like a fertile seed, planted somewhere in the back of her mind. She'd been toying with it for a couple of days now. And it was time to see if she could really pull it off. It wasn't that she planned to put this in the show. But it was something she wanted to attempt.

By late that evening, she was finished. She washed out her brushes, and without looking at the painting, took Michael out for one last quick walk, then took a hot shower and collapsed exhausted into her bed.

The next morning, she got up just as the sun was rising. Feeling like a stranger in her own house, she tiptoed over to the easel and took a peek at yesterday's painting. With the morning sunlight gently diffused through a thin voile curtain, it was as if the painting was specially lit. She stared at the image with wide eyes, wondering if she'd really captured the likeness or whether her memory had simply transformed itself, meshing into her latest creation. But even if the portrait didn't look like Anna, it somehow captured the girl's spirit. And that's what she'd wanted. Oh, she knew the little girl wasn't really an angel. No doubt, she could probably be a little tyrant if she wanted to be. What child couldn't? But there was something in that face, her countenance, her innocence . . . something Claire had been unable to forget ever since the day she'd met her.

Stepping back, she studied the picture more critically now. She wasn't sure why she'd painted a white bird in Anna's hands; she hadn't planned to in the beginning, but somehow it had just seemed to fit, with its feathery wings splayed open like a burst of living light. Really, this piece was beautiful. But then that was only *her* opinion. And she had been wrong before. She'd have to let Jeannie and Henri be the final judges.

She sighed, then shook her head. Why deceive herself? It was the public and the art critics who would be the final judges in this matter. And in all honesty it was the actual "patrons of the arts" who really determined whether any single work was a success or not. Because, despite what critics or contemporaries might think, it was that old bottom line that could make or break any show. She took in a deep breath and slowly exhaled, willing herself to calm. But the nagging fear wouldn't leave her. What if her show was a complete bust?

She filled her day with mundane chores, doing laundry, organizing a storage closet, walking the dog, paying bills. But by midafternoon she felt as if her nerves were all on edge. How would she manage to survive this opening? She fumbled to dial Jeannie's number, waiting impatiently until an assistant finally put her on the line.

"Jeannie?" she heard the urgency in her own voice.

"What's wrong, kiddo? You sound upset."

"I am! I mean, I'm totally freaked out." She took in a quick breath. "I just know they're going to hate me—my art. What *was* I thinking? *Angels?* Good grief! Why didn't you tell me that I was out of my mind? It's just way too sentimental, too weird. Oh, Jeannie—"

"Take it easy, Claire. It's going to be okay."

"I'll be a laughingstock. I'll probably never be taken seriously again. Is it too late to cancel the show? Can Henri get—"

"Relax, Claire. You're getting yourself all worked into a lather over nothing."

"Nothing?"

"Well, I'm not saying your art is nothing. But think about it— what is the worst that can happen? That's what my shrink always asks me. I mean, really, what's the worst case scenario here? That people won't like it? Won't get it? You won't sell anything?" Jeannie groaned. "Well, okay, even if that did happen, it wouldn't be the end of the world, would it?"

"I guess not."

"And I doubt that it would even end your career. People have pretty short memories when it comes to art. And besides, what if you hadn't painted those angels; where would you be right now?"

"Back at the cabin?" Suddenly Claire didn't think that sounded so bad—safe, secure, isolated.

"Yeah, and you'd be so down, you'd probably be ready to just give up."

"But if this show goes bust, I'll be ready—"

"I don't want to hear another word of negativity from you. You're killing my mood, and I need to be on my toes tonight. Now, let's change the subject. Tell me, when did you get into town anyway? And are you dropping Bowzer by my house?"

"We got here on Wednesday, and his name is Michael. I've got permission to keep him with me until Christmas."

"Great."

"But, Jeannie—"

"Only positive thoughts, Claire. I mean it."

"Right."

"Because just think about it, kiddo; it's like you're insulting whatever inspired you to paint those angels in the first place. Do you want to do that?"

Claire bit her lip. "No, not really."

"Okay then, this is what I want you to do. Go fill up that old clawfoot tub of yours with hot water and then add some really expensive bath salts—something soothing like lavender. Then put on a nice calming CD, light some candles, and just climb in and soak until the water cools off. After you're done, take a little nap, then get up and get dressed in something—uh, let me see—something heavenly. You got that?"

"I think so."

"And I'll come pick you up—"

"Oh, I can drive my—"

"No way. I'm not taking any chances. I'll be there around six—just to give us plenty of time."

12

‖‖‖‖‖‖‖‖‖‖‖‖‖‖‖‖‖‖‖‖‖

Jeannie's prescription worked its magic on Claire, and by the time she got up from her nap, she felt a tiny glimmer of hope glowing within her. Maybe the evening wouldn't be so terrible after all. And if it was, she could always feign a headache and duck into the back room to lie down. She searched and searched her closet for something appropriate—was it "heavenly" that Jeannie had said? She'd be doing well to find something that fit, didn't need mending, and wasn't completely out of style. All the while she pulled out items, she berated herself for not having gone out and gotten something special for this evening. What had she been thinking? Finally, she came to a dress tucked way in the back of her closet. Something she'd almost forgotten. She pulled it out and gave it a shake. She barely remembered purchasing it. But as she recalled, it was supposed to have been for Scott's younger sister's wedding about three years ago. The couple, however, decided to elope, and as a consequence, the dress had never been worn. Claire wondered why she hadn't returned it then, but she'd liked it and probably hoped she could use it for something else.

The dress was a champagne-colored velvet—almost luminous, and perhaps slightly celestial or heavenly, if there were such a thing in earthbound apparel. It was the kind of fabric that seemed to just melt in your hand, soft and luxurious, flowing. That was probably why she'd kept it. It felt like liquid gold—only warmer. She held the dress before her in front of the mirror. The style, thankfully, was classic—as appropriate for today as it was three years ago.

Feeling a little like Cinderella, Claire slipped on the dress. But instead of a fairy godmother, she imagined that angels had prepared her finery for her. And why not? Her spirits buoyed even more when she found a pair of shoes that actually went with the dress. And her hopes for the evening continued to climb as she successfully pinned her hair into a fairly nice-looking chignon, slightly loose with a few strands curling around her bare neck. Then she inserted the antique pearl drop earrings that had been left to her by her mother. Perfect. She considered a rope of pearls around her neck, but that seemed a little too much. Just the earrings and her usual wedding ring would be sufficient jewelry for someone who'd worn little more than jeans and sweats for the last year and a half.

Standing before the mirror again, she admired her image with an artist's eye. The color of the dress was almost identical to her hair. Perhaps another reason she'd picked it. She'd just finished adding a soft touch of makeup, the first she'd worn in ages, when the doorbell rang.

"Claire!" exclaimed Jeannie. "You look fabulous, dah-ling!" She laughed. "I'm serious, girl, you look stunning. Where'd you get that dress?"

"I found it in my closet."

"Shoot, I wish I could get so lucky." Jeannie tossed her cape onto the sofa and went to the refrigerator. "Mind if I get myself a soda?"

"Of course not. Let me get my coat and purse, and I'll be ready."

Claire had just located her coat when she heard Jeannie's scream. Running out of the bedroom, she nearly tripped over the dog. "What's wrong?" she cried.

"Oh, my word!" Jeannie was standing before the easel now. "This is absolutely gorgeous! When did you do it? And why isn't it in the show?"

Claire's hand was on her pounding chest. "Jeannie, you scared me to death! I thought you were being mugged or something."

Jeannie grabbed her arm. "I mean it, why isn't this in the show?"

"I don't know. I just did it. I wasn't even sure if—"

"Well, it's dry isn't it?" She gingerly tapped the edge. "Good. Grab some bubble wrap. We're taking it with us."

"But I'm not sure I want to sell it."

"Oh, Claire." Jeannie frowned at her, tapping the sharp point of her shoe on the hardwood floor.

"Really, Jeannie. I want to give it to someone."

Jeannie sighed. "Well, whatever. I suppose we can put a sold sign on it, but it *is* going in the show."

Claire practiced her deep breathing techniques as Jeannie drove them to Henri's gallery, praying silently that God would help her through this night. She wasn't asking for anything spectacular—mere survival would be sufficient.

"It's going to be okay," Jeannie assured her as she parked in back. "Leo's already written a rave review that came out in today's paper, but he'll be on hand just the same. And I've got a few other aces up my sleeve."

"Stacking the deck, are you?" Claire glanced uneasily at Jeannie as she carefully retrieved the painting from her trunk. "You afraid I might flop without some help?"

"No, I just like a little insurance; you could call it priming the pump."

Claire shook her head. "I think people can see right through your little devices, Jeannie. I mean, they're either going to like it or—" she controlled herself from using the word hate—"or they just won't."

"Claire! Claire!" Henri beamed as he met her at the door. He kissed her on both cheeks, then helped her to remove her coat and handed it to his assistant. "Oh, my!" He clasped his hands together. "You are such a vision—ah, the perfect companion to your lovely creations."

She looked right into his eyes. "So, really, Henri, be honest, do you like them?"

He pressed his lips together then nodded solemnly. "It is a very different type of show for me, but, yes, I do like them—very much so."

She knew that this was also his way of saying that he too felt unsure as to how the public might respond to her work. He, better than anyone, was well accustomed to the cynics and critics and snobs. And it was no secret that they could ruin an opening like this. For his sake, she hoped they wouldn't show at all—other than Leo that is.

Jeannie removed the bubble wrap from Claire's latest piece. *"Voila!"*

Henri clapped his hands. "Oh, it is exquisite. A prize! I know just where it will go." He turned around. "Andre! Come quickly." He whispered something to the man, then turned back to Jeannie and Claire. "Champagne?" he asked as a woman in a sleek black dress appeared with a tray. "And we have cheese and—" he waved his hands. "Oh, you know, it is the regular fare. Now if you will, please excuse me."

Claire leaned over to Jeannie. "He's nervous, isn't he?"

Jeannie nodded, taking a sip of champagne. "Let's give him a moment to place that last painting before we go in. You know how he likes the drama—to feel like the curtain's going up at the theater on opening night."

Claire swallowed. "I just hope it doesn't fall flat in the first act."

Jeannie scowled, then cautioned in a lowered voice, "No more negativity!"

"I'm sorry." Claire held up her hand. "I promise, no more."

Before long, Henri was ushering them into the gallery, waiting expectantly for their compliments and approval. And the truth was, Claire was impressed. His setup was flawless. The music was perfect. If the paintings flopped, the blame would be hers and hers alone.

"It's perfect, Henri," she said finally. "It couldn't be better. Thank you for taking such care." She looked around the carefully lit room. "Your gallery is really the best in the city, you know."

Jeannie held up her glass. "Best on the West Coast."

Claire laughed. "Best in the country."

Henri waved his hands as if to stop them. "Thank you, ladies. You make me blush."

People started to arrive now, slowly drifting through, quietly moving through the gallery in groups of twos and threes. Claire recognized a few of the faces and tried to be as friendly as seemed appropriate.

She knew the early showing was for serious buyers, those who'd been specially invited—the type of people who would narrow their eyes and study a painting for several minutes, as if trying to see into the mind of the artist who painted it. Henri always served the best of the champagne first, and he scurried about, greeting his guests, introducing people, and commenting on various aspects of the art.

Claire could feel her hands trembling as she stood in a corner and watched their faces, unsure as to what they thought—one could never be sure. These were the kinds of people you would never want to play poker against. Their ability to conceal emotion was uncanny. And Claire knew it would be useless to try to read them tonight.

Like a puppet, she came when either Jeannie or Henri called, shaking the hand extended her way, smiling—but not too widely—aware that she could easily send the wrong message whether she meant to or not. She hated these shows—always had. But these were her dues, and in the art world, they had to be paid.

"Mrs. Campbell," she said. "It's such a pleasure to meet you. I've read of your work with the children's center—so wonderful."

"Thank you, dear." The woman pointed to one of Claire's earliest angel paintings. "And what inspired you to paint that?"

Claire swallowed. "It's hard to describe where inspiration comes from exactly . . ." she struggled for words. "I could say it's from some hidden place deep within me, and that wouldn't be untrue, but sometimes there seem to be other forces at work too." She smiled, but not too big.

"I see." Mrs. Campbell nodded as if she understood. Odd, since even Claire didn't completely understand herself. "Very nice, dear," said the older woman, as if talking to a preschooler about a finger painting.

Claire couldn't remember when the evening started to become fuzzy and hazy to her, and maybe it was the champagne, although she'd only had a few polite sips. But it was a blessing of sorts, like a form of protective insulation wrapping itself around her. And it helped to get her through all the varied and sometimes thoughtless comments that casual observers often make.

But finally, about midway through the show, and long after most of the serious art world had gone their way, to dinner reservations or some Christmas party or the comfort of their own homes, she slipped into the back room and sank into Henri's deep mohair sofa, leaning her head back with a loud sigh. She closed her eyes and tried to get everything she'd heard the last few hours to slide off her—like water off a duck's back, as her father would say. She'd talked him into coming on another night, when it wasn't so busy. But suddenly, she wished she'd begged him to make it tonight.

It would help to have someone else in her court right now. Someone unrelated and uninvolved in the precarious and unpredictable world of art. He could hold her hand and reassure her that it would be okay. No matter, if everyone here hated her work, if no one bought a single piece, if Henri quietly cancelled the remaining three weeks of the showing. Her father would put his arm around her and tell her that he loved her anyway. At least, that's the way she imagined it tonight. In reality, he might say something stupid like, "Maybe you should go back to teaching." He did that sometimes. Oh, she supposed it was only his practical side. But it always deflated her. Yes, perhaps it was better that he wasn't here to see her flop tonight.

"Claire?" Glenda, the woman in the sleek black dress, was standing in the doorway. "Someone here would like to meet you."

"Yes, of course." Claire stood and smoothed her dress. "I was just taking a break."

Glenda nodded without speaking. Claire wondered if she just thought she was being lazy, a slacker, like she didn't really care about the outcome of the showing. Claire followed this graceful woman in silence, wondering who could possibly be interested in the creator of these strange works that really wouldn't look good on anyone's wall.

And then she saw them. She blinked at first, thinking she must be imagining things. But there they were, Garret and Anna, both smiling at her as if she were a long-lost friend.

"What are you two doing here?" she exclaimed, taking each of them by a hand.

"We wanted to surprise you," said Anna.

Garret cleared his throat. "Actually, I'd promised Anna some Christmas shopping and—"

379

"I made him bring me here." Anna nodded victoriously.

"She didn't *make* me." Garret smiled. "I wanted to come."

"Claire, these paintings are—" Anna paused as if looking for the perfect word—"they're awesome."

"Thank you, Anna." Claire glanced around then spoke quietly. "That's the nicest thing anyone has said tonight."

Anna frowned. "You mean they don't like them?"

Claire shrugged then forced a smile. "It's hard to say."

"Then these people are all crazy."

"Anna." Garret spoke in a hushed but stern voice.

"Sorry." Anna looked up at Claire, then spoke in a quiet voice. "That one over there." She pointed toward the entrance. "Is *that*—?"

Claire grinned. "Yep. You recognize yourself?"

Garret was shaking his head in what seemed amazement. "But I don't get it, Claire. I mean how on earth did you manage—"

"I relied on memory." Claire guided them over to the painting of Anna. "I hope you don't mind."

"Of course not." Garret stared at the painting.

"I love it," said Anna. "And the bird is just perfect. I can't even explain why; it just is."

Claire sighed. "I hadn't planned on the bird at first, but he just came."

"But it's sold," said Anna, the disappointment plain in her voice.

Garret laughed. "We couldn't have afforded it anyway, sweetheart."

"Excuse me," interrupted Henri. "Can I borrow the artist from you, for just a moment, please?"

"Of course," said Garret. "We didn't mean to monopolize her."

The next instant, Claire was whisked off to meet the Fontaines, a wealthy couple who were seriously considering the painting that was set in the evening.

"I just love the dusky feel to it," said Mrs. Fontaine. "It reminds me of something. But I can't quite put my finger on it."

"Do you like Van Gogh?" asked Claire.

"That's it," said Mr. Fontaine. "It's like *Starry Night*."

Claire smiled. "Yes, that's what I thought when I finished it. I hadn't really meant it to be. Although I must admit to adoring Van Gogh. But when it was finished, I could see it too."

"Claire," called Jeannie.

Claire turned to see Jeannie motioning to her. "Will you excuse me, Mr. and Mrs. Fontaine," she said.

"Of course." Mrs. Fontaine smiled warmly. "It was so nice to meet you."

For the next ten minutes, Claire was shuffled around from customer to potential customer like a pinball. But the whole while she tried to keep a discreet eye on Garret and Anna, afraid they would soon grow bored and leave. She couldn't help but notice how handsome Garret looked with his hair combed and beard neatly trimmed. Not that he hadn't looked handsome before. But tonight he looked more of a turn-your-head sort of handsome. Striking even. And she felt a slight flush climb into her cheeks as she accidentally caught his gaze upon occasion. She didn't really think it was just her imagination, but he almost seemed to be keeping an attentive eye on her too. Now, more than ever, she was thankful she'd taken the time to dress carefully. And yet she was troubled too.

As pleasurable as Anna and Garret's unexpected visit was, she still felt as if she'd been caught slightly off guard. And to experience such feelings of interest toward Garret was more than a little disturbing. She hadn't felt this way since—well, since Scott. And in a way, she felt as if she were betraying him now— just by *feeling* this way. She knew it was probably ridiculous and unfounded. After all, Garret was little more than a casual acquaintance. And even if he turned out to be something more, Scott, of all people, would surely want her to get on with her life. But still she felt unsure and slightly off balance. Finally, there came a lull in her introductions, and she knew it was time to return to Garret and Anna. She could tell by Garret's posture that he was moving toward the door. She knew it was time to say good-bye. And although it was something of a relief, it was a stinging disappointment as well.

"I'm sorry," she said as she rejoined them. "It got so busy all of a sudden."

"That's good, isn't it?" asked Anna.

"I don't know. But let's hope so." Claire glanced over her shoulder. "I'm so worried, mostly for Henri and Jeannie, that tonight's going to be a failure."

"But there are lots of people," said Anna hopefully.

"Yes, but so far, no sales." Claire sighed, then remembered Anna's portrait. "Other than the one, that is. And it's not for sure."

Garret nodded then spoke quietly. "And that's what pays the way, Anna. No matter how well we write or paint, we're always dependent on the folks who are willing to plunk down their money for our work."

He looked to Claire with what seemed compassion. "But it's easier for me, I think. The price of a book is a mere pittance compared to," he waved his hand, "all this."

Claire nodded. "I guess that's what makes me nervous."

Garret reached over and laid his hand on her shoulder. "Well, really, you shouldn't be." He looked her straight in the eyes, and for the second time she wondered about the actual colors she saw there—such a pleasant mix. "You are a great artist, Claire. And these paintings are bound to be a huge success. Just take a deep breath and relax. Let it all just come to you."

She felt almost as if he'd hypnotized her, and she just stood there for a full minute, just letting it soak in. Then she took a deep breath. "Thanks, Garret. I think I needed that."

"It's true," chimed in Anna. "You are a great artist."

Claire smiled—a big smile this time. "I'm so glad you two decided to drop in. I think I might actually be able to make it through the rest of the evening now."

"But is it true, you're not coming back to the cabin?" asked Garret.

"Yeah," said Anna. "We just barely got to know you—then poof, you're gone!"

Claire laughed. "Well, my work had been accomplished. Although I have to admit that I miss it already."

"Claire," called Jeannie again.

Claire nodded in her direction, then turned back to Garret. "I'm sorry—"

"No, we're the ones who should be sorry." He made another move toward the door. "We've been hogging all your time. Remember, you're the star tonight, Claire. Now, you get out there and shine."

She looked straight into his eyes for the briefest moment, mere seconds, although it felt like much more. Then she turned to Anna, afraid that actual tears now glistened in her own eyes, ready to betray feelings even she couldn't begin to fully understand. She gently squeezed Anna's hand, then glanced back to Garret. "Thank you, *both*, so much for coming."

"Our pleasure," said Garret.

"Bye, Claire," called Anna in a sweet voice as father and daughter exited together.

13

Claire knew she was quieter than usual during the ride home, but she had no words left—nothing she wanted to express, nothing she could say with any real meaning. Her mind felt jumbled—too many people, too many feelings. Overloaded. Yes, that was it. She felt like too many circuits had been operating at once and now she was drained, melting down.

"You okay, kiddo?" Jeannie glanced her way.

"Yeah, I guess."

"The show went pretty well, I think." Jeannie sighed. "Well, no big sales as yet, but sometimes it takes time. People need to go home and think about it, look at their walls, and the next thing you know a painting is speaking to them—they wake up the next morning certain they can't live without it."

Claire nodded. "Hope you're right."

"You sure you're okay?" Jeannie tapped her fingers on the steering wheel. "You seem a little depressed or something."

"Just overwhelmed, I think." Claire swallowed. "You know, after being alone—in the quiet—all those weeks, well, I . . ."

"Oh, I get it. Culture shock. Kind of like when the hermit comes back into society for the first time. Yeah, I bet tonight was a little taxing for you. Personally, I love these openings, but I must admit I feel a little frazzled afterwards. Still, I wouldn't give up this life for anything."

Jeannie continued to talk with enthusiasm, mentioning names of wealthy or important people—names that went right over Claire's head—people who might buy a painting or tell a friend or whatever. Claire wasn't really listening. She felt incapable of soaking in one more word, one more thought.

"Thanks for everything," she told Jeannie, climbing out of the car with weary relief. "Sorry I'm not much company."

Jeannie waved her hand. "Don't worry, kiddo. You did great tonight. That's what really matters. Now get some rest. Sleep in until noon tomorrow. Take it easy."

Claire nodded and closed the car door. As she slowly walked up the three flights of stairs, she remembered Michael. Hopefully, he'd been okay while she was gone. She hurried to unlock her door, suddenly worried that something might be wrong. But there he was, trotting happily toward her.

"Oh, you sweet thing!" she exclaimed, wrapping her arms around his neck. "How I missed you!"

Then she took him outside for a quick walk. The fog was thick tonight, not unusual for the Bay Area in December, but when she looked up at the streetlight now shrouded in heavy mist, she found herself missing the star-studded sky in the mountains—and the snow. She also found herself wondering where Garret and Anna were staying tonight. In the city? Or perhaps they had family or friends in a nearby suburb? Or did Garret have a house himself? She'd never thought to ask where they lived when not staying in the cabin. And once again she wondered if there was a wife, a mother, somewhere nearby. She turned and began walking quickly back to her apartment, irritated at herself for wondering on these things. What difference was it to her anyway? Garret and Anna *were* nice people, yes, and they had helped her in a time of dire need. But the relationship would surely go no further than this. Why on earth should it?

Back in the apartment, Claire realized she was pacing again. She went over to the bookshelf, which was still only half filled; boxes of books and various memorabilia were stacked nearby. She picked up a framed photo, just a candid shot that she'd managed to catch at Jeremy's soccer game, not long before the boating accident. Father and son were both smiling as they celebrated the win with a victory hug. Jeremy's hair curled around his forehead, damp with sweat, and his eyes shone, big and brown—the mirror image of his dad nearly twenty years earlier, or so his paternal grandma liked to brag. And Claire had no reason to doubt her. What a pair they were! And, as usual, she felt that old familiar pain in her chest when she gazed at the photo, only now it felt slightly different. As if the knifelike sharpness had left her or become dulled somehow, what with the passing of time and emotions poured out along the way. She knew it was right, and yet it felt totally wrong. Like a betrayal even. As if she had sneaked something behind their backs, or thrown away what was valuable, or simply run away.

"But you're the ones who are gone," she said aloud. "And you were the ones so bound and determined to go deep-sea fishing that day, even after I told you the forecast didn't look good. You were the ones with all the confidence and bravado, ready to take on the weather and bring home your trophy fish to hang on the wall above the fireplace." She set the photo down and sighed. She no longer felt angry at them, the way she used to during those rare moments when she allowed herself to remember that day and the way they so easily brushed off her warning.

She walked over to the window, the one that offered a view of the bay, on a clear day that is. Not tonight though. "I forgive you," she whispered into the glass that reflected her own image, although it was them she was seeing. "And I realize it's not your fault." She felt her eyes filling, but not with tears of rage this time. "You never intended to go out there and die. And you never meant to leave me all alone like this. It's just the way life happened." She took in a deep breath. "And I release you both now. I release you to celebrate eternity—to fly with the angels!" She smiled, tears slipping down her cheeks as she imagined the two of them flying with the angels, just like she'd done in her dream. And in that same moment, it was as if a heavy coat of iron mail began sliding off her shoulders. And she lifted her arms like wings, and leaning her head back, with fingers splayed, she took in a slow deep breath, then exhaled. And it tasted just like mercy!

14

||||||||||||||||||||

"Henri would love for you to make another appearance," said Jeannie. "If you can manage it, that is. The weekend traffic was pretty good, and the 'starry night' painting sold, and we've had several promising bites on others too."

"That's great," said Claire. Cradling the phone between her head and shoulder, she returned to her work in progress and picked up a brush.

"I know you're not that crazy about public appearances, but Henri really thinks it would help to keep this ball rolling."

"Yeah, I'm not much into that whole meet the artist sort of thing, but I'm willing to do my part"—she daubed a little more blue in a corner—"if you really think it'll help the showing."

"Oh, you're a darling. How about both Thursday and Friday nights? That's when most of the traffic comes anyway, plus it'll still give me time to run another ad in Wednesday's paper."

"Sure." Claire twirled the paintbrush between her fingers. "And I might even have another painting for you."

"You're kidding! Oh, I can't wait. What's it like? Can you tell me?"

Claire studied the nearly completed work. "Well, as you can guess, it's angels again. But this time it's more of a seascape, more blues than whites; it's hard to describe really."

"Oh, it sounds wonderful. Let me know when to have it picked up."

"And Jeannie," Claire considered her words. "I think it might be my last."

"Your last?" Jeannie gasped. "What? What are you saying? You're not—I mean, I know you were depressed—"

Claire laughed. "I don't mean my last painting—ever! I mean my last *angel* painting. I just have this feeling that I've reached the end of my angel era. I'm ready to move on now."

"Oh." The relief was audible. "Well, that's okay, kiddo. To be honest, I'm not even sure how big this angel market really is, but, hey, we're giving it our best shot. And so far, we're not disappointed."

"Good. I think you can probably send someone by to pick this one up by Wednesday."

The week progressed slowly for Claire. She found herself missing the snow and the mountains and, to be perfectly honest, Garret and Anna. Although she kept telling herself this was completely ridiculous. Good grief, she barely knew them. Had only experienced two very brief and somewhat unusual encounters with them. But still, she missed them and wished for the chance to know them better. Not only that, she felt fairly certain that Michael was homesick too. He seemed to be lagging lately, and his tail didn't wag nearly so often or so vigorously as before. The city was a poor place to keep a dog like him. She wondered if he might not even be happier in his old, albeit slightly neglectful home, penned up with the other dogs.

She stooped and stroked his head on her way out the door. It was her last night to make an appearance at the showing. "I'm sorry, boy, I have to go out again tonight. But I promise to take you for a nice long walk tomorrow. We'll go to the park and chase sticks or something."

She tried not to notice the lights and decorations for Christmas as she drove through the city. And, although it wasn't nearly as bad as the previous year had been—her first Christmas without them—she still felt lonely. Her father had invited her down to Palm Springs again, to join him and some of his retired friends for the holidays, and she'd told him she'd think about it, but somehow she just didn't think that was where she wanted to be this year. Not that she knew exactly.

Once again, Claire followed Jeannie and Henri around the gallery—the congenial marionette, jumping whenever they pulled the strings. She greeted potential customers, all the while smiling and conversing, trying to appear relaxed and comfortable when she was anything but. Still, there did seem to be a good-sized crowd moving in and about—even better than the week of the opening.

"Word's gotten around," whispered Jeannie as the evening began drawing to a close with only a few stragglers remaining behind, picking at what remained of the cheese and crackers and finishing off a bottle of cheap champagne. "To think we had this much business tonight, and just a week before Christmas—not bad."

"And Leo's review didn't hurt any either," said Claire. "Remind me to send him chocolates or something."

Jeannie laughed. "Don't worry, I already did. And you've had a couple other good reviews too."

Claire felt her eyebrows lift. "And no bad ones?"

Jeannie shrugged. "Hey, you can't please all the people all the time."

"I figured as much." Claire smiled. "That's why I still think ignorance is bliss when it comes to reviews."

Jeannie patted her arm in a placating way. "For some people perhaps."

After the gallery closed, Jeannie invited Claire to go across the street for a cup of cappuccino with her. "Unless you're totally exhausted, that is. As for me, I always need several hours to unwind before I can even think about sleep."

"Sure, that sounds good. As long as it's decaf."

"Well, Henri seems very pleased," said Jeannie after a pair of large mugs were placed on the table. "He sold another painting tonight and expects to sell another to the Van Horns tomorrow."

"Which ones?"

"Tonight was the foggy one. I'm not sure which one the Van Horns are interested in."

Claire smiled. "That is so cool—three paintings sold within a week! I hope the paintings last as long as the show."

Jeannie laughed. "Now, wouldn't that be something? Oh, by the way, someone inquired about consignments the other day. Do you want to consider it?"

Claire frowned. "I don't know if I could. I mean not with the angels anyway. It's not your everyday kind of painting, you know? It's like an idea just hits me, all at once like an inspiration, and I pour it out onto canvas—almost without thinking, although I know that doesn't make sense. I don't think I could have someone actually directing me in this."

Jeannie waved her hand. "No problem. I sort of hinted at that to the woman. Besides, she seemed pretty interested in your latest one anyway, the seascape."

Claire took a sip of coffee. She hadn't really wanted to sell that one, but after already hanging onto two of them, she felt she'd better let it go. Especially since that's what the picture had been about anyway—*letting go*.

"I've also had several people ask about the one with the bird in her hands. It's a shame you don't want to sell that one." Jeannie drummed her long painted fingernails against her coffee cup, making a ringing sound, almost like bells. "But you know, Claire, perhaps that's one we should consider having some numbered and signed prints made from, that and a couple of the others. Had you thought about that?"

"No, but it sounds like a good idea. If you really think they'd sell."

"I'll look into it first thing in the morning. I don't know why I didn't think of it sooner."

Claire had to laugh. "You are such a businesswoman."

"Good thing one of us is." Jeannie studied her carefully. "You seem to be doing better, Claire. Or is it just wishful thinking on my part?"

Claire briefly told her about her recent letting go episode and how she felt more at peace than ever before. "It was such a simple thing to do really. I don't know why it took me so long."

"Just a matter of timing, I suspect. You can't force some things."

"But I have been thinking about something . . ."

Jeannie's eyes lit up. "What? A new project? Tell me."

Claire smiled. "No, not a new project. Actually, I was considering going back to the cabin—I mean if it's okay with you—"

"You're kidding! You want to go back up there again?"

She nodded. "I know it probably sounds crazy, especially this time of year—"

"You're serious? You want to go up there now? Right in the middle of winter and just days before Christmas? Are you *really* all right, honey?"

Claire felt her cheeks grow warm. "Okay, Jeannie, I'll tell you something, but it's just between you and me, okay? Because I could be all wet and about to make a total fool of myself."

Jeannie leaned forward. "I'm in! Quick, tell me everything before I keel over from curiosity."

"Okay, do you by any chance remember a man and his daughter— they came in on opening night last week, and I spent some time talking to them?"

Jeannie's brows shot up. "Yes! A very handsome man—sort of a Robert Redford type, only I think this guy had a beard, didn't he? Now, I don't normally care for full beards like that, but as I recall it looked good on him. And a pretty little girl—" she snapped her fingers. "A girl who looked strikingly like a certain angel I've seen somewhere. Tell me more!"

Claire giggled. "Remember the Hendersons up in the mountains— the people you told me about?"

"The ones with the cabin not too far from ours?"

"Yes. Well, have you ever heard of an author—a G. A. Henderson?"

"Historical novels?"

Claire nodded. "The Hendersons' son. I met him and his daughter up there."

"Aha, now it's all starting to make sense. Do I smell romance in the air?"

"No, no. Not romance. But I did find them both, well, interesting. And I want to get to know them better. I mean, I hardly even know them at all, but . . ."

"Sometimes you know certain things . . . almost instantly . . ." Jeannie's eyes grew slightly dreamy. "It's like—you know, one of those things . . . you can just tell when you first meet someone that there's something more." She shook her head and chuckled. "Unfortunately it takes some of us years before we really figure it out."

Claire studied Jeannie. "You mean you've got something romantic going?"

Jeannie smiled coyly.

Suddenly Claire knew. "It's Leo, isn't it?"

"Now, don't you say a word to anyone. I'm not even totally sure myself yet."

"That is so perfect."

"Well." Jeannie set down her cup. "That settles it then."

"What?"

"You've *got* to go back to the cabin."

"I don't know. I mean, I was only considering it; I'm not really positive it's such a good—"

"No arguing. Now, when are you leaving?" She looked at her watch. "Good grief, I should let you get on your way right now; that way you can start packing tonight. You can leave first thing in the morning and be up there just past noon."

"But—"

"No buts. You better get going, kiddo. Look at it this way. It's still, what, three days until Christmas? And if you find out you're wrong about this guy, say in the next day or so, well, you can just cut your losses and hop in your car and get back to whatever it is you were planning to do for Christmas."

"I didn't really have any plans—"

"Well, then you'll just have to join Leo and me and some of our other single friends."

"But what if he's not there, or what if he's—"

"I said *no buts.*" Jeannie picked up her purse and started to stand. "Now, it's time for you to be on your way, kiddo. No argument. And don't worry, the showing will get along just fine without you for the next week. Just promise to keep me posted on this." She clapped her hands. "Oh, this is just too good! I can't wait to write the press

392

release—something like 'famous writer and artist soon to be wed'! How about on Valentine's Day? This is fantastic!"

"Oh, Jeannie." Claire shook her head in mock disgust. "You are such an opportunist!"

Jeannie frowned. "I thought you were going to say a romantic."

Claire laughed. "Well, how about if we make a deal? I'll pursue my romantic dream—as crazy as it seems—if you'll pursue yours, which happens to be practically sitting in your lap."

Jeannie stuck out her hand. "Deal?"

"Deal." And they shook on it.

15

Without allowing herself the luxury of even considering what it was she was about to leap into, Claire followed Jeannie's instructions to a T. She went straight home, began packing her things, and was ready to leave the following morning. But instead of leaving first thing in the morning, she waited around long enough for the gallery to open, then called Henri.

"I hate to bother you, Henri, and please feel free to say no, but you know the angel picture—the one with the girl holding the bird?"

"Yes. The one I am not allowed to sell?"

"Right. I wonder if you would mind if I took that one with me today. It's meant to be a Christmas gift—"

"Of course. You come and get it whenever you like. It might help some of the other paintings to sell, you know, taking away that un-available distraction."

"Yes." She considered this. "I can see what you mean."

So, before leaving town, she swung by the gallery and picked up the painting, then tucked it safely into the backseat of her Jeep. Even if Jeannie decided it was worth reproducing copies from, they could always borrow it back later for scanning.

"Well, here we go, Michael." She smiled at him as she pulled back into the traffic. "I hope this isn't a great big mistake."

But Michael's tail thumped happily, as if he knew that it wasn't a mistake at all, and as if he knew he was going home. While she drove, she kept a constant train of CDs going, all her old favorites, trying to fill the space and to keep herself from thinking about what she was actually doing. She was afraid if she really considered all things carefully and the limited chances of success, she would simply turn back and forget the whole thing. And she really didn't want to turn back.

It was afternoon by the time she reached the cabin. Michael was so happy that he leaped from the car and ran around in circles, barking wildly and rolling in the snow. She immediately went inside and started a fire. She knew the cabin would feel like an ice chest after sitting vacant for more than a week. Then, taking her time, she unloaded her things. She had already decided not to visit Garret and Anna today. She needed some time to settle in, to prepare herself and gather up her nerve. But she could take Michael for a nice long walk—she had promised him as much yesterday. Of course, she had expected it to be within the city limits at the time. Now, the space was limitless, or so it seemed.

With the fire stoked up and burning brightly, she bundled up in preparation for their walk. She tried not to remember their last walk— the time when they'd become lost and nearly frozen in the woods. But then it had turned out all right, all things considered. For how else would she have met them? Fortunately, there was no threat of snow today. The sky was perfectly clear and bluer than a robin's egg, and the snow shone clean and bright, recently dusted with a fresh coat of powder.

"All right, Michael," she said as she opened the door. "Let's go!"

Everything was the same as she remembered—only better. Much, much better! The trees seemed taller and greener, and the smell— why, the smell was almost intoxicating. Why hadn't she noticed that before? Air so clean and fresh, a person might become rich if they could somehow bottle it up and sell it as a health tonic in the city. She paused to notice the various tracks crisscrossing through the snow, the usual rabbits and squirrel and deer and birds. Oh, what a story something as simple as snow could tell! She continued on until she came to the dead tree, then stopped just to admire its flawless form once again dusted with glistening snow. Of course, she realized—

she must paint it! She walked around, considering it from various angles, finally deciding on the way she always found it on her walks, pointing to the right, as if indicating which way the trail went. She was glad she'd brought her camera to the cabin this time. She'd have to remember to carry it with her on all her walks. Who knew what other great things she might discover out here, things full of inspiration and worthy of painting—

Suddenly she stopped. Frozen in her tracks, she stared down at the trail before her. Her hand flew to her mouth, but in the same instant she told herself not to worry, that it was nothing really. Nothing that should concern her anyway. Not really. Still she stayed put. Michael paused up ahead, turning to look back at her, his head cocked to one side as if to inquire about why she'd stopped.

"It's okay, boy," she finally assured him, forcing herself to continue walking forward and averting her eyes from what it was that had so stunned her.

Three sets of footprints. There were three sets of footprints today. Two pairs looked familiar. She easily recognized them as Garret and Anna's—the same she had seen so many times before. But the third set, the new ones, looked to be a woman's boots—about the same size as her own. She knew this for certain on first glance. And in her mind's eye she could see the three of them walking together too. The happy family—husband and wife and child.

Well, of course, she chided herself, why wouldn't he have a wife? And why shouldn't sweet Anna have a mother? It was only normal. What had made her think otherwise? Certainly nothing he'd said, and nothing from Anna had misled her in this regard. It had simply been her own stupid assumption. The wife probably worked, maybe in the city. Perhaps she kept things together in their home while Garret went off to write in the woods. And why not? She knew plenty of people who lived somewhat independent lives—especially creative people. Oh, why hadn't she seriously considered this possibility before? She brushed away a cold tear that had streaked down her cheek, and fighting against the lump in her throat, told herself to be an adult. "Get over it!" she said in a sharp voice, causing Michael to turn and look curiously at her.

"Not you, Michael," she said in a friendly but forced tone. "You're a good ol' boy." Happy with this praise, he continued along, and obediently she followed him, moving her feet like a pair of leaden boots and wishing she were at the bridge so she could finish her walk, turn back, and go home—back to San Francisco.

She blew out a long puff of air, watching it turn into white steam as it hit the frigid air, then quickly vanished. And what difference did it make that he was married anyway? What was it to her? It certainly didn't change anything. Garret and Anna had still been good friends to her. Good grief, they had literally saved her life. So why on earth should she think of them any differently now? It was silly for her to react like this. Childish even. And, she told herself sternly, she would still give Anna that portrait—partly as a thank-you and partly as a Christmas present. A very valuable present, of course, but then Anna was special. And for some reason Claire felt she deserved the portrait. Sure, it wouldn't be easy to take it up to their door and perhaps risk meeting the mother—the wife—but then, it would be necessary. And maybe it was a good way for her to simply close this door and move on.

Claire paused at the bridge, taking a moment to touch it, then turned around and began walking quickly back, averting her eyes from the trail in front of her. But as she walked, she prayed. She confessed to God that she felt disappointed and sad by this new revelation. But she also asked him to help her move through it.

"You've gotten me through so much more than this," she said aloud as she walked. "I know you can help me with this too. I trust you."

It was just getting dusky when they reached the cabin, and despite her longing to get out of that place, to return to the city and to never, never look back, she realized the wisdom in waiting until morning before she made her final exodus. Besides, she needed to drop off the painting for Anna. She briefly considered calling Jeannie and telling her the disappointing news, but what if Jeannie used this as an excuse not to pursue her chances with Leo? Claire would wait until she returned to the city—or maybe even after the holidays. Why should she crash their happy Christmas gathering and be forced to share her pathetic story? Then, realizing that Jeannie might actually call her, she unplugged and turned off her cell phone. She had no desire to hear Jeannie's voice oozing with sympathy. That would only serve to unleash the sadness inside her—the sadness that she had, so far, managed to keep mostly at bay.

She went to bed early that night, worried that this most recent distress might disturb her sleep with restlessness or troubling dreams, but when she awoke the next morning, she felt surprisingly rested and peaceful. While she went about her chores of cleaning and repacking, and finally reloading the Jeep, she could almost feel Michael's confusion; he studied her with quiet canine curiosity—as if he somehow knew she was making a huge mistake. Perhaps he wanted to ask her if she really intended to take him back to the confines of that city, but being a dog, he simply remained silent but watchful.

She knew she had one more thing to do, and it would take everything in her to do it. She backed out the Jeep and pointed it in the direction of the Henderson cabin, and with unexplainable resolve willed herself to drive there. It took only a few minutes by road— unlike the snowy day when she'd followed their tracks through the woods. It was only as she pulled up that she noticed a different vehicle in the driveway—not the SUV Garret had driven her home in that day. This was a sensible, dark green Subaru—one of those wagon-types with all-wheel drive—very safe and good in snow. A family car, probably his wife's.

After parking her Jeep and practicing her smile—the same one that came in so handy during art showings—she opened the back door to retrieve the painting. It was too late to turn back now. She reminded herself of one of her dad's favorite sayings—what doesn't kill you will make you stronger. But even so, she fought back feelings of dread and foolishness as she tramped through the snow and onto the porch. Gritting her teeth, she knocked resolutely on the door, hoping against hope that Anna would be the one to open it.

"Hello?" said a pretty, dark-haired woman, thirty-something, petite, and wearing an oversized charcoal gray sweater—probably one of Garret's.

"Hello." Claire smiled, but not too big. "I'm sorry to intrude like this, but this is for Anna—"

"Oh, my goodness!" The woman stared at the painting. "Why that's absolutely beautiful!" She looked back at Claire, astonishment written all over her face. "Oh, excuse my terrible manners; I'm Louise; I'm—"

"Can you give it to her, please?"

"But won't you come inside and—"

"No." Claire firmly shook her head. "I mean, I would, but my dog's in the car, and we've got to be on our way; we're going back to San Francisco and—"

"But Anna's not here right now. They went sledding just a bit ago—Garret had been promising her and—"

"Oh, that's okay." Claire waved her hand. "Just tell them Merry Christmas for me and—"

"But, please, can't you come in and just visit for a few minutes?"

In desperation, Claire shoved the portrait toward this disturbingly friendly woman. Why couldn't she have been someone a little less likable? Claire felt her chin trembling now, a sure sign that she was about to lose it. "No," she said firmly. "No, I can't. I'm sorry, but I've really got to get going now."

Louise took the painting and shook her head. "This is such a wonderful present. I just wish you could stay a bit and—"

"Sorry." Claire turned and hurried back to her car, not even pausing to look as the woman called out to thank her and say good-bye.

Claire started her engine, pretending to intently study her rearview mirror as she backed out of the driveway, but mostly she was trying to see past the blurry curtain that was slipping over her eyes.

"Just relax," she said aloud as she drove back down the road and eventually past her cabin—rather, Jeannie's cabin. She took in several deep, calming breaths, then continued driving deliberately on—not too fast and not too slow. That really hadn't gone so badly, all things considered. She hadn't made a complete fool of herself. And Louise really did seem like a nice person—good mother and wife material. That was something, really it was. And before long, this would all be just a distant memory—perhaps she and Jeannie would even laugh about it, in time. "Remember the time I dared you, and you took off over the mountains hoping to find your true love," Jeannie would chortle, "only to discover that the poor man was already happily married?" And then they would throw back their heads and laugh.

But not today. There would be no laughing today. She slipped a CD into the player, careful to pick an upbeat one, turning the volume up just slightly. Then she reached over and patted Michael's head. "Hey, I still have you, boy." She tried to make her voice sound light and cheerful. Then more apologetically, "But I'm sorry you have to go back to the city now. I didn't mean for this to be such a quick trip. We'll figure out something better than that old apartment for you. I promise, we'll find something that has room for you to run around. It won't be so bad, really, it won't."

16

Before heading onto the highway, Claire decided to stop by the little store. It would be her last chance to say good-bye to Lucy and get a cup of coffee. Not the best coffee, to be sure, since Lucy was of the old school and believed the best coffee came from a great big red can labeled "mountain grown." No freshly ground Starbucks would ever be found in her little store, no-sir-ee, not as long as she still ruled behind the counter.

Claire parked her Jeep in the deserted parking area in front of the little store. Christmas Eve was obviously not Lucy's busiest time. In fact, Claire had wondered if she'd even be open today. "Want to get out and stretch your legs once more before we hit the road?" she asked Michael, holding the passenger door open while he jumped down. "I'll just be a minute."

Claire tried to smile as she opened the door, tried to appreciate the irony of the cheesy artificial wreath—a sharp contrast to the real, live evergreens growing in abundance all about the place. "Merry Christmas!" she called when she spied Lucy stooped over a cardboard carton in the rear of the store.

"Is that you, Claire?" Lucy stood up slowly, rubbing her back. "What on earth are you doing up here the day before Christmas?"

Claire considered her answer. "Well, I just had an errand that brought me this way again."

Lucy frowned. "So, you're just passing through then?"

Claire nodded. "Yep. But I thought I should stop by to say hello before I head back to the city. And I'll take a cup of your coffee for the road."

"You got some big plans for the holidays?" Lucy reached for the stained coffee carafe and started to fill a large-sized Styrofoam cup with what looked like very black and thicker than usual coffee.

"I'll probably just be with friends."

Lucy held out the cup. "This one's on the house, Claire. Merry Christmas."

"Thanks. How about you, Lucy? Do you have any plans for Christmas?"

The old woman laughed. "Ha. Not hardly. I'll probably just take home some old movies and park my tired body in front of the television."

Knowing that Lucy was a widow, Claire wondered if she had any family nearby but knew better than to ask, especially considering Lucy's obvious lackluster plans for the holidays. No sense in forcing the old woman to explain what could very well be painful to talk about. Besides, Claire knew as well as anyone how it felt to answer those kinds of questions. Who liked to admit they would be alone for the holidays? It sounded so pathetic. Besides that, such pitiful admissions only served to make the asking party feel bad, guilty even, as though it were somehow their fault that they hadn't been as unfortunate.

"Well, I better be on my way now. Thanks for the coffee, Lucy."

"You drive careful. And come see me again—next time you're in this neck of the woods, that is."

Claire went back outside, expecting to find Michael sitting patiently on the porch, just like he always did when she came to the store. But he didn't seem to be around. "Michael?" she called. She went over to the Jeep, thinking he could be waiting over there, but still no sign of the dog. Now she whistled, expecting him to shoot around the corner, but still he didn't come. Worried, she set her coffee cup on the hood of her car and began to look around, calling his name. Where could he have gone? It wasn't like him to take off like this.

She heard the bell tinkle on the door and turned to see Lucy peering out at her. "Something wrong?" called the old woman.

"It's my dog," explained Claire. "He seems to have taken off."

"He didn't head to the highway, did he?" Lucy looked toward the main road where a big semi was streaking by, its chained tires clinking in rhythm to the wheels.

Claire felt a jolt of fear run through her at the thought of Michael venturing onto the highway. "Oh, surely he wouldn't."

Then Lucy nodded toward a stand of pines behind the store. "Hey, there's some tracks going that way."

"Yes!" Claire followed them with her eyes. "And they look like dog tracks. I'll go see if that isn't him. But if you see him around, could you keep him on the porch until I get back?"

"You bet."

Claire hurriedly followed the tracks into the trees, not completely sure they belonged to Michael, but not convinced they didn't either. She continued calling his name and whistling. But the tracks just seemed to go deeper and deeper into the woods, and the more she looked at them, the more she wondered if they actually belonged to her dog at all. Finally, she bent down and felt of a paw print, but the impacted snow had a crusty edge to it, as if this trail was from the previous day. She turned around and began to jog back to the store, fearing the worst—why hadn't she gone up to check the highway first? Maybe he was trying to go back home. She felt tears sting her eyes as she started to run. What if he'd been hit? Oh, how could she possibly endure another loss right now? How much could one person take? With each step she prayed, silently begging God to spare her dog. It didn't seem too much to ask. This morning had been hard, but to possibly lose Michael too—that would surely push her over the edge.

She emerged from the woods to spot another vehicle now parked in front of the store. A dark blue Ford Explorer—and it looked a lot like the one Garret drove. And, yes, to complicate matters further, there stood Garret and Anna along with a couple of other people she had never seen before.

"Claire!" cried Anna, waving wildly. "We've got your dog here."

Claire sighed in relief and hurried toward them. Perhaps seeing them wouldn't be so bad after all, as long as Michael was okay.

403

"Lucy said you'd lost him," said Anna, as she and the dog ran over to join Claire. Michael looked perfectly fine, if not somewhat pleased with himself as his tail wagged happily behind him.

"What got into you, boy?" Claire asked as she knelt down and stroked the dog's head. "You had me really worried."

"We saw him walking by the road," explained Anna breathlessly. "I told Dad that I knew it was your dog, but he didn't believe me at first. Then I made him stop, and we picked up Michael and brought him over here. And then we saw Lucy, and she told us that you'd lost him."

"Thank you," said Claire, standing. "Once again, you came to my rescue." She tried to keep her eyes from glancing over to where she knew Garret was standing.

"Claire!" he called out, waving.

She looked his way and waved weakly. She longed for a quick and easy escape, some way to avoid what promised to hurt, but knew she must do the mature thing. "Hi, Garret," she called, mustering a bravado she didn't feel. "Thanks for picking up my dog. I really don't know what got into him."

He was walking toward her now, a big smile on his face. "Anna's the one who first saw him. And even then I thought it was simply hopeful imagining on her part." He laughed. "But she was right. And here you are."

"See, Dad!" She poked him in the arm. "I *knew* it was Michael."

"What are you doing here?" he asked, his eyes peering into hers with an intensity that threatened to undo her.

She felt a tightness in her chest as she averted her eyes and pretended to adjust her leather gloves. "I—I needed to take care of something—at the cabin." Then she remembered the portrait. "And, well, I had something to leave for Anna—"

"For *me?*" Anna's eyes lit up. "What? What is it?"

"Actually, I already dropped it by your cabin." Claire fumbled in her coat pocket for sunglasses, a good cover-up, just in case.

"Then you met Louise?" he asked.

"Yes." She slipped on the dark glasses and returned his gaze now.

He was still smiling, that same slightly crooked smile, and his eyes shone mostly blue in the bright sunlight, or maybe they were simply reflecting the blue of his parka.

"So, how long are you staying?" he asked.

"Oh, I'm on my way home."

"Already?" Anna's disappointment was plain in her voice.

"Yes, it's Christmas Eve, you know." Claire pressed her lips together. "I really should be going now."

"I'm sorry," said Garret, as he noticed the man and little boy now coming over to join them. "I guess I should've introduced you to my brother-in-law Doug and my nephew Hayden. We were all out sledding this morning."

"You must be the famous artist." Doug grinned as he shook her hand. "Anna's been going on and on about you. And my wife's been literally praying to meet you."

"Well, her prayers have been answered," said Garret. "Claire dropped something by the cabin just this morning."

"You're kidding! Man, I'll bet she was totally beside herself when you showed up!" Doug slapped her on the back. "Wow, I'm surprised she actually let you get away so easily."

Claire narrowed her eyes, studying him closely, unsure as to whether she'd heard him correctly or not. "You mean *Louise?* Louise is your wife?"

"Yeah, we came up here to spend Christmas with the family." He pretended to punch Garret. "We'd heard this guy was turning into a hermit, so we all decided it was time to come on up to the mountains and stir him up a little. The folks are coming too."

Anna grabbed Claire's arm, whispering urgently, "Please, can you tell me what it is?"

"What?" asked Claire, feeling slightly dizzy. She suddenly felt the need to sit down and put her head between her knees, or perhaps drink a cool glass of water or just breathe or something.

"What it is that you brought me," explained Anna, her eyes wide with anticipation.

"Oh." Claire remembered the painting. "But it's for Christmas. It should be a surprise."

405

"But can't you come back to the cabin for a little while?" begged Anna, gently tugging on her arm. "Aunt Louise is making chicken enchiladas for lunch."

Claire looked helplessly toward Garret, then over to her Jeep—her escape from all this. Of course, she *was* relieved to learn that Louise wasn't his wife, but did that really change anything? *Really?* Her strong reaction to meeting Louise this morning had both shocked and frightened her—she'd been unaware that she cared that much. And even now, she had no guarantees that there wasn't a wife—hiding away somewhere—ready to pop out at any given moment. And even if there were no wife, why on earth should she stick around and risk more pain? "I . . . I really should go," she said weakly.

"But it'll be lunchtime soon," urged Anna, sounding more mature now. "And you'll have to stop to eat anyway, won't you? Why not just stay a little longer and eat lunch with us?"

"We'd love to have you," added Garret. "And Louise is a really great cook."

"Yeah!" agreed Anna with youthful enthusiasm. "She's the one who taught me everything I know, which is pretty important since Dad's totally hopeless in the kitchen."

"I know Louise would be thrilled to have you," said Doug. He looked down to see his small son now hopping from one foot to the other. "Excuse me, but I think Hayden may need to visit the little boys' room."

"Please, come!" Anna peered up at Claire hopefully.

Claire looked at Garret and, despite herself, thought he looked hopeful too. "Well, I suppose I—"

"Yes!" Anna made a victory fist.

"Great," said Garret. "Why don't you go on ahead of us. We need to pick up a few things at the store, and then we'll meet you at the cabin."

Claire walked over to her Jeep, feeling almost as if she were in a dream. But as she opened the door for Michael, she realized what she'd just agreed to. What had she been thinking? What was the sense of putting herself into what seemed a very precarious position when she obviously lacked the emotional stamina to survive more pain?

Why hadn't she simply made her excuses and run? But how could she back out now? She drove back toward the cabin, feeling dazed. But as she drove, she prayed. And as she prayed, she felt a faint glimmer of hope—like maybe she could get through this after all.

"You're back?" said Louise as she threw open the door. "Oh, I'm so glad. Can you come in?"

Claire nodded dumbly as she was led inside. "I—uh—I'm Claire. I met Garret and Anna at the store—and your husband and son too."

"Oh, that's wonderful." Louise reached for Claire's coat. "And they must've convinced you to join us for lunch then."

"Yes. Anna wouldn't have it any other way."

"Well, good for Anna." Louise hung up Claire's coat, then turned to face her. "You seemed a little upset earlier. Is everything okay?"

Claire saw how Louise's eyes were almost identical to Garret's, same mixture of blue, green, and gray. Why hadn't she noticed this earlier? Perhaps she would have saved herself from a lot of unnecessary upheaval. She sighed deeply. "Can I be perfectly frank with you?"

Louise placed her hand on Claire's. "Of course, please do."

And so Claire began to pour out her story, explaining how she'd first met Garret and Anna on that snowy day, her confusing feelings afterwards, and then how her hopes had risen when they appeared at her showing. Finally she told about her challenge from Jeannie to come back here. "And now I feel like such a fool; I mean I totally lost it when I thought you were Garret's wife. I feel so stupid. And, believe it or not, it's not really like me to do something like—like this."

Louise put her hand over her mouth as if to suppress laughter. "Oh, this is just too incredible!"

Claire stared at her in horror. Did Louise think she was lying? Or perhaps something else? Something worse? "What is it?" she said quietly, preparing herself for the worst. "What's wrong?"

Louise waved her hand. "I'm sorry, Claire; forgive me. But, you see, Garret called me a week or so ago. He told me all about how this beautiful artist appeared on his porch in the middle of a blizzard one day. At first he made it sound like it was only Anna who'd been so taken in by you, but I could tell right away that his heart was involved. But then he said that he noticed you were wearing a wedding ring and so, he figured, erroneously as it turns out, that that was that. Then just a couple days later, Lucy, you know, down at the store, straightened him out on that account. And then he and Anna made that special trip just to see you at your opening. And, well, my poor brother's been wracking his brain trying to figure out a way to get together with you ever since."

"Really?"

Louise nodded with girlish enthusiasm. "Just don't say you heard it from me." She glanced out the window toward the driveway. "And one more thing before they get back: Garret's wife died of cancer about six years ago. It was very unexpected and tragic. He's never really had a serious relationship since then."

Claire swallowed. "Thanks for telling me all this."

"Well, I don't want to overwhelm you, but I don't want you running back off to the city prematurely either."

Claire smiled. "I guess maybe I could stick around a bit longer."

Louise squeezed her hand. "Good."

"Can I give you a hand with anything?" Claire glanced around the room, longing for something to do, something to keep her busy and distract her thoughts. "I heard you're a whiz in the kitchen, but I'd love to help."

"Sure, why don't you make the salad?"

Claire focused all her attention on cleaning and cutting and prettily arranging the salad ingredients into the big wooden bowl, and by the time she heard the front door opening, she thought maybe she could handle this. Just maybe.

17

Anna shrieked when she walked in the front door, causing both Louise and Claire to drop what they were doing and dash out of the kitchen just in time to see the girl staring at the painting that was now propped on a chair.

"Is this *it?*" Anna cried. "Claire, did you really bring this for me?"

Claire nodded. "I thought you should have it."

Anna shook her head. "I cannot believe it. This is so cool!"

"Are you sure about this?" asked Garret, his eyes concerned. "This is a very valuable—"

"I want her to have it." Claire folded her arms across her chest in what she hoped appeared to be a convincing posture but was merely an attempt to conceal her now trembling hands.

"It's very generous." Garret turned to Doug. "Come here, you've got to see this." Then he began telling Doug about Claire's showing in the city. Claire felt certain she could hear the pride in Garret's voice, and she turned away, hiding her pleased smile. The two men stood with Anna, admiring the painting.

Louise and Claire had barely returned to their final preparations in the kitchen before the elderly Hendersons arrived, and suddenly the little cabin was overflowing with laughter and voices. If the couple felt surprised to discover an unexpected guest, they didn't show it. Before long Claire felt almost like part of the family. She laughed as young Hayden galloped through the kitchen, chasing after Michael, who was having the time of his life.

Claire was beginning to feel more relaxed now, and lunch went relatively smoothly. The interesting mix of people and ages kept the conversation hopping from one topic to the next—a great relief to Claire since she already felt like she'd hopped onto a roller coaster today. She kept herself from looking at Garret too often, afraid that others at the table might notice and wonder, or that she might make him feel uncomfortable. But she did sneak an occasional quick peek, at the same time wanting to pinch herself, wondering if all that Louise had told her could possibly be true.

Finally, she felt it was time for her to leave. "Thanks so much," she said, getting up from the table. "It was so nice to meet everyone, and lunch was delicious. I'm glad Anna talked me into it. But I really should hit the road—"

"You're not thinking about going back to the city today, are you?" Louise's question sounded innocent enough, but Claire could tell by the glint in her eyes that she was up to something. "You don't really want to be making that long trip back to San Francisco on Christmas Eve, do you?"

"Well, I—"

"We're all going out to cut a tree this afternoon," Louise continued. "Can't you stay a little longer and go with us?"

"Oh, please," begged Anna. "Come get a tree with us, *please?*"

"It's quite an experience," said Garret. "Tree hunting with the Hendersons. Why, it might even inspire you to paint something . . . comical."

She smiled. "Well, I suppose I could stay a little longer." She glanced over to Michael who was now stretched contentedly by the fire. "And I know my dog's not all that eager to get back to the city." She laughed. "In fact, if I didn't know better, I might think he actually planned this whole thing by getting himself lost today."

"God does work in mysterious ways." Louise grinned.

"I better go back to the cabin first." Claire thought for a moment. "I need to change into hiking clothes, and if I'm staying the night, I'll need to get the fire going again—it's my only source of heat there."

Anna's eyes were bright. "Then you'll come back and join us?"

Claire smiled. "I guess so."

Garret walked her out to the driveway. "I'm glad you're going to stick around, Claire." He opened her door for her. "I was a little worried earlier. I mean you didn't seem all that glad to see us up at the store. I thought maybe I'd done something to offend you."

She shook her head. "Oh, no. I was just feeling a little rattled, I guess. You know, being in a hurry and losing Michael and all." She had no intention of telling him that she'd been upset because she'd assumed Louise was his wife.

"I'd really been hoping—actually praying even—for the chance to get better acquainted with you. It's occurred to me more than once how I might've come across as, well, a little unfriendly that day you were here at the cabin."

She shrugged. "Oh, I just figured you were absorbed with your writing. I know how it goes; I can be like that with my art sometimes."

"That wasn't really it though." He looked down at her left hand, then exhaled slowly as if he were about to say something he was unsure of. "I—I noticed you wear a wedding ring. . . ."

She looked down at her ring, watched as the diamond glistened in the sun. Why *hadn't* she removed it yet, tucked it safely away, before she returned to the mountains? Was it simply because she'd been in such a hurry, or was it something else? She looked back at Garret.

"Lucy told me that you'd lost your husband and son." He squinted up toward the sky now, pausing uncomfortably. "And I suppose it's possible, maybe even likely, that you're not really ready for—" He stopped himself, running his hand through his hair nervously. Then he shook his head and sighed, as if it were hopeless.

She attempted a weak smile. "It's okay, I think I understand." She looked into his eyes now. "I'm glad that Lucy told you about it. It's true, my husband and son were drowned—it was a boating accident—about eighteen months ago."

"I'm sorry."

"It's been a long hard process for me, getting through the loss, I mean. But coming up here to the mountains was a real breakthrough. And I honestly think I've finally let them go." She looked down at

411

her ring. "I'm so used to wearing this that I didn't even think to take it off. I guess I should."

"I know how you feel. Despite what people tell you, it's never easy to move on. But I do think it gets better with time."

"Yeah, and I feel like I've had some good help along the way."

He nodded. "We can't do it without help."

She studied him carefully, then surprised herself by her next question. "Do you believe in angels, Garret?"

The corners of his lips curved up just slightly. "Yeah, as a matter of fact, I do."

She sighed. "Good."

"So, you're going to stick around then? I haven't completely scared you off?"

She smiled. "I don't really scare that easily." Then she remembered something. "You know, I'd been thinking if I stayed here and was alone for Christmas, I was going to invite Lucy over—she's alone for the holidays and—"

"Of course, she can come spend the holidays with all of us!" exclaimed Garret. "I don't know why I didn't think of it sooner. She and Mom are old friends."

And so it was settled.

Claire spent most of her time during the holidays with the Hendersons. They included both her and Lucy in almost everything, doing all they could to make them both feel completely at home—like one of them—part of the family. It was a Christmas Claire would never forget.

The day after Christmas, Anna and Garret invited her to take a walk with them. She had expressed curiosity about their walking route, not mentioning how it had coincided with her own and perhaps even initiated this whole amazing turn of events right from the beginning. They started out from the Henderson cabin and followed a trail that cut through a thickly wooded area and emerged right along the other side of the dead tree—now she could easily see how the two paths converged. Anna and Michael happily led the way with Claire and Garret lagging just slightly behind. As they came to the bridge, Claire told Garret the meaning of the footprints in the snow.

She explained how she'd been haunted by them at first, inspired by them later, and finally how she was driven to follow them in an effort to put her mind at peace. She told him of her frenzied chase through the blinding snowstorm and how she still had no earthly idea how she'd ever made it safely to his cabin.

"Incredible." He shook his head in amazement.

"I know. It's almost unbelievable."

"But did you say that you actually *saw* our footprints on *that* day?" he asked, an odd expression on his face. "The day you got lost and wound up on our porch?"

"Yes. They were nice and clear to start out with. You know how we'd just had a few inches of fresh snow the night before? So, in the beginning the footprints were quite easy to follow, until it started snowing, that is."

He stopped walking and turned to face her, intently studying her, his hand gently resting on her shoulder. "But, Claire," he said slowly. "We *didn't* take a walk that day. In fact, Anna had been rather upset with me because we hadn't gone out for a walk for several days—I'd been too absorbed in my writing."

"But they were there." Claire stared up into his eyes, unsure as to why he would question her on something like this. "Honest, the footprints were there. I'm not making this up!"

He nodded. "Oh, I believe you."

"But you said you two hadn't walked—"

"That's right. We hadn't. But I have no doubt that you saw footprints that day. They just didn't belong to Anna and me."

She considered his words for a moment. "Are you saying . . . ?"

He pushed a stray curl from her eyes and smiled. "I already told you, Claire, I really do believe in angels."

Melody Carlson is the prolific author of more than two hundred books, including fiction, nonfiction, and gift books for adults, young adults, and children. She is also the author of *All I Have to Give*, *An Irish Christmas* and *The Christmas Dog*. She recently was nominated for a *Romantic Times* Career Achievement Award in the inspirational market for her books. Visit her website at www.melodycarlson .com.